THE

GEOMETRY

OF

LOVE

THE
GEOMETRY
OF
LOVE

Jessica Levine

SHE WRITES PRESS

Published 2014
Printed in the United States of America
ISBN: 978-1-938314-62-9
Library of Congress Control Number: 2013950805

For information, address:
She Writes Press
1563 Solano Ave #546
Berkeley, CA 94707

For Emily and Sophia

Part One
1987

1

I WAS IN THE OLD Barnes & Noble on Eighteenth Street—the original, quirky haven, half on one side of the avenue and half on the other—looking at the remaindered poetry, when I noticed a man wearing two collared shirts, a red one on top of a white one, with the sleeves pushed up. I'd once known someone who dressed like that.

"Michael!" I cried out.

He looked up. He was unshaven and slouched as he'd always been, and a little heavier and grayer, but still handsome enough to stand out in a crowd. A tall man, with a large, important-looking head and an arresting gravity of expression. Just what you'd expect a struggling composer to look like.

"Julia!" he exclaimed.

We stared at each other across the remainders table for a long second. I knew Michael well. While a graduate student at Yale a decade before, he'd shared an apartment with my boyfriend, Ben.

"Wow," I said, as he came over and gave me a hug.

"You look beautiful! I almost didn't recognize you. I mean, you were always beautiful, but now, with the makeup and the shorter hair, you're gorgeous."

"You look good too," I said. "But what's that?" I dared to touch the long scar starting at the jawbone and running down the left side of his neck. Yes, we were once that familiar with each other. The last time I'd seen him, that warm September night, we had a sushi dinner and ended up making out on the steps of the New York Public Library.

"Another gory chapter in the endless soap opera of my life," he groaned and glanced down at the table. "Looking at poetry? Anything good here?"

"Probably. This is where the best poets come to die," I said.

"So, what's the story? You living in the city now?"

"No, in Princeton. Ben got a job teaching there." Pride swelled my voice a bit.

"I bet they like his British accent there. So you two are still together..." He reached for my left hand and examined it. "But no wedding ring."

"No, not yet."

"Hmm...But you must be thirty-one or -two by now...Let's go get a cup of coffee."

We stepped out of the air-conditioned store into a blast of September heat intensified by eddies of steam rising from the cracked sidewalk. As we crossed the street he cupped my elbow in a gentlemanly gesture at odds with his disheveled appearance.

"So what kind of work are you doing?" he asked.

"Secretary in the math department."

He gave me a questioning look. "Okay...I remember you played the piano and wrote good poetry. That poem that won the prize—I remember that."

I blushed. An erotic sonnet of mine won a prize my senior year and made me uncomfortably famous on campus for a semester.

"I don't write anymore," I said.

"How come?"

"I don't know. Nothing to write about."

"Somehow I don't see you satisfied being a secretary."

"One has to make a living, and there just aren't that many options in Princeton."

"So you took what you could get in order to be with Ben."

"Yes. I wanted to live together." I shrugged, ashamed of my old-fashioned agenda.

"And what are you doing in the city today? Visiting your parents?"

"Yeah, had lunch with my mother," I said. I'd been up to Seventy-

Sixth earlier and had found her sober. "And also, I'm looking at an apartment today. My dad has been suggesting I take over his accounting business. He had a heart attack a couple of years ago and wants to retire."

"Okay. So you and Ben will have to commute to see each other?"

"I don't know. I'm not even sure I want to move in. This is the first apartment I'm looking at."

"You'll move in," Michael said. "The desire is written all over you. And then why shouldn't Ben move in as well and commute out to teach? That would make the most sense. He has a cushy job teaching two or three days a week, right? And it's only an hour out to Princeton."

He had this uncanny way of imagining my life, *inhabiting* it, so that he could solve my problems.

"We haven't gone into the details yet. You know how hard it is for me to make decisions."

"Wait a minute—does Ben know you're looking at an apartment today?"

"Actually, no," I said. "I'm just testing the idea. I just wanted to see what you could get for eleven hundred a month."

I felt uncomfortable because Michael had caught me doing something furtive: I'd looked at ads, contacted the agent, made the appointment— all without telling Ben, though of course I would have to eventually, if I rented a place. And Michael knew me well enough to continue unmasking me. He would see that I was using my dad's business as an excuse to push the boundaries of the relationship I was in.

"You haven't told Ben because he wouldn't want to move in. Because the commuting would take time away from his precious writing and research." Michael spoke with that mix of fondness and sarcasm he'd always used when talking about Ben. "So you would just see each other on weekends."

Michael was right. That was exactly the kind of objection Ben would make, and I would tolerate it, because his focus and ambition had been the very qualities that had attracted me. But if Ben's drive had once been something I hoped to emulate, now it was the thing that made him less available to me. Thus it often happens that the traits that make someone initially attractive turn into the Achilles' heel of the relationship.

"But," Michael continued, "it sounds like you two are working it out, as I once predicted—right?"

We reached a coffee shop and Michael opened the door for me. Settling into a booth, I felt the sticky burgundy vinyl against my perspiring, bare arms. I glanced sideways at the tempting display of pies and overdone layer cakes under glass domes on the counter. On the wall behind the counter, local celebrities grinned in black-and-white photos bearing supposedly authentic signatures. Looking back at Michael, I took in the annoying beauty of his mouth, the expressiveness of his lower lip. Something in me shimmied in reaction, like a bird bruising its wings against the bars of its cage.

"I said," he repeated, "you're working it out, *as I predicted...* You do remember, don't you, that I predicted that?"

"You were always a great believer in predictions, especially your own," I responded, smiling.

"Touché," he said.

Our waitress came over.

"What's the story on the apple pie?" Michael asked.

"We make our own," the waitress said. She wore a gray plastic nametag on her chest that read "Mary" in clean white letters.

"Really?" Michael asked. "No one makes their own anymore." He was implying that the shop was special, that *she* was special.

"Well, *we* do," Mary said. I had to admit she had a pretty smile.

"I see you're still flirting with waitresses," I said as Mary disappeared.

"You call that flirting?"

"You wouldn't?"

"No, I wouldn't. I wasn't trying to pick her up."

"Maybe she was trying to pick you up. I remember your story about the French woman in the train compartment."

"After my divorce, I had to keep myself busy in order not to fall apart. In those days, the crazier the better."

I nodded. I would never forget the wild women he'd told me about, like the Canadian stewardess he'd screwed in an airplane lavatory or the English girl who'd given him gonorrhea. His story about the French woman—he'd edged a foot up into her skirt and she'd grabbed it and moved it in a way that was just right for her—was, perhaps, the most perturbing for its bizarre, quiet eroticism. Then there were the heartbreak stories: an impulsive marriage made at twenty and ended at twenty-one, his ill-fated romance with my cousin Robin, and others. I used to listen, wondering when Michael would stop this ceaseless sexual sampling that brought him so much disorder and suffering. But remembering his stories now, after ten years of a monogamous relationship with Ben (in other words, with a sense of the thinness, the drabness, of my own experience), I had a different reaction. With the sorrowful feeling that I hadn't used my twenties well, I could appreciate both the exuberance of his instincts and the wider wisdom he'd gained from a painful love life.

"I was done with pickups by the time I got to Yale," he went on. "And these days I'm too busy working." He described how, after quitting graduate school and moving back into the city, he'd gradually pieced together a musician's livelihood, giving lessons and getting gigs. "The competition here is fierce, and, economically, I'm always on the brink of disaster. Sometimes I think I should get out of New York and move to California."

"You think things would be better there?"

"Everything's better in California," he said.

"You believe that?"

"Sort of. At least you're closer to nature."

"You'd miss New York."

"Yeah, but so what?"

The waitress returned with the pie and two coffees. "Here." She placed the pie with a definitive click in front of Michael and waited, arms crossed, for the verdict.

He tasted it. "Excellent," he said, raising his eyebrows for emphasis.

Mary raised her eyebrows in return and sashayed back to her post behind the counter.

I rolled my eyes.

"It really is excellent," Michael said. "You want to taste?" He extended a forkful.

The cinnamon sparkled in the glaze over the apples, but I shook my head no. I avoided sweets. And eating from his fork seemed too intimate a gesture.

"And are you still composing?" I asked. I used to get mesmerized watching him at the piano, shaping tornadoes of feeling into flowing structures of sound.

"Stopped after the last heartbreak," he said. "After this—" He pointed to the scar on his neck.

"You want to tell me what happened?" I asked.

"Some other time," he said.

"I can't imagine you not composing," I insisted.

"I need a muse. If I'm not in love, I can't compose. I need to compose *for someone*. And if the love has an element of suffering in it, then I've got it made."

Even as he laughed at himself, making me laugh with him, I envied him his muses. I'd had a brief experience of that kind of ecstatic stimulation only once, during my infatuation with the junior I wrote the sonnet for. What bliss it must be to have a lasting source of inspiration! To be like Andrew Wyeth and have Christina sit in a field for you or like Pierre Bonnard, whose paintbrush vibrated every single time he stuck his wife in a bathtub. Nice work if you can get it, but I couldn't imagine such good fortune for myself. How many women got to have muses? Could a woman have a muse without also being one? I thought of George Sand and Chopin, Georgia O'Keeffe and Alfred Stieglitz, of Yoko and Lennon. They had all suffered, but they'd been compensated with results.

I stared at Michael's scar again. It was a raised, pale and fibrous line of tissue called a keloid, like the scar I'd developed the previous year after having a benign ovarian cyst removed. Recently I was having a worrisome ache in my abdomen again, this time on the opposite side. It could be another cyst. I needed to make a doctor's appointment.

"So you lost your muse after *that*?" I asked, gesturing toward his neck.

"Yeah. A little suffering can be good for an artist, but a truly catastrophic love affair is the kiss of death. So it's an endless cycle—I produce while a relationship is going and run dry when it's over. I mean, if I don't have someone, well, I can still compose, but it becomes more and more mechanical until I get so bored I can barely do it anymore. It's what I need to do, though."

"What's what you need to do?"

"To compose even if there's no muse. To find the muse inside myself." He looked at me gravely. "That's the task, isn't it, Jul?" he asked, using his old nickname for me.

"I suppose." I squirmed, aware of my failure as a poet. "And then, after that woman, what happened?"

"You mean, what was the next chapter in my love life?"

I nodded.

"Nothing," he said. "I haven't been in a relationship since. I've been completely celibate for five years."

"You're kidding," I said, processing that he was available, while I wasn't.

"I can't be bothered if it isn't going to be the real thing. I'm too old to be casual. I'm a middle-aged man now. Look." He pointed to his receding hairline.

"You're not middle-aged!"

"I am indeed. I'm forty-one. But what about you? Have you been faithful to dear old Ben? Let's see—the seven-year itch should have struck three or four years ago."

I blushed. "Well, you can have the itch and not scratch." A few years before, I'd had a minor flirtation with a guy I'd met in a business class.

"Sounds uncomfortable," Michael said.

"If you wait long enough, it goes away."

"Your loyalty was one of the things I always admired about you."

"I don't know if it's loyalty or some weird kind of symbiosis." If I hurt Ben, I would feel his pain as my own. There was something not quite right about this way of loving, which repeatedly inhibited my freedom of action.

I remembered my appointment with the real estate agent and looked at my watch. "I've got to get over to that apartment I'm checking out."

"I'll go with you," Michael said. In a familiar movement, he swung his black canvas bag on his shoulder, then stretched his neck a bit in the opposite direction. "Wait a minute, I've got to cancel my next lesson." He put a few dollars down on the table and headed to the telephone near the restrooms at the back of the coffee shop.

Restless, I stood up and walked over to the front door. As I waited for him, my fingers went for the mints in the little crystal bowl next to the cash register. I would allow myself two. The pastel colors made them satisfying before you put them in your mouth. Michael took his teaching very seriously, and I felt flattered that he was canceling a lesson to spend more time with me. But maybe his canceling didn't have the import I wanted it to have. Like a jazz musician alternately jesting and crying on a saxophone, Michael had always lived with an easy impulsiveness.

As we walked toward Fourteenth Street, where I was meeting the agent, Michael recalled some of the good times we'd had my senior year:

the night we went to see *Teacher's Pet* at the Yale Medical School film society, the New Year's Eve he came to my mom's cast party.

"And then there was that summer night we listened to jazz in Damrosch Park," he said. "Remember that?"

We'd met at the fountain in Lincoln Center and listened to an outdoor concert while eating meatball heroes. That was when he told me he had decided to quit graduate school. The decision made sense to me. And his leaving New Haven opened up the possibility of my moving in with Ben.

"That whole summer was fun," I said. The summer of '77: Ben was in London with his family and Michael had broken up with Robin, so Michael and I saw lot of each other—maybe too much, which was why things ended the way they did that September night on the library steps. The back part of my mind tried to make sense of what had happened— because I never had been able to before—while Michael moved on to a new topic, talking about the jazz scene in Manhattan until we reached the brownstone on West Fourteenth Street that was my destination.

The real estate agent, a small man dressed for success in a suit that smelled of dry-cleaning fluid, led us up several flights of stairs to a one-bedroom apartment at the back of the building. I was immediately charmed by the quality of the light coming in through the tall windows. Both the bedroom and the living area looked over a small backyard, where potted trees and flower-filled planters stood in a circle around several black metal chairs. Some wild-looking bushes grew in a square of dirt. Sitting on the windowsill, I was enchanted by the little garden, while Michael interrogated the agent. How was business these days? Were rents ever going to stop their astronomical climb? Michael had a knack for engaging strangers in conversation. Amused, I let him do all the talking.

As I watched Michael do his thing, I realized that he hadn't had a cigarette since I ran into him. Nor did he smell of tobacco anymore. So, he'd given up smoking as well as pickups. In two small ways at least—and maybe there were others yet to be discovered—he'd taken hold of himself.

He looked in my direction, and our eyes met. "Maybe we could have a moment to talk it over?" he said to the agent, who agreed to wait for us downstairs. The agent clearly thought that Michael and I were "together," and Michael was enjoying the pretense immensely.

The agent stepped out, and Michael threw me an inscrutable look. We had been pretending for over an hour that we'd never made out on the steps of the library, but now that we were alone in this private space I had a momentary impulse to run and throw myself at him, in order to pick up exactly where we'd left off—*but hey, woman, that's not where you want your life to go.*

"So what do you think?" I asked.

"It's expensive, but not more than anything else these days, and quiet, and close to the subway—"

"I love the garden—"

"And that wall is just crying for a piano," Michael added, gesturing at an empty white space.

"I haven't played the piano in years."

"But you'll want to start again once you have your own place."

"You predict it?" I asked, returning to our old joke.

"I predict it," he said, smiling. "You can rent something for not much, you know."

I looked at the wall. "A piano would look nice there, wouldn't it?" Somewhere in the attic of my house in Princeton there was a portrait of me at Michael's piano that my other cousin, Anna, had done the winter of our senior year. I imagined hanging it over a rented upright; I saw Michael and me sitting on a bench side by side.

As though intuiting my vision, he added, "And I've been studying this technique I could teach you. It's really turned my playing around…"

I sat down again on the windowsill to gaze at the courtyard. I could feel him looking at me, thinking about me, maybe even—was it my imagination?—desiring me. I was in a tumult, and one should never make a decision in a tumult.

"The thing I'm wondering," Michael continued, "is whether you feel confident about your strategy here."

"My strategy?" I looked up at him.

"Vis-à-vis Ben. You're trying to push him, aren't you?"

"What do you mean?" I asked, feigning innocence.

"To ask you to marry him, to start a family. Your taking a job in New York—even if it is with your dad—and getting your own pad will seem like a threat to him. An ultimatum. *I* see what you're doing, even if he doesn't."

Michael was describing motives that I hadn't fully articulated to myself. I looked out the window and down. I loved that little garden.

"I can't make any real money in Princeton. And my father is seventy," I said. "He's got a client list that takes years to build up. It's a good opportunity."

"Right. Which has nothing to do with you and Ben," Michael said.

"Why would I move into the city if I was in a hurry to get married and have kids?"

"My point exactly. It's a case of brinkmanship. It's your way of delivering an ultimatum."

"Did I mention that we bought a house together?"

"Yeah, I know. You adore him and he's still your white knight, right? The white knight of the subways…" Years ago Ben had come to the rescue of a woman who was being harassed on the West Side IRT and I'd admired his courage. "But you're not going to start a family without the wedding ring, are you?"

I wanted a child eventually, but I also felt conflicted about marriage, which, in the spirit of my generation, I saw as a bourgeois trap. *All the little boxes*, went the song.

"And so, if my moving into the city is a strategy, what do you think of it?" I asked.

"Powerful but risky. You're giving him room to play around."

"He's not the type that plays around."

"Hmm, maybe you're right," Michael said, remembering his old friend. "Of course, it gives you room to play around, too, doesn't it?"

"I suppose."

"Not that you're the type, either," he added, cool and neutral.

We fell silent. Then he spoke again. "It's blissfully quiet here, you're near the subway, and you've got a low building across so you'll have light all day."

"I wish the bedroom had a better view," I said.

"Now, now, Julia," he said, making a naughty-you sign with his finger. He knew my way of finding a flaw in order to defer action. "You know this is a great apartment."

"Yes," I said.

"Besides, if you take it, we could hang out together again."

I nodded.

"And if you don't take it," he went on, "someone else will by tonight. Apartments like this go fast in New York."

"You're right," I said, convinced by his logic. Normally, I would have looked at fifty apartments before making a decision of this importance, but now I reached into my bag for my checkbook and watched my hand fill in the blanks.

I looked up and saw that inscrutable expression on his face again.

"That's better," he said. "Now we're cooking."

2

DOWNSTAIRS A MOMENT LATER, I gave the check to the agent and arranged a move-in date.

"How do you feel?" Michael asked, watching the agent walk away.

"A little shaky," I said.

"It's the adrenaline. You need to walk—where to now?" he said.

"I've got to get up to Penn Station to catch the train back to Princeton."

"You and your trains," he said, in what I took to be a reference to the night we kissed on the library steps and then had to run to the station so I would get there in time.

"Sorry," I said.

Walking up Sixth Avenue, we reached the plant district where trees in enormous plastic pots turn the sidewalks into a lush tropical forest and storefronts are jammed with plants tolerant of central heating and indirect light. Drops of water fell on my forehead, coming from either dripping air conditioners above or an automatic sprinkler system misting plants.

"Just look at this!" Michael stopped and waved his long arms up at a dense canopy of foliage arching overhead. "I wish I had my camera with me."

I loved walking around New York with Michael—the way he noticed things. Ben wasn't like that.

"I never understood what your fight with Ben was about," I said, knowing Michael would take my non sequitur in stride. The fight had happened right before he moved out of their apartment.

"He got upset when I decided to quit graduate school. He said I was giving up too easily, which wasn't exactly true. I'm a composer—I wasn't cut out to be an academic. You understand what I'm talking about— you have an artistic temperament." He brushed aside a leafy branch of a banana tree.

I winced. "I told you I'm not particularly artistic anymore. I'm a secretary now."

"Oh, Jul, Jul. What's to be done with you?"

"Actually, my official title is 'budget manager.' I manage the department's funds."

He sighed. "The artist in you needs to be prodded, that's all," he said. "You've always needed to be prodded. The minute I met you, I could see it."

"We were talking about your fight with Ben," I said.

"The whole time we were in graduate school, Ben always thought he knew what was best for me. I certainly knew more about literature than he knew about music, but I never told him what to do. Does he still have that bossy streak?"

"It isn't that he's bossy. He just cared about you. He thought you were a genius and wanted you to succeed."

"Yeah," he said distractedly, ignoring the compliment. "In any case, the argument was probably about something else. We had fun hanging out together, but on some level he hated living with me because I was such a slob. I think he just got sick and tired of it."

It was true. Ben and Michael had been a kind of odd couple, with Ben keeping order in his bedroom and the living areas, while Michael's room verged on the revolting, with soiled clothes heaped in a corner and sandwich crusts in greasy paper bags on the window sill. After the break-up with Robin, his personal hygiene became erratic: he shaved twice a week at most and sometimes forgot to shower or brush his teeth.

"Are you still a slob?" I asked.

"Comes and goes. Has to do with being single," he said. "I try to pull myself together for work."

We reached Penn Station and, passing a stand with the best pumpernickel bagels in New York, stepped onto the escalator and glided downward. The appetizing aroma of fresh-cooked dough mixed with smells of hot train tracks, disinfectant, and the urine stench of the Reagan-era homeless, resulting in a sweet-and-sour olfactory symphony.

Checking the departure board, I saw I'd missed my train by ten minutes and had almost an hour until the next one.

"Let's go get a beer," Michael said. He guided me into a bar on the upper platform, where we found a table in a dimly lit corner. Michael liked bars—the grubbier, the better. He cultivated the persona of a lowlife, perhaps to take distance from his father, a distinguished musicologist at Columbia University.

The beer, when it arrived, was pleasantly cool.

"Does your mother still drink like a fish?" he asked.

I was taken aback. We'd never talked about my mother's drinking. "Sometimes," I said—nothing more than that.

He raised and dropped his eyebrows, then wove backwards in the conversation. "So, tell me more about why you stopped writing and playing."

"I don't know. I stopped having anything to write about. And why play the piano when I wasn't getting any better? It all started to seem pointless."

"Pointless. Big word. With psychological and metaphysical implications."

I shrugged.

"And what you meant to say before—the itch you didn't scratch—is that you were tempted to be unfaithful, but not seriously."

It was the way we had always talked—weaving back and forth between topics.

"As temptations go, it was serious enough. I was going through a moment of feeling dissatisfied with Ben and had the urge to step out. But then I had a revelation. I realized that all relationships have their ups and downs and that I simply needed to hold fast with Ben. I was like Dorothy in *The Wizard of Oz*—I had everything in my own backyard, with Ben, so what was all the fuss about?"

There I was talking about Ben again, laying out my damn philosophy of happiness via compromise, even as I longed to ask Michael about the night we made out. *What was it for you, did you miss me afterwards?* The desire we'd felt that night and the decade of silence afterward kept on going in and out of focus in my head.

"Hmm," he said.

"I can't describe how powerful this revelation was," I went on. "I just—" I hesitated, wondering whether Michael would appreciate the importance of what I had to say. Our eyes met. Of course he would understand, he always had. "I decided to be happy. I mean, I decided to choose happiness with a known quantity over a fantasy."

"To cultivate your little garden, so to speak."

"Yes, exactly."

"And you're sure you don't need to be married and have children to enjoy that garden?"

"I haven't worked that one out yet," I confessed.

His attention, fixed on me, created a bubble around us blocking out the sights and sounds of the bar and train station.

"And do you think anybody can do that—choose to be happy?" he asked.

"Well," I said, "happiness is what we want, fundamentally, as human beings, isn't it?"

"I'm not sure about that," he said.

"What is it we want, if not happiness?"

"More."

"More of what?" I asked.

"More of whatever we've already had, whether it's good or bad for us. We're creatures of habit and repetition."

His world-weariness triggered my sympathy even as it struck me as self-indulgent.

"Well, I believe that our thinking can influence our desires."

"So you just thought away that itch of yours?"

"The way I'd put it is that I used good judgment to protect my happiness." I spoke confidently, then, remembering "the library steps," stopped myself. Had I used good judgment that night? Was I using it now in sharing so much with him? I probably sounded self-satisfied, if not downright hypocritical.

But he was neither ironic nor disparaging. He just said, "Hmm," and sat there, mulling over what I'd said.

"Don't you have a train to catch?" he asked, finally. Stopping me with a gesture when I reached for my wallet, he placed a few dollars on the table.

"It's my turn to pay," I objected.

"Forget it, Jul," he said.

We exited the bar and plowed through the crowd to the track entrance, where we stopped and looked at each other. *Even with the two-day stubble and the ridiculous two shirts one on top of the other and the slouch—my God he's handsome.*

Michael lightly put a hand on my waist. My skin absorbed his touch as though thirsty for it.

"Let's have dinner together—the three of us—as soon as you move in," Michael suggested.

"I—I don't know," I said. And then I blurted it out. "After that night, I told Ben what happened between us."

"Immediately?"

"He figured it out before he even picked me up at the train station. Remember how I took a later train? A two-hour-later train?"

"And you confirmed his suspicion? Of course, you did the right thing."

"He was really angry," I said.

"It was just a kiss. We were just friends saying good-bye."

Just friends saying good-bye? "Right," I said, hardly convinced.

"Maybe you shouldn't tell him you ran into me today," he said, hooking me again.

"That's what I was thinking," I said.

We looked at each other, barely breathing. In his light brown eyes I saw the illuminated reflection of my own hazel ones.

"But…we'll see each other again, right?" he asked. "You'll call me once you've moved in?"

"Yes," I said.

"Promise?"

"Promise."

"Okay, I'm counting on it."

Michael took me in his arms and gave me the bear hug I remembered so well, the hug that turned me into comfortable jelly and ended with a small squeeze within the larger one. I felt my breasts press up against his ribs—his now slightly padded ribs.

And he let me go, casting me into the crowd that straggled down the sooty-breathed stairway to the platform below. The train waited, its silver doors open. I stepped over the narrow abyss between the car and the platform, and the doors closed behind me, their rubber rims bouncing against the last passengers squeezing in. Thus they had closed ten years before, at Grand Central, when Michael had said good-bye not at the top of the stairs but on the platform below, standing with one foot in the train car, his back against the furiously bouncing door, as though about either to get on the train with me or pull me back out. Who was I kidding? That kiss had not been the "accident" that I, for a decade, had imagined it to be—it had been a cutting-in-two good-bye. I'd buried it determinedly in the long ago, but now here it was again, erupting from my dense, volcanic heart.

3

I RODE HOME WITH a clenched feeling in my lower abdomen, where I'd had the surgery. Outside the train, over the industrial landscape of northern New Jersey, blue gaseous plumes rising from mammoth chemical tanks melted into a dirty pink sky. An occasional tree struggled up, between steel cylinders and belching pipes, into a mauve blanket of grit-granulated smog. Inside the car businessmen dozed or drank beer. Tired from all the walking I'd done, I closed my eyes, but I was too agitated to sleep.

Ten years before, on the night of the library steps, I got home two hours late.

"That was an awfully long dinner you had with Michael," Ben had said when he met me at the train station.

"Oh, we ended up taking a walk and chewing the fat for a long time," I'd said. Chewing the fat—what a ridiculous expression.

I got into the car and Ben looked at me again for a long moment before pulling away from the curb. There wasn't much light coming in from the street, but I knew he'd seen enough to guess that something had happened. When we got home, he took me by the shoulders, his thumbs against my clavicles.

"Did you do something with Michael?" he asked.

I confessed immediately. "Yes. I kissed him."

I'd never seen Ben so angry. He wanted to know if I'd slept with

Michael, and I said no. He asked if I had been flirting with Michael behind his back all spring. I said, no, I was just spending time with him while you were studying. And that was the truth: Michael was sharing Ben's apartment, and Ben didn't want me in his bedroom while he plowed through Shakespeare and Milton for his doctoral exams—he said it disturbed his concentration. So I did my homework sitting in the living room, listening to Michael play the piano. When he stopped the two of us would chat and have tea. That was all there was to it.

"Are you in love with him?" Ben continued, and I said no, it was just a good-bye that got out of hand—and that was truly how I wanted to think of it. And then Ben forbade me ever to see Michael again, and I said I wouldn't, I didn't want to. Which was also true. It seemed simpler that way.

So why had I confessed so readily to—what? a kiss? I couldn't stand having a secret from Ben; it felt like it would spoil the intimacy between us. To put it mathematically, the equation at that point in time was: pain of keeping a secret from Ben > (greater than) pain of not seeing Michael anymore.

Ten years later, the math wasn't so clear. I couldn't tell Ben that I'd run into Michael that afternoon. I didn't want another scene. I didn't want to rehash what had happened ten years before. And I didn't want to hear Ben forbid me to see Michael again, because I wouldn't obey.

And so I decided, for the first time in my relationship with Ben, to keep a secret from him.

Well, the second time—there was that flirtation with the guy with the red moustache.

My conversation with Michael kept running through my head. He was right about my moving into New York. I was playing a high-stakes chess game with Ben, hoping to get him to agree to the life I wanted—marriage, Manhattan, maybe even (though I was no longer sure about it) a baby. But through some odd twist, it was my wanting to live closer to Michael that had pushed me to play. I had just signed a lease on impulse, and I wasn't an impulsive woman.

The train crossed the Raritan River in New Brunswick and the view mercifully changed to suburban sprawl—houses with plastic siding, trees, backyards with inflatable toddler pools. Soon I'd be home and everything would be okay, as it always was. I've always had this ability to pull back from things emotionally when I move away geographically.

As we pulled into Princeton Junction, I stepped out onto the open end of the car and saw Ben on the platform looking for me. The wave of pleasure I usually experienced taking in his long, lean figure now mixed with apprehension about concealing my meeting with Michael. And there was the matter of my signing a lease without consulting with him first.

"How was the trip uptown?" he asked, giving me a kiss.

"Fine," I said.

"Subways okay?"

"Yeah, fine," I said. "I wish you wouldn't worry about it." Ever since Ben had rescued that woman on the subway, he worried about me.

"I don't worry. I just—"

"Worry."

We laughed together.

"Parents?"

"I had lunch with Mariel," I said. "It was fine." *Fine* was code for *sober*. "How was your day?"

"I worked all day," he said.

Ben hadn't been into Manhattan with me for months. He only took breaks for things close to home, like cooking or digging up a square of lawn in the back, where he was planning to create a stone patio. In his sixth year of teaching at Princeton, he was coming up for tenure, and he wrote in every spare moment, including weekends, in order to finish his second book. The goal was worthy. If achieved, tenure would mean security of employment at Princeton for life. Though his devotion to his work sometimes robbed me of his company, I admired his ambitiousness and supported his quest, which might provide him with the financial security he felt he needed in order to start a family. Or maybe he would support me and I'd finally become the poet I'd once hoped to be.

Both parenting and poetry were, of course, at odds with my moving into the city to take over my father's business. But I needed to get out of Princeton in order to satisfy my need for economic self-sufficiency. My dad had shown me how to shelve dreams in order to take care of practical matters. He'd once played various wind instruments in addition to the piano, performing in small clubs and dreaming of greater success, only to put his saxophone and clarinet away in order to focus on making money.

"But writing poetry is different," he once said to me. "You can do it in the cracks of the day. Look at Wallace Stevens, how he wrote those poems in his head while walking to his insurance job."

Well, I wasn't Stevens. If I had been born a decade or two later I might have been able to imagine combining raising kids, writing, and having a business. But at the time I thought that these paths were mutually exclusive and combining even two things from my list seemed like a recipe for a nervous breakdown. The way I saw it, Sylvia Plath hadn't stuck her head in the oven because she was mentally ill, but because she was overwhelmed and her husband kept disappearing. I didn't have the female role models to help me be a supermom multitasker.

Ben drove by campus and headed down Witherspoon and out on Cherry Hill Road toward our house, which lay in the "country" between Princeton and New Hope. When we first moved there, I felt like a Woody Allen character who has a panic attack every time he leaves the cacophony of New York for a quiet night in the country. Then slowly I became unhooked from the constant stimulus of the city, and our house began to feel like a welcome retreat. As we drew closer to home in the falling darkness, I was aware of the trees interlacing their dried September green above our heads, and I looked forward to falling asleep with the layered orchestra of crickets and rustling leaves outside the window.

The downstairs of our house had an open plan with a sunken living and dining area furnished in neutral tones. From the foyer I could see that the table was set with soup bowls and a salad. Dinner was ready. Ben was a good cook, although dependent on recipes, which meant he usually made enough for six or more people. Tonight he ladled out minestrone, which he served with a chunk of whole wheat bread from the health food store. I smiled as he sprinkled a handful of chopped parsley into my bowl. He'd taught me to love the freshness of the bright green on a long-cooked dish. He had an appreciation for contrasts of flavor and texture that struck me as very European. It was part of who he was, not a skill set he'd picked up from a cooking show.

It was too warm an evening for soup, but I didn't mind. Fortunately there was a breeze coming in through the open window. I blew on my steaming bowl.

"I have news for you," I said halfway through the meal. "I rented an apartment today."

His face got very still. "You what?"

"I rented an apartment on Fourteenth Street."

He put his soupspoon down. "That was sudden."

"Is it really? I've floated the idea before," I said. In fact, I'd thought about it more than I'd talked about it. "I just decided that I need to learn the ropes of my dad's business *before* something happens to him, not wait till *after*." I plodded on, trying to make my explanation as convincing as possible. Instead, I stumbled on a sore point. "After all, it's not as if things were going anywhere *here*."

I didn't know whether I was talking about my job as secretary in the math department or about our not yet having gotten married. I wanted to blame him for my feeling stuck, even as I dimly knew that I tolerated our lack of official commitment because part of me wanted more freedom.

Ben fell silent. He had an aggravating way of ruminating in order not to spill his gut reactions, so that I never knew how he really felt about anything.

"Well, say something," I said.

"What am I supposed to say? I didn't expect you to come home with that kind of announcement. I thought that you'd want to talk about it more first, *for example*, what kind of apartment to take." He gave "for example" an irritating emphasis.

"What do you mean, *for example*, what kind'?" I asked, repeating his emphasis. "You haven't shown any interest in moving in with me and commuting out to teach, so I took a small apartment. A one-bedroom."

"I thought you'd at least want me to see it before you signed the lease—"

"Things don't work like that in New York. It would have been gone by tomorrow."

Ben sighed. "Of course. You're right. But why West Fourteenth Street? It's not a straight shot from there to your father's office."

"I like the idea of being close to the Village. It's fun. And it's a straight shot uptown on the subway to Penn Station—to get back out here."

I watched him process my message that we would continue to see each other. We knew other couples who had adopted "modern" commuting arrangements after realizing they could be committed without spending seven days a week together.

"So when do you move in?" he asked, calming down.

"October first."

"So what will we do—one weekend here, one weekend there?" He wanted to be fair, but I could see he was worrying about how my move would affect his work.

"That sounds reasonable," I said. The way he said "we" comforted me, in turn.

"Sorry I jumped the gun. I guess the idea of being out here by myself with all the stuffed shirts and dead wood"—he meant his staid fellow faculty members—"isn't so appealing."

"You'll be okay," I said.

"I want you to be happy, to find what it is you're supposed to be doing with your life."

"I appreciate that."

"And do you think," he asked, sounding tentative, "there might be enough space in your apartment that I could have a desk to work at when I visit?"

"It could be arranged, if you're good."

"If I'm good?" he echoed, catching on to the salacious implications.

"If you're *real* good."

"You mean I'll have to work for my keep?"

"You bet you'll have to work." I had successfully shifted the tone of the exchange.

"Come here, you saucy wench," he said, pushing back from the table. I loved the way his British accent elongated the "aw" in "saucy"—it made me feel like I was a tavern harlot in a Chaucerian tale, and right then being a tavern harlot felt good. I've always had a weakness for men with foreign accents: English spoken any way that isn't American becomes my entry ticket to a fantasy set on the broad beaches of South Africa, or near the coral reefs of Australia, or in a ruined Indian temple. Although the Southern Hemisphere accents are intoxicating, in the end I prefer pure British.

I sat on Ben's lap, facing him. I took his face in my hands. It was rough with evening stubble, but I admired its smooth oval shape, the relief of the cheekbones, and the discreet sensuality of his mouth, fuller at the center, narrow but long in a smile at the corners. The angles of his profile combined British refinement and Jewish gravity. His eyes were the refracted, dense green of moist grass. He made me feel safe; and I needed to feel safe in order to be intimate with someone.

Ben put his arms around me, and his hands traveled under my shirt to unsnap my bra. I placed my arms around his neck and enjoyed the feeling of his hands moving forward toward my breasts, stroking them. Over the past few months—was it since my surgery or because he was finishing a book?—we'd been making love less often, and I missed it. My afternoon with Michael began to recede as I felt the happy bulge in Ben's pants. Unzipping him, I pull his erection upward.

"That's better," I said.

"Much better," he said. "You tired?"

"Not too tired, if you do all the work."

"I had an easy day. I'll do all the work."

In the bedroom a moment later I faced him and said, "Undress me."

Having asked him to "do all the work," I imagined a woman in nineteenth-century dress, her layers of frocks pushed away, maybe a little ripping of those endless undergarments. Somewhere in the scene, a bowl of strawberries. And she lets herself be taken, typically in some absurd place, like a bower or a dip in the moors, or maybe a horse-drawn carriage, the sound of hooves covering her moans of pleasure. "And he took her"— I'd always loved that expression in old novels. And that's what Ben did when he explored me and found I was wet already. He pushed in slowly and then, nestling into my neck, began his work faster.

"Just enjoy yourself," I whispered. It was my way of telling him that I was so excited he could go straight to it and his long, free swinging movement would cause my climax to happen by itself. That's how it usually went with us because we'd had so much practice. There had always been an easy perfection to the way we made love.

But as he began to move, my arousal faded, and my body didn't respond as expected. The memory of the day was creating interference.

"You want to come some other way?" he asked when he was done.

"No, I don't think so. It's that pain," I lied, referring to the stitch in my abdomen. "It distracted me." The truth was that, for some mysterious reason, the pain always went away when we had sex.

"You should get that checked out. Soon."

"I'll make an appointment."

After the bedtime rituals and a little reading, after Ben had fallen asleep beside me, I lay awake with a wanting of what, I didn't know. I missed the intensity of the sex that Ben and I had during our first couple of years but the yearning was more than sexual, it was an itchy kind of restlessness. In order not to think about Michael, I got up and wandered around the house, looking for a distraction, like a snack or a magazine. Soon I found myself standing in Ben's office, staring down at the work on his desk.

He was writing about Ezra Pound. It was Ben's interest in modern poetry that had made me think he might be a muse for me, might be a man interested in whatever came out of my brain, the way Leonard had been for Virginia. Whenever she finished a novel, he'd lock himself up in his study for a weekend and read it straight through from cover to cover. Then he'd emerge and say, Virginia, you've done it again, you're a genius. One would think that that kind of emotional support would be enough to cure any kind of mental illness. Well, it didn't cure Virginia, but Leonard was still one in a million. And it certainly hadn't worked out that way with Ben and me. I couldn't remember what had gone wrong. Had he criticized my poems—maybe even constructively—and I'd been so sensitive and defensive that I retreated as a consequence? Or had there be an edge to his comments—a put-down in the tone of his voice or body language—because he felt threatened by my talent or envious of it?

I'd stopped writing after college. Which is to say that I stopped writing around the time I moved in with Ben, so I was tempted to blame it on him. But the truth—which I'd only see decades later—was that I'd been so lacking in self-confidence as a young woman that I'd just given up. Only thirty years later, after seeing the sea change in women's writing, would I understand how meager the stream of women's literature had been previously, how it had suffered from lack of role models and social support. And my mother certainly hadn't helped me learn a positive attitude about female creativity. As she aged and acting parts grew scarcer, her diatribes about how the arts were run by men grew more bitter and drunken. I had neither the acumen nor the optimism to see beyond what she taught me.

When I met Ben, some part of me must have hoped that Ben's support would make up for what I never got either from my parents or the culture at large. And I was disappointed when it didn't happen.

Though we'd entered the computer age, Ben still did his first draft by hand. I sat down and admired the European quality of his handwriting, which was as even and tightly woven as a fishnet. There was a sense of intensity and speed in his slightly compressed script—the loops were tall and fine, each and every one of them, with a thread-fine bit of a trail at the end of the words. Looking at it, you would never have known how embattled he was with himself—with being both a Brit and an academic. He once said to me, "Baruch atah Adonai that I'm Jewish. Otherwise I'd be a complete stereotype."

I started to read what he'd written about Pound. I couldn't understand Ben's interest in obscure poetry or his tolerance of the aging poet's anti-Semitism. Ben used to say, a critic has to rise above such things, which always brought me to two opposing conclusions at the same time. One, that Ben was a superior being, endowed with a nobility of spirit that enabled him to consider poetry as a disembodied manifestation of meaning, image, and rhythm. And two, that Ben had a gigantic blind spot, a fundamental inability to connect with the way things were. It was the same quality that caused him to make minestrone on a hot night. He was *thinking* "autumn, therefore cold" instead of *feeling* "hot day."

I bent over to look closer. As always, his argument was brilliant and entertaining, and if I had kept on reading I'd have become convinced that Pound was worth the time, but I pulled away. As an English major I'd certainly read my share of literary criticism; however, my "artistic temperament," as Michael called it, rebelled against the critic's dissection of literature and implantation of thesis and meaning—an operation that substituted argument for feeling. In my immature way of looking at things, analytical thinking belonged to the realm of math, science, and psychology, but not poetry.

I pulled myself away from Ben's desk and went into the living room, where I flung myself on the couch. There was no way around my need to dwell on Michael and how we'd parted ten years before.

After eating sushi on that warm September evening, we walked up Fifth, past shoe stores, luggage outlets, and jewelers, all gated and locked up for the night, and the occasional cafeteria still open for the rush-hour crowd. Even though I'd told Ben I'd be on the eight o'clock train and it was already seven-thirty, I dragged my feet.

"When's your train?" Michael asked.

I looked at my watch. "In a half hour, or an hour and a half, if I catch the one after."

"In an hour and a half, then," he said.

I went to a phone booth and called Ben and told him that I'd be on the next train. When I hung up, Michael gave me a funny little look and

said, "Let's go sit by the lions," and it was on the way there that I put my hand in his pocket. He squeezed it and began stroking the back of my hand with his thumb.

"I guess I won't be seeing you much anymore," I said.

"Why shouldn't you?"

"I'll be in New Haven; you'll be in the city."

"So?"

"Everything'll be different."

"You're right," he said. He slumped, and the corners of his mouth dropped.

We sat down on the library steps, under the south lion statue, and I began to cry.

"Hey, Jul, Jul," he said, taking my face in his hands, "I'll always treasure our friendship. You know that."

"Kiss me," I said, and he did.

Yes, I initiated it.

"A curse upon Ben for finding you first," he said between kisses, the kind you have when you're in public and you can't take off clothing so you take the layers off the face instead—the masks, expressions, words—until you're naked, eye to eye, breath to breath. His lips softened as they danced around my lips, his tongue played with mine, his teeth gently seized and released me. We hung from each other's lips like hummingbirds that feed from a lily—such was the intensity of the contact, the speed of the heart, the sweetness of the nectar. My hand traveled into his thick black hair, my womb was a fist of desire that needed only privacy to pull him in. But his apartment was way uptown.

"You'll miss your train," he said.

We stood up and began walking toward Grand Central, and as we crossed Fifth, holding hands, Michael stopped and, standing on the double yellow line, swung me toward him to kiss me again. I folded myself up against his chest and cocked my head for another kiss. Behind his shoulder, the river of red lights extending for miles downtown began to turn green, with the lights at the corner turning first, then the lights on Fortieth, Thirty-Ninth, and so on, one gigantic yes all the way to the bottom of the canyon that is Fifth Avenue. And as I pulled away I saw a mass of taxis and cars waiting at the now green light and I heard their angry honking as we just stood there, feeding off each other. The entire city saying *go ahead*, and yet I would get on that train, we would say good-bye. Flailing in our own stupidity.

The memory of that evening got me aroused all over again. The desire rolled right through my pelvis, ending in butterflies in my stomach. Goddamn it that we hadn't had sex, that I'd gotten on the train.

I didn't ascribe any meaning—like "love"—to my body's reaction to running into Michael that day. I only recognized that, in order to get some sleep, it was necessary to do what I needed to do, by myself, in order to release the tension. Stretching out on the couch and pulling a throw over me, I let my imagination carry me back to that warm, magical night on the library steps, while my hand knew exactly where to go and what to do.

4

THERE WAS A DELICIOUSNESS to having my own apartment that I hadn't expected. A couple of weeks later, after Ben had helped me move the basics in, unpack, and make the bed that looked so little—we'd bought a double instead of the queen we had "at home"—we had dinner and he took the train back out to Princeton and I found myself alone. I was thirty-two and I'd never lived by myself. With Ben gone, I had a moment of being spooked, like a child who's left without a babysitter for the first time. I went over to one of the bedroom windows and opened it and looked up and down. There was no fire escape but someone could let himself down from the roof with a rope and crash into my apartment and rape and murder me. Crazy Hitchcock scenario. I left the window open a crack for air circulation, and a feeling of elation came over me. I breathed into my new, glorious freedom and levitated right then and there.

Maybe I'd needed to move into New York in order to disrupt the symbiotic aspect of my relationship with Ben—the way what he felt always became what I felt and what he needed always made sense to me. The way his priorities and desires diluted mine. In my own place I could at last be sovereign over all parts of my life, the wretched as well as the blessed.

In those first moments, I didn't do much with my new freedom except get into bed and set down next to me, in the place where Ben might have been, a couple of books, *The New Yorker*, and a tray with a dish of nuts and raisins and a mug of herb tea. I tried to settle in, but something was missing. I got up and grabbed a notepad and added it to the pile—I had that restless feeling that preludes notable words in the brain and the worlds they birth with their pungent oranges and bright greens, passions of rain and moods in falling snow, shimmering deserts and forests in flower. Maybe I'd stopped writing poetry around the time I moved in with Ben for lack of privacy. Maybe being apart would help get me going again. Not that I had anything to say. Yet.

I thought of calling Michael but I wasn't ready. There was something I had to take care of first.

I made an appointment with Dr. Sarler to discuss the mysterious abdominal ache. The pain I'd had before the surgery had disappeared for six months after removal of the cyst; its reappearance on the opposite side suggested a cyst might have grown on the other ovary. I'd already had the requisite ultrasound—noninvasive but unpleasant because it required drinking an impossible eight glasses of water—but it had revealed nothing. The question was what to do next.

I asked my mother to meet me at the doctor's office on East Eighty-First, between Park and Madison, to offer moral support. Mariel's ministrations were hit-or-miss in most areas of life, but in medical situations she was reliable, able to provide a steady stream of distracting chatter. When I arrived I found her already there. She got up and hugged me, her wiry arms a little too tight around my ribs. I was wearing my urban black; she was all dressed up, as though we were going to a party— tight purple pants and a wrong-decade orange-and-red paisley top that looked terrific on her. She could wear any color or pattern, in or out of fashion, and look fifteen years younger than she really was.

When I was in college, my mother used to greet me with a comment like, "You'd be so beautiful if only you'd wear a little makeup." Now she simply said, "Your eyeliner isn't right at the corners. And you look like you're dressed for a funeral."

"Mom, I'm dressed the way I'm always dressed."

We sat down and she reached for my hand.

"Don't worry," she said, "I'm sure it's nothing."

"You don't know that it's nothing," I said. Can you ever believe an actress?

"I have a strong feeling that it's nothing. And soon we'll be on that plane to California."

We were scheduled to fly out to San Francisco soon for a family reunion to honor the ninetieth birthday of my great-aunt Iris, matriarch of the Lipski family.

"I'm not much in the mood for the trip right now," I said.

"You'll have a ball," my mother said.

I sighed and looked around. There were three women in different stages of pregnancy, waiting for Sarler's partners I hoped. In my teens I'd been fascinated with pregnancy and childbirth, and when I became involved with Ben, I began to dream regularly about having his baby. In the uncomfortable week before my period, I was especially susceptible to such dreams. But whenever I brought the issue up, Ben's nervous reaction silenced me, and I continued to use my diaphragm religiously.

The nurse came out and called my name. I followed her to the examination room, leaving my mother behind.

"Undress from the waist down, please," she said, putting a flimsy sheet of paper on the table. "The doctor will be in soon."

I undressed and sat on the table, placing the paper modestly over my lap. On a shelf stood a plastic model depicting a cross-section of a pregnant belly. It looked impossibly uncomfortable. I stared at the upside down fetus developed enough to be recognizable as a baby. The pink of the bisected uterus. The squashed intestines, bladder, and rectum were bisected, but the fetus was whole—suggesting the splitting of the woman's body to create new life. Since my surgery, I had developed a visceral hesitation about pregnancy. I was lost in disbelieving contemplation of the model when Dr. Sarler knocked and walked in.

I'd only known Sarler for the year since the surgery he performed. Tall with jet-black hair and much too handsome to be a gynecologist, Dr. Sarler spoke with a South-African English accent that made him even more intriguing. I thought it very clever of me to have a devilishly attractive gynecologist, which was exactly what this kind of anxiety-provoking situation required.

"Still having that pain?" Dr. Sarler said. "Scoot yourself back. Okay, open up...It's possible, though very unlikely, that you're sensitive enough to feel another cyst growing, something small enough not to show up on the ultrasound."

He sat on a wheeled stool and moved down between my legs, reaching for the speculum on the tray next to the table. The speculum touched my vulva and I screamed—it was burning hot.

"Sorry. The tray was too close to the lamp, and I can't feel the temperature with these gloves on. Here, let me cool it down."

This guy had been my savior the year before so I was ready to forgive him. I took a deep breath and relaxed.

"Everything looks fine inside. Any pain during intercourse?"

"No," I said. "The pain actually stops during sex."

"It's a handy evolutionary trick," he said. "The ovaries pull up and out of the way during sexual excitation."

He slid the speculum out and stood up in order to palpate me. I gazed up at him adoringly. After the surgery, he had told me that my cyst was the size of a grapefruit, and I'd imagined the battle to remove it as a heroic one—surgeon against mammoth growth, armed with only his modest scalpel. It was a dermoid cyst, solid instead of filled with fluid, which is why it couldn't be lanced and had to be surgically removed. When he'd explained that dermoids are oddities in that they contain bits of hair and teeth, I'd thought—*okay, so that's what my body decided to grow instead of a baby.*

With a couple of gloved fingers inside me Sarler poked around, like a woman looking for something in a handbag, while his other hand pushed on the front of my abdomen.

"Ouch," I said. Obviously my ovaries weren't in a pulled-up position.

"I don't feel anything new here. Everything seems to have healed very well," Sarler said, unapologetic. "I'm feeling your uterus now," he continued. "You know, I couldn't feel this clearly before, when the cyst was in the way, but now it's clear—has anyone ever mentioned to you that your uterus is in an inverse position?"

"An inverse position?"

"It's upside down."

"Upside down?"

"Yeah, it's tipped in the opposite of what's normal. Not harmful in any way, but it could make it harder for you to get pregnant," he said. "If you want to have a baby, I wouldn't put it off indefinitely. It could take time."

Just what I needed to hear.

"Okay, why don't you get dressed, and you and your mother can come into my office." He placed a box of tissues on the examination table beside me and left.

A few minutes later my mother and I convened in his office where he sat behind a huge desk with a glass top, his back to a wall of leather-bound volumes thick with knowledge and authority.

"I recommend we do a laparoscopy," Dr. Sarler said. " It's a simple procedure in which we make a small incision in the navel and insert a thin scope so we can look around. You'll be in and out of the hospital in a couple of hours." He smiled at me reassuringly. "And while you're in, we'll also do a D and C."

Used for abortions as well as to check the lining of the uterus, the D and C—dilation and curettage—consists of scraping the inside of the uterus. It's one of those procedures that was obviously invented by some sadistic nineteenth-century gynecologist who never washed his hands. And Dr. Sarler tacked it on, as though it were some kind of dessert. I'd begun to perspire.

"Are there other options?" my mother asked.

"Not if you want a diagnosis."

My mother looked at me.

"Okay," I said. "Let's go ahead with it."

The word "incision" must have made me turn white because Dr. Sarler added, "Julia, whatever it is, at your age, it's probably not life-threatening. It's probably another cyst or endometriosis."

I nodded. Endometriosis—where the lining of the uterus somehow escapes and migrates in patches to other organs surrounding it, leading to bleeding and scarring, chronic pain and possibly infertility—hardly sounded like a happy possibility.

We left his office, stopping in reception to schedule the procedure. The nurse informed us that there had been a cancellation the next morning, if I wanted to do it straight away.

"Might as well get it over with," my mother said, and I nodded to the nurse, thinking that Ben could take an early train into the city and meet us at the hospital.

My mother and I were walking toward Madison when I stopped in my tracks.

"I just realized that tomorrow is Wednesday, and Ben teaches on Wednesday. He won't be able to come."

"It's such a small procedure—do you really need him there? I'll take you back to the apartment afterwards," she said, meaning her apartment, which was around the corner from the hospital. "It doesn't make sense for you to go back down to Fourteenth."

I hesitated, for the first time unsure about my commuting arrangement with Ben.

"Why disrupt his teaching week?" my mother went on. "You can spend the night with us and then he can come in Friday night as usual."

"Well, if it's just a two-hour 'thing,' I should be able to go downtown on my own," I said, suddenly confused.

"You'll come back with me," she said.

"But I'm going back to my place now," I said. I had a date with a certain book.

When I got back to my apartment later, I immediately threw myself on my worn copy of *Our Bodies, Ourselves*, caving in to the desire to know all the gory details of whatever they were going to do to me. Fifteen minutes later I was completely distraught. How did women ever get the idea that it might be reassuring to read all the things that could possibly go wrong with the reproductive system, then read all the things that could possibly go wrong with medical attempts to fix that system? Oh, right— it's not about being reassured, it's about being knowledgeable. Knowledge is power—supposedly. Problem is you never know quite enough.

I called Ben in Princeton and brought him up to date. I sat on the windowsill in the living room, looking down at "my" little garden.

"Well, why don't I just cancel my class tomorrow?" he offered. "Then after the procedure you can decide whether to stay at your parents' or go back downtown."

I was touched. "That's really sweet of you, but there's no reason to disrupt your teaching week," I said, echoing my mother. "I'm going to be in and out in two hours."

"Are you sure?"

"I'm totally sure." I was an expert at saying the exact opposite of what I felt.

"Well, I'll come in on Thursday," he said.

"No," I said, determined to be brave and generous. "You'll come in Friday night, after your class, as usual."

"Wouldn't you rather I came in for the procedure?" he said, backtracking, and we went through the whole thing all over again.

Ben was generous and considerate. He wouldn't have minded coming into the city for the procedure, yet the more he insisted, the more perversely I dug my heels in. Of course, I would have liked him there—he could be helpful in a calm way that ordered things, that brought the terrible into the realm of the manageable. But, having made the decision to separate out a bit, I wanted to test my new independence. Besides, I knew that if Ben did cancel a couple of classes, he would want to make them up later in order to fulfill his duty to his students. And he would get so stressed rejuggling his schedule that it would undo, from my point of view, the benefit of his presence.

There are people who are able to remain calm when "going in for a procedure," but I wasn't one of them. After talking to Ben, my chest felt tight and I fought with myself to breathe.

I thought about Michael, how you could count on him to babysit you through anything that required courage, and dialed his number.

"You've taken your time about calling me. When am I going to see you?" he asked.

"I don't know," I said. I told him about my pelvic pain and the procedure scheduled for the next day.

"Are you frightened?" he asked.

"Of course I'm frightened," I said. "I hate doctors and I hate hospitals. I believe they're out to get you."

"But you know they're not?"

"I don't know what I know."

"Well, there's nothing you can do except give yourself over. Right?"

"Give myself over," I repeated dully.

"Let's plan something for Thursday. Something fun. How about we go rent you a piano? There's this place on West Fifty-Eighth…"

We made a plan to meet. And then he started talking about how he'd found himself on Fifty-Seventh Street the day before and had wandered into an art gallery with some gigantic, wild paintings and then after that into Hammacher Schlemmer where he'd tried out the automated shoe-shiner and the vibrating mattress pad. "And afterwards I asked myself which testifies more to the human imagination, the gadgets at Hammacher Schlemmer or the art gallery, and I couldn't really answer the question."

He was babbling to distract me—and it worked.

After hanging up, I reflected that it was one thing not to have told Ben about my accidental meeting with Michael, quite another to be silent about a planned rendezvous. But the thought flickered and disappeared. I didn't care to see how contradictory my impulses were—how I was simultaneously trying to force Ben to make a deeper commitment to me while needing to "explore other directions," how I was considering having a baby with Ben while gravitating toward Michael. The only thing I was sure of was that the equation had flipped and now read: pain of keeping a secret from Ben < (less than) pain of not seeing Michael again.

The next morning I went uptown and met my mother in the hospital lobby.

"You haven't eaten anything this morning, have you?" she asked.

"No," I said.

Fortunately, the laparoscopy didn't require any horrid pre-op procedures, like the enema and pubic shave I'd experienced before my previous surgery. Walking to the waiting area, I barely listened to my mother's patter, distracting myself instead by thinking about Michael—what were my feelings really, what were his, where would it go? Registration was a bit of a blur, and the next thing I knew I was in a gown on a gurney, terrified and being sedated.

The body doesn't like being tampered with. The body doesn't like being probed, cut, scraped, pricked, inflated, or scoped. The body does appreciate the anesthesia, but some part of my mind remained aware enough to yowl internally, because when I came to, I heard myself screaming, "Is it over? Is it over?"

My mother was standing next to me in post-op. She said to me, "Everything is fine. It's only scar tissue. I'm so relieved."

"But—is it over?"

"Yes, it's over."

Dr. Sarler came in. "You'll be able to go home in a few minutes. Everything is fine. You have some scarring from your surgery last year. Pelvic adhesions are very common among women, I'm afraid. I'll see you in my office tomorrow and we'll talk about it." And he left.

As I slowly became alert, I processed what he'd said. If it was "only" adhesions, did that mean the achy feeling would go away? Or did it mean it wouldn't? He hadn't said anything about the pain. Nobody cares about your pain, except you. I quickly regained full consciousness, but Sarler was gone and I'd have to wait till the next morning to get answers. I got up and dressed.

"How do you feel?"

"I feel fine," I said. I was a little wobbly but otherwise okay. Perhaps because of the residual effect of the anesthesia, the pelvic pain was gone. I got back into my black outfit. It wasn't just my New Yorker costume. Today the black pants would shield me, in case the pad the nurse had left me didn't suffice.

Outside, the Manhattan streets flowed generously with energy, and soon I was walking confidently, my arm passed through my mother's. My parents' apartment was only a couple of blocks away, and I bravely declined the taxi Mariel offered. The wind put its cold hands on my cheeks, bringing me into greater alertness.

"It's nothing," my mother announced to my father when we walked in.

"Nothing?" he repeated, surprised.

She explained about the adhesions. Her use of "nothing" grated on me. When the anesthetic wore off and the pain came back, the diagnosis would be of little comfort.

I went into my old room and lay down for a nap. It was more of a storage room than a bedroom now, with two dark armoires for my mother's many outfits, and a wall where my father's musical instruments stood neatly in their black cases. There were a couple of oil paintings done by my aunt Linda. I closed my eyes and slept off the remainder of what they'd used to drug me.

It was around six when I woke up. Ben would be home. I called him and gave him the report.

"So it's nothing," I concluded, using the same irritating language my mother had used. "At least nothing serious."

"That's good news," he said. "I guess."

"I know. I don't know what to make of it, either."

"So you'll call me again tomorrow, after you meet with Sarler?"

"Of course."

"What's your mother making for dinner?" he asked.

"It smells like chicken."

"Your mother makes a fine chicken," he said.

At dinner my parents talked about the situation in Nicaragua as though nothing unusual had happened that day. I could feel the aching returning as the anesthetic wore off.

"I loathe him," my mother said. We knew she was talking about Reagan, though she never used his name. "He's turning Nicaragua into the next Vietnam."

"I'd say that what he's doing is turning the CIA into an auxiliary branch of the US Army," my father responded.

"Well, nothing new *there*. That's been going on for decades."

"It doesn't matter," my father said. "The people will prevail. They always do."

"What are you talking about? Of course they don't. Look at China. Weapons prevail, not people. This is the century of dictators."

"What do you mean, 'look at China'? Before Mao, the hordes didn't have anything to eat. Now they do."

My parents had basically the same political views, so they had to argue about broader topics, for example, whether the lot of the average human had improved over the past hundred years, whether Communism was possible without corruption, whether there would ever be another president like FDR. Whether the general drift of history was toward good or evil. The easy philosophical questions, in short.

These dinner debates always made me feel like an eight-year-old again, bewildered by the intensity of their political passions. And I shouldn't have been at the table alone with them. I was thirty-two. I belonged at a dinner table with a husband and a child or two. The thought passed again that if I'd gone through a pregnancy earlier, maybe I wouldn't have developed that cyst.

"You can't believe anything you read in the paper, anyway," my father said. "The media is totally corrupt, like the government."

"No," my mother said. "The government is a lot more corrupt than the media." She removed a shoe—one of the ballet flats she always wore— and slammed it on the table for emphasis. The gesture signaled that the four glasses of wine she'd had were kicking in.

My mother had been sober during my early childhood, when regular acting jobs kept her happy. Her sobriety did me little good, because I experienced a miserable loneliness when she went out at night to work.

Then, when I was around twelve, she started striking out at auditions for parts that were clearly meant for younger women. She decided to accept television commercials, which she loathed. She'd come home bitter and angry and would pour herself a glass of wine and place it in the kitchen cabinet, where she kept refreshing it for the rest of the day, while ranting about the lack of good parts for older actresses. She was home for dinner now, but I was miserable for different reasons.

Although the evidence was right before me, I didn't understand she had a drinking problem until I was in college and my cousin Anna, who came home with me one weekend, whispered to me something like, "Wow, your mother drinks almost as much as mine." That's a reconstruction, because the truth is I can't remember what she said exactly. It was one of those moments when you're presented with information so wild that your brain garbles what you're hearing. Still, I got the general gist of it. I had to face the fact that my mother wasn't just "temperamental"— she drank. However, I never used the word "alcoholic" in my head or with anyone else. That was the word I used for Anna's mother, my aunt Linda, who drank every single day, from noon until bedtime, and made a fool of herself in public with her slurring and stumbling and rages. In comparison, my mother, who drank sporadically, in response to specific situations, seemed in the range of normal for someone so frustrated. I forgave her because I felt sorry for her. I couldn't imagine what it would be like to have to give up the thing you love most—the thing that makes life burst at the seams with juice, that makes you sing the colors of the day. Like a dancer who can no longer leap because of a broken ankle, she had to keep the energy inside herself, and drinking was the only way she could reduce that aliveness to a manageable level. Otherwise, she might have exploded. Maybe she'd have been better off if she'd never had the experience of channeling her talent so successfully into Ibsen, Shakespeare, and Irving Berlin.

"Mom," I said, "put your shoe back on." The shoe was sitting on the table, the toe an inch or two off the edge.

She looked straight at me, saw the criticism in my eyes.

"Okay," she said, suddenly the good girl. She stood up, and tentatively, testing her motor coordination, picked up a dish.

"I'll clear the table," my dad said, coming to the rescue.

Mariel nodded, looked at me again, and, a little unsteadily, walked out of the kitchen, grabbing the newspaper off the counter on her way. I gave my father a look.

"She had a rough day," my father said when she was gone. "What's the big deal if she has a couple of drinks?"

My father was always ready to defend her, perhaps because he drank, too, though it barely seemed to affect him.

"*She* had a rough day? I'm the one who had the procedure."

"That's right. And you were knocked out for the duration. It was your mother who sat in the hall doing the worrying."

"Jesus Christ!" Now it was my turn to get up and leave the room. On the way to my bedroom, I passed through the living room where my mother was sprawled on the couch and already drifting into a nap, with the paper open over her chest. It never ceased to amaze me how my parents, whom I considered basically rational, could see everything backwards after a couple of drinks.

When I woke up the next morning, my mother was sleeping in, and I decided I wouldn't wake her but go back to Sarler's by myself.

"You sure you want to go alone?" my father asked.

With affection I took in the concern on his aging face, marked by a long Jewish nose both dignified and caricatural. When I was a little girl he used to give me that same look and say in wonder, "What hath God wrought?" (even though he didn't believe in God). He always made me feel loved and secure.

"Yeah, it's no big deal."

We were having breakfast together at the kitchen table as we'd done thousands of times. My mother still went to bed late as she used to do when she was in shows, so the early morning belonged to my father and me. He always had an English muffin with marmalade, and I had cold cereal.

"That's right," he said. "There's no malignancy, that's the main thing."

I realized then that he and my mother had probably been worrying that I had cancer. But as I was thirty-two, the thought had barely crossed my mind.

"Don't forget to get a painkiller," he went on. "That's the thing about going to see doctors—you always forget to ask the most important question. Then, once you're out, it's too late."

"Okay."

"And I'll see you on Monday, right?"

"Yes."

That was when I would start working for him.

Sitting in Dr. Sarler's office, I listened as he described what he'd seen inside my belly.

"You have scar tissue around both ovaries. On the right side, where you're having the pain, the ovary is stuck to the bowel. The other ovary is stuck to the broad ligament on the other."

"The broad ligament?"

"It's inside the abdominal cavity, like this." He picked up a pad of paper and made a simple drawing of my insides. A circle for the ovary, a loop for the intestine, a couple of parallel lines for the ligament.

I let it sink in.

"But the cyst was on the left ovary," I said. "I don't understand why there are adhesions on the right one as well."

"When I did the surgery on the left one last year, I opened up the right one, too, to make sure that there weren't any cysts in it. Some surgeons are beginning not to do that, but I still think it's wise to check."

I swallowed what he said whole. It would take me years to register the full extent and absurdity of the violation. He had sliced open a part of my body that was healthy, thereby creating permanent scarring. He might have asked me before the surgery which I preferred—the risk of missing another cyst by *not* checking or the risk of creating a new problem by bringing in a knife. I was so grateful to him for "saving" me that it didn't occur to me until a decade later that I ought to have sued him for making the decision for me.

"So what about the pain? Can you remove the scar tissue? Or separate the organs?" I asked.

"Scar tissue is tricky. If you try to remove it, you get more bleeding and just create more scar tissue. The only instance in which we try to remove it is when there are fertility problems. Which brings me to the next issue." He paused.

"Yes?"

"The scarring has probably compromised your fertility. The fallopian tubes are fine, but the adhesions will be in the way of any egg on its way to the opening of the tubes, which also increases the possibility of an ectopic pregnancy." He scribbled another absurd drawing and held it up for me: the circle again for the ovary, a couple of lines, closer together this time, for the tube, and some cross-hatching for the adhesions.

"Which means?"

"Which means that if you want to have a family, you should get started earlier rather than later. It could be difficult for you to become pregnant, given the scar tissue and the peculiar position of your uterus."

Did he really say "the *peculiar* position of your uterus"? Or *particular*? He was about to pick up his pencil again, but I stopped him. "Don't bother," I said. The last thing I wanted to see was his rendition of my upside-down uterus.

He crumpled up the sheet of paper and threw the drawing of my insides into the wastepaper basket.

"So you might want to have a talk with that boyfriend of yours," he said. Assuming that every woman wants to have a baby, he clearly disapproved of Ben's dallying.

"Yes," I said, taken aback by the personal advice.

Sarler had met Ben when I'd had the surgery the year before and knew that we'd been together for ten years. "Where I come from," he'd said, "that would be called common law marriage."

"In my practice," he went on, "I'm now seeing too many women who've waited too long, so think about it."

Was he saying that, at thirty-two, I'd already waited too long? Even as he infuriated me, I had the thought again—this time clear and sad. *He's right. If I'd had a baby in my twenties, I wouldn't be having these complications now.* I'd made the mistake not of waiting too long, but of assuming that my fertility would last until my late thirties, at least.

Sarler closed my folder to signal that our appointment was over. As I stood up, a dull tugging in my abdomen reminded me of my father's reminder to get a painkiller.

"But what about the pain?" I said.

"Now that you know it isn't life-threatening, it may gradually recede from your awareness. The body has a way of getting used to things."

"Well, while I'm waiting for it to 'recede,' what do you suggest?"

"I know that ovarian pain can be intense, like a toothache. We could put you on oral contraception, which suppresses activity of the ovary—"

"I've been on the pill, and it made me really sick—"

"Let me give you something, then."

He handed me a prescription for Percocet. I moved toward the door, and he stopped me.

"I forgot to mention sometimes women with adhesions feel better after a pregnancy—if you can get pregnant. You see, everything is stuck together right now, but a pregnancy can loosen the scar tissue by stretching it out. Another reason to have that baby sooner rather than later."

I looked at him in disbelief. Childbirth is a risky thing. I'd heard enough stories—about one woman who'd torn up into her rectum; another who'd spent her pregnancy in bed and had difficulty walking for a year afterwards; a third who'd developed lupus after her child was born. And what if, like a third of pregnant women, I had to have a Caesarian? How many new adhesions would that create? Maybe one day I would try to get pregnant, but not as a solution to my pain.

"Right," I said, and walked out.

Outside, I stood on the pavement for a moment, catching my breath, and looked upward. Standing in the narrow, rectangular canyon of a Manhattan side street, I could only catch, framed by apartment towers, a slim slice of blue in which clouds feathered out in gently curved parallel lines, like the bleached ribs of a dinosaur skeleton. That's how it is in New York. Most of the time you only see a small piece of sky framed by concrete.

5

WHEN I GOT BACK to my apartment, I sat on the windowsill in the living room and called Ben. He listened to my report, asking the occasional careful question.

"Sarler seems more interested in my fertility than in my pain," I concluded, playing with the leaves of an ivy plant I'd bought and set next to the phone. It connected me to the courtyard garden below.

"Well, he's an obstetrician. He wants more business." Ben said.

It was typical of Ben to joke when I broached this delicate subject.

"His point being," I continued, "that if I want to have a baby—if *we* want to have a baby—we shouldn't put it off indefinitely, because it could be difficult."

There was a pause in which the music made by the planets was less than sweet.

"It's not something I can think about before the spring," he said. *Spring* was his code word for the tenure decision his department would make then. Could I blame him for not wanting to have a pregnant girlfriend/wife on his hand if he lost his job?

"I know you want to talk about it," he went on, "and we can talk about it if you want, but to *act* on it—I don't have the courage right now."

"We'll talk about it then, I guess," I said.

"Yes, we'll talk about it later."

Depression came over me as I hung up. *Talk about it later* seemed emblematic of the way we dealt with the future.

I didn't think the tenure decision was as important as he did, insofar as starting a family was concerned. Millions of people have babies every day without job security. Besides, Ben was brilliant. I believed—but he didn't, unfortunately—that if he didn't get tenure at Princeton, he would be grabbed up by some other university. I guess I'd hoped that the diagnosis of difficult fertility would have spurred us on, giving us the courage to overcome our ambivalence and get me pregnant. After all, Ben would make a good provider and a great father—he was affectionate, reliable, entertaining—and I might (possibly) be an adequate mother. But now I could only wonder whether we would ever make the necessary leap of faith.

Ben's father was a jeweler in London, and his older brother worked in the business with his dad. For Ben—who was always dodging one stereotype or another—failure in academe would mean the horror of returning to Britain to become a "little Jewish jeweler" bent over chains and watches with a magnifying monocle soldered to his forehead.

He also dreaded the increased anxiety that goes with parenthood. He'd once said to me, early in our relationship, that if we ever had children we'd have to have three in order to have an "extra" one just in case. "In case of what?" was a question I didn't have to ask. His younger sister had died at age nine of some rare cancer, and when I met his family I understood the cloud that had overshadowed his childhood. All the calamities that can befall a child and, by extension, her parents and siblings—birth defects, disease, abuse, accidents, death—were not, in Ben's mind, theoretical possibilities. The way he saw it, parenthood was an open invitation to bad luck—a view I understood a little better now that I'd had some bad luck with my own health. "If you're reasonably okay—employed and in a happy relationship—why flirt with disaster?" he once said to me.

Ben's doubts fed my own hesitation. Maybe I'd read too much feminist literature. The women of my generation, coming of age in the seventies, saw marriage as an instrument of patriarchal oppression. We still wanted babies, but we were frightened that marriage would rob us of the freedoms attained in the previous decade. Many of us ended up never having children because we rejected marriage while being unable to imagine parenthood without it. Indeed, my absurd logic went like this: I don't need marriage because Ben and I are as committed as any couple could be. But I can't have a baby until we get married. Since I'm not getting married, I can't have a baby.

There was a sticky, stagnant quality to my confusion, and the more I tried to untangle things, the deeper I went into the muck. Children happen as often as they're planned, emerging from the momentum of life itself—a momentum that Ben and I continually undermined with debate. Perhaps if I'd known women who drew joy from motherhood, I might have had been able to follow my instincts. But I didn't. My mother was certainly of no use there. Like my dad, she encouraged me to put my financial independence first. "Besides," she once said to me, "if you don't have kids, you don't know what you've missed, so what's the problem?"

The message I got was that if she hadn't had me, she wouldn't have missed me. Children weren't that important.

Of course there remained a problem in the form of a deep yearning, which was why I stewed miserably for a while after talking to Ben.

Fortunately, I was meeting Michael at the end of the day.

I walked into Beethoven's Pianos on West Fifty-Eighth Street and found Michael seated at one of the many uprights crowding the room, practicing—maniacally, I thought—the andante movement of a Mozart sonata. He seemed oblivious to other people in the room, yet, when I approached him, he turned his head around and lit up with pleasure. Swinging his whole body around to face me, he sent the sheet music he'd placed on the piano bench beside him flying across the floor.

"Uh-oh," he said, stooping down to collect the music.

I squatted next to him to help.

"Hi," I said. Our eyes met and he dropped the music he was holding.

"I'm such a klutz," he said.

For a brief moment, I was in my power.

"How are you feeling?" he asked. "What did they find?"

I brought him up to date. Michael had had so many girlfriends that you could trust him to grasp the details of any kind of female problem. And he was always easy to talk to.

"Well, maybe now that you know, you'll be less anxious," he suggested.

"And maybe if you're less anxious, you'll have less pain—like the doctor said."

"I hope so." I shrugged, breathed into the spasm, and felt it let go a bit. I had some way of contracting around it, and if I could learn to release that, I'd feel better. "Have you been here long?" I asked.

"A while," he said. "I've found something for you. And it's rent-to-buy." He led me over to a chestnut-colored Wurlitzer upright and sat down to demonstrate. "It's great. Listen."

In a hilarious sequence, he moved from a Bach inventio (his posture controlled and tight), into Chopin (darkly romantic, eyebrows forward), then a madcap blues riff (jazzy, loose shoulders), and finally a schmaltzy John Denver song (sagging and hangdog).

"Oh stop," I pleaded. "Laughing makes the incision hurt." I had a single stitch in my belly button.

"Okay, you try it." He stood up from the bench.

"No," I said, "I haven't played in years…"

"I don't believe that," he said. "Your dad has a piano, right?"

"Well, yeah." Of course I had played, just not very well.

"Come on."

I sat down, played some fragments of pieces that I used to practice long ago. Then I improvised a bit, self-consciously, because improvisation wasn't my forte. The piano had a lovely timbre, just a shade softer than bright, with a fine, subtle resonance. But I took my time in deciding, circulating to some of the other instruments, while Michael followed me around with a smug expression on his face. He knew he'd found the best piano, and he was waiting for me to make that discovery myself.

After the tenth piano I returned to the Wurlitzer.

"You're right," I said.

"Of course I'm right," he said. "Let's find the guy and wrap this up so we can go get something to eat."

I put a deposit down and arranged a delivery date.

"You're very good at helping me spend my money," I joked to Michael.

"I enjoy being helpful," he said, grinning.

I suggested the veggie place on the north side of Fifty-Seventh. With its little booths, it felt like an old-fashioned diner.

"Hope you don't mind eating vegetarian," I said when the food came. It looked good. I had chili over brown rice; he had lasagna.

"No, it's great. I need to get lean...So you feel okay after the procedure?"

"Yeah. Maybe it's residual anesthesia, but the pain has subsided a bit." Then I told him about the fertility issue.

"Why don't you just not use whatever you use not to get pregnant and see if you do?" he suggested. "Isn't that how a lot of gals get pregnant? And then they say to the guy, sorry, honey, I guess I skipped some pills last month, or sorry, honey, I forgot to put the goop in my diaphragm."

"Did you ever get a woman pregnant?"

"Not that I know of," he chewed thoughtfully, perhaps wondering why so-and-so had never called him back. Then he looked back at me sharply. "But about *you*—why not?"

I thought about how vulnerable leaving my diaphragm in the drawer would make me feel.

"This would be a fine moment to get pregnant," I said, "right after I've moved into the city."

Michael shrugged. "It depends on your priorities. What do you really want, Jul?"

"I'm pretty mixed up, actually. Kids seem like so much work...for one person, anyway. And if Ben isn't fully behind it—which he just isn't—it would all fall on me."

"I know what happened to Ben's sister, but he needs to move beyond that and get on with life," Michael said. "He'd be such a great dad. And family's the only thing anyone's really got. Friends come and go, but family's there forever. Personally, I'd give anything to have a kid."

"Really?" I said, surprised.

"Sure. Do you know I even have a baby fund? I've been saving up money for years in the hope that—" He looked away again. "But women don't see me as daddy material."

"They don't?"

"Well, do *you*? Honestly?"

I blushed. It was true. I had a hard time seeing him as a father.

"No, I don't."

"Why?"

"Well, because..." I didn't want to hurt his feelings.

"Because I've had too many relationships? Because I don't seem like the kind of guy who can make a commitment? Because I'm a musician and I don't have job stability or make enough money? Or is it because I'm a slob?"

"Michael!" It was true that everything he mentioned contributed to my inability to see him as a father. I remembered his bedroom in New Haven—the remains of sandwiches in crumpled paper, the dirty laundry on the floor, the LPs stacked without covers. He was the kind of creative person who lived so completely in his head that he was oblivious to his environment.

"In any case, I seem unable to find 'the One,'" he continued. "I'm fated to always fall in love with a woman who's already taken. You want me to tell you about my last relationship?"

I looked at the scar on his neck. "Yes, please."

"I made the mistake of falling in love with a married woman, a brilliant cellist who could do anything—classical, jazz, even pop. You don't expect that from a cello. We were doing it at her place, her husband came in, reached for a kitchen knife, and—that's how it happened." He made a little gesture with his neck, moving the scar forward toward me.

"You were doing it at her place?" I asked incredulously.

"I know—not very smart. He was supposed to be out of town. And I could have been killed. Why didn't we hear her husband come in? Well, it's a biological fact that people in the act of coitus gradually lose their sense of hearing as they approach orgasm. So we didn't hear her husband open the door and walk into the apartment."

He'd always had an almost clinical way of talking about sex. I was used to it.

"And he attacked you?"

Michael nodded.

"With a steak knife. They didn't do a very good job sewing it up in the emergency room," he said.

I shuddered. I was attracted to Michael's passionate nature but I didn't want to have anything to do with the danger and melodrama that went along with it.

"God! And then what happened with—what was her name?"

"Karyn. Oh, her husband forgave her, and she stayed married. Adulterous women usually do. I read a statistic about that once, in a magazine. It seems they crave the excitement of a lover but in the end prefer the stability of marriage."

I raked it over for a moment. "You mean her husband actually *saw* you guys doing it and he was able to forgive her?"

"Maybe it turned him on. For all I know, he's still using the memory of that primal scene as an aphrodisiac." He sighed. "We had a physically very passionate relationship, but at the same time, that was the least important part of it. There was a huge connection between us on an artistic level. She was my muse, my source of inspiration. She had a brightness inside her—it made me want to compose. And she was really in love with me. Sometimes I wonder whether, if I'd been in a parallel situation—if I'd had a girlfriend or wife to fall back on—Karyn and I might have been more careful and carried it on indefinitely. If I'd been in a square instead of a triangle, I might have felt less vulnerable and not acted so stupidly."

"So she couldn't bring herself to leave her husband?"

"Any woman, given a choice between a solid guy with a steady job and an impoverished musician, will choose the solid guy. Women are genetically programmed to avoid risk—you know, they need security for the baby."

"How 'solid' could this guy have been if he attacked you with a knife?"

"He was a lawyer with a six-figure income."

"That's solid, all right," I admitted.

"She has two kids now."

"I'm so sorry."

"It broke me into pieces. I told her she had to leave him, I even threatened suicide, but after he attacked me, she became frightened of him. Why would any woman want to stay with someone capable of that kind of violence?" He shrugged. "Anyway, I learned my lesson: nothing good ever comes from secrecy. That's why"—he leaned forward, staring into me— "that's why I think you ought to tell Ben that we're seeing each other. I mean, that we're friends again."

I was startled. "But I thought we'd decided—"

"I've thought it over. We don't have anything to hide, right? That kiss ten years ago was an accident, right? You know what I think? I think the three of us should get together and do something fun—like drive out to the island and have an old-fashioned clambake."

"A clambake?" I was stunned and, yes, somehow disappointed that he didn't want to keep our relationship a secret. The way he glided over our kiss hurt me, although I didn't know myself what it had meant. "I don't even know what a clambake is."

"You dig a pit in the sand, gather some stones and seaweed—it's a lot of fun. Anyway, it's time, don't you think, for Ben to 'forgive' me for dropping out of graduate school?"

"Well, obviously, but what am I going to say? I told you, he'll be upset. He won't want me to see you anymore."

"Even to be just friends?"

"Even to be just friends."

"Of course, we stepped out of bounds, so he's justified in being suspicious. That's why it's so important for us to reinstate a three-way thing."

"I wouldn't even know how to broach the subject."

"We'll figure something out."

After eating, we walked over to the Columbus Circle subway station. He was going uptown and I was going downtown, and we parted inside the station, between one staircase and another, with the smell of piss and subway soot wafting around us.

"Good luck working for your father, and I guess I'll see you when you get back from California," he said. "Ben going with you?"

"No, he's finishing an article for the tenure case."

"Have fun," he said.

Then, in what had become a familiar, troubling ritual, we hugged a little too tightly, I felt my sternum against his firm belly, and we parted.

Later, I kept on hearing those two absurd words in my head— "clam bake." I had a hard time picturing Ben, Michael, and me standing on a beach throwing clams into a smoking pit. Was it Michael's way of showing—or pretending—that he wasn't harboring even the trace of a sexual fantasy about me? I felt rebuffed. Well, he was messy and unreliable, as artists tend to be. It would be unwise to get involved with him.

Three days later, I was in Princeton, walking along the Raritan Canal with Ben. I'd taken him away from his desk to one of our favorite places to visit in the fall, and we ambled in silence, gazing at the reflection of yellow ochre and sienna on the silken surface of the water. The foliage flared brightly on either side of the mirror that ran between the riverbanks. Rural New Jersey felt sweet after a few days in the city, and I enjoyed the contrast between city and country that went with commuting. Maybe that's what I needed to be happy—contrast between places, activities, and maybe even men. We never held hands when we walked, I don't know why. In Ben's silence I imagined his worry about his professional future or him tinkering with a piece of writing he was working on. My own silence was stillness and movement, like the moment itself, with its slice of concealment and fluttering, of color exploding in the wind, of contraction against the cold of the season. The elms rustled as I held my second meeting with Michael close to my chest—an uncomfortable, but not unbearable, secret.

We stopped to watch some ducks swimming close to the edge. The quacking, both soothing and amusing, ruffled us out of our quiet places.

"I want to apologize for being flippant on the phone," Ben said. "The information that Dr. Sarler gave you, obviously it's important for us. We have to talk about it."

His reopening the baby topic took me by surprise.

"I know you're anxious and confused," I said.

"I wish I knew what we should do. I wish I wasn't so afraid."

I nodded. "I think everyone is afraid about having kids. It's such a big change."

"We're more afraid than most people," he said.

"Yeah."

"Where does that leave us, then?"

"I could be happy with whatever we decide," I said. "To have children or not. If we didn't, I could think of myself as 'childfree', not childless—free to do whatever I wanted—or what we wanted—" The words felt true as I spoke them.

"Like traveling?" Ben asked. He knew I regretted not having been more adventurous and traveling in college and in my early twenties, the way Anna had.

"Yes, like traveling. And doing something interesting with my work life." I paused briefly before continuing. "The thing that's hard for me is the indecision. Not knowing where we're going. I feel a need for a road map. Because not knowing makes me feel confused and even more anxious."

"It's your moving into New York that makes me feel confused and anxious," he said.

"Oh, Ben." I went into his arms. "I haven't abandoned you. I'm just in the city working for my father."

"Really?"

"Really."

"I wish I were going to San Francisco with you," he said. I was starting work for my father on Monday, then leaving for California on Friday.

"It's all right," I said.

He held me tight. I held him even tighter, fighting whatever it was that, like a gigantic vacuum, was pulling me away from him. The truth was that I was looking forward to a trip without him. I needed some distance and wanted to talk to Robin about Michael. With ample life experience and professional training as a therapist, she was the wisdom carrier among us. And she'd been Michael's lover ten years before. Surely she'd have some advice for me.

6

IT WAS A CRISP OCTOBER morning when I went to my father's office, dressed in my usual Manhattan black. Black pants, shirt, jacket. A single departure from my usual dress code, a headband around my head with a black-and-white floral print, inaugurated this new chapter in my life. My father's office, on East Sixty-Eighth Street between Third and Second Avenues, was on the second floor of an old brownstone with wrought-iron plant holders and painted plaster stairs leading up to the front door. I had helped my father during tax season for years, and every detail of the place was familiar—the work area looking out over geraniums onto the street, the kitchen and bathroom off a long, dark hall, and the tiny room with file cabinets at the back of the building. I arrived to find Betty, my father's assistant, at her desk. My father sat on the couch, consuming a bagel and cream cheese.

"I thought you weren't supposed to eat cream cheese," I said.

"Low-fat," he said. "And it tastes low-fat. Kind of dry." He licked a blob off the corner of his mouth and wiped it with a paper napkin. He gestured toward his desk with his chin. "It's yours now."

I hesitated.

"Go ahead," he said.

I sat down in his chair.

"If you get stuck with anything," he continued, "Betty knows the answer."

Betty and I had lunched and shopped together a number of times over the years. In her mid-thirties, she would serve as my guide not only to my father's business but also to Grown-Up New York, a very different place from the city I'd known as a child—a jungle in which one was always searching for a dentist who caused no pain, restaurants with fast but decent lunch food, and a dry cleaner for that vintage sweater with the beaded embroidery.

"So you're my new employer?" She spoke with a semisweet Queens accent.

"No, I think my father's still your employer," I said.

"We're going to give it a trial period before we make it official," my father explained. He returned to his bagel and opened up *The Wall Street Journal*. After leafing through the paper, he pulled out his copy of volume five of *The Remembrance of Things Past* and settled in. My father knew something about everything. He could explain electricity, why ice floats, and the structure of the *Niebelung*. And he was still adept at the piano. His one intellectual flaw was his uncritical belief in Communism; he was as blind there as the rest of the lefty cohort of that generation.

An hour later, he went home and Betty and I were alone.

"Boss-in-training, then?" she said to me with a little smirk. "You old enough?"

"Now, don't you dare," I said, wagging a finger at her.

"Anything you need to know, I'm here for you," she said.

We laughed.

I loved being self-employed. Not having anyone looking over my shoulder, not having to punch in and out or account for every hour taken off from work to do something personal.

Still, I was uncomfortable because part of me knew that I could have aimed higher than my father's business. In college I'd been deeply involved with music for a couple of years, then had double-majored in English and math. The college career counselor said I was a renaissance woman and a number of careers were open to me. I could become a teacher of English, math, or music at a university level, or a teacher of all three in a grade-school context. I could go into applied mathematics and technology. There was journalism, editing, publishing. There was business. An MBA is a handy thing, he said, if I wanted to make money. I listened with little confidence to the counselor, a middle-aged bearded fellow who'd clearly fallen into career counseling because he couldn't get his own act together.

Ten years later I hadn't done anything except drift because I'd never been good at knowing what I wanted or needed. A young woman in the 1970s with a fancy BA could go places her predecessors couldn't have. Such a woman, if she'd been well nourished by feminist writers, as I had, *should* have done something of note. But the education and the reading hadn't helped me break with the female habit of making relationships my highest priority, and for a decade I'd drifted in Ben's wake, following him wherever he went. Now, even as I sought a little autonomy vis-à-vis Ben, I was turning to another man—my father—in order to feel secure.

A few days later I was on the plane for San Francisco. My mother alternately played solitaire and studied a script for an upcoming audition. It was the weekend after Black Monday and my father picked his way through *Business Week* and the *Journal*, highlighting important facts and charts for me. I understood enough about economics to follow the financial news, but he liked teaching me.

We separated after retrieving our bags. My parents rented a car and set off for a hotel downtown, while I took a taxi to the Richmond district. My cousin Anna and I would stay there with Robin, who had bought one of those little San Francisco houses that seem packed together extra tightly as though to hold each other up in a quake. I arrived to find Anna already there and Robin nursing her housemate's baby, Matthew. After a wild youth, Robin had settled into a domestically stable if unusual arrangement. She and a friend had decided to get pregnant at the same time in order to raise their children together. No, they weren't gay, she explained repeatedly. They were a kind of miniature commune.

"Both babies nurse with both of us—which the doctors told us would never happen. But what do they know?"

Robin was the only one of us second-generation Lipskis who had a child. She had never been able to commit to a relationship with a man, but she'd made the leap into motherhood with surprising ease.

"Where's Gloria?" I asked, and at that moment the front door swung open and a woman with long, dirty-blonde hair came in with Robin's baby girl, Serena.

"Welcome," Gloria said and unceremoniously placed the infant in my arms.

It was my first encounter with Serena, who'd been born the previous spring. True to her name, she looked up at me with contentment, unruffled by the newcomer staring down at her. Buffeted by waves of fear and desire, I held her close to my heart and gazed at her tiny blue eyes framed by dark, thick lashes. I'd been looking forward to a weekend of escaping my personal obsessions, but here was one staring straight at me. "My little niece," I whispered. She was so beautiful it hurt to hold her. Yes no yes no went the brain and the womb.

Anna moved next to me to look at her, too.

"Do you want to hold her?" I asked. I was relieved when Anna took Serena from me.

"She's splendid," Anna said. There were tiny, annoyingly sentimental tears in her eyes.

"My mother has really gone overboard this time," Robin said about the party scheduled for the next day. "At least a hundred and fifty people, and a six-piece band. Catered, of course."

Iris lived in Nob Hill, on the ground floor of a three-story townhouse owned by my aunt and uncle, who occupied the two floors upstairs. The party would take place in their gargantuan living room, which enjoyed a glamorous view of the city and the Golden Gate Bridge that served to remind the entire family that the California Lipskis were the branch of the tribe that had evolved the furthest from our shtetl origins to an elegant lifestyle congruent with our essential worth. I anticipated world-class food, jazz, and an inspiring parade of cocktail dresses.

"And what's up with you?" I asked, turning to Anna.

"I'm moving to New York," Anna said, looking at me. "I got a job at the Metropolitan."

"Really?"

"Assistant curator, European art."

"Wow," I said. "When do you start?"

"After New Year's. I'm moving back in December. Maybe for good."

"Really?"

I couldn't help being skeptical. Anna had always been on the move, more than once pulling me into her orbit. After her junior year in Paris, she invited me to travel around Italy with her, and for two months we careened, as close and quarrelsome as sisters, from Milan to Venice, then south to Rome, where we visited our eccentric aunt Doris, who lived there. After graduation, Anna continued to follow the impulses dictated by her wanderlust. She returned to Paris, then Rome, where she taught English to support herself and had a love affair that ended so disastrously I needed to visit Rome a second time to perform a rescue operation. Italy was followed by a teaching fellowship in Hong Kong. I envied the way she kept perfecting her languages as she moved from country to country. When she came back to the States, she kept moving around, following different boyfriends who never "worked out." Somewhere in all this, she managed to get a master's degree in art.

"I'm looking forward to being back home for a while."

I might also look forward to it, if her current boyfriend was tolerable. "You with anybody these days?" I asked.

"No, the last one was another dud." She smiled wistfully. "But I think working at the museum might be lucky for me."

"Lucky?"

"She's looking for a rich husband," Robin said, laughing.

"Well, why not?" Anna countered. "A rich spouse is the modern artist's equivalent of the Renaissance patron."

"Speaking of Anna's men," Robin said teasingly, "guess who I ran into? Val Findlay. He has a beard now. We had lunch a couple of times, and I invited him to the party. I hope that's okay."

"Why wouldn't it be?" Anna said. "He was never one of 'my' men."

"No," Robin said, "but he had a soft spot for you, I always thought."

When Anna took her class on the nude at Yale, Val agreed to pose for her. For a month he was in our living room, completely naked, his flaccid dick always in exactly the same position, just slightly to the left. When Robin and I would walk through the living room, he didn't blink. Either he had no inhibitions or he was so infatuated with Anna that he didn't even notice us.

"But if Val really is that infatuated with Anna," I used to joke, "you'd think his dick would get hard with her staring at it all the time."

"Performance anxiety," Robin would say.

Who knows whether Val was infatuated with Anna or not. As for Anna, she could be very private about her relationships, so much so that when, in the spring of our senior year at Yale, she broke up with her high-school boyfriend, I never knew exactly why. Did she secretly lust after Val? Or was there someone else? For a while I entertained the paranoid fantasy that she had a crush on Ben. My jealousy led me to believe that she would be attracted to anyone I was, because she was a larger-than-life double of me whose personality realized those parts of mine struggling to emerge: she created art easily, whereas I got blocked; she found a boyfriend early, whereas I had to wait for years. She was smart and creative, tall and fascinating.

"So what's Val up to these days?" Anna asked Robin.

"He's a professional photographer. He's going to take pictures at the party and bring his camcorder, too."

Anna looked at me. "Things okay with you and Ben?" she asked, changing the subject as though to prove there had never been anything between her and Val.

"Things are basically good." It was a simplification, not a lie.

"It's time to put these babies to bed," Robin said, for they were both asleep now. It was with relief that I watched Anna and Robin go up the stairs carrying the babies, but the convivial dinner that followed—the four of us at a round table over the kind of vegetarian sauté Robin had taught me to make in college—was interrupted, as was the evening and the night that followed, by crying and the sounds of Robin or Gloria tending to a little one. Later on, sharing the foldout couch with Anna, I was disturbed by an achy feeling in my abdomen, like PMS but worse, a provocation of a place in the body that was half-dead, half-wild with life wanting to happen. *I should have stayed in a hotel, away from this.* Around two a.m. I took a Percocet and fell into a deeper, hallucinatory sleep, in which dreams of pregnant women shoving babies at me tugged at tissue and fluid.

Light finally broke and I woke up to see Anna next to me, her auburn hair tangled all over the pillow. She opened her eyes and looked at me.

"Jet lag," she said. "I could use another three hours' sleep."

A baby cried upstairs.

"Dream on," I said.

But the crying stopped and we both fell back asleep, only to be woken by morning bustling in the kitchen, the smell of coffee and pancakes on the griddle.

Ben called during breakfast. The kitchen was noisy with four adults and two babies at the table, and Robin shooed me upstairs, where I could talk in the quiet of Gloria's room.

Ben sounded depressed. "I wish I were there," he said.

"It's all right. It's kind of nice to be with my cousins, without you." I knew he'd take my rudeness the right way.

"You mean in your family gynocracy?"

"Yeah." I chuckled.

"I love your family, and I'm missing out."

"You're doing what you need to do to get the packet in," I reminded him. "Packet" was our word for the pile of documents he had to submit for the tenure process.

"I feel like I'm in prison," he said.

"I admire you," I said. "Your tenacity and resolve."

"Thanks," he said. "I appreciate your support. I know I've been less available for the past six months. As soon as this is over, things will get back to normal. I promise."

After hanging up, I sat on the bed for a moment, feeling ashamed of ever having resented his involvement with his work. Because I'd felt neglected, I had abandoned *him* by moving into the city, when he was doing what he needed to do in order to survive economically. Moreover, his will to make something of himself had motivated me to take over my dad's business in order to give some shape to my own life.

Robin's head appeared at the doorjamb. "You've got to finish breakfast and get dressed. There's a party today, and we're cooking."

In my family we always cook a lot before a party, even if it's catered, because the paid-for food might be disappointing, and it's wise to have supplements. So we cooked all morning, with a brief walk over to Clement Street, to trawl through the Chinese grocery stores for some fresh scallions, Japanese noodles, and black sesame seeds. There was a low, heavy fog that Gloria promised would clear by early afternoon. Serena and Matthew were bundled next to each other in the stroller, and Gloria stopped to reposition the blankets right under their chins.

Gloria practiced acupuncture before it became popular. Soon I was telling her my "female complaints" and, passing the stroller to Robin, she offered to take my pulses. Pulses in the plural, she explained, because there were six organ systems she could contact with three of her fingers on my wrist. And so I let her "listen," my hand in hers, as we stood in front of a vegetable stand heavy with bok choy, yu choy and wrinkled cucumbers called bitter melons—shades of greens warming the northern palette of urban neutrals under a gray sky.

"You have liver stagnation," Gloria said. Catching the startled look on my face, she added, "No, nothing is wrong with your actual liver. The stagnation has to do with how the chi, or energy, is flowing from the liver through the meridians. It's the energy being stuck that causes the discomfort. You know, some women have pelvic adhesions but no pain. We can do a few needles when we get back to the house. You open to it?"

"Uh—sure. Why not?" It would have been narrow-minded of me to refuse.

"And why don't we find a formula for you…"

Leaving the babies with Robin and Anna, Gloria led me into a Chinese herb store. As she browsed the boxes of patent formulas inscribed with Chinese characters, I hovered over the bins of dried sea horses and fish, shriveled mushrooms, wizened ginseng—samples of the entire natural world desiccated to various shades of brown, beige, and taupe, exuding a musty smell that was oddly comforting.

"Here," Gloria said, grabbing a little green box covered with Chinese and English writing. "This will help you." She was so positive in a blonde, California kind of way that I believed her.

When we got back to the house, Gloria had me lie on her bed and went to get her needles. With the babies napping, the house was quiet, and Gloria's room, with its wood-poster bed and white curtains, felt peaceful. Necklaces and earrings hung neatly from nails above her dresser, and three crystals hung by the window on nylon threads, casting rainbow-colored spots of light on the pale green walls.

"Is this going to hurt?" I asked when Gloria returned.

"Hardly at all. A tiny prick, then nothing."

Gloria rolled up my sleeves and pant legs and inserted needles here and there. Again she felt my pulses, then pushed my shirt up and, asking "May I?", unzipped my pants. A few needles pricked my abdomen.

"If you'd get some acupuncture when you got back to New York, I think you could get a handle on this," she said. "There's also a wiriness to your pulse that suggests some emotional aspect to whatever's going on."

"That's possible."

At first I felt nervous as she pinned me with threads of steel. Then something happened, a kind of whoosh of relaxation from head to toe, and I fell asleep.

I was awakened by the click of a glass of water set on the bedside table and the feel of her fingers on my wrist again.

"That's better," she said. She cocked her head as though really leaning in to hear my pulses. Then she removed the needles.

"I feel better," I said. The achy feeling was gone.

"Yes, we moved the chi that was stuck there." Gloria opened the green box she'd bought on Clement Street and took out a little brown bottle inside that held irregularly shaped, dark pills. "And the herbs will keep it moving smoothly. Here. Take eight."

I opened the bottle. The pills smelled musty and spicy, like the store itself. I swallowed them hopefully.

It was just the beginning of my California weekend.

7

WE WERE WRAPPING UP the soba noodle salad when Val rang at the door. Taking in the perfunctory hug Anna gave him, I concluded she'd spoken the truth—Val had never been one of her men.

"Hey, Julia," Val said to me, extending a hand that was as thin and wiry as the rest of him. His beard, trimmed short, looked soft; his forehead and neck had a healthy, Mediterranean tan. He had the kind of interesting, rugged handsomeness that can lead to an easy time with women.

"You've improved," Val added. I felt agitated by the flattery. Ben was far away. So was Michael—but why should Michael matter in this equation?

In the background, Anna was helping Gloria gather equipment for the babies while Robin executed a last-minute diaper change.

Val leaned against the wall, staring at me. "I'm looking forward to meeting your—aunt? grandmother?"

"She's my great-aunt but she's always treated me like a granddaughter. My grandmothers both died when I was little."

"Listen, why don't you ride with me?" he asked.

"Why don't you," shouted Anna, who was obviously listening in from the landing upstairs. "I'm riding in the back of Robin's car, between the babies."

"I'm parked illegally," Val shouted up.

"Then get out of here!" Robin shouted down.

Outside, the sky had cleared to a perfect blue, as Gloria had promised. The sun was sauna-hot now, the air still cool. It was two in the afternoon. The party, in deference to Iris's aged friends who petered out early, would start at three.

I watched Robin and Gloria, with babies, lead Anna toward their car. Val had a rusted, olive Volkswagen bus parked in front of their driveway. Glancing into the back of the bus, I saw a mattress with an Indian bedspread on it, a sleeping bag, a pillow, and a box of photographic equipment partly covered by an old wool blanket.

Val and I climbed into our seats and buckled in.

"So what's the story on the bus?" I asked. I'd picked up that phrase, *What's the story*, from Michael.

He glanced sideways at me, pulled away from the curb. "I travel around," he said. "Photographic expeditions. Soon I'll be going up to the Sierras."

"Do you make a living at that?"

"I do pretty well between this and that. I get assignments and sometimes teach. I take groups of photography students into the wilderness. What about you—still baring body and soul in poetry?"

That damn sonnet followed me everywhere.

"No," I said, "I've given that up." I told him about how I was taking over my father's business.

"I bet you'll take it to the top," he said.

"I don't know what that would mean."

"Why don't you go into financial advising? Target rich New York women, the ones who make big bucks in their divorce settlements. You'd get rich yourself, then you could do what you want with your life."

"Hmm," I said. "You've got a creative mind."

"I've got a very creative mind," he said, giving me a flirtatious look.

As we rode past the shops on Clement Street, then through fancier neighborhoods with Victorian houses painted in bright color schemes, I caught glimpses of the brilliant bay to the north and east. We arrived at my aunt and uncle's to find that they had arranged valet parking for the guests.

"Ritzy family you got," Val commented.

"Just this branch of it," I said.

The parking attendants, in ridiculous red jackets vaguely reminiscent of the Queen of England's royal guards, hovered by the van as Val opened the back door to grab his equipment. As he leaned over, his pants rode down a bit, revealing the elastic of his brief and his tanned lower back. With the feeling of doing something vulgar, I stared at his naked skin, then forced myself to look away.

"You wanna help?" he asked, placing a black vinyl bag over my shoulder. He hoisted two more bags over his own shoulder and gathered a loose tripod in his bent arm.

We entered my aunt's house and went up the two flights to the living room. The walls of the staircase were, like the entire house, crowded with paintings, drawings, and prints by contemporary artists. Framed and grouped, they made for a sophisticated, moneyed effect. Between two abstract canvases, a hyperrealistic painting of a San Francisco street scene depicted parking meters in front of a bakery window.

Upstairs we found thirty or forty guests had already arrived. My mother and my aunts Linda and Sarah were leaning over the hors d'oeuvres, rearranging the caterers' table setting. Linda's husband, my uncle Carl, who was some kind of scientist, examined the display, as though hunting down some exotic toxin. Gazing at his rotund figure, I imagined that he lived his life pulled in opposite directions by his enormous appetite and his fear of food poisoning. Right behind him, my father was talking to my uncle Herbert, whom he privately called "a rich son-of-a-bitch." Neither of my parents liked Robin's dad, who was rumored to have serial affairs behind my aunt's back.

Then I saw the guest of honor seated in a bay window with the Golden Gate Bridge in the background. Iris was dressed in a heavy-looking, black lamé dress patterned with crimson and purple flowers. She had further adorned herself with some large gold pieces—a chunky snake bracelet with ruby eyes, a pin shaped like a fist holding a cluster of gemstone flowers, and a diamond necklace. It was a mystery how she'd accumulated this stuff— my great-uncle Isaac couldn't have been rich. A furniture merchant and painter in Brooklyn, he sold sideboards and chests that he decorated with elaborate floral designs. When he began to drink later in life, he started inserting body parts into his decorations—a breast inside a flower, an erect penis peeking out from behind a leaf. This eventually led to disgrace and ruin. Iris's jewelry must have come by way of her subsequent boyfriends.

I approached and took her aged, veined hand. Her grip was still firm.

"It's so wonderful to see you," she said. "I appreciate it, you know, all the effort going into this." She let go of my hand and put her arms out to me for a hug. I fell into it, like I did when I was a little girl.

"Dear Iri." I used the nickname we'd all had for her when we were little. "I'm so happy to be here. You look beautiful."

"And is the handsome photographer your escort?" she asked.

"This is Val, a friend from college."

"I'm making a video of the evening," Val said, shaking her hand. "May I interview you in a while?"

"I'd be delighted," she said.

Val wandered off, and I sat next to my great-aunt.

"And Ben couldn't come?" she asked.

"No, he couldn't," I said.

"I've heard you're commuting now…But things are okay with the two of you?"

It was becoming a question I could barely stand. "Things are great," I said.

I took her hand again, gazing at the intricate marbled effect that the capillaries and veins made under the translucent skin. Then I reached over and played with the giant snake bracelet the way I used to when I was little and she would come to New York and take Anna and me to the Metropolitan Museum of Art for lunch.

As though reading my mind, she said, "I think I've got one more trip to New York in me yet."

"I hope so."

"When I think of New York now, I think 'cold.' Did I ever tell you the story about how my mother and I, in our first years in America, shared a single coat?" It was her only story of immigrant hardship; I'd heard it many times. "So in the winter we could never go outside at the same time. We had to take turns." She looked back at Val, who was interviewing someone across the room. "I wonder what kind of questions he's going to ask me." She posed for me. "Is my makeup okay?"

She had too much rouge on, and the eyeliner on her creped lids was unevenly applied. "It's perfect," I said.

The afternoon wore on. Guests trickled in steadily. The elderly ones were all out of breath from the two flights up the stairs. My mother came up to me holding a glass of wine and kissed my cheek.

"I don't see why Sarah couldn't have thrown the party some place at ground level or with an elevator," she said, with that indignation she got in her voice when drinking. "They could afford it. Just look at these old folks. They're about to keel over."

Val appeared, just in time to rescue me from my mother.

"You have to take me around, introduce me," he said.

"You never struck me as the shy type," I teased.

"I'm not," he said. "I just want your company. Come on."

I followed him obediently while he filmed interviews with the guests. He was full of questions: *Do you have any stories about Iris you'd like to share? How do you feel about being here today?* An extrovert having fun, Val didn't need any help from me. But I enjoyed watching him. I collected a plate of miniature hors d'oeuvres and began popping them into his mouth while he worked, my thumb and index finger taking in the sensation of his warm lips and soft moustache and beard. I was flirting with him in front of my whole family, but it would never get back to Ben. The women in my family might judge each other, but we never tattled.

Val and I looped back toward Iris, and I got to hear the story about sharing the winter coat all over again. Then he reached Anna, who balked at being filmed.

"Hey, Anna, you owe me," Val said, referring to the nude portraits.

"I don't know what to say. What do you want to know?"

"What's it like having a matriarch in the family?"

"The thing about matriarchs," Anna said, "is that they're both a blessing and a curse."

"Go on," Val said, "I'm interested."

"You know, Iris is ninety now, she's lucid and healthy and a wonder, but on some level she's becoming a burden. I don't know how my aunt Sarah feels about shouldering the entire responsibility for her. My mother seems to have pretty much checked out about it, that's for sure."

Her mother had crept up behind her, listening. "Sometimes checking out is the path of least resistance," Linda said. "A form of self-defense."

"Mom, what I meant was—"

"I know what you meant. And of course you're right." My aunt Linda, with her frizzy Jewish hair, clay-rimmed fingernails, and classic red lipstick, looked like a bohemian forced out of her lair and into civilization at gunpoint. Only the gold locket around her neck suggested she might have once been a good girl. "I have no filial sense of duty. I'm here under duress." She grimaced, took a sip of something on the rocks. I could count on Anna's mother getting a lot drunker than mine.

Val squirmed, glanced out the window. The sun was setting and the colors coming up around the bridge reflected in crisp metallic colors on the bay.

"Okay, thanks, let's stop there," he said. He swiveled away from the mother-daughter pair, saying to me in a low voice, "I've had it. Let's take a break," he said. "Come on."

"What?"

"We've got an hour or two of daylight left. Let's go for a drive."

I hesitated for a fraction of a second only, exchanging looks with Robin, who, from the other side of the room, gave a subdued nod as she saw us leave together. She would know I'd left and with whom. That somehow made it okay and safe, like in college, when she would pick up a guy at a club—no, we used the word "disco" back then—and make sure I saw them leave together. Except for tonight it was the other way around, and it felt terrific. Like a skier taking off, I followed Val out of the living room and down the stairs.

8

"WHAT DO YOU WANT to see?" Val asked.

"I don't know. Anything. I never see much when I come here. I usually just hang out with my family."

"Been over the bridge?"

"Not yet," I said.

"Okay, then." The ride down the hill was so steep that it felt like diving. One bounce and we'd be in the bay. When we reached bottom, Val headed toward the water, winding through the city with the quick expertise of a driver who knows the whereabouts of all the one-way streets and no-left-turn signs.

"Great," I said. "I get to experience your manic driving style." I didn't want to admit that I occasionally suffered from motion sickness.

"I want to get to the other side of the bridge while the light is still good."

"As long as you're not worried about safety."

"I'm a safe driver," he said.

As we headed through the Presidio on Route 101, the Golden Gate Bridge kept disappearing behind clusters of trees then reappearing, each time growing larger and brighter like some gargantuan orange toy that was being inflated.

As we passed through the toll and rode north across the bridge, I watched the pedestrians crossing on foot or leaning over to gaze down at the water.

"I want to do that," I said.

"We'll park on the other side."

I craned my neck to look back at the sand-colored palette of San Francisco receding behind me, its windows reflecting the low sun in gold glints painful to the eye. To the right, the Bay rippled back, huge and flat, toward the Berkeley and Oakland hills sparkling in the distance. Ahead of us rose the Marin headlands, intoxicatingly green and close. In Manhattan, you had to travel huge distances to get out of the concrete jungle; here it was on the other side of a bridge.

We parked and walked back to stand on the north side of the span. Holding onto the rail, I could feel the vibration caused by the cars crossing behind me and the push of the wind—strong and cold and clean. With a girlish instinct, I grabbed Val's arm. He swiveled toward me, put his other arm around my waist.

"You got a boyfriend?" he asked.

"Ben—the same one I had at Yale. What about you?"

"Yeah, I got a girl up north. We've been together five years."

He looked at me inquiringly. Then with a quick gesture he grabbed me, drew me close, and kissed me. My lips took in the warmth of his mouth and the feeling of his beard; it felt like his kiss came with a blanket. He put a hand behind my head to steady it and kissed me harder.

"You taste good," he said.

"So do you."

A stronger gust of wind pushed me closer to him, and I screamed happily.

"Let's get out of here," he said.

We walked back to the van and climbed in. I didn't ask myself what I was doing or why; it was as though I'd stepped into someone else's story.

Val suggested we drive down to Sausalito to get something to eat and, exiting the highway, we wound down through the steep hillside town to the water's edge. The bay had a dark pearl shimmer in the falling light, and the city of San Francisco had receded to a flat crenellated skyline of gray against blue. We parked and, holding hands, wandered into a pizza place, where we sat at a table squeezing each other's knees. The encounter was escalating with exciting rapidity. I've always needed to check a guy out thoroughly before touching or kissing him, as though men were a dangerous, other species. But for some reason I felt okay with Val, maybe because I'd known him in college, maybe because I was so far from New York. When I got on the plane home, I'd leave all this behind.

"So where do you actually live?" I asked.

"Near Mendocino."

"Mendocino?"

"North," he said, not about to explain California geography to me. "I have a piece of land I'm building on. In the redwoods. I grew up there."

"I didn't know that. And where do you stay when you're down here?"

"I park on some friends' property, here in Marin, and sleep in my van. Someday I'll get a place in San Francisco. My friends have a farm close by. You want to see?"

That was the moment when I decided to go ahead with it, without any sense of how far "it" might go.

"Sure."

Back in the van, we drove north on 101, exiting onto a back road in a rural area. We passed a small shopping center, then turned onto another back road, over a hill and down. He turned into a driveway and parked. The air had a pungent smell.

"What kind of farm?"

"Mostly goats," he said.

He turned off the headlights, stepped into the back of the van, pulled me back with him, and began kissing and undressing me. The moon gleamed in just enough for me to see Val's face in the dark. A goat bleated. A shadow of pain in my abdomen reminded me that I couldn't completely escape my life or my body. And I didn't have my diaphragm with me, and straight people were starting to worry about AIDS, so shouldn't we use a condom? What did I know about Val, really—how many women he'd been with? But I felt comfortable as he explored me. With tenderness and enthusiasm, his hand then his lips, cold from the autumn night then gradually warming, moved over my breasts. His beard and moustache moved lightly against my thighs. I felt knocked down, cleansed, and renewed by the ocean of his attention. The van became tropical, as the windows clouded over with steam from our breathing.

"Can I put myself inside you?"

I balked. "I don't want to get pregnant."

"You're not on the pill?"

"No," I said. "Don't you have a condom?"

"Actually, no, it's not like I do this all the time," he said. "Please—"

"No," I said. "Can't we go get some? Isn't there a drugstore at that shopping center we passed?"

"What? I'm just going to pack this up"—gesturing to his erection—"go to the drive-through condom store and yell out, 'Hey, one box of rubbers to go, please!'"

"Why not? I'll run in and get them, if you want. We have the whole night." I stood firm. It would be absurd to get pregnant by someone besides Ben, when I didn't even know whether I could get pregnant. I wasn't going to take any chances.

"Oh, come on," he said, drawing me closer.

"No." I said firmly.

It never crossed my mind that it might cross *his* mind to force me. Fortunately, my trust was well placed. He just looked at me and burst out laughing.

"Okay, you win," he said. He pulled on his briefs, pushing his erection down under the elastic waistband.

"You're not easy," he said.

"But I'm worth it, right?"

"Oh, yeah, you're worth it."

I'd begun dressing, too, when we heard a hard banging against the driver's door.

"What the hell!" Val exclaimed, pulling his jeans up fast, and then the banging was followed by bleating. Laughing, Val flung open the door to reveal a curious he-goat, horns front up, black eyes glinting in the dim light that shone out on him from inside the bus. "Look at this fella!"

We laughed hysterically as Val, planting his heel between the animal's horns, worked hard to disengage us from the goat, which seemed determined to climb into the van. Finally Val started making loud noises and flapping his arms wildly, and the frightened animal pranced off. Still chortling, we drove back to the shopping center, where I jumped out, ran into the drugstore and bought a box of condoms. Twenty minutes later we were back where we started, sans goat, naked in the van under an opened sleeping bag, laughing again. We laughed so much that whole evening and night; I'd never been with anyone who made me feel so light inside. We laughed and then touched each other until the laughter turned back into sexual yearning.

But there came a moment of gravity after he ripped open a condom package and slid the rubber down over his erection.

"Are you sure you want to do this?" he asked.

"You weren't asking that a half-hour ago," I said.

"When you were in the drugstore, I had a moment to think. It'll change you." As he rolled toward me, my peripheral vision caught the swinging movement of his erection. "You and that boyfriend of yours. You'll have a secret from him. Unless you intend to tell him."

"No, I don't intend to tell him. And you?"

"No, I won't tell my girl." He looked away for an instant. "To make it easier, I'll—I'll pretend—to myself—that this happened long ago, when we were in college, before I met her." He hesitated. "Maybe it should have happened then."

And then I realized—idiot that I was—that he had been attracted to me back then, but with my head in the clouds about Ben, I'd been unaware.

"All that matters is that it's happening now," I said. I was being driven by something besides attraction—my fascination with Michael, my stalemate with Ben, my confusion about my life. Val could have been someone else and served just as well; there was something lurchingly impersonal about what I was doing. At the same time, I was delighted that it was Val. He was a terrific guy, a stroke of anomalously good luck.

"I don't want to think about anything else," I said.

I slipped my palm under his balls and got on top of him. He hooked his ankles over mine and a moment later he was inside me and I was saturated with the crazy deliciousness of things that break out of the blue, through the numbness of habit-worn senses.

We were awakened the next morning by the sounds of goats bleating and humans talking. Sitting up and looking out the van window, I saw a thirty-something couple dressed in plaid work shirts and down vests milking goats. We got dressed and went out, and Val introduced me to his friends. Claire and Robert greeted us while the milk ran over their hands and into the buckets with a tin sound. Wherever I went that weekend, there was someone or something producing milk. I gawked at a process that seemed far from natural, maybe because, as a fifties baby, I'd been bottle-fed, of course.

Val led me inside and we breakfasted on face-puckering, homemade goat yogurt, heavy bread, and thick coffee, and then we showered together. *I never shower with Ben, why is that? He's always in a rush to get back to reading.* We lathered each other up and kissed under the powerful shower head, and I had the same feeling I'd had standing in the wind on the Golden Gate Bridge and when we'd made love in the van—instead of feeling I'd done something wrong, I felt purified, refreshed. Maybe it was the fact that we'd used condoms and there was no drip, no mess. Like Shake 'n Bake—nothing to clean up afterwards.

I borrowed a pair of Claire's too-big boots and Val grabbed one of his cameras and we went out. The farm was on a gentle slope facing south. With fingers interlaced, we walked up to the top of the hill where a grove of oak trees was losing its leaves and some silver-green pittosporum fluttered in the morning sun. It reminded me of a dream I used to have as a kid, of a field going up to a magical forest with a thick carpet of pine needles, where I walked expecting to meet Eeyore or Winnie-the-Pooh. Val and I stopped short of the woods and, turning around, headed back down to a corral where a single cow and a couple of horses chewed hay, their breath making clouds in the cold. He kept stopping to take pictures of me. The way he looked at me was almost as delicious as his sexual attention.

"I have to do a wedding in the city at eleven," he finally said, breaking the spell.

"I need to get back, too," I answered.

We left the farm and headed back, south along 101, across the Golden Gate, and through the city toward Robin's. We were mostly silent, one of us occasionally reaching out to touch the other on the arm or thigh. At a stoplight a block from Robin's, Val said, "Well, let's kiss good-bye here, then," and for a split second I felt again the warmth of his beard and the quickness of his tongue. I was sad the adventure was over, but overjoyed that I'd had it. Maybe there really was such a thing as a seven-year itch, and I'd gone too long without scratching mine. Now that I'd stepped out, I'd feel better and all this foolishness about Michael would be over with.

"Thank you," I said when we reached Robin's. "Thank you so much."

Val smiled wistfully. "No, thank *you*."

I opened the van door and he added, "I'll wait to make sure someone's home."

I went up to the door and knocked on it, and when Robin came and opened it, I turned around and waved at Val. He gave me a wave and pulled away from the curb and was gone.

"Did it every occur to you that I might worry about you?" Robin asked, looking upset.

It was the last thing I'd expected. How many times, when we'd shared an apartment in New Haven, had she stayed out all night with someone new?

"I don't get it," I said. "Why would you worry when you knew I was with Val? It's not like I picked someone up in a bar."

"Ben called again last night."

"Did you cover for me?"

"Of course I covered for you. I said you went out to dinner with your parents after the party."

"Thanks."

"Speaking of Ben—what were you doing with Val, anyway?"

"What do you mean, what was I doing with Val?"

"I don't care about fidelity, but you do. I mean, that's just not like you."

Robin thought of me as sexually repressed because I lost my virginity late and had been faithful to Ben. But I've never been a prude. Choosy and romantic, perhaps, but not a prude.

"Well, I decided to do something not like me for a change," I said, and then the next thing I knew I was sitting on the couch weeping, and Robin was stroking my arm to comfort me. I wanted to be back on the goat farm with Val. I didn't want to be back in my life.

"What's going on with you, sweetie?" Robin whispered.

"Oh God, Robin, I'm so mixed up." I stopped myself. "Where's Anna?"

"She and Gloria are out for a walk—"

It was safe to proceed. "I ran into Michael last month—"

"Michael?"

"Michael Chambers."

Robin took it in. "How is he?"

"The same," I said. "You're not in touch with him anymore?"

"We send each other cards at Christmas."

"Oh," I said.

"What—are you—attracted? Or did you sleep with him?"

"No, no! It's impossible. He'd never—he's been too wounded in triangular situations. "

"But you're attracted."

"Yeah."

"You didn't have an affair with him after I did, at Yale?"

"No, of course not. I was really involved with Ben. It was a completely platonic friendship." I'd never told her about how I'd kissed Michael good-bye, and I wouldn't mention it now.

Robin sniffed. "You should stay away from him. He's very messy. It would end in disaster."

"You think so? Did you know he has a baby fund—he's saving up to have a child?"

"He had that baby fund at Yale. Contributed five dollars a month, I think. As though that could make a difference—"

"You're wrong. When you start saving early, the effect of compound interest—"

Robin shook her head. "Get real. Can you imagine Michael in a committed relationship? Can you imagine Michael with a regular income? Anyway, what about Ben? Does he know you're seeing Michael?"

"No, of course not."

"You and Ben have been together for ten years—that's unheard of these days. You don't just throw away a relationship like that. I don't know anyone who's been with anyone for ten years, married or not."

"I love Ben, but—uh—" Exhausted from lack of sleep, I was suddenly inarticulate.

"You need to see a therapist," Robin said. "Or maybe you and Ben need to see a couples counselor together. Why don't you guys get married?"

"He hasn't asked me. Besides, look at you," I said, waving a hand at her breasts that nourished two babies, one hers, one not hers, and no partner in sight. "You're a fine one to tell me to get married."

"That's the point. Someone in our goddamn family should get married!" Robin shrugged. "As for me, I wanted to have a child, so I've cobbled something together. Listen, I want you to see a therapist when you get back to New York."

"I don't know how to find one."

"I can give you the name of someone I was in school with. It really couldn't hurt."

"A little dent in my bank account, that's all," I said. I didn't want to become a whining woman addicted to therapy.

"Julia, it's your *life* we're talking about," Robin said.

"Please don't tell Anna," I said.

"You think she'd be judgmental?"

"Yes, because she never liked Michael, so she wouldn't understand."

Robin laughed. "Yeah, I remember the time he knocked over her painting."

It had been an unforgettable incident. Anna was painting Val's portrait and I was in the open kitchen making dinner when Michael came to the house to pick Robin up for their second or third date. While waiting for Robin to come out, he stood in the living room and critiqued Anna's portrait. He didn't like the orange in the flesh tones—orange wasn't a popular color, he said, so why would she want to use it? Anna countered by explaining that the orange was a bit like one of those weird jazz chords that's both ugly and beautiful at the same time. I was just trying to be helpful, Michael said, and, turning around, accidentally knocked the canvas over with his shoulder bag.

"Klutz!" she screamed, running to the painting that had fallen, like the proverbial buttered toast, wet side down onto the one piece of carpet that wasn't protected by tarp. Robin came out and helped clean up. Soon the whole place smelled of turpentine, but the paint wouldn't come off the rug.

"Remember the way Anna hounded him afterwards to reimburse us for the damage deposit?" I asked. "She sure was angry."

"How could I forget? Anyway, cross my heart it'll remain confidential: I won't tell Anna. So what do you think?" Robin asked, bringing me back to present. "You want a phone number? I know a good therapist in New York—she's even downtown."

"Okay," I said. "I'll try it."

9

BEN, ANXIOUS TO SEE me after my trip to California, came into the city Tuesday night. I wondered what it would feel like to see him, to have sex with him, after having slept with Val.

Going home after work, I could hear Ben inside the apartment as I put my key in the lock. I had a moment of paranoia, wondering whether he might have seen or read anything in my apartment that would have clued him into my infidelity. No, I hadn't left any evidence around. Val had given me neither memento nor keepsake. My diaphragm was exactly where I'd left it, a flying saucer grounded in its slim blue container, parked in the shade of the bedside table drawer. As for my diary, my nosey mother had led me to self-censorship early on, and I'd had the habit, since high school, of making enigmatic diary entries. If he looked, Ben would find nothing incriminating. *Sparkling party. Hilly drives. The golden Golden Gate and the moment of the magic blanket. The night, like a goat telling jokes, etc.* Not that Ben, ever honorable, was the type to snoop.

As soon as I walked in, he turned off the stove, where he'd started dinner, and grabbed me and pulled off my shirt. Happily, living apart had proven to be a remedy for the cooling that had come over our sex life in the previous year. Ben's hands felt almost hot as he ran them over my breasts and pulled me into the bedroom. I reflected, as I rolled away from him in the bed and inserted my diaphragm, that using condoms with Val—thank God I'd insisted—had left me feeling oddly inviolate. My lips, my skin, my privates were unchanged. I was, except for the contents of my memory—in other words, except for a slight alteration in the structure and function of my brain—*exactly the same*. And the grooves in the gray matter were so deep and labyrinthian that I could trust them to engulf my secret. For a moment, I wondered why people made such a fuss over adultery.

Then, as I turned back toward Ben, remembering Val and feeling Michael in the wings, a wave of nauseating guilt washed over me. I wanted Ben to erase Michael, erase Val with his lovemaking. I wanted the simplicity of loving and wanting one person only. I'd already done something foolish in California, and I wanted to stop it right there, before I lost him. The stupidest thing I could do would be to take Ben, as a lover, for granted. As rain pelted the windows—a cold sound against the hiss of the radiators in the background—I reached for Ben, yearning for the familiar yet exciting way we'd always been together.

"Take me by storm," I said to Ben as he wrapped his legs around mine.

"I'm going to spread you and fuck you till you weep," he said.

He popped my breasts out of my bra, yanked my panties off.

My night with Val had been exciting, but he didn't know my body the way Ben did. Ben knew, like a military strategist, how to surprise me with a gesture or a word that would throw me into a state of blissful submission to my desire for him. He knew exactly how I liked to be kissed, stroked, and penetrated. He knew how to drag me out past the waves and through the tunnel into the pulsing octopus. He was mercilessly generous in his gifts of pleasure.

I started seeing the therapist Robin had recommended. Sandra Horowitz had a sweet, open face framed by short, dark curls; her Manhattan accent had Brooklyn overtones she tried to suppress. We sat across from each other in two black leather chairs, and I did what I was supposed to—I blabbed. She didn't say much during our first session, in which I told her about running into Michael, about my parents, and my conflicted feelings about motherhood. Somehow I managed not talk about Ben very much.

She said so little that I wondered whether she was bored.

Maybe it was to get a reaction out of her that, in my second session, I fessed up my adventure with Val.

"So this happened right before our first session," she said. "I'm surprised you didn't mention it last time."

"Well, yes." There was something accusatory in the way she scrutinized me, so I proceeded to defend myself. "I didn't mention it because it didn't seem really relevant—I mean, to my situation with Michael."

"And today it does?"

"The way I slept with Val reminds me of the way I lost my virginity," I said.

"Oh?" She came to attention. Who doesn't perk up for a losing-virginity story?

Cautious and dreamy, I found myself a virgin in my senior year of college. I almost did it with Brian—the guy I wrote the sonnet for—but the encounter ended in fiasco. We were in the middle of foreplay when his suitemate came back and started throwing up after drinking, and that was the end of that. I went back to my own dorm, and Brian avoided me after that night; I'm not sure why. I stopped dating for a while after that. When other men presented themselves, I discouraged them, maybe because I didn't consider them "men" really, and that's what I wanted—a grown-up who could initiate me properly.

And then I found myself, along with Anna, in Ben's discussion section of Contemporary Poetry. A graduate student in his mid-twenties when I met him, he qualified as a grown-up. I worked myself deeper and deeper into a sexually desperate infatuation until Anna and Robin invited him over for dinner in order to help me out. When our plumbing failed, the party ended up taking place at Ben's. That was the night I met Michael, but I was completely focused on Ben. Undergraduates didn't normally socialize with graduate student instructors, so the gathering began with a sense of constraint, then grew wilder and wilder, culminating in our throwing out the window—we were all under the influence by that point—a bunch of scratched LPs that Michael couldn't bring himself to get rid of, though they were unplayable. Ben flirted with me nonstop, and I expected he would ask me out soon after. But the weeks passed, Thanksgiving rolled around, and he still hadn't made his move.

I returned to New York for the holiday, depressed and convinced nothing would happen with Ben. My mother was hosting the family gathering that year, and I ran errands for her, which meant going up and down in the elevator and flirting with Rodrigo, the handsome Puerto Rican on duty that weekend. "You look a little forlorn, Miss," he said. "I bet I could make you feel better. What about stopping by at lunch hour…?" The proposition took me by surprise because we'd always had a distant, polite relationship. Something on my face must have screamed "desperate."

Thus I ended up in a basement apartment, getting deflowered by the elevator man between an errand to D'Agostino's and a trip to the liquor store.

It was a scene out of *Lady Chatterley's Lover*, updated for late-seventies Manhattan—the sheltered Jewish princess finally yielding her body to a member of the working class. Amber-colored, smooth, and muscular, Rodrigo positioned me in his huge bed and fucked me until the blood pounded from my teeth to my toes. Unfortunately, he had decorated the bedroom with garish psychedelic posters. In the one facing the foot of the bed, a unicorn was flying off into a blood-red sunset. I studied it afterwards, while he served me coffee in bed.

The next day my mother and I took the subway down to Macy's to do the requisite shopping. She was giving me a makeover at the Clinique counter— "you know, your eyes are on the small side and a little eyeliner wouldn't hurt"—when I saw Ben and Michael meandering from the men's department through cosmetics toward the exit. Ben suggested the four of us have lunch together, and on the way to the deli at the corner of Seventh Avenue and Thirty-Fourth he asked me out for our first date.

I narrated all this to Sandra.

"Ben and I met the next day at the Cafe Dante. It was snowing and the Village was beautiful." I looked out the window at the brick wall of the building next door. Ten years later, Thanksgiving was approaching again. "We had our first kiss on a bench in Washington Square. It was incredibly romantic. In fact, it would have been perfect if I hadn't slept with Rodrigo the day before."

"So you regret Rodrigo?" Sandra asked.

"No," I said. "It was too much fun to regret."

We gazed at one another from our identical black leather chairs—she, waiting for me to continue, and I, waiting for her to direct my blathering.

Next to each of us stood a tiny coffee table, mine with a box of tissues, hers with a glass of water and a pack of gum. Only years later would I decipher these clues to her secret—that she suffered from dry mouth induced by antidepressants. A depressed therapist purporting to offer counsel—if that isn't a case of the blind leading the blind, I don't know what is.

"And what does this have to do with Val—or Michael?"

"Well, it's the same pattern, don't you see? Because I'm hot for one man I can't get, I end up going to bed with another who isn't the one I've been wanting. I never get what I want."

"Maybe 'not getting what I want' is a story. And a story that isn't true. Because you did get Ben, and it's possible you could get Michael, too, if that's what he wants and what you want, too."

"I must really want him. My mind keeps on spinning around him."

Sandra chewed her gum thoughtfully. "Is it possible your attraction to Michael is symptomatic of some other problem in your life? Is it possible that something is missing in your relationship with Ben?"

"Is it possible I'm attracted to Michael just because I'm attracted to him?" I countered. "Didn't Freud once say that sometimes a cigar is just a cigar?"

"I told you I don't consider myself a Freudian."

"Ah," I said. "Right." Sandra didn't have much of a sense of humor. "So?"

"Well, yes, I guess I'm tired of waiting."

"Waiting? For?"

"Ben has always kept me waiting. Waiting for him to ask me out on that first date. Waiting for him to ask me to move in with him—it was only when Michael moved out, that he asked me to move in. Waiting to get married. Waiting to have children."

Sandra said nothing—the therapist's continuance signal par excellence.

"But I've agreed to wait," I added, "so maybe I don't have the right to complain."

"So rather than talk to him about it, you're getting interested in another man?" Sandra asked.

"That's too simple," I said.

"Well, then go on about the waiting."

"I guess," I said very quietly, "I'm angry about it."

"You don't sound angry," Sandra said.

"Well, how angry can I let myself be when he's simply satisfying the demands of his job? And sometimes I think part of me hasn't minded waiting."

"Oh?"

"I'm tired of waiting but I'm not sure I want to get married. Is that a conflict or a contradiction? I don't know." I sighed. The effort of wrapping language around my confusion was exhausting.

"This is where couples counseling could be useful."

"No, it's not that I don't know whether I want to marry Ben—I don't know whether I want to marry at all."

"Yet you still have the feeling of waiting for it?"

"Because everyone I know is looking at us and wondering—when are Julia and Ben going to get married? Even my cousin Robin, who's sort of a hippie, asked me, 'Why don't you guys get married?' It makes me feel pressured and I end up not knowing what I want."

"Hopefully our sessions will be a space in which you can figure that out."

I stepped out of Sandra's building into a sparkling dusk. The stoplights and streetlights, the neon signs of the still open stores, the white headlights of oncoming cars and the red tail lights of disappearing ones, twinkled like sequins thrown onto an evening gown of gray organza. I headed toward a dinner date with Michael.

It would have made more sense to see Sandra *after* seeing Michael, instead of before, but the schedule abetted the game I was playing as I analyzed the situation in therapy, then continued doing what I wanted. As I walked a little faster, the usual ache in my abdomen turned into a sharp stitch, reminding me to look into acupuncture, as Gloria had suggested. Moving through the urban checkerboard as one does through life— never as the crow flies, but always by indirection—I zigzagged southeast toward the Second Avenue Deli. I'd never eaten in a fancy restaurant with Michael, who preferred coffee shops, little pizzerias, and pita joints with sticky tables. A Jewish deli was about as upscale as he'd go; bright and noisy, it suited the platonic intimacy of our renewed friendship.

He was seated, bent over his agenda, when I got there. That first glimpse of him when we met always released a latch in me, admitting pure joy, like a glittering stream into a secret garden.

He stood up when he saw me and planted a quick kiss on my cheek. "I'm ravenous," he said. "What are you having?"

"The brisket," I said. Pathetic that *gedempte fleish*—soft meat—was one of my only connections to my religion of origin, and a taste that stood in the way of my being a vegetarian.

After we ordered, Michael reached for something in his shoulder bag. "I'm getting more organized under your influence. Look—" he said, showing me his agenda.

"Under *my* influence?"

"I think of you as a very organized person."

"Is that a compliment?"

"Shut up, you, and look here!" he said, shaking his agenda at me, with that mock wrath I found so amusing. "I've rearranged my schedule of lessons by neighborhood. Mondays and Tuesdays—my neighborhood, Upper West Side. Wednesdays—*your* neighborhood—downtown." He bowed to me.

I bowed back.

"Thursdays, Lincoln Center—"

"The *arts* district," I said, with a mock British accent.

He bowed again. "And Friday—East Side."

"Why don't you have the students come to your place instead of chasing them around town? Don't a lot of music teachers do that?"

"The mess, Julia. Remember the mess."

I nodded. I hadn't seen his apartment uptown, but I remembered the chaos of his room in New Haven.

"Anyway, I'm impressed," I said. "You've got a full roster there."

"Only one student missing," he said.

"Who?"

"You."

"Me?"

"Yes, you. Remember I told you how I've been studying this new technique. Don't you want me to show it to you? How's that rented piano of yours, anyway?"

The Wurlitzer had arrived and now stood against the empty wall, but I'd played it little.

"I could use it more," I said.

"Well, then?"

I said nothing, and our long pause was filled with the sounds of the

Second Avenue Deli—loud conversations, clattering plates, the squealing, swinging kitchen doors. Michael hadn't been to my apartment since I'd moved in. We always met in public places.

"You're uncomfortable about having me over to your place," he resumed, "because you haven't told Ben yet that you're seeing me, have you?"

"No, I haven't," I said. It was true that at the back of my mind was the fear that if Michael came over, Ben might surprise us by coming in from Princeton unannounced.

"Well—"

"Any ideas about how I should go about it?" I asked.

"No," he said. "If we were in a novel, someone could throw a party for us. Then I could say to Ben, hey, nice to run into you again…"

"Sounds more like a lousy TV show than a novel," I said. "I thought you wanted to be straightforward."

"I do. I want everything aboveboard."

"Okay," I said, "I'll figure something out."

"So when can I see that piano of yours and give you a lesson?"

"Next time we meet," I said. "After Thanksgiving."

Ben came into the city Wednesday evening to spend the holiday weekend with me and my family. He walked in ruffled and irritable.

"You wouldn't believe how crowded the train was," he said. "And I had to fight my way out of the station. I hate holidays."

My heart surged toward him, wanting to soothe him. "That's not true. You love holidays."

"You're right," he said, immediately looking more cheerful. "And they'd be perfect if it wasn't for other people."

"What can I do for you?" I asked.

"Get in bed," he said.

After we'd engaged in our ritual—which was beginning to feel like the questionable mortar of our relationship—and dinner, Ben settled in on the living room couch with a pen and his Ezra Pound manuscript and books. Restless, I pored over *The New Yorker* movie listings. Some Russian film, probably incomprehensible, called *Dark Eyes* was playing around the corner at the Quad. On Third Street they were doing Mamet's

House of Games. I wasn't wild about Mamet. I would have liked to see Jean Renoir's *The Rules of the Game,* playing on Bleecker Street. But if I went to the movies, it would be alone: I wouldn't be able to tear Ben away from working on his tenure packet—damned tenure packet was how I thought of it, always adding *but he has to, it's his job that's at stake.* I felt stuck—and in my own apartment. It didn't seem right to go out by myself to play; at the same time, with Ben on the couch, I couldn't relish the peace of being alone and doing exactly what I wanted to do. The apartment suddenly felt small. I realized how much I treasured having my own place.

I stared at Ben for a moment, confused. We'd just made love, and now I was wishing he wasn't there. I went into the bedroom and turned on the TV.

We went up to my parents' mid-afternoon the next day. My mother prided herself on being an unconventional woman, but when it was her turn to host the family Thanksgiving dinner, she always had a fit of conformity and made a meal of turkey with the traditional condiments, all of which she would do her best to ruin because she hated "cooking what everyone else in the damn country is cooking." She also hated the tradition of the midday meal, which she thought plebeian, so we would eat around six. "The turkey's never done before then, anyway," she'd say, when the truth was that having the meal at the end of the day gave her an opportunity to get crocked before serving it all up.

Mariel always invited the "Long Island branch" of my family—Anna and her older sister, Evelyn, and their parents, Linda and Carl—as well as several old friends—Harold Lassen, aging poet laureate of Brooklyn, his wife Christina, and the aging painter Romero Tella and his wife.

Harold took me aside, as he always did, and asked me whether I was writing any poetry.

"That sonnet you wrote was so good," he said. "I just don't understand how you could have stopped."

We were sitting on the living room couch. Harold usually was not so accusatory.

"I just did," I said, a little sharply.

"Maybe it's out of loneliness that I speak—the loneliness of my profession—or some misplaced paternal feeling, but I want to see it again in you. Because you—*you* are the next generation."

"You know, Harold, there are plenty of other poets making up the next generation. I'm really not needed," I said and sent Evelyn, in the armchair across from me, a pleading look to be rescued.

"She's got a good head on her shoulders," Evelyn joined in, leaning forward. "She's going for the money."

"Bah! Money!" Harold said. "Who needs it? I make almost nothing as a poet and I've got this Polish princess of a wife"—he gestured toward Christina, a slim, gently faded blonde who'd reached sixty without working a single day in her entire life—"who loves me anyway, in all my glorious poverty."

"I thought she came from money," Evelyn said bluntly.

"Well, yes, but not *that* much money."

Evelyn laughed and winked at me. "Harold," she said, "I'm going to steal my cousin away from you for a minute. Go fix yourself another drink."

Only Evelyn could interrupt conversations and order people about like that. Always dressed in designer black "pieces" that made my own garb feel like a mechanic's outfit, she epitomized style, power, and success. Before becoming a successful interior designer, she'd had a job at Sotheby's that had made her a woman, literally, of the world. She still traveled abroad frequently and had, in luxurious hotels in unusual places, affairs with married men, which she pulled off without a hitch. In another era, she might have been a French countess with a stable of discreet lovers.

Evelyn led me by the forearm to the loveseat by my dad's piano. "What's up with you?"

"Nothing much. What about you? Still living the wild life?"

"No, I'm taking a break. I've had it with married men—these sex weekends are fabulous but I can't stand the logistical complications, the waiting by the phone afterwards—there's just so much fucking crap. I never know from one minute to the next where I stand."

"Sounds rough," I said, though hardly sympathetic. I thought of doing it with Val in his van. The goat had been hilarious, but I wouldn't have minded a posh hotel room with a marble bathroom in Stockholm or Gibraltar.

"You making money these days?" Evelyn asked, interrupting my reverie.

"It's going fine," I said.

"You don't know any good women financial advisors, do you? I've really taken a hit recently."

"You and everyone else," I said, reminded of Val's suggestion that I should go into financial advising for women.

"I can't stand the condescension you get from men in financial services. Drives me nuts."

"Yeah," I said. "The world could use more women in that area." There was no reason why I couldn't take evening classes at Baruch College and move in that direction. Eventually the stock market would turn around and I'd be ready for it. To hell with all these men in my life. It would please me to be obscenely rich and successful. That's what I needed to focus on— me, specifically me making money. My mind, under pressure, whirled in multiple directions. Remaking my professional profile. Michael. A poem about Michael. My mother in the kitchen, probably getting drunk.

"Let's go check the turkey," I said.

On the way to the kitchen, we passed my uncle Carl, who was grilling Ben. How long would Thatcher stay in power? Would Elizabeth ever step down so her son could ascend the throne? Wasn't Prince Charles in an absurd position? Carl, his fingers laced over his large belly, looked at Ben with mock accusation.

"I think that, deep down, the British adore their queen," my uncle said. A scientist and a logical thinker, he enjoyed studying irrational popular attitudes.

"Off with her head is what I say," Ben said, winking at me as I walked by.

As expected, my mother and my aunt Linda were seated at the kitchen table, deep in scotch and soda. On her own, my mother moderated her inebriation by sticking to wine. When she was under Linda's influence, the sky was the limit.

"The turkey, Mom? Have you been checking the turkey?" I asked.

"Goddamn that turkey," my mother said.

"Fuck the turkey," seconded Linda.

"Mom!" Evelyn said.

I pulled the turkey out of the oven. There it was, in its old, speckled pan, steaming and sizzling—and looking very dry.

"We'll slice it and pour some gravy over it," Evelyn suggested. "We'll just serve it that way. It'll be delicious."

"I don't know how to make gravy," I said.

"Don't we take the giblets and put them in a blender or something?"

Ben appeared into the kitchen. "This can't be that difficult," he said.

"Let's find a recipe."

A man who knew how to find information, Ben was undaunted. Soon the three of us were doing a comparative study of gravy in *The Joy of Cooking* and *Fannie Farmer*. The giblets did end up in the blender, but there were a couple of steps before and after. Fortunately, Ben had the presence of mind to taste all the dishes before they were served. Quickly he adjusted the cranberries with more sugar, the vinaigrette with more oil, and the mashed potatoes with more butter. My mother had perversely tried to ruin everything, but Ben, exhibiting grace under pressure, had saved the Lipski Thanksgiving, and not for the first time.

After dinner, Anna and I retreated to the little love seat I'd occupied with her older sister a few hours before.

"What are we going to do with our mothers?" she asked me. With her heels under her thighs, her auburn hair, and her long-waisted body, she leaned against the sofa back looking like an Ingres odalisque.

"Nothing," I said.

"I'm going to look at an apartment on Seventy-Fourth, near Columbus. I think this is going to be the one for me."

"That's around the corner from where John Lennon was shot," I said.

"Yeah. So?"

"I dunno," I said. Whatever apartment she got, it would be nicer than mine because she had an artist's flair for decoration and arrangement.

"Look at Ben and my dad," Anna said. "What do you think they're talking about?"

They were leaning toward each other, discussing something intensely.

"An hour ago it was the British monarchy."

"Anyone who can hold a conversation with my dad deserves a medal," Anna said. "Something with lots of ribbons and maybe a couple of bells jingling from the bottom."

Carl was a demanding conversationalist, but Ben always made the effort—and with a smile—to connect with everyone in my family. I would never find another man as good as this one. Still, that didn't stop me from doing what I did next.

"Hey," I said, "I wonder if you could help me out with something." I dropped my voice and leaned toward her.

She dropped her voice and leaned in toward me. "What's up?"

"I ran into Michael Chambers recently."

"Really?"

"You remember how Ben and Michael had a fight—"

"Yeah, I know—when Michael dropped out."

"Listen," I said, "would you mind doing me a favor? If I had a party, like a Christmas party, would you bring Michael? I mean, you could call him, or he could call you, and you could arrive together..." I saw her frown. "I know you never liked him that much—"

"No, it's not that. I'm just wondering what you're up to."

She was sharp, and I'd have to step carefully.

"Michael wants to be friends with Ben again." I wasn't as prepared as I should have been and felt like I was making it up as I went along. "And I'd like it, too. If you brought him, it would just make it easier. All you have to do is walk in with Michael, saying 'Look who I ran into,' and I'm sure Ben would be happy to see him again."

"Why don't you just say *you* ran into him?"

"It wouldn't work as well, don't you see? With me, he might argue against it, but if you just showed up with him, it would be a fait accompli—" Inexperienced at subterfuge, I blushed at the mess of a story I was telling. Fortunately, our corner wasn't well lit, and Anna was staring off into space instead of at me.

"Do you think he'd really argue against it, after all this time?"

"It's possible."

"Okay," she said. "I'd be happy to do what you want."

Later that night, after Ben and I took the subway back down to Fourteenth Street, I lay in bed next to him, telling myself that my maneuver was well-intentioned—it was, after all, what Michael had requested. Nothing good comes from secrecy, he'd said. If that was true, Jesus, maybe I should just ask Ben's permission to have an affair with Michael. No, crazy idea. Ben would never agree to an open relationship. But maybe Michael would eventually succumb to his desire for me, and we could have an affair under Ben's nose, the way in those Henry James novels adulterous couples openly parade around together. The Prince and Charlotte, Chad and Madame de Vionnet—they all got away with it, at least for a while. Could I be happy with "a while"? Could I handle the inevitable discovery, the final twist in the plot? Isabel Archer realized her husband once had an affair with Madame Merle when she walked into the living room one day and noticed that, although Madame Merle was standing, her arm on the mantel piece, Osmond was sitting: the deepest intimacy was suggested by this violation of the Victorian convention that dictated, if the woman stood, so should the man. James, like Michael, believed that secrets always come out. I wasn't so sure.

Finally, I decided that, whatever happened or didn't happen, putting things in plain view would be the best way for them not to be seen, just as, in the Edgar Alan Poe story, the purloined letter is "hidden" in plain view, on a mantelpiece. That tale was linked in my mind to a nursery school episode. We had a game that involved one child hiding a red plastic cup with the teacher's help, while the other children went out of the room. When my turn came, my teacher suggested placing the cup on the tip of the flagpole erected above the window. I was delighted when the children came back into the room and not one looked up and saw it.

Of course, in the Poe story, detective Dupin is a lot smarter than the kids in my nursery class were. How smart the people in my life were remained to be seen.

10

IN HIS GROUND-FLOOR office on Ninth Street, Frank McCloud, LAc (licensed acupuncturist), stood next to me, staring off into space as he took my pulses. Thin and straight, he incarnated health and longevity. Walking in, I expected a preliminary medical interview, but instead he directed me right onto a treatment table. The gentle koto music in the background (Japanese) didn't quite jive with the scrolls on the wall (Tibetan) or the silk jacket he wore (Chinese), but the general Asian effect was soothing.

"You said on the phone that the pain is in this area." He gestured with his free hand to the lower right corner of my abdomen.

"Yes."

I'd gotten McCloud's name from Michael, who'd sought acupuncture after his neck injury. Michael had warned me Frank was a wizard at reading pulses and would lay my soul bare in the process.

"There's some liver stagnation and a wiriness in the pulse, of the kind that can be put in motion by emotional issues." He glanced at me.

"I've been a little tense recently. I'm in a muddle about something—can't make decisions."

"And I'm feeling a kind of guardedness in the nervous system, at a deeper level that goes really far back."

"Meaning?"

"Far back in time. Childhood. Probably related to your upbringing. Or the way your particular organism received that upbringing."

"Ah." As my body lay there, an indiscreet traitor, I remembered how, when my mother drank, I used to brace myself for whatever "eccentricity" might follow.

"Whatever is happening now is connected to very old patterns." He pressed his fingers deeper into my wrist.

"I'm looking into that with a therapist," I said, meaning "end of subject." Raking over things with Sandra once a week sufficed.

"I understand," he said. "Well, let's get things moving." He pressed the lever of a dispenser and caught the paper-wrapped needles that fell out. "I use disposable needles, the finest that are made."

I stared up at the ceiling, then closed my eyes. He hiked up my pant legs and sleeves, then moved around me, palpating my arms and legs for tender spots. I barely felt the pricks as he inserted needles. He deftly unzipped my pants, folded and tucked the open flaps inward, targeted a few points on my belly.

"Your mind will feel a lot calmer after this. Maybe you'll be able to make some of those decisions. Or change some of those patterns."

"Maybe."

"For the moment, if you could just focus on your breathing, on bringing it down into your belly…"

He turned the light down and left the room. It was hard to focus on my breathing when my mind was in perpetual flight, but gradually, pinned to the table like a giant butterfly, I fluttered into stillness and drifted deeper.

Leaving Frank's office an hour later, with Chinese herbs in my bag, I noticed that not only was my pain gone, but my mind felt clearer. As I walked back to my apartment, I found myself—for the first time, really— thinking about my dad's business and where I might take it. I had the beginning of an impetus to make something new of it—and of myself, in the process.

But a day later, my mind gave in to its craving for intense feeling by gravitating back to Michael. Zoning out with acupuncture was fine and good, but part of me didn't want to be calm. My system craved imbalance and disruption, extremity and intoxication—the elation when the forest blooms, the chaos of the sky at sunset, the sea of spuming feeling.

So I asked Michael to come to my apartment for the first time since I'd moved in. I went home a little early and changed outfits several times, finally choosing a ten-year-old plum sweater with a V-neck that I associated with Michael. Maybe I'd worn it that night when Ben was studying and Michael and I went out to see *Teacher's Pet* with Doris Day and a weathered but still irresistible Clark Gable. I hadn't worn the sweater much, as though wanting to preserve it.

At seven, Michael walked in with a bag of Chinese takeout and set it on the dining table. "Here you go," he said. As he took off his leather bomber with the fur collar and looked at me, I felt as though we were two magnets of the same pole, kept apart by a force field. If one of us flipped around, we would come together violently.

"That top looks familiar," he said.

"It's very old," I said.

He cleared his throat. "Okay, let's eat."

I brought out the old Woolworth plates my mother had given me and he put the little white boxes out on the table. He had ordered two of my favorite dishes, vegetarian mu shu and prawns with snow peas, and two of his, hot-and-sour soup and Szechuan eggplant. Wondering whether he'd remembered my preferences, I realized I was remembering his. We started eating. I loved the way he bent over his plate, focused on flavor.

"Wow, this is good," he said, then looked at my sweater again. "You wore that top the night we went to see *Teacher's Pet* at the Medical School film society."

"Did I?" I said innocently. "You have a good memory." Suddenly I was embarrassed by just how deep the V was.

"That was a fun evening—the crowd was pretty raucous, wasn't it?"

The student audience, men and women alike, had whistled and jeered every time Doris, in a pencil skirt, swung her hips around for Clark's benefit. But it was the moment afterwards, in Michael's car, that I remembered best. So did he.

"We had some kind of deep conversation in the car, didn't we?" he said.

"Yes," I said. "We had a lot of deep conversations."

"You were wondering what was going to happen with you and Ben after you graduated—"

"At that point I was planning on moving back into the city to look for work and wondering whether a commuting relationship with him would work—" I was finishing my undergraduate work at Yale, but Ben needed to stay on to write his doctoral dissertation.

"Wondering about commuting—" he laughed at me.

"I know, life repeats itself. *I* repeat myself," I said.

"I remember telling you that your relationship with Ben would be like a Möbius strip—it would keep going infinitely."

We'd sat for a while talking before he started the engine. He'd torn a long narrow strip of paper out of a notebook then had gone into his explanation:

"Okay. Here's your strip. Now we put the two ends together to make a loop. But first you flip one end over like this, 180 degrees, before you attach it. Am I doing this right?" He held the two ends together between thumb and index. "And then what you've got is really a one-sided circle of paper."

"So?"

"It's a metaphor, don't you see?" he said. "For you and Ben. Let me show you." Brushing my leg, he fumbled for a paper clip in the glove compartment, then clipped the ends of the strip together. Taking up a pen and resting the twisted donut against his knee, he began a line that he continued until it had covered both sides of the paper and returned to its starting point.

"Isn't that cool?" he asked. "I think your relationship with Ben is going to be like this Möbius strip. Every time you feel you've gotten to the end of it—emotionally or sexually—you're going to find yourself back at the beginning, with the feeling of things being new."

I stared at the Möbius strip.

"I hope you're right," I said.

"You'll be together forever—unless of course he works himself to death first."

We sat in the dark car, considering each other. Quietly my eyes penetrated the gloom to feed on the eyes I knew to be a warm brown, the thick black hair that made a widow's peak just left of center on his broad forehead, the discreetly sensual mouth. Quietly I felt him examine me in turn, and not so quietly I repressed an impulse to lean toward him and change my future. Then he turned the car keys in the ignition, and the moment was gone.

I'd been so young. Only twenty-one.

"You went on about it," I remembered, "actually constructing a Möbius strip for me, as though I wouldn't have known what it was—me, a math major—"

"I guess that was pretty patronizing of me. Sorry. But you have to admit the metaphor was a stroke of genius."

We finished eating, and he went over to the kitchen sink to wash his hands.

"Piano time," he said. "I want to play this little gem you've rented—rented to buy, I hope?"

"Yes, I'm buying it."

As he sat on the piano bench, his whole body settled into place, as though becoming part of the instrument. Joy flooded his face as he extended his hands to touch the keys. He moved through some chords, brought in a minor melody, improvised a bit.

"This instrument is so sweet…" he said, his eyes sparkling.

I nodded. Listening to him play made me want to play again, too.

"So this technique you've learned…" I asked.

"It's called 'swing and drop.' Let me show you. You play with the whole body, using the weight and movement of the whole arm for each note. Watch how the hand swings as I go from the index finger to the thumb here. And watch how the thumb just drops to land. Now I'll do it the other way."

As he went back and forth between two notes, the hand followed the soft rotating movement of forearm and wrist. "It's both precise and free. Why don't you try it?" He scooted over a bit on the bench to make room for me.

I sat down and looked at him. His face was eighteen inches away from mine.

"Watch my fingers again. Now you try."

I extended my right hand and tried the drop. It felt awkward.

"Free the wrist, try it again. You notice," he said, "how it's the weight of the whole hand that's playing the note, instead of just the finger bearing down on it?"

"Yes, it's a little tricky."

"Try it again, and let yourself feel the rotation coming from here"—he touched a spot on my forearm—"and here." He touched the back of my hand. His slightest touch reverberated through my body.

I did a few more "drops," then stopped and looked at him. "I like it—it's starting to feel good—but obviously requires practice."

"Because you're used to your fingers acting separately, instead of as a unit with your arm—and your body."

His eyes moved to my neck, and he reached for the carnelian pendant I was wearing.

"That's beautiful," he said. "Unusual." As he took the pendant up between his fingers and examined it, I felt the warmth of his hand resting on my sternum. "Where did you get it?"

"Some Balinese store," I said.

He looked back up at me, stood up abruptly. "Let me grab something for you," he said, getting his music bag. "I bought you some Scarlatti."

"Scarlatti?"

"It's playful, challenging, and simple at the same time—it's perfect for starting up again. Here, try it." He opened it up for me and I began to play with him standing behind me. My sight-reading was rusty, and I heaved a sigh.

"You play it for me," I said.

"Scoot over," he said.

I moved to the left to make room for him on the bench, and as he sat down I took in his dry, grassy scent. At Yale, when I did my homework on his living room couch, I loved watching, listening, *feeling* him play, and here I was loving it again—the sense of plunging into a fourth dimension that was rich and harmonious and sweet.

"The fingering here looks tricky," I said, pointing to a couple of measures at the top of the page. "How would you do it?"

"Here, let me write it in for you." He played it using one sequence of fingers, then another. He grabbed a pencil, wrote down the fingering, then scribbled a note in the margin.

"'Rock when possible?'" I smiled, reading what he'd written. It sounded like a general instruction for life.

"You want to rock the hand, with a rolling motion, right here—try it."

I obeyed. For so many years I had played sporadically, with a feeling of despondency and self-criticism, and now Michael was taking my arms and physically reconnecting me to the beast of hammers and strings that I'd loved in childhood. I was in such a state of sensory arousal, with hyperawareness in every nerve ending, that I could feel the music vibrating under my fingertips.

"You're giving me a piano lesson, for free," I said. "I should pay you."

"You can make me dinner next time," he said.

"All right."

That evening, the air between us grew denser, the light brighter and clearer. Even as the mutual focus tightened, panic washed over me in waves. I was afraid not only of hurting both Ben and Michael, but also of getting hurt myself. One thing I knew about Michael: he didn't have a history of commitment. If I had an affair with him and everything exploded, I would be alone, winner losing all. It hit me that the smart thing would be to put myself out of harm's way, and—here was a new idea—the best way to do that would be to put *him* out of harm's way.

Yes, that was the solution. I couldn't take it anymore—the anxiety and uncertainty, the desire and the guilt.

The next day I shared my plan with my therapist. I'd changed my therapy day to Thursday, in a weak attempt to look more honestly at what was happening.

"'Put him out of harm's way?' What do you mean by that?" Sandra asked.

"Find him a girlfriend," I said.

She raised her eyebrows. "What? Play matchmaker?"

"Why not? He might really like this woman who works for me, Betty. And then there's my cousin Evelyn, who's his age and seems ready to settle down. He's suffering because he's single, and I can feel that I'm falling into this thing with him because his energy needs to go somewhere—"

"And what about *your* energy?"

"My energy?" I fell silent.

"Julia, I really need to ask you again, how are things going with Ben?"

"They're okay, I've told you. Sex is still great, when we have it—and when I put Michael out of my mind."

"So, sometimes great sex and then otherwise the relationship is 'okay.' Is okay good enough?"

"Okay means okay. I don't expect fireworks year after year. I'm a realistic person. And Ben is wonderful—"

"Ben is wonderful and you love him, but is he a good *fit* for you?"

"A good fit?"

Ben, wonderful and loveable, but not a good match for me—what did that mean? I understood the individual words in her question, but not the sentence they made together.

"Something seems to be missing."

"Doesn't every relationship have something missing? I don't expect one relationship to satisfy all my needs—do you?"

"No," Sandra said. "But if you know what's missing, then there's a greater possibility of finding it inside or outside yourself, in your partner, the one you've got now or another one, or maybe in your friendships…"

"Are you suggesting my matchmaker idea isn't a good one, because I need to investigate him for myself?"

"I'm suggesting that you're not getting what you need in your relationship with Ben, and that's why you're looking elsewhere."

"You don't think it's possible to love two people at the same time?"

"No more possible than it is to read two books simultaneously, or watch two movies at the same time."

There was a flaw in her logic, but I couldn't put my finger on it.

"Michael makes me feel less lonely."

"Do you have friends, Julia? You never talk about your friends."

"Yes, I have friends." There was a woman who lived in Princeton, a sculptress whose studio I liked to visit. In New York, I had a friend from Yale, who liked to go to flea markets with me, and a couple of friends from high school. "But I don't see them very much. They don't satisfy my craving for—whatever it is I'm craving."

"Because it's you who has to satisfy that craving. You are the creator of your own life and experience."

"I know that's what I want—to realize myself—but how? And even if it is 'all about me,' as you say, still, I can't help thinking that who I'm with is important."

"But maybe not as important as you believe it is. In long run, Michael is a passerby in your life, just as Ben is."

"Ben—a passerby? I don't think so. And Michael? A passerby? It feels more like a head-on collision with a semi-truck. That's why I want to put him out of the way."

"Back to the matchmaker idea."

"Yeah."

"The important thing, Julia, is for you to be honest with yourself."

"I *am* being honest with myself, and the truth is that I feel a lot of contradictory things at the same time." I felt impatient. As a therapist, Sandra ought to have understood the way the mind can hold opposing thoughts, and the heart opposing feelings.

"Go on."

"I want him—for myself. At the same time I don't want to hurt him. He's been in this type of situation before. Maybe he even told me that story about the affair with the married woman to warn me that he couldn't go there again. Not that Ben would ever attack anyone with a kitchen knife. But I don't want to break Michael's heart."

"And you think you might?"

"I might, yes, if—if, for example, I had an affair with Michael, and he started hoping I'd leave Ben for him. Because I don't know if I could."

Sandra said nothing.

"That's why," I continued, "the safest thing would be for Michael to get involved with someone else and for me to refocus my energy on Ben."

"Safety," she said, "is often very important to people with an alcoholic parent."

"My mother isn't an alcoholic, she drinks. It's a little different."

"Is it?"

"This is what I hate about therapists. A couple weeks ago, I told you my mother sometimes drinks too much, and now you're constructing my whole character around it. Besides, what's wrong with wanting security?"

She chewed her gum thoughtfully. "Nothing. Nothing at all."

11

ONE OF MY SOCIAL duties, as Ben's consort, was to attend the holiday party given by his department at Princeton. I'd skipped it the previous couple of years, feeling rebellious, but now that we were commuting, it seemed important to show up. As Ben was helping to organize the party, rather than have him pick me up at the station, I took the "dinky" or shuttle train that connects the main line to downtown Princeton. The word "dinky" still conjures for me the quaint world of Princeton—the dark-shingled Nassau Inn, the little lingerie store run by sexless crones, and the pancake house with its striped French awning.

From the dinky station it was a short walk to campus. A cold mist rose from the grass in translucent, mauve layers as I crossed the green. Walking into the party, I saw familiar faces—the eccentric, kilt-wearing chairman, the eminent scholar of Victorian fiction (a mother of four said never to sleep, like the prolific authors she studied), and the medievalist who wrote about baseball to prove his breadth of vision. I nodded to the pert departmental secretary who always talked about moving on to do a graduate degree but never did. Then there were the graduate students— the guys intensely talking about Derrida, and the women in black cocktail dresses, nervously trying to impress their professors.

I scanned the crowd for Ben. He walked in from the departmental kitchen, bearing a paper plate loaded with French bread, cheese, and grapes. He looked sharp in a charcoal jacket over a black cashmere turtleneck and a pair of black corduroy pants. Just seeing his good posture, the legacy of years of fencing lessons, made me feel more balanced. He put the plate down on the food table and approached me. I put my arms around his neck, and his kiss came to me at a soft angle, like a trumpet vine flower. Sandra was wrong, my desire for Michael wasn't the result of something "missing" from my relationship with Ben; it was a separate thing, an emotional inconvenience that would be resolved once he was safely parked somewhere.

"You look beautiful," he said.

"You look handsome," I said. "I see our tenants are here." When I'd moved into the city, we had sublet the two bedrooms downstairs to three graduate students in English, George and his wife Helen, and another woman named Mary Jo.

The three of them stood to the side, quietly sipping apple juice, undoubtedly afraid to get drunk in front of the faculty. Mary Jo was wearing a double-threat little black dress with a neckline so low and a hemline so high that both her breasts and ass threatened to pop out when she leaned over the buffet table. I wondered whether Ben found her attractive, and I remembered Michael's warning, the day I ran into him, that Ben might play around if I moved into the city.

Ben saw me looking at them. "I've made my contribution here setting up. Let's go home and do it before the kids get back," he whispered. He always called our tenants "the kids."

"You'll have to wait," I teased. "I just got here and I'm going to circulate a bit."

I walked over to our tenants.

"How are you guys doing?" I asked. "Everything okay at the house?"

"It's very quiet," George said. "I'm getting a lot of work done." His pattern was to study late into the night.

"The right front burner on the stove still isn't working quite right," Mary Jo said.

"I'll look at it again," I said. "Maybe we need to get the repairman out again."

The conversation jerked forward in stops and starts. Then I was pulled aside by the secretary, interrupted by the Victorian scholar, and finally head to head with the kilt-wearing chairman.

"So you're gracing us with your presence," he said. "To what do we owe the honor?"

I was jolted by the resentment in his voice, though it was typical of Princeton that the chair would keep track of my absences from departmental functions.

"I—I," I stuttered.

Ben came up behind me and said, "Julia is now a successful businesswoman in Manhattan."

The chairman gave me a veiled look, clearly suspicious of anyone who chose to live her life outside the University, in the Real World.

"Power to you," he said simply and moved away.

A slim woman with a very short haircut, wearing an oversized man's suit, came up and touched Ben's sleeve.

"Is this Julia?" she asked him.

"Yes, and Julia, this is Lisa Gould. Lisa was just hired."

"What's your field?" I asked.

"Gay studies."

"Wow," I said. I was surprised that Princeton had done something as radical as a gay studies hire. "I hope you're happy here."

"Thanks."

It was hard to imagine her happy. The smile seemed forced, and she held her shoulders up tight. "Excuse me," she suddenly said, glancing across the room, and darted away, moving toward a woman close to her age, with the same haircut.

"That must be her partner," I said.

"Yes. Her name is Dana." Ben dropped his voice. "Rumor has it that she's mentally unstable and that Lisa has her hands full taking care of her."

"Really?" I gazed at Dana, feeling a surge of sympathy for anyone who followed her partner to Princeton. "Well, if she's not crazy now, she will be soon, anyway."

"It's not that bad," Ben said. "Brie, wine, ivy, and money."

"You're the one who complains about it all the time, calling your colleagues 'stuffed shirts' and 'dead wood' and all that."

"Come on, let's get out of here."

Grabbing my hand, Ben pulled me out of the party. It was cold and dark out, and we ran to the parking lot.

"So what's the story with Mary Jo? I think she has designs on you," I teased. "And you probably have the *hots* for her..."

"How could I have the *hots* for someone named Mary Jo?" he responded, imitating my emphasis. "Please! Mary Antoinette, maybe, but Mary Jo? You must be pulling my leg!"

"I must be—what—your leg?" I reached across and, placing my hand on his thigh, began to slide it upward. He took my hand and kissed it, and for a brief moment I looked forward to bedtime.

The darkness grew thicker as we left the streetlights of the town and, passing the silent headquarters of the Educational Testing Service, turned right onto the road to New Hope. As a child, I'd often fantasized about a life filled with the rural pleasures I'd missed growing up in New York— dogs and cats and maybe a horse, opening the windows to the smells of spring and walks through snow-covered woods. Then, when I left home and felt lost in New Haven, then Princeton, I began to believe that I could only be myself in New York. But the house in Princeton still gave me a taste of what I'd missed as a child, and I was glad it would be there for me if my New York plan didn't work out.

Ben turned into the driveway. There was the white front door of our little house, lit up by the iron porch light. Stepping inside, I switched the lights on, and our large living room with its brick fireplace and overstuffed second-hand furniture came into view. Everything looked neat and a little shabby in a homey way I treasured.

As we went upstairs, I knew we would get undressed and make love. Part of me wanted to, and part of me didn't.

I had read in some woman's magazine that the way to manage wandering desire is to redirect it into one's principal relationship, and as I took off my clothes, I set myself the task of rechanneling my erotic energy from Michael toward Ben.

Part of me was wishing that I was undressing for Michael, not Ben. Part of me was rebelling, saying, *I don't really feel like doing this now, because when I do, there's always the feeling of something not being met.*

But I kept on undressing, and when I'd taken all my clothes off, and Ben had, too, I got into bed and felt our bodies come together with the familiar warmth. When he took my head between his hands and said, "You sweet thing," and his hand moved down between my thighs, I remembered what it felt like to be loved by him—I felt that in some way it *was* sufficient and even wonderful.

And the two feelings—the feeling of it being sufficient and the feeling of wanting to get the hell out of there in order to get something else, something more—kept on alternating as his kisses followed his hand and the arousal washed over me. Was I making love with Ben because I wanted *him*, or because I needed to have sex and he was available? The question receded when he got on top of me and, moving in a technically perfect way, took me over the top of the wave, leaving me, on the other side, in a place that was simultaneously sweet and fulfilled, sad and hungry. I'd had my ecstasy but my heart continued to itch. I couldn't quite understand it—the combination of sexual pleasure and then the empty feeling inside—the feeling, somehow, that true *contact* hadn't been made, that I hadn't gotten what I needed. Maybe Sandra was right—something was missing. But was it something in the relationship? Or was there was something missing in *me*—the ability to connect fully? Maybe *I* was the obstacle to the intimacy I needed.

We'd been together long enough that, after making love, we usually didn't while the time away lying in each other's arms. Instead, Ben would shift gears, saying, "I'd like to read a bit before going to sleep," and reach for his book. But tonight he held me longer. He took my left hand and pretended to read my palm. "I see a lot of sex in your future," he said. And then he added slyly, "And babies, too."

It was the first time he had ever talked about sex and babies in the same breath. I was so startled I couldn't respond. Then he kissed my fingers one by one, starting with the thumb. When he got to my ring finger, he drew an imaginary ring around it and gave me a questioning look. I felt both delighted by the hint and irritated by his indirection.

"How many?" I asked.

"Three, but if that's too many, one or two."

"There's a big difference between one and three," I said. I remembered Michael and felt the confusion come up again. Was it possible that I didn't want to talk about marriage or babies? Now that Ben was finally advancing toward me, why was I retreating? Restless, I got up, went over to the closet where I still had some clothes hanging.

"So, you think Lisa is going to make a good colleague?" I asked. Departmental gossip provided an easy way to change the topic.

"Yes, she would seem to be very civic-minded, like someone who will pull her share in terms of committee work and so forth. And what an accomplishment—getting a job in gender studies here, in the ivory tower of conservatism. I'm amazed it worked out." He didn't mind my changing the subject. Maybe he was even relieved.

"What do you mean?"

"The job was advertised as twentieth-century British lit, and she refashioned it to her own liking."

Rustling through my outfits, I knocked a hanger off the pole.

"What are you doing?" Ben asked.

"Looking for an outfit for the holiday party I'm thinking of having in the city," I said, enjoying the sound of the first person singular. "Maybe one of those parties where you ask everybody to bring somebody, so you can meet new people."

"Oh?" he said.

"Yes," I said. "It will be a kind of housewarming slash Christmas slash welcoming Anna back type of thing," I said.

"And Chanukah?"

"Sure, if you want," I said. My parents had never celebrated Chanukah, and I hadn't known what to do with the menorah the first time Ben brought one home and set it before me. I continued to rummage around in the closet, pulling one black skirt, then another, out of my dull wardrobe.

"Are we going to have a tree here or in New York?" Ben asked. We always had a Christmas tree.

"I don't know," I said. "Why not both?"

"Why not both," he repeated, with a drop in his voice indicating a melancholy about our commuting. Looking at him, I glimpsed sadness in his eyes, but then it was gone. It was hard to know how Ben really felt about anything because he was so private. And, sure enough, he switched gears again.

"Remember those ornaments you made? I wonder where we put them."

"They're in the hall closet, I think."

Ben got out of bed and followed me out of the bedroom. The hall closet was jam-packed full of boxes and valises, but it took us only a moment to find a carton marked "Xmas stuff." Back in the bedroom, he set it on the bed and opened it. Inside were metallic ball ornaments on which I'd glued strips of lace and sequined trim.

"These are so beautiful," he said. "You're so creative."

I picked one up and turned it, examining the precision with which I'd attached the sparkling strips of fabric.

"Occasionally," I said. "Only occasionally."

In New York, I lived for my meetings with Michael, yet still thought of playing matchmaker. Our next meeting confirmed this was the right thing to do.

We'd agreed that I would cook him dinner in exchange for a lesson, but I hadn't had the time after work, and, when he came in with sushi-to-go and a bottle of cold plum wine, his generosity was easy to accept.

"Since you've been a good girl, I've got something special for you," he said. He set the food down and, opening up his black shoulder bag, took out some composition paper covered with his spidery musician's scrawl. "I've written my first piece in five years."

He went over to the piano and, sitting down to play, drew himself in and upward in a postural gesture of coming-to-attention so familiar to me. Reaching for the keyboard with the smoothness of someone who knows exactly where he's going and what he has to say, he cracked open into a composition that rose and fell like jagged lightning advancing and receding on the horizon. The music had moments of gorgeous melody and moments in which melody was smashed like a tree twisted in a storm. There was joy in it and defiance of the fragility of joy. It was the act of a man turning himself upside down and inside out, like a bulb planted with the wrong end down that flips itself over magically at the spring equinox and sends its first green sprout toward the sun. Michael had in his piece put some very intimate part of himself on display, and I was touched by the faith implicit in the enterprise. If a composer doesn't believe that someone out there will be generous enough to listen and try to understand his work, he can only dread humiliation.

"Wow!" I said. As Michael swiveled around on the piano bench to look at me, proud and beaming, I was certain for a burstingly ripe second that I was that someone out there for him—that I was his muse. He had written the piece for and because of me.

"And you mean to tell me you hadn't written anything at all in five years?" I asked.

"It was that business with Karyn," he said. "I was so devastated afterwards that I ran dry."

He turned back toward the piano, began improvising. His words scorched. For, like Karyn, I was already taken, and he could never love me, because that could only bring another heartbreak. If I were his muse, I would be an untouched one.

I listened to him play, remembering what he'd told me about his affair with Karyn: "It was physically very passionate but, at the same time, that was the least important part of it." I felt haunted by his confession of love for this other more powerful and talented woman. I wanted to know more.

"But why," I asked, interrupting his playing, "why *did* you go back to her place that day to have sex? Didn't you realize you could get caught?"

Standing up, he went over to the table to pour himself some plum wine, then sat down on the couch about a yard away from me.

"Of course I knew we could get caught. I think I *wanted* to get caught. I wanted her to leave her husband—that's why I brought the thing to a head." He stopped, looking confused, as though it had been recent. "I *wanted* to break up their marriage. What I did was unforgivably destructive and, maybe this is over-interpreting, but I think I wanted to do to some other man what my best friend did to me when he exploded my marriage."

"Go on." I was barely breathing.

"I felt horribly guilty afterwards. In fact, one day I walked into a church and went into confession. I said to the priest, I'm not Catholic, but would you listen to me please and forgive me? I was in a crazy state of mind."

"You went to confession?"

He smiled. "Yeah."

"Your marriage...You never told me the whole story."

"Okay. This is what happened. I was at my parents' vacation place in Ontario with my wife. It sounds funny to say 'wife' because we were kids, still in college. So we were up there alone, my parents hadn't come up yet. Then my best friend shows up for a visit. One day I go down river by myself to get some supplies, but change my mind because the water looks active, and I end up fishing instead. I go back, real proud of myself because I'd caught a really big trout, and I see the camper door's shut. I creep up and peek through the window. The curtains are drawn but there's just a bit of a crack between them, and I see my wife's on top, my best friend's on the bottom with his hands on her bare ass."

"Didn't they realize they might get caught?"

"They thought I was going to be gone all day getting supplies. Just think—if I hadn't caught that fish, the rest of my life might have been different."

"So then what happened?"

"I waited politely—God only knows why—till they finished, then I knocked on the door. The worst part was that she climaxed just before he did. I mean, she came while they were screwing, which was something she could never do with me. At twenty-one I wasn't a great lover, I guess. Anyway, I knock on the door and swing it open, she grabs the sheet and pulls it up over her tits like she's in a cheap movie, and I start yelling and throwing things. They packed in a jiffy and left camp together. My father walked me through the divorce when I got back to New York." He took a breath. "So you see, I have a long history of triangulated situations."

I stood up, agitated. "What ever possessed you to leave them alone together? Didn't you have any suspicions?"

"Of course I did. I guess I was testing her."

"And so you make a connection between that and Karyn?"

"Sure. I wanted to make some other man suffer the same torments of jealousy that I'd been through. Of course—this is the irony—I only ended up being victimized all over again." He craned his neck slightly, as though reliving the slash of the knife.

"And you feel sorry for yourself," I said. "You use your divorce and Karyn and everything that happened in between as an excuse to give up and stop looking for someone."

He looked startled. "Go on," he said.

"You're just drowning in self-pity." I was so angry I paced the floor. The way he wore his broken heart on his sleeve infuriated me—what woman could resist so much woundedness? I felt manipulated. "You've just given up so you can enjoy being miserable."

I sat back down on the couch, exactly where I'd been before, except that the yard between us now seemed a lot wider. The pelvic pain, which had lessened with Dr. McCloud's treatments, grabbed me again.

Michael sank deeper into the couch, staring off into space.

"You're right, of course. You're so astute, Jul." He wasn't defensive. Maybe that's why he got wounded so deeply. "I've been walking around as though I'd been damaged for life. I should get back in the ring."

He stood up, went over to the brown paper bag, and started unpacking the sushi dinner. I went into the kitchen to get some plates. Our both thinking so hard filled the silence with static.

We sat across my little table, eating sushi. Then he spoke.

"It's been so long," he said, "I almost have the feeling of, do I remember how to do this? The dating thing, I mean. And even though I'm out and about all the time, right now there doesn't seem to be anyone I could ask out."

"I'm going to have a holiday party," I said, "and there'll be a couple of women there you might like to talk to. My cousin Evelyn and this woman I work with, Betty."

"Setups of that kind never work out."

"There's that pessimism of yours again."

He laughed. "Okay. But what about Ben? What's he going to think about my turning up? You never solved that."

"You can come with Anna—pretend *she* ran into you, instead of me."

"Anna never liked me very much, especially after I critiqued that orange painting of hers."

"Critiqued and knocked over," I reminded him.

He winced. "Yeah."

"That was a long time ago. I talked to her about it and she's willing to help out."

"Really?'"

"Then you and Ben can be friends again—and you and I can be aboveboard, which is what you wanted, right?"

"Yeah…I guess it's time for everybody to forgive everybody," he said.

"Yes," I said. "Absolutely." I breathed into my belly to soften the spasm. I needed to shift the conversation away from relationship issues. "That piece you just played for me, Michael, it's really amazing."

"Thanks. Now it's your turn."

"What do you mean?"

"To share something with me."

"I don't have anything. I told you I don't write anymore."

"Well then, why don't you trot out the famous sonnet? I'd like to read it again."

"Enough with the sonnet already. Anyway, I don't have it here."

"I don't believe that. You wouldn't move into the city without your sonnet."

"You win," I said amiably and, getting up, went over to the filing drawer under my desk. "It's in here somewhere." I took it out, glanced at it, placed it next to him.

Michael swallowed, wiped a little red egg roe off his mouth with a napkin, cleared his throat with a theatrical "Ahem," and read out loud:

"Sonnet by Julia Field

It's dusk now; climb ahead; race the last stair.
Let hands still cold-bit draw the curtain soft.
You light the candles, my cheek in your hair.
We roll the covers down, close in our loft.
The clothes slip off us as the chalk peach falls.
The tangled hues of wheat-felt marble dance,
and sea velvet, warm and wet, sways and calls
deep and deeper: soon we won't have the chance.
Embedded in parting, desire should cry.
But now we'll touch into the night; ride high
the quivering wave that unfurls and leaps;
fill to burst this moment, threatened but fired;
swim drunk together until we're too tired
(to think of the purple cabbage or hope it keeps)."

There was a moment of silence. "It's damn good," he said.

"Yeah, it is, isn't it?" I was pleasantly surprised.

"I'm not sure about the 'wheat-felt marble' image, but the 'purple cabbage' is great.'"

"Fuck you," I said, and crumpling up a napkin, threw it right at his broad, majestic forehead.

When Michael brought me two more compositions the following week and played them for me, beaming with pride, I felt sure I was his muse. And I began to feel that he was mine. The next day, during my lunch hour, I wandered into a stationery store and bought a small notebook with a hard black cover. As I stepped outside, some words in my head demanded to be recorded. Leaning against the storefront window, with the display of file folders and staplers behind me and my handbag tucked under my arm, I wrote:

Inside the long quiet day,
I wait for the voice
that gives me joy.
I hear the music
you make in my life.

As a beginning, it wasn't very good, but I knew that I would have to produce some bad poems before getting back to the good ones, and I didn't mind. I was too elated by the return of my poetic voice to continue torturing myself with the judgment of mediocrity. I had, finally, to accept myself for what I was—not the kind of poet who gets inspired by plums in the fridge or a jar in Tennessee, but one who needs passion to get going. And Michael was the provider.

For years my voice and heart had been muffled by a cotton batting made of self-doubt and self-deprecation. But now Michael was stripping that batting away as I did the same for him. Joyfully I watched our friendship bring him back into the world of self-expression, as, glowing like a toddler who has just learned to walk, he played me a new composition every time we met. I didn't tell him I was writing again, too, because my poetry was about him. But that was all right with me. What mattered was that he was my inspiration, that I was creating bits and pieces of verse that, like a mirror made of mosaic-sized shards of glass, served as adorning reflectors of my life. Certainly I could suffer the hardship of an unrequited attachment when the reward was stepping so much more fully into what I had to say.

12

I BEGAN TO INVITE people to my party. I called Evelyn, Betty, my friend Theo from Baruch, and other friends I hadn't seen in a long time. Ben invited people as well.

With my matchmaking scheme underway, I felt more in control. Even my abdomen felt better, almost normal. I would find Michael a girlfriend. I would focus on Ben. Things—people—would fall into their proper places, one at a time. I took my calm, like a dog takes its bone, to Frank, wondering whether he would feel the changes in my pulse.

"It feels better this week," he said.

He inserted the needles in my arms and legs as I stared at a painting, set on dark brocade, of the Medicine Buddha, a figure in lapis blue that sat cross-legged with one hand holding a bowl.

"What's in the bowl?" I asked, nodding at the scroll.

"The wisdom of the dharma—the medicinal teachings of the Buddha, which dispel greed, hatred, and ignorance. According to the Buddha, all illness is rooted in spiritual confusion."

"So if I sort things out, I'll be cured?"

He chuckled. "Of course it's not so simple. But any tension—or conflict—in the mind affects the body." He inserted the needles in my belly last. Although it was my third treatment with him, I still instinctively tightened when he approached my abdomen.

A needle went in below the belly button.

"I don't like that one so much."

"Here, this will help."

He lit a stick of compressed mugwort and passed the glowing tip over my abdomen. The warmth felt good. But as pleasant as it was to be rebalanced and cared for, I had only to remember my account balance to feel uneasy. Seeing both Sandra and Frank was extravagant. Resolving to spread my appointments further apart, I closed my eyes and dozed off.

Finally I called Anna, who had just moved into her new apartment on West Seventy-Fourth Street, and invited her.

"Everyone is bringing someone to the party," I said, "and your job is to bring Michael and say you ran into him in a bookstore." I gave her his phone number. "He's expecting you to call him." It was good having a cousin I could count on.

"All right," she said. "And can you come up this weekend and help me unpack?" she added. "I'm drowning in boxes."

"Of course." I agreed because it felt good that she could count on me, too.

Anna's apartment echoed mine—a one-bedroom with southern exposure—except hers was nicer, with higher ceilings flaunting decorative molding. In the living room, large enough to double as an art studio, the couch in the corner was barely visible behind a mound of oversized boxes filled with paintings. She hadn't finished unpacking but was already painting at an easel set up over drop cloths.

"Let's hang some things up," she said.

"How do you find the time for it?" I said, staggered by the quantity of canvas.

"Oh, there's plenty of time, after dinner and on the weekends. It really"—she waved her hand at the paintings, drawings, and collages— "keeps going by itself, like a clock with a battery in it. It doesn't need winding—just keeps ticking away."

Her work was jammed with fantastical animal forms—creatures with two heads or three ears, giraffes with short necks, homunculi with fur, monsters with spikes, and on and on, in breathless, inventive proliferation. The paint had been put on in layers, with a profusion of bright colors overlaid by minute, print-like characters in black and white. Many of her compositions were divided into interlocking sections by thick, dark strokes that worked, like so many angry impulses, to crunch and compact her humor and exuberance into hieroglyphic capsules.

This was not the painter of nudes and still lives that I'd known in college. I was mesmerized and jealous of her productivity. She had no blocks, no self-doubt. Or if she did, they were quickly swept aside by the daily resurgent impulse to *make something new*. And she didn't seem to need a muse to generate flow.

"Wow, you've been busy," I said. "Animals everywhere."

"I was a cave painter in another life," Anna said.

"You've got a lot of two-headed creatures," I said.

The artist nodded. "I suppose that's because I'm a two-headed creature. I have one head that's orderly and wants a neatly arranged bourgeois life, and another head that wants to be a wild animal like this—" She pointed to a snarling leopard with wings.

"So you've got one head working at the Metropolitan looking for a rich husband, and another head living like this." I waved my hand at her unconventional living room.

"Don't you think that's a recipe for success?" she said, laughing.

"Why not?"

We hung paintings for an hour, then Ben, who'd been uptown at Columbia having coffee with a colleague, arrived, and the three of us went down to a place on Columbus called Jeremy's, where the tables were sticky from syrupy brunches, but there was a pleasant atmosphere of yuppies on their day off having a good time.

"I can't believe that the two of you are still together," Anna said, sitting across from us at the table. "How do you do it?"

Ben and I looked at each other.

"It's true love," Ben said.

"With a good dose of persistence and patience thrown in," I added dryly.

"Seriously," Anna said, "there must be some secret to it."

"Both people have to want the same thing. That's all," Ben said. "Both have to want to be in a committed relationship and both have to believe that the relationship is worth making sacrifices for."

I looked at Ben in wonderment. He was articulating my unspoken belief that commitment was a kind of third—and higher—thing in a relationship that had its own power. His words reminded me of what deep roots this higher thing had in my being.

Anna sighed. "That's so beautifully put. I want and believe those things, too, but I haven't found a man who does, too. I split up with my last boyfriend as soon as I realized it wasn't going anywhere."

"What do you mean?" Ben asked.

"I've had it with these guys who won't commit—they make me so angry. Steven was never going to want to get married, and—" She stopped, remembering that Ben and I weren't yet married.

"It's okay, Anna," I said, grimacing at her gaffe.

"Shit. But with you guys it's different—you don't need to get married…"

"Guys are slow," Ben said. "Sometimes it takes them a long time. It's taking me a long time, but I'm getting real close—"

"It will be totally anticlimactic if he ever *does* get around to it." I tried to sound affectionate instead of resentful.

Anna looked uncomfortable. "Well, maybe I just haven't found the right guy. When I think back on the boyfriends I've had, the truth is, they've all been flawed."

"Everyone's flawed," Ben said.

"I know," she said. "But I want perfection. Actually, someone decent, who wants to have a baby with me, would do."

Her quest for the perfect man aggravated me. "So tell us about your job," I said.

"Well, I have this job in museum heaven. I get to the Metropolitan at a quarter to nine and have fifteen minutes to walk through the museum by myself before I start work. And every day I say to myself, what an amazing place…"

She babbled on. I barely listened as I wondered whether Ben was hinting at marriage again because he intuited a threat. Don't they say that, over time, couples begin to read each other's minds without knowing it? Then they act accordingly, in a kind of unconscious dance, mutually mesmerized by what their deeper minds are receiving from their partners. I glanced sideways at him. Maybe he even knew, *really* knew—but how would he know? Not from my cryptic diaries, not from anything I'd said or done. Because I hadn't done anything wrong. My whole relationship with Michael was based on fantasy, and on a fantasy I was nipping in the bud.

"…What do you think, Julia?" I heard Anna say.

I snapped back to attention on hearing my name. "What do I think about what?"

"You weren't listening—what were you daydreaming about?" she asked, as Ben's eyes narrowed on me.

"Gee, I don't know," I said. "I really don't know." I looked at her, then him, and swallowed a forkful of scrambled eggs.

There was an empty lot on Fourteenth Street between Ninth and Tenth Avenues where Christmas trees were sold, and on the way home Ben and I picked up a six-foot pine tree and carried it back to my apartment, where it exuded a clean, scratchy smell. We decorated it together, though really, as Ben said every year, there was no reason for him to help, since I always rearranged everything he put up—moving ornaments to the right or left a couple of inches, re-draping the lights, redistributing the tinsel to get everything just right. We drank eggnog with whiskey in it, and Ben made the same toast he always did, "Have yourself a nice Jewish Christmas." I was tired of the joke, but I pretended to be amused. It was something I knew how to do, because my mother had taught me, by always smiling at my father's tired jokes, that a woman's ability to keep responding to her man's wit contributes to the health of a relationship.

My party was set for the following weekend. Ben went back out to Princeton to correct papers. Of course, he could have corrected them in my apartment in New York, but he said he worked better in New Jersey; there were too many distractions in the city. I didn't try to persuade him to change his mind. I was finding that kind of conversation, in which I would try to get more out of him and he would resist, increasingly wearisome. Besides, I was so deep in my obsession with Michael that, even with the resolution of not pursuing it to consummation, I was happy to have another week to myself to sort things out.

I'd settled on cousin Evelyn as a logical choice for Michael. She had artistic qualities; she was articulate and engaging and a sexy dresser. Add to the package that she made a bundle of money working for one of the more prestigious interior design firms in Manhattan. In her late thirties, she was tired of serial affairs with married men and desperate to find a man who was truly single. She would be perfect.

I spent the week fantasizing about Michael and Evelyn pairing up. Evelyn's ample earnings would allow her to support Michael financially, freeing him up from some of his teaching and performing responsibilities so that he could compose more. With Evelyn backing him up, Michael's music would be performed by the Philharmonic in no time. And I could play "auntie" to the children they would inevitably have.

The idea of Michael having a child with someone beside me brought me up short. It seemed impossible that he might go that *irrevocably* into a relationship with another woman.

Still, on the whole, Michael-and-Evelyn-together seemed like a constructive fantasy.

Friday night returned again, and Ben came back in on a late train. The next morning we went over to Balducci's where I spent too much money on dips and cheeses. I felt hyper leaving the store and walked up Sixth Avenue with my legs bouncing beneath me. The energy turned into irritability as we cleaned up the apartment and arranged the table.

Ben noticed. As I was putting a tablecloth over my little dining table, he came up from behind and kissed my neck: "Do you need to unwind a little—take a break?"

His voice was sweet, but the idea of getting into bed with him when Michael would be over in a few hours was unthinkable, even if I was hoping to set him up with another woman. A stormy sea was rising, and my insides felt sloshed by the waves. I certainly couldn't have sex till the boat stopped rocking.

"No," I said, "I'm too nervous—about the party."

"Why? Our parties always go great."

"Just am, that's all," I snapped.

I went and got dressed. I liked to dress casually when giving a party, in order not to outclass my guests. Putting on some jeans and my plum sweater, I stood in front of the mirror, glanced out toward the living room to make sure Ben wasn't watching me, and yanked the V-neck down a bit.

Once dressed, I went back to helping Ben. By six o'clock we had the dining table covered with cheeses, hummus, fruit, sausage chunks with toothpicks in them, plates of little pumpernickel squares with lox and cream cheese, dolmades, and, in the middle, a large tray of spanakopita.

The kitchen counter was crowded with wine, beer, soda, a couple of bottles of hard stuff (Scotch and whiskey) and plastic glasses. As the guests arrived, I wondered whether they would all get along. We had invited a hodge-podge of people, including some of Ben's colleagues at NYU and Columbia (academic literary types) and a few friends I'd made at Baruch (practical, business people). To top it off, there'd be Betty and my two "artistic" cousins, with Anna bringing Michael, as planned.

Evelyn came in wearing a black leather miniskirt, a black cashmere top with fake fur trim, and, tied around the waist, a silk scarf with a black-and-white architectural design on it. She brought one of her coworkers, a tall, thin guy I assumed was gay.

Betty arrived wearing skin-tight purple silk pants and a soft-looking, V-neck sweater with a silk bow at the cleavage. "I'm sorry I didn't bring anybody—no one available, just no one," she apologized. As I gave her a welcoming kiss and took the proffered wine, I beat myself up for not having dressed more glamorously.

Theo arrived. I hadn't seen him in a while and had forgotten how good-looking he was.

"So good to see you," Theo said.

He wrapped a hand around my wrist and kissed me hello. As his moustache brushed my cheek, I remembered the night when some error in judgment, or maybe just curiosity about what it would feel like to kiss someone with facial hair, had led me to agree to go to his apartment after class, and we'd made out for an hour before I ran away.

Fortunately, he'd forgiven me and remained a friend—and a valuable one since he had a photographic memory of anything having to do with the tax code.

As Theo passed into the living room, I saw Anna on the landing, with Michael behind her. In high heels Anna was as tall as Michael, and she towered over me as she walked in. My heart skipped a beat. At the same time, I felt Ben approaching from behind.

Anna gave me a hug. "Look who I ran into in Brentano's," she said, gesturing toward Michael.

She seemed completely comfortable with the dissimulation.

"Wow," I said to Michael, "I haven't seen you in a while. What have you got there?" I gestured to a stack of booklets he had under his arm.

"Christmas carols," he said and, stepping forward, gingerly kissed me on the cheek.

"My God," Ben said to Michael. "Look at you—you've grown up. You're shaved and everything." Ben looked happy. They might be friends again.

"Hey, good to see you," said Michael. They exchanged a big hug.

In a kind of minuet, I stepped back and the two of them stepped into the living room together. They leaned toward each other and talked intensely, with eyebrows dancing and heads nodding. What were they talking about? Would I really get away with this absurd scheme of having Anna bring Michael to the party?

Anna looked at me, raising her eyebrows.

"Good job," I said softly.

She shrugged and glanced around the room. "Are there any guys here who know how to make money?" she asked.

"Well, the guy in the tweed jacket is a professor of economics…"

"Oh, really?"

"I think he makes a lot in various consultancies. And then Theo over there is doing well…"

Anna moved off into the crowd. Her auburn hair was pinned up and a long strand of fake pearls ran around her pale neck several times. In a black, vintage dress with a beaded, low-cut neckline, she looked gorgeously nineteenth-century. I watched her penetrate the crowd with a mission.

Theo came back up to me. "Great to see you."

"Thanks. So, how's work going?" I asked.

"My boss is an asshole," he said. "But besides that, everything's great."

"Well, you know the solution to that one," I said to Theo.

"What's that?"

"Become your own boss."

"Oh, *that* solution!" Theo laughed. "Hey, it looks like we both need more wine."

I followed him into the kitchen, where Ben's guests, a Shakespeare scholar from NYU and a Spenserian from Columbia, were talking about their undergraduate students.

"I think the general level has improved," said the Shakespeare scholar.

"I disagree. At Columbia, things have been going steadily downhill for a decade now," said the Spenserian.

Theo glanced sideways at the two professors. "You've got several different worlds going here," he said, pouring me some more wine.

"It's very important," I said, "to get drunk at your own party. That way you're guaranteed to believe it's a smashing success."

"In that case," Theo said, adding another inch of red to my plastic cup.

Out of the corner of my eye, I could see that Michael was now in deep conversation with Evelyn. The fake fur trim of her sweater framed her neck in a way that was classic, seductive. He leaned toward her at an angle that suggested attraction. *I've made a terrible mistake with this idiotic matchmaker game.* I looked back at Theo. I had never, not for half a minute, imagined that I was in love with Theo.

"So how's your business going?" Theo asked.

"I'm thinking of turning it into a woman-oriented firm," I said.

"Oh really? In what way exactly?"

"The idea would be to serve women who are in the process of separating and divorcing from their husbands. A lot of them wake up one day and find their finances are in a mess." I was making this up as I went along.

"You're going to move into financial consulting, then?"

"Yeah," I said. "Especially for women, for divorced women."

"That could be very lucrative," he said. "If you just get the ones who've taken their husbands to the cleaners."

"I'd like to aim for a good mix," I said. Outside the window, a few snowflakes were falling, shining in the light emanating from my apartment. I thought of the first time Ben kissed me, on that bench in Washington Square. It had been snowing that day, too. For so many years, the memory of that moment had held huge erotic power for me. Now it was fading fast.

"It sounds like a great idea," Theo said. "You could make a real reputation for yourself."

"Yes. Eventually I'll have to expand, I think. Hire more people. Move into a larger office." I imagined a firm employing a dozen quick-witted women and a stream of female clients coming in through the door. I could go whole days at the office without seeing a single man.

"Feminism in action," Theo said.

"Do you know what my father once said to me about feminism?" I said. "'Anything that's good for Julia is all right by me.' I always thought that was so sweet."

"I can see you as a financial planner. But you got a lot of course work ahead of you to get that certification."

"I know."

With my peripheral vision working hard, I caught that Michael had moved on to Betty now. What an obscenely huge silk bow at the tip of the V of her sweater. My mother always said that low-cut sweaters worked, and she was right. Men had peripheral vision, too. *Jesus why did I invite all these women? It's inevitable—he's going to choose one of them. I'm such an idiot.* Betty's little face was turned up toward Michael with rapt fascination. Just the size of the man was sexual—like a bull or a stallion. I wondered for the first time whether his "equipment" was proportionally large, whether I'd be able to accommodate it if I ever had the chance—which I wouldn't anyway. So what. Betty reached for a pen. She wrote on a party napkin and handed it to Michael, who put it in his wallet. *He's got her number already. What an operator.*

"You know there are a number of eligible women at this party," I said to Theo. "Have you met them all?" Taking his arm, I guided him toward Evelyn.

I'd delivered Theo to Evelyn when Ben came up to me. "Great party, don't you think? Good mix of people! Are you having a good time?" He spoke loudly over the din, which seemed to be growing by the second.

"I've been too busy to have a good time."

"Stop working so hard. It's taking care of itself."

A couple of hours later, some guests left and the crowd thinned. The noise level dropped. Michael handed out the Christmas carol booklets he'd brought as guests settled in. He sat down at the piano and started to play "God Rest Ye Merry Gentlemen," and soon two-dozen voices were singing along.

I let myself sink into the couch.

I'd positioned myself behind Michael and a little to one side, so that I could see the back of his head, with its thick hair, as well as the left side of his face and a small piece of the scar on his neck.

I opened my booklet to the right page but neither looked at it nor sang. I just sat staring at Michael.

Suddenly I had a revelation, as though from an angel that looked like an Italianate Venus. I floated above the room, knew how things were supposed to be. I saw that Michael and I were each, for the other, the missing piece, and that we would never be happy until we recognized that fact. We'd made a horrid mistake ten years before, when, after making out on the steps of the New York Public Library, we'd run with meteoric speed—as though afraid of the power of what we'd unleashed—to put me on the train back to New Haven. Why in God's name couldn't I have taken a later train and let our story unfold? A cataclysm would be needed now to set things right.

Michael moved on to "Joy to the World." I looked at Ben, whose self-confident, booming voice could be heard singing above the others. What I felt for Ben was—after all!—not passion, but a stoical tenderness so deep that I couldn't stomach the idea of hurting him by leaving him for Michael. An impulse rising tsunami-like from the deep would be required to redirect my life. Or maybe Fate would intervene. Ben might be "removed" by some twist of fate—*he* might leave *me* and fall in love with somebody else or something might "happen" to "remove" him from my life…

No, that was the stuff of film noirs, not of life. That was also the thinking of a cowardly heart. The only way out was to let things with Michael come to a head and then to leave Ben—if that's what Michael wanted, too—

If only Ben wasn't so good in bed.

I sank deeper into the safety of the couch. Everything had turned inside out. Michael and I were connected, always had been, by some thread which was bringing us back together again. We had some special form of communication, which I could feel right in the middle of my crowded living room, as though our lives had always been tied together and running parallel, even before we'd first met.

I closed my eyes as alternating currents of desire and anguish, intensified by drink, washed over me. A shivering started in my chest, and I reached for the wool throw draped over the arm of the sofa. The music stopped and, looking up, I saw Michael rise and cede the piano bench to the Spenser scholar, who picked up my volume of Scarlatti and began sight-reading it with an easy perfection that, in my musician's jealousy, I found obnoxious.

Michael headed toward the kitchen, then swerved and came and sat down next to me on the couch. Without looking my way, he pulled one end of the blanket over his lap and reached for my hand under its cover. I felt his long, warm fingers, which I knew so well from watching them on the keyboard, melt into my palm and stroke the back of my hand, and my entire body was warmed by the contact, as though I had slipped under a down comforter and into a bed where he was lying, waiting for me. Then, spontaneously, simultaneously, we both turned our heads and looked at each other. Two fireflies signaling to each other in the dark.

I squeezed his hand hard and then, with that peripheral vision of mine operating again, I quickly let go of him as I saw Ben moving in our direction.

The party began to wind down. I was happy when Evelyn and Betty were gone. Michael and Anna were heading toward the IRT together, as they both lived on the Upper West Side.

Ben stopped Michael at the door. "I'll be in the city for the next couple of weeks. Let's get together for a drink."

"Great idea," Michael said, "absolutely."

They hugged, and Michael was gone.

"It was a successful party, don't you think?" Ben asked me later.

"It was great."

"Great to see Michael again," he said.

Our eyes met and did a little dance. Would he cross-question me, would we have to review that awful night in '77 when he guessed I'd made out with Michael?

"Yeah," I said.

"And, uh, for you, when you saw him, was the old magic still there?"

"Oh, come on," I said. "That was just something that sort of happened. You know that."

Ben nodded and fell silent. His fear of knowing what I really felt for Michael combined with his weird British respect for "privacy" insured that any investigation wouldn't go far. But there was something I wanted to know.

"Why *did* you guys have that fight when he quit graduate school?"

"I don't have a lot of patience for people who are self-destructive, I guess. It killed me to see him wasting his genius. I don't mean his dropping out of the doctoral program—I couldn't care less about that. But seeing too many women, running around all the time, not getting the work done because he was smoking too much pot. Even a genius can't compose when he's completely stoned."

"Did he smoke that much?" I remembered Michael smoking weed only at parties.

"All the time. But not when you were around. He knew you'd disapprove, and I guess your approval meant something to him." He looked at me sharply, then looked away. After a moment, he looked at me again. "I don't know if he still does—smoke pot, I mean."

"I wouldn't know either," I said.

We put away the leftover food, corked the open wine. I hid my face behind a rigid mask of calm as Ben changed the subject to talk about his colleagues at Columbia. Something enormous had happened: I'd gotten away with my plan to bring Michael back into our circle. And yes, for a couple of hours I'd suffered as he collected phone numbers from the women I'd stupidly wanted him to meet, but that misery had been dispelled when he took my hand under the blanket. Inside, I was buzzing, exulting. This was real now. It was life calling to me. I had to go with the flow.

When I got into bed later and Ben turned off the lights and rolled away from me onto his side, he became a ghostly presence compared to the man I'd seen sitting at the piano, the touch I still felt on the back of my hand, the look I'd met when we turned toward each other. As I slid between the sheets and closed my eyes, my winter pajamas seemed to dissolve and what I felt instead was the sensuality of the sheets against my naked skin and the warmth of Michael's body embracing mine. When sleep came, dreams had me interposing myself between Michael and Evelyn and Betty or placing my head on his lap and feeling his hardness. Then, toward morning, I flew out the window with a feeling so physically vivid that I thought, *This is what New Agers mean when they talk about astral travel.* I glided down to the courtyard, my feet making a slight crunching sound in the snow as I landed. I picked some berries improbably growing on a raspberry bush and put them in my bathrobe pocket. Finding some pruning shears in my other pocket, I cut the plant down, beneath the level of the snow.

Then I flew up out of the courtyard and into the sky, I sailed over the plant district and Macy's, up the West Side, with Central Park down on the right, and finally over Amsterdam Avenue, all the way to Michael's apartment. I went right through his window and landed on my knees next to his bed. Sensing my arrival, Michael opened his eyes and lifted the bed covers to make room for me, and I saw his erection poking out of his flannel, striped pajamas.

I sat straight up in bed, awake. Surely this was a premonition, surely something would happen now! But there was Ben sleeping next to me, still trusting and loving me. Nausea washed over me as I considered the stalemate I was in—with myself.

I rose, went into the living room, took in the sour smell of the wine cups we hadn't gathered. Looking out the window, I saw patches of crusty-looking snow in the garden below glinting in the dawn light. I went for paper and a pen, and wrote:

My love is like a raspberry plant.
I must keep pruning it back
if I want more berries.

13

A FEW DAYS LATER, Ben and Michael met for a drink uptown on Columbus Avenue. Ben came back to my apartment afterward, curiously reticent, until I prodded him for an account.

"He chose one of the seediest bars in Manhattan, of course," Ben began. The Upper West Side hadn't been gentrified yet, and you could trust Michael to lure Ben into its tawdriest dive. "What is it about the American bar that's so dismal? Anyway, he told me what he's been doing. I told him what I've been doing. He still has his little ironic sneer about academia, but I don't begrudge him that." Ben stopped, reflected. "We don't really have much in common anymore."

"You don't?"

"Not much besides my liking music, his liking books, and—" he stopped himself.

Our both liking you—was that what he was about to say?

"But—" Ben started up again, tacking in another direction. "We're in two very different worlds, now."

"And you can't be friends with someone in a different world?"

"That's not what I meant. Rather, once we lived together and went to the same university, so naturally we were chums. And perhaps we will be again now, but in a different way."

Not wanting to seem overly curious, I didn't press for more information, and the topic was laid down delicately, like a glass ornament on a glass table.

After spending a Christmas with a French family when she was in her early twenties, my mother adopted the French *réveillon* as the gold standard for Christmas Eve. So when Ben and I spent the holiday in New York instead of London, she took out Julia Child and put together a French menu. Mariel had always been proud of her "European sensibility," which raised her, at least in her own eyes, above the level of the common, uncultivated American and allowed her to console herself with the fantasy that, if she had to be a Jew, at least the Lipskis had sophisticated forbearers, old European families in high-ceilinged homes with fine furniture and heavy silver menorahs and Kiddush cups. My conversations with Iris, however, had led me to believe that my ancestors had been shtetl Jews who lived in cabins with dirt floors and chickens in the backyard. The reality had probably been closer to *Fiddler on the Roof* than to *The Garden of the Finzi-Continis*.

Like many secularized Jews in New York, my mother saw no contradiction between her heritage and a lavish Christmas dinner. She wanted to be a citizen of the world, and no one could been more helpful to her quest than my British boyfriend—my British *Jewish* boyfriend. Ben was superior by virtue of nationality and education. By becoming a member of our family, he bettered us. By extension, he bettered *me* as well. I, Julia Field, was a worthier, more loveable daughter because I'd chosen the right man. Well, who knows what Mariel really thought, but she certainly worked hard to impress him. This year, she hunted down the most authentic *bûche de Noël* she could find, she set the table with a red cloth, she roasted some pathetic-looking quail, and she fussed over a true vinaigrette with shallots. Then, as though to sabotage the Christian or French effect, at the last minute she decided to whip up some matzo ball soup as a first course.

"Here," she said, moving the mixing bowl with the matzo meal in my direction. "You know what to do."

I went to the fridge for an egg, moving in the shadow of impending depression. In the living room, Ben was talking politics with my dad, which I appreciated, because my father's Marxist politics could be hard to take. If only Anna and her parents could have joined us, as they did at Thanksgiving, but my aunt Linda would have nothing to do with Christmas. Just my parents, Ben, and me, year after year—our lonely foursome. Where was the young life that was supposed to grace this picture? My longing for a child swelled and heaved like a wave about to crest, even as I waited for the sign I expected from Michael after he'd taken my hand. I needed to be patient; knowing that Ben was in the city with me for winter break, Michael would stay away until the coast was clear. Or maybe, now that he'd had a drink with Ben, he felt paralyzed.

"How's Ben doing? Is he getting nervous?" my mother asked, referring to the approaching tenure decision.

"He's been kind of quiet about it ever since he submitted the tenure packet. The wait for the department's decision must be driving him crazy."

For the past couple of weeks, Ben had been distant except, irritatingly, when he wanted to have sex. I didn't know whether this was a typical male pattern. He barely conversed with me, barely touched me. He kept himself separate, living in his head all the time except for when he needed a sexual connection. And it was becoming increasingly difficult for me to be present for those fifteen minutes; it took an immense effort of concentration to keep mind and body together for the act and not think about Michael. I'd imagine that I was in bed with some third person, like Jeremy Irons, or, even better, that I myself was some other person—that tavern harlot, for instance.

I worked the egg and tablespoons of water into the meal, barely able to concentrate on what I was doing. I felt suspended, as though I wouldn't be able to breathe or sleep or eat until the situation with Michael came to a head.

I glanced sideways at my mother. In a printed shirt and long skirt, sipping white wine, she was the picture of happiness. Because Ben and I were in New York and not in London. Because she was already sloshed.

I dropped the first tablespoon of batter into the chicken broth. It assumed a flat pancake shape that would displease her.

"You should be doing this," I said to her. "When I do it, they never come out round."

"They don't have to be perfectly round."

I dropped another tablespoon into the broth.

"But I'm nowhere close to round," I said. "These look like flying saucers. Yellow, mushy flying saucers."

She came over and peered at my work.

"You're right," she said. "You're making flying saucers. Here, let me." And she yanked the wooden spoon out of my hand.

On the first Wednesday morning after the end of winter break, Ben was back in Princeton, and Michael called me at the office.

"I know we usually have dinner together Wednesday night, but I'm too exhausted. I canceled my lessons downtown today."

"You getting sick?"

"No, I'm fine, just really tired. The holidays were exhausting." His depressed tone made me worry he was losing interest in me. "I'd love to see you, but I'm too tired to come downtown."

"Why don't I come uptown for a change? I'll stop on Broadway and pick something up for dinner." It was easy to take the bus crosstown from my office and then a subway uptown.

"I don't know. My apartment—it's gotten really bad," he said.

"You mean—messy?"

"Yeah."

"I don't care."

"Well, come, then. I really want to see you."

After work, I rode across town then uptown feeling uncomfortable. Although Michael had said he wanted to see me, there had been a reluctance in his tone. His fatigue sounded more than physical.

It was my first visit to his apartment. I got off the West Side IRT at Ninety-Sixth Street, picked up some fried rice and a prawn dish (for me) and some hot-and-sour soup and Szechuan eggplant (for Michael) at Jade Villa, then walked over to his building on Amsterdam and One Hundredth Street. Taking the elevator up to the tenth floor, I found his name, M. Chambers, under 10B. I rang, and he opened the door and pecked me on the cheek. He was hunched and unshaven, wearing a stained red flannel shirt over a frayed white one, with neither completely tucked into his pants.

"Don't say I didn't warn you," he said, frowning.

His room in New Haven had been a mess, yet I wasn't prepared for the disorder and filth in his living room. There were sheets of composition paper on the floor, books on the couch, and notebooks piled high on the little card table he used for eating. The remains of a recent takeout dinner sat on the ledge of the window in a grease-stained Chinese box. A viscous layer of dust covered every surface, including the piano.

Moving jaggedly, he cleared off the table, piling the books on the floor to make room for dinner. Obviously his taking my hand under the blanket at the party meant a lot less than I thought. We unpacked the Chinese food, opened the boxes.

"Szechuan eggplant, good choice. Hot-and-sour soup, fried rice— nice combo, Jul…You know I had a drink with Ben?"

"Yes, he told me about it."

"What did he tell you?"

"Not much, actually," I said. "How did it go?"

"It went fine." He waited until I served myself from each box before helping himself copiously.

"That's all? 'It went fine'?"

"It was good to catch up," he said.

"All right, then."

"So, how was your holiday with *the man*?" He met my eyes as he referred to Ben.

"It was fine. We spent Christmas with my parents, as usual. And you?"

"Same old, same old. Dysfunctional parents snapping all the time. Fun to see my brother, though. Hey, we haven't done a post-mortem on your party," he said.

"Yeah, so what did you think? I saw—uh, I saw you wrote down a couple of phone numbers."

"Yeah. Well, Betty, you know, I don't think I'll call her. I don't think that would work. But your cousin Evelyn has class."

"Have you called her yet?"

"Uh, no. But I still have her number."

"What are you waiting for?"

He gave me a dark look. "Wanna beer?" he said, going to the fridge.

I fell silent. The energy danced chaotically between us, as though whizzing particles were banging up against my stinging cheeks. We continued to make small talk. When we sat down at the piano bench after dinner, I felt there was a force field between us. Clearly, Michael's drink with Ben had sobered him up, reminding him that we were in a triangular situation and I was unavailable.

We had reached a miserable dead end. And that was what I'd thought I wanted.

My father sliced through the January cold to visit me in my office. Bending over my desk, peering at folders and papers and my computer screen, he said, "Julia, are you on top of things?"

"What do you mean?"

"I mean, you did send out the end of year tax letter in December, right? And you're beginning to schedule people for tax season, right?"

"Yes, of course."

The truth was that I'd sent the letter out a little late, and not as many people were calling as I'd hoped. Maybe some of my father's clients had decided they would rather take their business elsewhere than work with Mr. Field's female successor. Or maybe they had decided to do their taxes on their own because of the recent stock market crash. The truth was I hadn't been doing my best. I looked away, ashamed that I was being sloppy at work because of my miserable obsession.

"Julia, you can make a go of it—if you apply yourself, that is. The one thing I want to see before I die is you economically independent. Not just self-sufficient thanks to some minimum-wage job, but earning a real living—the kind where you can put some money away in the savings bank, where, if necessary, you can be on your own."

I glanced at him in surprise.

He went on. "You limited your job opportunities by choosing to live with Ben after graduation. Made yourself dependent on him with that underpaid secretary job."

"I know that."

"Of course, I hope you and Ben are going to have a happy ending, but if it doesn't, you need to be prepared."

"Well, moving into the city to run your business hasn't exactly been easy on our relationship."

"I'm aware of that. But sometimes separation brings clarity, for both parties."

Walking to the subway later over a sheet of ice sprinkled with kosher salt, I mulled over my father's words. What *would* it be like to be on my own? I had a flash of Ben skidding on ice and having an accident on Route 1. There it was again—the film noir scenario, this time more vivid: Ben dead, his head bashed in, the highway police and ambulance circling in—what could be more horrible, what could be more not what I wanted, even if it meant that then I'd be free to be with Michael? Stopping in the middle of the sidewalk, I tried to inhale. My attraction to Michael, which opened up the possibility of a split with Ben, brought home the full economic import of what I'd been doing with my life. My father was right: by staying in New Haven then following Ben to Princeton, I had for a decade sacrificed not only the opportunity but my very will to advance my earning power.

Someone jostled me and, as I skidded a bit, the grains of salt looked like hail. Had hail fallen, instead of snow, in the middle of January? I retrieved my balance, continued walking. If nothing else, I would be successful with money. I swore it to myself, then and there.

Michael called midweek to ask if I wanted to meet him in the Village to hear the up-and-coming jazz pianist, Louis Willard, play with his band. I said yes, and we arranged to meet at the club a half-hour before the show.

Classes had started again after winter break, and Ben was safely in Princeton.

It was a bitterly cold night and, thinking that we might have to wait on line outside, I put on two scarves, a little one I tucked into the collar of my coat and a second, larger wool shawl I wrapped around my head and shoulders. I was so bundled up that Michael didn't recognize me when we met.

"Have you ever heard Willard live?" he asked me. "He's prodigious." He kissed me one inch to the right of my mouth.

"It's freezing out here."

"It's worth it, you'll see," he said. Our exhaled breaths mixed in the icy air as he pulled me closer, drawing the folds of my shawl together at the front of my neck. "Got to keep you nice and warm," he said.

I didn't know why he was being more affectionate with me, but I was happy not to repeat the awkwardness of our last meeting.

We stood on line with a motley crowd of jazz aficionados. A man in front of us, with a long gray beard and a Russian type of fur hat, smoked a pipe. Watching him warmed me up. A homeless person approached the line and began to work it methodically from head to tail. When he reached us, the urine stench cut through the pipe smoke. Michael shook his head forcefully in the negative, and the panhandler moved on.

Inside the club, we were lucky enough to get seats with a view of the keyboard. I ordered a glass of wine, and Michael a whiskey. The smell of tobacco and booze, the dim lights, and the jabbering of the audience contributed to the pleasant expectancy.

Then Willard walked out. Tall, black, and portly, he stood by the piano to receive immense applause. His eyebrows had the thick, forward definition one often sees in charismatic performers. The clapping bounced off the walls of the small club like tennis balls in a court. Then the bass player, the guitarist, the drummer, and the saxophonist came out one at a time, to lesser applause.

The music began.

One had to travel at the speed of light to keep up with Willard, whose improvisations swirled forward in spellbinding patterns of increasing speed and density, as though propelled by a preternatural nucleus of energy. My mind repeatedly lagged behind, dropping the ball, but, glancing sideways at Michael, I saw he was following every move, taking mental notes and finding inspiration.

Two hours later, it was snowing outside and there was a fresh dusting of white on the icy sidewalk. The late night whiz of taxis on Seventh Avenue made a soothing, muted whoosh. After the smokiness of the club, the cold air felt clean like an astringent splashed on the face after a shower.

"What did you think?" Michael asked.

"It felt to me like he was showing off," I said.

"What do you mean?"

"It was like the jazz equivalent of a classical recital in which the performer plays only the hardest pieces to demonstrate his technique—there was no soul, no self-expression."

"You've got to be kidding me! It was *all* soul, *all* self-expression!" Michael looked at me in disbelief.

"It seemed very solipsistic to me." I enjoyed getting a rise out of him. "I mean, I know something about jazz, and I couldn't follow what he was doing."

"Well, you don't have to *understand* it to appreciate it."

"That's true of a lot of music. But with this, it seemed to me like the kind of intellectual performance that required understanding." I sounded like an egghead in a Woody Allen movie.

"Jesus!" he burst out in irritation. "The man puts his entire being on display and you call it ego."

"Obviously, you've listened to his music before, so you found it more accessible than I did."

Michael didn't know how to respond to that one. He stopped and pulled out a pack of cigarettes.

"I thought you'd stopped smoking," I said.

"I have," he said, with the cigarette dangling from the corner of his mouth. We could have been in a French film noir, with him being Belmondo and me Jeanne Moreau. Except that we weren't plotting to murder Ben. "But I allow myself one after going to a club. I was virtuous enough, not smoking in there." He struck a match, and I watched as a gigantic snowflake collided with the flame, extinguishing it before it reached its destination. Intent on his smoke now, Michael ducked into a doorway.

I stepped into the doorway with him and leaned against the building as he took out another cigarette. Suddenly I felt tired, chilled to the bone. We had no future together of any kind. The worst part of the whole thing was that the wonderful feeling I used to have with him, of being truly and completely myself, was disappearing because I now had to hide my feelings, and the hiding made it difficult to be authentic around him. It's hard to be hopeful about anything in January, and, on this dark, cold night, spring seemed to exist eons away, in another order of reality, a parallel universe. Maybe Michael and I just weren't meant to be. After all, what could I hope to offer him compared to the talented, passionate woman who had preceded me—compared to Karyn? Relinquish hope, all ye who enter here.

Michael lit up and drew a deep breath of smoke.

"That's a filthy habit," I said. "Why don't you just give it up for once and for all?"

"You don't have to dump on me just because you didn't like the show."

"I liked the show. I was just giving you a hard time for the fun of it." I looked away, toward a nearby lamppost. The snow swirled in the cone of light it projected, like a meteoric shower in slow motion, revealing the dense nature of time when every second provides agonizing conflict.

"The only way to stop smoking is to start doing something else," I heard him say and, out of the corner of my eye, I saw him drop his cigarette and crush it with his heel. I saw his arm reach for me and pull me toward him, and I felt his hands slip under the shawl around my head and his lips touch mine. Finally a long kiss, like the one ten years before on the steps of the New York Public Library. A little smoky this time.

"Thank you," I said.

Michael said nothing, only continued to kiss me.

"Come home with me," I said.

"Yes," he said.

A melting came over me. I was ready to obey desire—this knocking at the door of the soul, this call to waking and living. Desire, the ferryman taking me where I needed to go. Desire, this thing that springs up from the genitals and ends in all four chambers of the heart—or is it the other way around?

We walked holding hands. My place was only a couple of blocks away.

"That was a silly argument we had," I said.

"Of course it was. Just tension building up." He stopped to kiss me again. I was in paradise.

When we got up to my apartment, we took off our hats and coats and scarves and sat on the couch. Michael's face, between kisses, was marked by a terrible, almost religious gravity. And Ben was light-years away, because my first, passionate love for him had been so long ago. In the here and now, there was only Michael and the ritual we would engage in that night.

"Give me a minute," I said.

"All right," he said.

I rose and went to my bedside table in the bedroom, where I got my diaphragm. In the bathroom, I squirted a dab of spermicide into the hollow and spread it around. A bit shaky, I fumbled putting it in and had the impression that it wasn't sitting properly. Taking an extra minute to reach inside, I checked that it covered my cervix. I washed my hands and went out to find Michael.

He was standing next to the couch, putting his coat on.

I was shocked, like a military wife receiving a message that her husband has died.

"What are you doing?"

"I'm leaving, Jul," he said. "I'm going home."

"Why?"

"You know this isn't the right thing to do."

"It feels right to me," I said. "Doesn't it feel right to you?"

Michael sat back down with a huge sigh. I sat down next to him. Obviously, he didn't feel like kissing me anymore.

"I'm feeling hungover already," he said.

"So the only reason you kissed me is that you had a couple of drinks at the club?"

He shook his head no. "You know my story. I've been in this kind of situation too many times before, and I can't get involved in this kind of thing again. I don't think you're going to leave Ben, and even if you did, then I'd have the burden of breaking you guys up."

"You speak as though Ben and I were married."

"You're as good as, from what I can tell, and you will be soon, officially. I predict it."

"I see," I said. "We're back to your fucking predictions."

"I just don't have the energy for this. I mean, tell me, honestly—are you planning on leaving Ben?"

"I hadn't gotten that far in my thinking—I wasn't even sure until this evening that you had these kinds of feelings for me."

"If you were unhappy with Ben, you would've left him already."

"Not necessarily," I said. "Everything's been so unclear."

"Everything?"

"Except that—I feel like you're my soul mate," I said.

That brought him up short. "Yeah, I feel that way, too," he said, then found his momentum again. "Whatever the hell that means. I mean I feel that way, but I've felt that way before."

"Thanks."

"You know what the story is with you? You haven't had enough experience with guys, and now you're thirty-two and moving toward settling down, and here I come, kind of your last chance, so why not get it on with me and have a little fun? That's what you're doing. It's plain as day."

I felt both unmasked and misunderstood. There was no denying, after my trip to California, the extent of my sexual restlessness. But my need for sexual adventure was only one piece of the pie. The rest, sweet and spicy, was that Michael was unique and that I wanted him specifically.

"You're not being fair—" I began.

"Listen, I know the score. You want to have a secret affair with me to see if it'll 'work out' between us. You want to 'try it out.' Because, even though you're all lovey-dovey about me, you've got your little doubts—isn't that the case?"

"I don't know," I said. But the truth was that he'd hit the nail on the head, and the proof was that I'd interrupted the flow of things to insert my diaphragm. Goddammit, if only I hadn't, we'd be in bed already! But no, I was always making little computations about my safety. And the fact that Michael understood me better than I understood myself kept me abjectly off balance.

"You and Ben have ten years of history already, and more than just history. Commitment—the kind that doesn't need a marriage license. You'd have to be crazy to throw all that away to be with someone with a relationship record like mine."

Michael was speaking the truth. I'd wanted him to sweep me off my feet, but he had wanted *me* to make the first move by leaving Ben, and I was paralyzed by my own cautiousness.

"Besides," he went on, "there's the small matter of betraying Ben. How would you feel about it if we actually did it? How would you feel if he found out? How would *I* feel about it—punching my old buddy in the stomach?"

Deep down, he was more honorable than I'd ever imagined.

"So why did you kiss me?" I asked.

"I had to," he said. "We both knew it was coming, and I wanted to get it out of the way."

"Out of the way for what?"

"So that we could go back to the friendship we had before."

"Go back? But I've always wanted you. I wanted you ten years ago when we were at Yale."

Even as I spoke I knew I was rewriting history. My attraction to him at Yale had always been under the surface—until the famous kiss on the library steps. Michael gave me the skeptical look I deserved.

"There was an attraction between us, okay, but to go from that to saying that you 'always wanted me'—that's quite a leap."

"Is it?" I said.

"I think it is."

"But you had feelings for me back then, didn't you?"

"To begin with, there was the matter of Robin—remember Robin, your cousin? I was having an affair with her—remember? And then, how could I have feelings for you—Jesus, how could I even ask myself what my feelings were, when you and Ben were screwing in the bedroom across the hall from me? God, what a racket you guys made sometimes!"

I blushed, realizing for the first time—how could I have been so stupid—why Michael had often played the piano when Ben and I made love. My embarrassment lasted only a second, however.

"But what about that summer when Ben was away and you and I saw each other in New York? What about that night we went to the concert in Damrosch Park? What about the night we made out on the steps of the library?"

"I remember that night. And I remember that I made sure you got on your train back to New Haven, which is where you belonged."

"No. We made a mistake, that's why this is happening to us again. I shouldn't have gotten on that train. And now we're being given a second chance."

"You know," Michael said acidly, "I really don't think there's anybody up there orchestrating our romantic opportunities for us."

Was that what it boiled down to—whether we believed in the meaningfulness of a coincidence?

"You know what I think?" he went on. "You *want* me. You *desire* me. But whether you really *care* for me remains to be seen. I can't help thinking that if you did, you wouldn't want to hurt me by getting me involved in this type of situation."

"If you feel that afraid, you shouldn't have kissed me tonight."

"Maybe you're right," he said. "Maybe I made a mistake, in which case I apologize." He stood up again and zipped up his leather bomber. "Let's let things simmer down a bit and then we'll talk—okay? In a couple of weeks. Call me—no—I'll call you." He walked over to the door. And then, with his hand on the knob, he swiveled back to look at me. "If it wasn't for all this crap, you'd be my best friend—you know that?"

"Yeah," I said. "I know."

"And you're my only best friend," he added angrily. "That's why I'm not going to let you fuck it up."

"You're not going to let *me* fuck it up?"

"Yes, you," he shouted. "Because the whole thing was your idea."

And he left, slamming the door shut behind him.

I slept little that night, my abdomen knotting itself tighter and tighter as I sobbed. Then I'd be hit by a wave of indignation and would pound my pillow. "Fuck you, fuck all of you," I screamed. "Fuck me for being so stupid."

Through the blinds, the night landscape of the city twinkled, indifferent to my woe.

My period came the next morning, a week early and accompanied by intense cramps. I called Betty and told her I couldn't come in. Then I made myself some coffee, poured in some whiskey and went back to bed.

Michael was the only person who knew where to find the magic switch that turned the light on inside me. I couldn't let go of wanting him, for fear of the light being turned off again.

But I had my notebook.

Rearrange the Night

Tomorrow I'll look at the pieces
and put them back together.
For now, I would slice the night sideways
and put my heart between two blankets
of forgetting.

But "heart" is so vaporous
that it cannot be put,
can only suffer the heaviness
of damp and shadow thickening
the dark.

I must find some other fix,
must dig in some other place
like a breathless gravedigger
who knows how and where to bury
his pain.

The old stories have power
until we beat them dead.
And yet I would rather die myself
than murder this one a second
time around.

"I'm in so much emotional pain I feel like everything in me—my brain and all the systems in my body—are just going to shut down." I sat in Sandra's office, weeping hysterically.

"You know, that feeling is a flashback," Sandra responded.

"You mean—to being alone in my crib, screaming for my mother at two in the morning?" I was one step ahead of my therapist by this time.

"Something like that. Because of course no one can turn the light on inside you *except you*."

"And my feeling of connection with Michael?"

"You're familiar with the concept of projection?" she asked. I nodded, and she went on. "It happens like clockwork in romantic relationships. A new person to love is like a blank screen, you see what you want there or what you need."

"So romantic love is a misguided attempt to get something that was either gotten or not gotten in the infant state? Then why is it that this is so *particular*? Why is it that I got from Michael something I've never gotten from Ben or anyone else?"

"Did you really get it? Or did you imagine you did?"

"I think I really did. The way he saw me and was curious about me, the way he wanted to know me."

"Well, since it seems you're not going to get it from him anymore, then wouldn't we be better off asking how you can get it from yourself? Or what parts of you were seeking to come alive through him?"

"Why ask that, since they won't come alive now? Ever, ever! Because he was the only one with the key." I was discovering I had a gift for melodrama.

"Now you're enjoying feeling sorry for yourself."

I did a double take. That didn't seem like the kind of thing a therapist should say.

"I'm not enjoying it! Feeling sorry for myself is really painful."

"I'll say what I've said before, that Michael is only a passerby in your life and that what you're looking for is some part of you that's missing."

"You don't think that people can help each other find the missing pieces? Isn't that what love is about?"

"Of course that's what love is about. That's also what therapy is about. You don't need Michael to get where you want to go. Besides, it sounds like he's not interested. Or capable."

"So you're going to help me get there instead of Michael?"

"Isn't that what you hired me for?"

"The problem is that I want *him* and not you."

"When you first came to see me," Sandra said, "you said you needed help in deciding about Ben."

"Right now I can hardly think about Ben, let alone decide about him."

"But he'll be here Friday night, won't he?"

"Yeah."

"Are you sure you don't want to consider couples therapy?"

"Yeah, I'm sure. How many times are you going to ask me that? If we did couple therapy everything about Michael would come out, and I don't want to hurt him."

"Sometimes pain brings people into a new intimacy."

I looked at the clock on Sandra's table. I had ten minutes left but I was ready to leave now. I took out my checkbook.

"Leaving already?" Sandra asked.

"You're not helping me today," I snapped.

"I'm sorry," Sandra said.

It was Betty who helped me in the end.

I couldn't keep myself from crying at work, and soon she had the whole story out of me.

Betty reflected. "I've seen this kind of thing happen to people before they get married—"

"But Ben and I aren't—"

"Of course you are. And you're going through the last fling syndrome. Somebody's all ready to walk up to the altar and then suddenly—ka-boom!—they get interested in someone else. Seems to be some kind of panic that's triggered by the finality of marriage. Not that I would know anything about that, of course. And then, you didn't get to have the fling. You probably wouldn't feel so bad if you'd actually had the affair." She paused. "Or maybe you'd feel worse if you and Michael did it. 'Cause you'd miss the sex with him."

"I was born under the sign of frustration," I said, blowing my nose.

"But you once told me that you and Ben had a good time in bed."

"We do," I said. "Though sometimes I wish...it could be more emotionally intense."

"Well," Betty said, "Ben strikes me as a very private kind of person. But—I'm sorry—I just don't see how you can describe yourself as frustrated. Look at me. I haven't had sex in two years."

"You're right," I said. "I don't know what's wrong with me. You know what makes me really angry? After kissing me, Michael pretended that I was the one who initiated it. And I wasn't. We were standing there"—in a doorway, that snowy night— "and *he* put his hand out and reached for me and kissed me. He started it."

"So he started it. Big deal. Men start things; then they retreat. Let me tell you something," Betty said. "A man may pursue you like you're the Queen of Sheba and then fuck you with gusto ten different times in ten different positions, but when things fall apart, he'll be quick to say: '*You're* the one who wanted it, *you're* the one who started it, it was all *your* idea.'"

"Is that true?" I asked naively. Talking to Betty always made me realize how lacking I was in life experience.

"Yeah, it's true. I know, because I've gotten that line again and again."

I thought it over. Ten times in ten different positions. I should have been so lucky! The truth was that there was one position more than others that came to mind—Michael's humble servant, on my knees. Maybe this was what was meant by female subservience—the impulse to put his pleasure before mine. No, that wasn't right. Because there was a second favorite position in my fantasy life—I was on top, enjoying him. And what was the common denominator between the two fantasies? I was active; he was passive. I sighed.

"What are you thinking?" Betty asked.

"I'm thinking maybe he was right. I was the instigator."

"No," Betty said forcefully. "He's not right. He just got real scared. Trust me. I know."

"Maybe I'll never see him again," I said.

"That's ridiculous," Betty said. "You know what I think? I think you're going to hear from him soon. I think you guys are still going to get it on."

"You think we're going to get it on, and you also think Ben and I are going to get married? Isn't there a contradiction there?"

"I don't see one. Do you? Who says you can't love two guys at once?"

"A lot of people."

"Well," Betty said, "they don't know anything about the human heart."

14

GRADUALLY A KIND OF numbness came over me. Michael had wounded my pride. He had rejected me, and I hated him for it. Of course, he was justified. It was true that I had wanted to "test" him out before breaking up with Ben.

I took comfort in Ben, in the way he looked up from a book and smiled at me, the way, when I got off the train at Princeton, he grabbed me and hugged me tightly, the way he moaned when he came inside me. Like Professor Higgins in *My Fair Lady*, all I could say was, I'd grown accustomed to his face. And there he was for me to fall back on after my adventure with Michael. Reliable, trustworthy. Isn't that what women want?

One night Ben called me from Princeton sounding excited. He'd received the good news: he'd been awarded tenure. He now had job security for life.

"Even since I got the news," he said, "I've been almost shaking with relief."

I had a physical reaction, too, experiencing a sudden heaviness, an unwinding that left me light-headed and flaccid of spine. I'd known he would get tenure, so it felt like an anticlimax.

"That's great," I said. "That's wonderful."

"Make a reservation someplace romantic, where we can celebrate when I come in Friday night."

I usually enjoyed Ben's festive spirit, but this time I didn't feel like celebrating. Waiting for tenure had put our lives on hold for years. Why had I let Ben set the timetable for my life? But it wasn't productive to dwell on the past. I needed to move forward. I called Jane's Fish Restaurant in the West Village and made a reservation.

I had requested a quiet corner, and the maître d' led us through the crowded main room to a private nook. Hanging on the white wall above the dark wainscoting, a swordfish grinned at us. We sat down and began tearing at the sourdough bread the waiter brought. Ben chose a bottle of champagne with the ease of an old pro, then looked at me and shrugged.

"First time I've ever ordered champagne," he said. "Who knows if it'll be any good."

"Who cares?" I asked.

I'd congratulated Ben again when he'd walked into my apartment, but now that we were face to face a third, "official" round, however perfunctory, seemed appropriate. I waited for the bubbly to arrive and be poured.

"You did it," I said, raising my glass.

"Yes, I stormed the walls of the American university system, and I conquered." He grimaced as we clinked glasses. The prospect of a lifetime of Princeton stuffiness was, for a moment, sobering. "If ever I were to get a job offer somewhere else, I mean, in England, how would you feel about moving there?"

His mind was already moving ahead to the next challenge. I thought about it as I sipped the champagne, which was working very fast. English tearooms. The Thames. Wandering through the little streets of Bloomsbury and Marylebone. Sending my kids to British schools. Living farther away from my parents as they began to age. "We're just fantasizing here, right?"

"Well, yes."

"You feel homesick?"

"A bit."

"What about my business—"

"You could sell it. You could write poetry in London," he said. "I'd be happy to support you."

We had never discussed that scenario explicitly, although I had often envisioned him giving me the freedom to do what I really wanted to do. Still, I hesitated.

"I could write here if I put my mind to it."

"There are too many distractions here. Wouldn't you like London?"

"The question being," I said, "will I continue to follow you? I stayed in New Haven to be with you, then followed you to Princeton, and now you want to know whether you can count on me to be willing to—to—do that again."

I could hear him clear his throat over the background noise of the restaurant.

"The question being, rather—will you *be* with me? Will you, Julia, consent to be with me for the rest of our lives?"

Awkwardly, he reached into his jacket pocket and placed a small box on the table.

I looked at it.

"Open it," he said.

Inside the box sat a platinum band with a small sapphire at the center and two smaller diamonds to either side. Shocked, I looked sideways and met the eye of the grinning swordfish. I had waited so long for Ben to ask me to marry him that for a moment I thought he was joking. Or had he sensed a threat in the wings and was rushing in to secure me? No. There was a simple explanation: his newfound security had emboldened him.

"You serious about this?" I asked.

"Of course I'm serious. Damn it, that wasn't the response I was hoping for. I'm asking, do you want to get married?"

"Of course I want to get married," I said. I could dream all I wanted about Michael, but he was gone now. And Ben was here before me.

Ben fumbled the ring out of the box, asked for my hand, and slipped the ring on my finger.

"Voilà," he said.

I'd never understood the way women fall in love with their hands once they've got a rock to show. But there I was, in rapturous contemplation of the jewelry on my finger. I couldn't have been happier with it. Ben had known that I wouldn't want the conventional big diamond. The blue of the sapphire was deep and glittering like the East River on a crisp, clear day, when the sun throws sparkles on the water at a slant. The dark, cold color resonated with me, as though something frozen inside me was finding its reflection here.

He reached across the table and took my hands in his. Later on in the evening, back at the apartment, he'd want to make love, and part of me would hold back, because inside, although bruised and battered of heart, I still yearned for Michael. It would require a certain effort to focus on Ben—to feel him, be with him—but we'd been lovers for so long that I could hope my response would be somewhat automatic.

Looking up at his face, I was touched by the love in his eyes. Eventually, everything would be okay.

15

"AND YOU SAID YES?" Sandra asked.

"Yes. My parents are totally delighted, as you can imagine." My mother had crushed my ribs in joyous embrace.

"But are *you* pleased?"

"Yeah, I'm pleased, though I'm still miserable about Michael."

I looked at her pleadingly, as though she might have a bandage she could apply to my heart.

"It's the encounter with reality that's so difficult," she said. "The destruction of your fantasy life."

We both fell silent. She reached for a stick of gum.

"You know," I said, "I find your chewing gum really annoying. There's something unprofessional about it."

"I'm sorry," she said. She reached for a tissue and discreetly spit it out. "My mouth tends to be dry. I'll sip water instead."

As we continued to dissect and analyze, my being there felt pointless. I wanted her to fix me, but she could only keep me company. I would leave the room in the same amount of pain and confusion as I'd been in when I'd arrived.

I was happy when I looked in my bag at the end of the session and found that I'd forgotten my checkbook.

"You can pay me next time," she said.

"Actually, I'll mail you the check. This is my last time." I made the decision right then. "I feel I've resolved what I came here to resolve. The thing with Michael is over, and I'm marrying Ben. So—thank you."

She looked startled. "Are you sure you don't want to come back for a wrap-up?"

"I'm sure," I said, standing up.

"I've enjoyed working with you, Julia. Feel free to come back anytime." She stood up, too, looking off-balance, and extended a hand.

I was going to shake her hand, then, impulsively, I grabbed her and gave her a hug. I'd miss her support, but I was done. I hated paying for conversation. Had I gotten anything out of therapy? I wondered as I left. Or had it all been a kind of theater? A bordello of the heart, in which the therapist played the whore and the client purchased fleeting satisfaction? I'd gone to Sandra needing help in making a choice between two men, but the men had made the decision for me. And in the end, my self remained a thing disordered and *unorderable*, which no amount of inquiry could tidy up.

Anna asked me to lunch at the museum. I agreed, though I didn't feel like seeing anyone. I'd have to tell her about my engagement to Ben…Well, maybe getting away from my desk would do me good.

I walked up Lexington, then across town on Eighty-First. The recent snow had melted, and the crunching of salt on the remaining ice underfoot satisfied the ear. At the museum, I took the long flight of stone steps into the lobby, then made my way past the guards through the back corridors of the Met, where I found Anna in a windowless office with a couple of spider plants, a sleek wooden desk, and a bookcase stuffed with art catalogs.

"Hi." She stood up to give me a hug. She looked elegant in a long, rust-colored cardigan that played off the red in her hair. My jealous admiration of her beauty magnified my love for her.

We headed for the museum restaurant through the endless galleries filled with the Greek pottery that had driven me crazy with boredom as a child.

"You seem happy," I said.

"I'm almost intolerably happy," she said. "I can't fall asleep at night because I'm so happy."

"Really?" I asked.

"I'll tell you the whole story when we get our food." She visibly enjoyed the suspense she was creating.

Back then, there were only two places to eat in the museum—the sterile, school-style cafeteria in the Children's Museum downstairs, which was to be avoided, and then the adult cafeteria upstairs, set in a grand, white-stone courtyard with overdone pillars, where we went now. The rushing and splashing of water from the bronze, spouting muses in the rectangular fountain softened the clattering dishware and conversational din. Potted bushes and birdcage chandeliers completed the luxurious effect, which was then undermined by the food counter with its tired-looking silverware and jello-filled parfait glasses.

As we got on the line, Anna noticed my ring.

"Hey, did Ben pop the question?"

"Yes," I said.

"When will you have the wedding?"

"Sometime in the summer. I'm thinking we've been together too long to make a big deal of it."

"Congratulations," she said. "I'm so happy you're making it official. He's a real prize, you know that?"

"Yes, Ben is wonderful," I said. In spite of losing Michael, I felt pleased with myself. "Remember our lunches here with Aunt Iris?" I said.

"I'd always have some kind of extravagant dessert," she said. "With lots of whipped cream."

Slowly we made our way past the salads, lukewarm mashed potatoes, and cheese sandwiches. I chose a salad; she reached for a turkey sandwich.

We found a table and sat down.

"Well?" I asked. "Tell me."

Anna was glowing. I expected a tale about some new love interest. For years, I'd followed her amorous career with a little envy, because I wasn't free to play the field, and a lot of relief, because I didn't have to. She bore the breakups much better than I ever could have. In the end—until my recent meeting with Michael, that is—I'd enjoyed my safe little place with Ben and wouldn't have traded it for anything.

"This is it," she said. "I'm absolutely sure this time. This is it."

A shadow of skepticism must have crossed my face because she went on, with added force. "Really, Julia. In my heart of hearts, I know this is going to work out."

There was such gravity in her voice that I had to take her seriously.

"Okay…"

"Michael," she said.

"Michael?" A large blunt object might as well have hit me in the shoulder. Had Michael actually gone and…behind my back? But of course! And why not? He was free. And I had even—for a short while—encouraged him to start dating again.

"I'm seeing him," she said.

"You're seeing Michael—romantically?" I found it difficult to speak, as though steel wire had been threaded into the muscles of my jaw. What I wanted to ask, but couldn't, was whether they had already slept together.

"You seem surprised."

"I remember your not liking him at Yale."

"Really?"

"That time he knocked over your painting, and the stupid criticism he made of it—remember he didn't like the orange?"

"Oh, that—" she shrugged. "I kind of liked that he was so brutally honest."

"Really?"

"He was right about the orange. It was sort of a vomit color."

"Oh," I said. "But you were so angry—"

"Well, he was with Robin, and I hated being so attracted to someone who was already taken."

"Was that why you broke up with Doug?" I asked. Senior year, she'd finally dismissed her high school boyfriend.

"There were many reasons."

"So what did you actually think—or feel—about Michael back then?"

"I remember having the sense that he could be right for me. At one point I had a kind of premonition in which I saw the two of us together in a home, with a child. In the past few weeks that vision has come back to me a hundred times. But at Yale, there was the frustration of not being able to get to him, of things being in the way."

"'Things'—meaning Robin."

"Yes."

"That's why you seemed pleased when they broke up. And I thought it was because you judged him not good enough for her."

"I hoped he would notice me. But he didn't. He says he was too depressed to notice anyone for a long time."

I reviewed her history mentally. After Doug and graduation, Anna had gone abroad and enjoyed various adventures in Paris and Rome. Then she'd returned to the United States for a series of lame boyfriends, one or two years with each one. In short, she'd had so many heartbreaks that there was no reason to think that this story would be lasting.

She read my mind.

"I feel I've come full circle. I've gotten everything out of my system that I needed to get out—all the experiments and running around—so that now I can settle down. And the beautiful thing is that I feel I'm finally over—certain things."

"You mean—Italy?"

Her eyes avoided mine.

"There's no point talking about it. I don't know why I brought it up."

Long ago, in Italy, she'd had her heart broken by her Latin lover. And Michael had had his heart broken by a married woman. Okay, let the two of them with their fucking broken hearts comfort each other.

"So, how far has this gone—with Michael?" I took the tiniest bite out of my salad. It was hard to swallow.

"We've talked about having kids. He seems as interested as I am."

A premonition about having a child with Michael was one thing. Having a conversation with him about it was another. She might as well have hit me with another blunt object, in the other shoulder.

"Kids?"

"Gosh, why are you so surprised?"

"Isn't this all kind of fast?" A marbled mist invaded my brain. "When did it start?"

"When I brought him to your Christmas party. It's true it's only been a couple of months, and it probably seems impulsive. But we both want the same thing, so why shouldn't we just go for it?"

"Why not," I repeated dully, computing how many more minutes I had to keep my composure.

"I worry about a child getting in the way of my painting, but, at this point in life, one's fertility goes down day by day. I mean, even as we speak our fertility is going down. Seeing Robin's baby in San Francisco really woke me up."

I looked at her, aghast.

"Well, I want to have a child sooner or later—don't you?" she asked.

"Actually, I'm not so clear about it anymore," I said. The question made me aware again of that nagging abdominal pain, which—suddenly I understood—was about my conflict, my arguing with my instinct to reproduce, my tussling with Ben. But I was engaged now. Ben and I could proceed. So what was the problem? "The more I think about it, the more confused I get."

Anna, like all people who have just fallen in love, was only interested in herself.

"Do you know that Michael has a baby fund? That he's been saving money for years to have a family?"

"Yeah, I know. Hard to imagine him settling down, though. I mean, you realize, don't you, that he's had a horde of lovers? A lot more than you have."

"He was looking for the right person. Anyway, he's sown his wild oats. He's ready now." She leaned forward, grinning. "Hey, you and Ben, me and Michael—we could have a double wedding—like in the movies."

"I don't think so."

"Maybe not. Can you imagine our mothers planning a wedding together? That would be pretty funny."

The conversation went on like this, with Anna more and more lit up by the minute. I looked at my knife, judging it too dull to impale myself on. And the fountain was too shallow for drowning. And earthquakes don't happen in New York, so the chances of being buried alive in a crumbling museum were slim.

"I thought you wanted to find a rich husband," I said.

"I realized I wasn't after money, really. What I want is the freedom and emotional support to do art and have a child."

"You've always been full of surprises, that's for sure." She was a ship charting an unpredictable course, and she'd run into me.

"Yeah, I know."

Finally and thankfully, we finished our meal and made our way out of the restaurant, back through the gallery with those damn Greek urns, and to the lobby, where we parted.

"I'm so happy for you, Anna," I said.

"Thank you, Julia, for asking me to bring him to your party," she said. And still glowing, she turned her back on me and headed back to her office.

I crunched my way over salt and crusted snow back to my office, cursing her, cursing Michael, cursing myself. I almost wished I hadn't said good-bye to Sandra. On the other hand, it was a relief I didn't have to share this final humiliation with her. And to think I'd brought this misery upon myself by using Anna in my idiotic matchmaking scheme! No, my bungling went back further than that, to our high school years, when I'd persuaded Anna that we should try to go to the same college. If Anna hadn't lusted after him then, she wouldn't have wanted to hook him now. I was in search of an ultimate cause for my suffering when suddenly I wondered—had Michael secured Anna in order to make our situations more parallel? Now he had someone to "fall back on," just as I did. The idea that he would embark on a story with Anna to make it safer to have an affair with me was absurd—or was it?

"Jesus, what happened?" Betty asked when I got back to the office.

I told her the whole story and waited for her wise pronouncement.

"He's scared shitless by his feelings for you, so he's running as fast as possible in the opposite direction," she said.

"You think so?"

"It's obvious."

"I really feel like calling him," I said.

"I wouldn't if I were you," Betty said. "This might be a good moment to hold onto your dignity."

"My dignity?" I said. "You gotta be kidding."

16

I WAS IN THE OFFICE the next day, staring at my engagement ring, when the phone rang. I picked up. It was Michael.

"Hi, Michael," I said.

Hearing his name, Betty pointed to her open mouth to indicate she was going to lunch and, grabbing her coat and bag, made for the door.

"Hi," he said. "We haven't spoken in a while."

"Yeah, I know." Hearing his voice, I felt my anger come up. "I had lunch with Anna yesterday."

"I want to talk to you about that—"

"I don't get it. How could you move so fast after what happened between us?"

"It makes the situation more equal," he said. "Don't you see? You have someone to fall back on, and I have someone to fall back on. More of a square and less of a triangle."

"And that's why you and Anna are talking about starting a family together?"

"Can we have dinner? I'll explain everything in person. Why don't you come over after work?"

"Why should I?" I said, though of course I wanted to see him.

"We need to talk and then—spend the night with me," he said, his voice dropping. "Tonight."

"You sure?" Warmth flooded up between my thighs and into my belly.

"We should have one night together, just a single night, don't you think? Isn't that what you want? I've thought it through, and I think that's what we should do."

I sat there, holding the phone to my cheek as though it were his face.

"You think we can stop after one night?" I asked.

"Yes, if we agree to it beforehand—if we swear to it. It's the only way not to get hurt."

"You're crazy," I said.

"What time will you be here?"

"Around five thirty," I said.

"Okay," he said. "See you then."

And we hung up.

A couple of hours later, as the energetic bus driver hurtled the rush-hour crowd across Central Park, I stood gripping the ceiling handle and swaying back and forth. With each curve in the road, I collided with the handsome, suited businessman next to me.

"Sorry," my neighbor said. He had, on the last curve, swung into my breast. I didn't mind. Maybe he worked for a Madison Avenue advertising firm and lived in a palatial prewar apartment with a balcony and a view of Central Park.

"That's okay," I said.

Studying him out of the corner of my eye, I noticed he wasn't wearing a wedding band, and I wondered whether he had a sense of humor and liked old movies, whether he lived on the surface of life or plumbed the depths. In New York you're surrounded by men whenever you step out onto the street. If Ben found out about my night with Michael and decided to break with me, well, so what? I wouldn't be alone for the rest of my life.

I realized I didn't have my diaphragm with me. Well, again, so what? I remembered Dr. Sarler's drawings of my reproductive system. The chances of my getting pregnant were slim. And I wasn't going to blow this window of emotional opportunity.

Opportunity for what? What was I doing? Ben had just asked me to marry him—I was wearing the fucking engagement ring and taking a bus to screw a man who had once been his best friend.

Sorry, honey, I apologized mentally to Ben. *Sorry, sorry, sorry, but I just have to do this.*

With a spasm of yearning for something dead and gone, I remembered that snowy Saturday when Ben and I first kissed on a bench in Washington Square. Quickly we agreed to go back out to New Haven early the next morning so we could make love in his apartment. I hardly slept that night. Sunday morning we met at Grand Central to catch a 9:00 a.m. train. As we rode the train kissing and touching each other, I was exploding with desire. When we got back to his apartment, we got naked, and everything happened in a kind of whoosh.

I'd been in love those first few months. It was, I thought, the "kind of love that it takes a lifetime to measure." I read that line or something like it in the *Alexandria Quartet*, I think, and was struck by the idea of a love so enormous that it would take decades to discover all the different aspects of the beloved's being. And with each new aspect revealed, you would fall more deeply in love. Isn't that what everyone dreams of? Wasn't that what I'd thought I had for a good five, or was it seven, years? Or was it until that moment I'd run into Michael in the bookstore? Had I been lying to myself? No. For a while it had been real.

And now I was going to kill my love for Ben with clear intention. This was not an impulsive act. It was premeditated murder.

Maybe I was going to commit this murder because it was the only way I might experience again the magic of first love, which I couldn't have with Ben anymore. There was no going back because our love had been eroded by the wear-and-tear of time. Or maybe I simply needed to free up the parts of me that were stuck.

I didn't know why I was doing what I was doing, and as I got off at the Broadway stop and transferred to the uptown subway, I stopped analyzing. I was in the grips of an obsession and the only thing I could do was follow through.

When I stepped into Michael's, he kissed me on the cheek with a sheepish look. I was surprised to see how he'd tidied the place up. The dining table and windowsills had been cleared of plates and food, books and papers were in neat piles, and a clothes-drying rack with several damp sweaters stood in front of the radiator. The clean smell of washed wool hung in the air.

He'd probably cleaned up for Anna, not for me.

"I'm ravenous. Let's go get something to eat," he said, grabbing his leather bomber with the fur collar.

"Okay," I said.

Suddenly I felt a little shy, but in the elevator he put his arms around me and gave me a long kiss.

"So you really want to spend the night with me?" I asked.

"Of course," he said.

Kissing him was incredibly sweet, as was holding his hand on the way to Jade Villa.

When we sat down and picked up the menus, he noticed the ring on my finger.

"The sapphire's nice," he said.

"Thanks," I said, embarrassed.

"Saw that coming."

"All right, Michael. Okay."

"When's it going to happen?"

"This summer."

"Hmm..."

Wishing I'd left the ring in my office, I returned to studying the menu. Soon we'd ordered and he reached for my hands across the table. I thought, even as I felt his fingers on my ring, *I'm never going to let go.*

"So start explaining," I said. "What's going on with you and Anna?"

"Well, I think I could be happy with her. I feel I could actually make a commitment to her."

"But you're not in love with her?"

"I read an article recently about arranged marriages. It was in *Psychology Today*—I was in the dentist's office—about how in societies where arranged marriages are the norm, people are just as happy, maybe even happier than they are in the West, where we choose our own mates—"

"Michael!" I let go of his hands.

"I'm desperate, Jul. I'm turning forty-two and I've had a string of disastrous relationships, and I won't be able to focus on my work—my creative work—until I'm in some kind of domestically stable situation. And I love children. I mean, I love teaching other people's kids, and why shouldn't I have my own? That conversation we had in the bar in Penn Station, when you talked about deciding to be happy—that made a real impression on me. I realized I had to make the same decision. And the way you and Ben have committed to each other has inspired me. I finally got it through my thick head that lasting love is something that's constructed, not just pulled out of thin air, like a rabbit out of hat. And I'm grateful to you, because you made me see that."

"How can you take Ben and me as a positive example under the circumstances?"

He didn't hear my question. "Anna and I are in similar situations. We both want to be in a committed relationship, and we both have come to believe that a lasting relationship is worth making sacrifices for."

I was astonished. Those were the words Ben had spoken the day we'd had brunch with Anna, who had obviously repeated them later to Michael.

"And we'll be able to help each other creatively. I need—Julia, *I need*—to be supported emotionally as a musician. Because success as an artist isn't just a product of talent. The right circumstances are necessary. You need to be gifted, of course, and you need drive and training, but mostly, *mostly*, you need support—"

I wanted to scream, *I could offer you that support*, but I didn't.

"—I want to be one of the lucky few who not only does what he wants to do in life, but is good at it, too. I mean, look out the window." He gestured at the throng on the Broadway sidewalk. An obese black woman with two small children, one of them in a stroller, was passing by. "She's probably on welfare and would give anything to land a job as a supermarket checker. The checker would give anything to be the floor manager. The manager wishes he'd had a chance to go to law school. And the lawyer wishes he could have been an artist. And the artist—" he paused.

He was rambling all over the place, and I was ready to strangle him.

"The artist," he continued, "is ready to kill himself because he can't pay the rent."

"I'm not sure how you and Anna together are going to pay the rent," I said.

"We'll trade off. We'll be compatible, I think—"

"But you're not in love with her?" I repeated.

"As I said, in this article I read—"

"So now you're making life decisions based on *Psychology Today*? You don't think love is important?"

"I could love Anna. I'm attracted to her and I find her interesting and fun and all that good stuff. There's no reason I shouldn't love her, eventually."

"Okay, what does all this mean? You're arranging your own marriage?"

"Yeah, you could put it that way. I mean, isn't that what you did with Ben?"

"What?"

"Yes, you were wildly in love at the beginning. But then, when that wore off, you made the mental computations and decided he would be a good bet—reliable, stable, a good daddy, yada yada." The mu chu arrived and he reached for a pancake and carefully filled it, sauced it, rolled it, while I looked at him in stunned silence. "And those same computations are what's keeping you from breaking up with him now."

The truth in what he said struck me dumb.

"And for some reason," he went on—with a bit of malice, I thought— "Anna's computations have led her to think I would be a good bet for her."

"She thinks you've sown your wild oats," I said.

"I guess only time will tell, huh?"

He was eating like a horse, while I could barely swallow a single bite.

"You're accusing me underhandedly of...not having faith in you?"

"That's one way of putting it. Listen, Julia. You see me as risky, but the truth is, from my point of view, you're risky, too, because of Ben and that ring on your finger, and I just can't—*I just can't*—risk another failure. It would drive me over the edge. I mean, really over the edge, if you know what I mean."

I nodded. He was referring to the suicidal feelings he'd had after breaking with Karyn.

"But you feel hopeful about Anna?"

"Actually, yes, I do," he said brightly. "I feel very hopeful."

"I don't think we're going to spend the night together, after all." I felt bruised and depressed.

"Don't be ridiculous. Of course we are." He raised a hand to hail the waiter. "Sir, some plum sake, please." I wondered whether the "sir" was ironic—along with everything else about him. He turned back to me. "It's something we need to do, so let's do it. You'll feel better after a little wine."

"You're being so businesslike about it," I said.

"No," he said with force, then added, in a completely different register, "it's anything but business for me, Jul." I felt his knees under the table squeeze one of mine in his. "Honey," he said, "you believe me, don't you?"

The way he said "honey" turned me to mush. I nodded.

We finished dinner quietly and walked back to his apartment. The feeling of his hand in mine, the kisses he gave me in the elevator, the feeling of anticipation as we entered his apartment—all are inscribed in my memory with a bold, broad hand.

As soon as the door was closed, he said, "We have to swear first. Swear that it's this one night only."

"All right," I said, feeling like a child about to engage in a blood-brother-and-sister ritual.

"What should we swear on?" he asked. "Since we're agnostics, we can't swear on the Bible."

"I don't know. You got any poetry around? Byron or Sylvia Plath? And Beethoven for you?" I grinned.

"I'm serious about this. Don't you see? After you leave tomorrow, I don't want to be asking myself if you're going to break your engagement for me—because you wouldn't. You've never offered to leave Ben. I told you—I won't let myself be put in a position where I'll feel that tonight you're 'trying me out.' I refuse to go through that kind of suffering. So it's got to be just this night and nothing more."

"But—"

"And if you were to tell me now that you were leaving Ben, how could I trust you?"

"All right," I said.

"Let's sit on the couch. You ready to swear? Put your hand on your heart—there. Think of something so dear to you it feels sacred."

"Okay," I said.

Silence. Then he spoke first.

"So—one night only. I swear to it, on my music," he said.

I took another second to formulate my vow. "One night only. I swear to it on the life of the child I hope to have someday."

"Good enough," he said.

He grabbed my hand and led me to the bedroom, and I followed him, letting go of everything that wasn't of the moment—my guilt toward Ben, my fantasies about the future, my desire to have some control over this man now taking me into his bed.

He pulled my sweater up over my head and unzipped my pants and then, too impatient for me to undress him, he was suddenly completely naked, lying in bed with a huge erection, while I sat on the edge of the bed in my underwear.

"Should I take everything off?" I asked shyly.

"Yeah, take everything off."

I took off my bra and panties and then, with the sense of being terribly, vulnerably naked, and with a shiver that was part excitement and part fear, I slid into the bed next to him and he pulled the covers up over us as I moved into his arms.

"Michael," I said.

"Jul," he said.

We came together in a wave of warmth, our hands moving quietly over each other. There was a small knot in my throat from the forbidden words of love I needed to keep to myself. I could only say his name, "Michael, Michael," as he gently squeezed me and gazed into my eyes and sucked on my breast. "What is it? Tell me," he said and I just kept repeating, "Michael, Michael"—his name over and over again, like an incantation taking me to a deeper surrender. Then suddenly a more violent passion burst out, wild and broad like a thunderstorm over water, and he was around and inside me, kneading my breast, caressing my face, spreading my legs, and caressing the inside of my thighs with his as he slid into me like a diver into a lake. I was wide and wet and huge, in a place of absolute receptivity that yawned open even further when he hooked his right arm under my left knee and, bending my leg, opened me further. Every muscle in my body softened in a yielding deeper than any I'd ever experienced.

But the best part, perhaps, was right after we came, when he stayed on top of me and inside me as long as he could, kissing me tenderly and whispering my name. The velvet, baritone notes of his voice, each word like a question drawing me out, each syllable investigating my heart. His eyes, continuing to stir and probe me, to want and hold me.

When people rescue injured wild animals with a plan to free them later, they must be careful to limit the animals' contact with humans, so that a bond does not form which might "imprint" them. If the animals do become imprinted, they can no longer be released back into the wild.

We're not so different in matters of the heart. There are experiences of connection so deep they mark and change you forever. After excessive joy there's the knowledge that everything to come can only be less than; that the happiness experienced is now gone forever, carried away by the torrential river of time; that the rest of life, as a result, can only disappoint. The bliss becomes a traumatic initiation into the ultimate insufficiency of life. Whatever the future has to offer, one thing is clear: it won't be enough.

Of course, at the time all I knew was that there was something I needed to experience in order to touch some place in my emotional being that had never been touched before. I expected that such an experience would yield some kind of permanent satisfaction. I never thought it might become an obsessive memory that would feed my longing indefinitely.

And yet, as though I had some premonition of the empty feeling to come, in the long, sweet night that followed I memorized everything about him. How he moved against me like a river, how he moved inside me like a song. The temperature and rhythm of his hands. The way he held his huge body above me with the lightness of a bird. The way he melted under me, his body conforming to mine as I yielded and held him. And the exact, deeper register of his voice, the slow, exact tenderness of it as he asked, "How about this? Does it feel good?"

It felt beyond good. And we kept on making love and going back to that place of beyond good until, completely exhausted, he could no longer stay erect and I was completely sore; and then still clutching each other, we dozed off as night gave way to dawn. And in my dreams our coming together kept repeating itself, and the rhythm of our breaths together felt like the rhythm of our union, only more languorous, as it rocked us into a sleep imbued with the motion and smell of sex.

Surfacing the next day, shortly before noon, I had a moment before he woke up to reflect. Maybe it was for the best that we'd made a pact to be together for a single night only. Could I bear receiving such exquisite joy, could I tolerate being so sensitive to another human being and needy of his love on an indefinite basis? The intensity of my feeling for him was almost unbearable. And unbearable pleasure could only give way to unbearable pain and loss, if we were to continue and watch it inevitably fade. Perhaps best to truncate it like this, cleanly and sharply; then at least we'd have a perfect memory.

One thing I knew: how I would carry this experience in the future would largely depend on how we parted. I had to stand by what I'd sworn to the day before and leave him with all the tranquility I could muster.

Thus it was that when he rolled toward me and opened his eyes, I'd already prepared my mask of cheerfulness.

"Thank you," he simply said.

I answered the same. "Thank you."

We got up, and I showered while he made breakfast. I was beginning to feel numb, as though I were anaesthetizing myself to prepare for the pain of separation.

But sitting across from him at his little table, the words slipped out of me, "So what now?" I had the tiniest sliver of hope he might change his mind.

He didn't take it as any big question about our relationship. He simply looked at the clock and said, "My first lesson is in half an hour. We need to leave soon."

My heart shook under the numbness like an earth tremor shifting snow. I wanted to say to him, *I'll call Ben and tell him it's over because I'm in love with you*, and I reached over to take his hand.

"I'll—" I began

He shook his head. "No. Because I lack the confidence, don't you see? I don't feel confident I can make you happy, that's the problem."

"But you feel you can make Anna happy?"

"There's no other guy with Anna."

I took the words in and sank to a deeper deadness of body, heart, and mind. It was comforting to know that in the future I could move into numbness when the pain became too intense.

"All right then," I said.

"What will you tell Ben if he tried to call you last night?" He was an animal smoothing over his tracks in the forest.

"I'll tell him I unplugged the phone and went to bed early."

"That sounds reasonable," he said, looking at the clock again.

If he looked at the clock one more time, I'd explode.

"Let's get going," I said.

We went out into the hall, and he pressed the elevator button energetically. Then we had the awkward wait for it to arrive. It wasn't a fancy building, and the insufficient lighting, worn carpet, and old paint were infinitely depressing.

"Michael—"

"I'm glad we did this," he said. "Now we have something sweet to remember each other by. It's nice."

The elevator arrived right then, with a couple of faceless people in it, and we got in and rode down not looking at each other, not touching. I thought of reaching for his hand and giving it a squeeze, but what was the point? Our story was over now.

We walked out of the building and toward the bus stop at Broadway and One Hundredth Street. He pressed forward as I followed, one step behind.

"I hate being late for a lesson," he mumbled.

Suddenly the lumbering, farting 104 bus was there, and he gave me a quick kiss and turned away to climb the steps.

As I watched the bus disappear, then walked toward the Ninety-Sixth Street subway stop, I realized that not once in that whole long night and morning, had either of us spoken the words, *I love you.*

Is this love then?—This gray place
after the sparkled night
where you have left me
alone.

Loss has a head
and feet too.
It walks into
the howling cavern
and finds music there.
Down the slope
where nothing grows
it slides on its ass
stopping now and then
to stare at the horizon
with binoculars.
Loss is hungry
for a sighting of hope.

I tried to anchor myself in the thought that eventually I would feel better, that I would find my balance again with Ben. But there was one thing that hurt more than others. As I cycled between numbness and pain, I found myself parched for the words not spoken. Michael was seeing my cousin, yet still I wished he had verbalized his passion for me. Only words could satisfy my hunger, could tell me where I stood exactly in the pantheon of lovers that had crossed his path. Instead, all I had was the memory of our lovemaking, which I parsed for its deeper meaning. I wanted to know *how much*—how much he cared for me, how much it hurt him to give me up, how much he would miss me. It was in search of those quantities that I kept on reviewing our encounter, looking for an answer that would silence my questioning.

When night rolled around, I hunted through the leaves of darkness for the shadows he had left behind. I stayed up late writing. Poetry was the closet in which I hung my longing, and the words, like hangers, were often sharp.

I expected Ben in the city the next day. I had wondered for many months what it would feel like to be with Ben after sleeping with Michael, whether I would feel altered, guilty, furtive.

I felt fine.

I didn't feel like I'd done anything wrong. I was happy to see him, as I always was.

I wondered, as I had after sleeping with Val, why people make such a fuss over infidelity. During the day, I had moments when, in a half-death of the heart, I could barely remember what it felt like to have Michael inside me. With my eyes open, I couldn't acknowledge the magnitude of the loss. But in my sleep agitated by yearning, my night with Michael kept coming back to me. The length and shape of his body next to mine, the way he smelled slightly of dry grass, how he reached for me in the dark and we made love yet again, toward morning, in a state of half-sleep.

One night I had a dream about Ben—that *he* was the one who had been unfaithful, that he was having an affair with a woman in some faraway city, a place with hills and cobblestone streets and a view of the sea, like Istanbul or Lisbon. My world turned inside out. Horrified, I kept asking him, do you want to leave me? What does this mean? And he kept saying, I have to think it through. I felt jealous, hurt, abandoned. Adrift after a massacre, on seas strange, sorrowful, and threatening. It was some combination of guilt and empathy, of course, that had reversed things in the dream. I woke up and remembered how much I loved Ben, how I'd wanted never to hurt him. I'd had the thought a hundred times before, but now it had a different meaning. The one night I'd had with Michael, which had left me wanting so much more, which seemed so little the further time carried me away from it, now turned out to be more than enough. I concluded that everything had happened the way it was supposed to. I had found the perfect solution in having only one night with Michael—I could keep it a secret, and no one would get hurt.

One Saturday in late April, I came home from the Korean grocery store and, opening my mailbox, found a stiff, ivory-colored envelope addressed to Ben and me from Mr. and Mrs. Carl Field, Anna's parents. Walking up the stairs with the letter between thumb and index finger, I readied myself for what I guessed was inside.

Without saying hello to Ben, who was reading on the couch, I sat down next to him and opened the envelope with a quick rip.

The honor of your presence is requested at the wedding of Anna Field, daughter of Mr. and Mrs. Carl Field, and Michael Harold Chambers, son of Mr. and Mrs. Bruce Chambers, at 3 p.m. on…

I read it several times to make sure I'd got it right.

"What's that?"

"An invitation to Anna and Michael's wedding," I said.

Ben scooted closer to look over my shoulder. "That was precipitous. Memorial Day weekend. So they're beating us to the altar," he said. "Wouldn't you know—just like the son-of-a-bitch."

"Yeah," I said. My hands holding the card were shaking.

"You know," Ben said, "we don't have to go."

"What?"

"We can invent an excuse, say we can't go because we need to be in England for my parents' wedding anniversary—or something like that."

I looked at him blankly, afraid.

"Julia," he continued, "I knew all along that you were still infatuated with Michael."

"Is that what you call it?"

He shrugged.

"How did you figure it out?" I asked.

"The night of your Christmas party—the way you didn't sing along."

"And do you want to know what happened after that?" I asked.

"No," he said. "I don't."

We fell silent. I wondered how much he'd suffered.

"Why didn't you say anything?" I asked. "Weren't you afraid of losing me?" It saddened me that he hadn't been more possessive, although it had given me the freedom I needed so badly.

"Of course I was afraid. I was terrified. But after I'd taken so many years to make a formal commitment to you, the least I owed you was a chance to work through any ambivalence you might have about me. Who was I to stop you from having your moment of doubt when it had taken me so long to work through my own?"

"You did take a long time," I said. "It almost wore me out."

"I'm sorry if I made you feel taken for granted." He passed an arm around my shoulders, drew me toward him. "Because I don't. I treasure you more than anything in the world."

"I still don't understand how you could have just stood on the sidelines—"

"Is there anything I could have said or done that would have changed anything?" he asked.

"No."

"I saw that it had to take its course. I didn't want to compete with a fantasy. So I decided to let you have the space you needed to take it wherever it had to go."

"Thank you. Tell me—were you very jealous?"

"Insanely," he said.

As he leaned his head on my shoulder, tears in his eyes, I was flooded with tenderness. He'd been so private about his jealousy. I felt tears running down my face, tears of love now. I was feeling it again.

"Oh Ben, I'm sorry I put you through this. When I think how close I came to ruining everything—" I reached for his hand. "You've been generous."

"No. *You've* been generous. And patient. Anyway, we're even now. I just want you to know that the next time this happens, if there is a next time, I'll punch the bugger in the jaw."

I smiled. "I just want you to know that, through the whole thing, I never stopped loving you." It felt good to say those words and to feel, finally, that they were true.

"I knew that. That's why I never stopped hoping." And he gently kissed me on the lips.

Part Two
2004

17

I WAS SURPRISED, ONE Monday night in Manhattan, to pick up the phone and hear Michael's voice. He never called me, and we hadn't had an extended conversation since the night we'd slept together.

"What's wrong?" I asked.

"I need you to help me," he said. "Anna has left."

"She's left you?" I was shocked.

"I wouldn't say she's left *us*, but she's left…A few years ago she started doing retreats at a Buddhist monastery, and this time she went and extended her stay by a week." He paused. "And then another."

"So what's going on?"

"I think she's thinking of taking vows, possibly becoming a nun."

"You can't be serious. Did she actually tell you that?"

"Not in so many words, but I have a strong suspicion."

"But she has a twelve-year-old daughter," I countered.

"I know. That's why I want you to come out and help me get her back."

The winter after they got married, Michael and Anna moved to San Francisco. I was surprised that Anna would give up her plum job at the Met so soon, but the move turned out to be good for both of them. In California Anna went back to teaching English as a second language and made the connections she needed to start exhibiting her art, and Michael was soon teaching at the San Francisco Conservatory and having his compositions played by local orchestras. In the years that followed, I saw him occasionally at family reunions, where we avoided each other in an intricate dance, maintaining a distance of some feet between us and only conversing when a third party was present. After a while, the Michael of flesh and blood who was married to Anna became a distinct entity from the man—friend, lover, musician—who lived in my head. I had to accept the facts: by following the advice in *Psychology Today*, Michael had arranged himself a successful marriage.

Several years passed and they had a baby girl. Sometimes Anna came to New York with Esther, but without Michael, in order to visit her parents, and I always had some satisfying time alone with my niece.

Anna continued to be prolific as an artist, and I envied her creativity until she developed MCS (multiple chemical sensitivities) as a result of exposure to art supplies, which began to cause her asthma and severe headaches. She stopped painting and began seeking less-toxic art forms. It was her distress that led her to become interested in meditation. Dealing with her illness, she became withdrawn and strange, and we fell out of touch. But I cultivated my long-distance relationship with Esther, and it gave me joy to be her Aunt Julia.

The abdominal pain I'd had gradually went away. Maybe my body adjusted to the scar tissue, maybe I learned to block out the pain, or maybe getting married and feeling secure helped. I don't know. I stopped using birth control but didn't get pregnant. I began fertility treatments and had an ectopic pregnancy—the embryo hadn't reached the uterus and was lodged in the fallopian tube. After surgery to remove the affected tube—leaving a second scar on my abdomen—our old ambivalence about parenting came up, and we abandoned the quest.

The truth was that Ben and I were both putting our energies elsewhere. As he became distinguished as a teacher and scholar, Ben's responsibilities on campus increased; moreover, his desire to move his stodgy department in a more progressive direction led him to a greater involvement in university politics. Allied with the Victorian scholar and Lisa of gender studies, he militated for change against a conservative faction led by the kilt-wearing professor and the medievalist. All this made him less available to me, but I made good use of my time alone. When I stopped writing poetry again, it was for a worthy reason—in order to focus completely on my business. I took the necessary courses and became certified as a financial planner. As my female clientele grew, I started writing a book I'd later call *Women, Be Rich*. Gradually I became another person—a woman of achievement, who valued her autonomy and professional success.

I felt proud of myself. The publication of *Women, Be Rich* brought me wealth and notoriety. I was invited to be a guest on radio talk shows, I was interviewed and quoted, and my clientele grew steadily. With two incomes and my book royalties, Ben and I had plenty of money to go to the theater, decorate our two homes, and travel. These were good years, when we explored Europe and Asia, visiting the cities that came into vogue in the nineties and first years of the twenty-first century: Barcelona, Prague, Lisbon, Shanghai, Ho Chi Minh City. Being together in strange places, isolated from our usual social contacts, suited us. While our first passion became more and more lost in the past, we still had an affectionate relationship.

It feels like an injustice not to say more about Ben and the contentment I did have with him. What is this impulse to write only about extremes— the extreme of passion, the extreme of loss? Whatever Ben was, he wasn't extreme. He was simply there for me, the tree at the center of things. The tree I took for granted.

I minimize the meaningfulness of my marriage by compressing its story into a few pages. It's the stories we choose to tell that define us, so, in some way, by not saying more about Ben, I suppose I'm trying to change who I am or, at least, how I see myself.

Over the years I went back and forth between two ways of understanding what had happened with Michael. In gloomy moments, a "romantic" interpretation led me to believe that I'd been a fool to let him go. I imagined that if I'd ended up with Michael, my life would have taken a different direction—instead of a successful businesswoman, I would have become a distinguished poet. In a misty dream of another life, I saw myself at public poetry readings, mesmerizing audiences and receiving praise, while Michael (sitting in the front row or more discreetly in the back) supported me with a subtle nod or glance.

Then there was another, "reality-based" interpretation: I had chosen Ben because he supported me in my quest to realize myself as the successful professional I needed to become. The freedom of our commuting relationship, the way he modeled dedication to career, the emotional stability he offered me—all these created the fertile conditions that enabled me to put myself out in the world and gain recognition. From this perspective, when Michael got me to move into New York, he'd simply been another catalyst encouraging me to make something of myself.

The "romantic" hypothesis led me to feel I'd made a tragic mistake in not breaking up with Ben in order to be with Michael. In contrast, the "realistic" hypothesis left me feeling that I'd acted in my own self-interest, that in choosing Ben I had insured my peace of mind, economic security, and self-esteem. The choice presented what we now call a no-brainer: most often, I opted for the second hypothesis, which made me feel wise and clever. As for my poetic talent, well, I was accountable for what I hadn't done with it. As Sandra put it—and maybe this was the only thing I'd gotten out of therapy—Michael, like Ben, was a passerby in my life. In the end I was responsible for what I did with my days on earth.

"I can't believe she would be so cruel to Esther," I said. I had two things to process: one, that I was on the phone with Michael again, and two, that Anna had left her daughter. Whatever Anna's reasons, Esther was likely to experience her mother's open-ended retreat as abandonment.

"Could you come out to visit?" Michael pleaded. "Buddhaland—the monastery—is two hours north of San Francisco. We could drive up there with Esther, and you could talk to her. Maybe you could find out what's going on."

It was late June, the slow season for my business. Ben and I had scheduled a European vacation for August, so theoretically it was feasible.

"Maybe I should call or write her first?"

"They don't allow phones or e-mail—"

"So what's your take on it?"

Michael began to ramble. Anna, he said, had become involved with this Buddhist sect for a variety of reasons. Meditating was good for her health: it seemed to calm the asthma attacks. Whereas the air in Berkeley was damp and laden with irritants, the environment at Buddhaland was dry and free of the substances, botanical and chemical, that triggered her asthma. She felt better there.

"So why do you want me and not Robin to talk to her?"

"I asked Robin, and she doesn't want to. Listen, are you going to do me this favor or not?" He had that tight, irritable edge I knew well.

"I'll do you the favor."

"When can you come?"

"I'll look for a flight now. How long should I come for?"

"I don't know. A long weekend. Or a week."

Hanging up, I wondered how Ben would take my going off to visit his old archrival. Well, he'd have to be okay with it. This was about Anna and Esther, anyway, not about Michael.

I went online, bought myself a ticket for Wednesday. Then I called Ben and presented my trip as a fait accompli.

I'd never told him that I'd slept with Michael, and he'd never pushed to know. But Ben wasn't an idiot.

"I don't like this idea," he said. "Michael's like a bad penny that keeps coming back."

"It's something I'm doing for Esther."

"Well, I suppose it's best for all of us if Anna and Michael stay together." It was like Ben to be supportive, even in this bizarre situation. "I don't like it, but maybe you're the one to do the job."

"That's what Michael seems to think," I said.

"What's she doing in the monastery, anyway? How narcissistic can you get?"

"She's desperate, I guess."

"Well, all right then. Don't forget to take the Dramamine before the plane takes off. You know it's useless if you wait until the nausea hits."

"I know."

"And get into San Francisco, have some fun."

It made me sad that he didn't offer more resistance.

A wave of anxiety came over me as the plane took off from JFK and swerved away from the Manhattan skyline outside the window. I felt myself being pulled up by the roots from everything that anchored me and made me feel safe—except that the city I lived in, three years after 9/11, no longer felt secure. The idea of being with Michael, even with Esther as chaperone, stirred me up. And I had a particular reason for wanting to stay on an even keel: Ben and I had recently begun discussing adoption. Ben seemed open not only to the idea of adopting but also to moving into New York if we started a family. My longing for a child, which I had shelved after failed attempts to get pregnant, had resurfaced after my mother's death the previous year. With both my parents gone (my father had died a few years before), I felt an anguished disorientation. I needed a child to point me toward the future. We had visited a social service agency that facilitated adoption and were looking at our options.

I didn't know whether, when I saw Michael, I would desire him or hate him or just find him plain annoying, and I had a hard time getting my mind to shut up as I examined the implications of the information he'd given me about Anna. Was their marriage in trouble? Wasn't I the wrong person to intervene? And what about Esther? How was she handling her mother's absences? By the time the San Francisco skyline came into view, my stomach was unsettled, in spite of the medication I'd taken.

But when I finally saw Michael and Esther waiting at the baggage claim exit, I remembered I was there to help. In the man that waved to me with a flat gray expression on his face I saw a husband and father in crisis. He was wearing two collared shirts one on top of the other, as he always did, one dark blue, the other crimson, with the shirttails sticking out from under his suede jacket. His being unshaven made him seem even older than the fifty-eight years he now was, and his lower lip protruded ever so slightly, presaging a less-than-attractive old age. I could handle this.

Esther, standing next to him, came up to his chest. The last time I'd seen her, a couple of years before, she'd been on the chubby side. Now, nearing thirteen, she was long and lean, an adolescent sprout. Her shoulder-length black hair was wavy and unkempt, like her father's, and she wore the inevitable jeans and a T-shirt with a message under a zip-front hoodie bearing another message.

She gave me a big hug, and I held her tight and tried to twirl her around.

"Oh, you're too big for this now," I said, struggling with her size.

"But I still like it."

Michael and I pecked each other on the cheek. We might as well have been on either side of a parking lot, that's how distant it felt.

"We're parked outside," he said.

Esther strode ahead of us, pulling my rollaboard. As Michael and Anna lived in the East Bay now, I had flown into the Oakland airport, a small facility with a parking lot right next to it.

"Be careful of cars pulling out," he called to Esther as we walked toward his car.

There was always a moment of internal disjunction when I saw him being a good father. I'd had a hard time imagining him in that role, but it suited him perfectly.

I was surprised to see he had an SUV.

"You succumbed," I said, pointing to the mammoth.

"Soccer dad and all that," he said. "It works if you've got five kids and another mom or dad and somebody's dog. Not to mention traveling with a band to a weekend gig down the coast."

The floor of the passenger's side was covered with empty paper coffee cups and sheets of paper from Esther's homework.

"I should have cleaned this out," he said—without much conviction, I thought.

"I'll help you, Dad." Esther fished around in the back and found a paper bag and began stuffing it.

It didn't seem appropriate to discuss Anna in front of her daughter, so Michael and I made small talk as he drove, while, in the backseat, Esther lost herself in text-messaging her friends.

"That book of yours," he said, "it must be making you a lot of money."

"I'm doing well," I said.

"*Women, Be Rich*," he chuckled. "Love the title. Could you write another one and call it, *Musicians, Be Rich*? What do you think?"

"I'll think about it."

Getting off the highway in Berkeley, Michael drove past a cement factory and a salvage operation through a neighborhood where stucco bungalows alternated with tiny, ornate Victorian houses. The occasional palm tree reminded me I was in California. The houses grew larger as we made our way across the flats of Berkeley and up into the hills through treacherously winding streets lined with fifties-style, dark wooden structures with broad windows. Finally, we pulled into a driveway.

"Here we are."

Over the years I'd always seen Michael and Anna in neutral locations, like funerals, my parents' apartment, or Aunt Linda's on Long Island. Somehow I had managed to avoid stepping into any of their homes. But now I was in one. The house Michael had bought and shared with his wife, my cousin.

Perhaps because it was the kind of midcentury shack I imagined Henry Miller lived in when he came to California, I felt myself riding on a wave of déjà vu as I stepped through the front door into a small living room with a shabby couch and brick fireplace. The house was as bright with light and color on the inside as it was dark on the outside. The light entering through the large square windows flooded the saturated hues Anna had chosen for the walls—Pompeian red in the living room, yellow ochre in the kitchen to the left, Persian blue for the hallway up the half staircase to the bedrooms. On the walls crowded with art, I recognized a couple of paintings from Anna's New York period, when she'd set her canvases in motion with swarms of animal forms. To the side, the small upright piano, heaped with music and composition paper, could have been the same beat-up one Michael had played when he was a graduate student at Yale. But now there was the addition, at a right angle to it, of an electric keyboard hooked up to a computer.

The house was small, but the view out over Berkeley and the silver expanse of the bay toward San Francisco made me take a big breath. A thin tongue of fog had slid in under the Golden Gate Bridge and rested right on the water. At the northwest end of the bay, the late afternoon reflection of the sun hurt the eye with its brilliant assault.

Michael carried my valise up a quarter-flight of stairs to a landing. To the left was the bedroom he shared with Anna, to the right the one where Esther slept.

"It all looks very—orderly," I said.

"I try to keep it that way for Esther's sake. It's hard work, actually, because I'm still a slob. What it means is that I'm always cleaning up after myself." He veered to the left and put my valise down next to the king-sized bed in the master bedroom. "You and Esther can sleep together here, and I'll sleep in Esther's room," he said.

"Yahoo!" Esther cried. "Girls' night!"

She disappeared into her room, and Michael and I looked at each other with an odd blankness.

"She'll be texting her friends now, to give them a blow-by-blow account of your visit," he said. "I try to control her gadget time, but it's a losing battle."

I looked at the bed. It was clear which side was Anna's: her night table had a clock, a box of tissues, and a stack of books. On Michael's table was a messy pile of CDs and spiral-bound composition paper.

"It's freezing here." I shivered.

"I should have told you how cold it gets here in July. You can borrow one of Anna's sweaters. I'm sure she wouldn't mind." He walked over to her dresser and opened a drawer.

She had chunky sweaters and featherweight ones. Long cardigans and short V-necks. I had finally given up my New York black, but only for a wider range of neutrals—navy, brown, charcoal. Anna's drawer, in contrast, was filled with saturated colors from the entire spectrum.

"This looks good," I said, sliding a deep burgundy turtleneck over my head.

"Want to help me set dinner up?"

I followed him back downstairs and into the kitchen, a colorful space with terra-cotta Mexican tiles on the floor, a splashboard of modernist, hand-painted ceramic tiles, and huge windows over the counter, looking out toward the bay.

"This is lovely," I said.

"Anna did it. Picked out the tiles, found cheap labor to install them. She has a real gift for decorating."

"I know."

He picked up an open bottle of red wine sitting on the counter.

"Do you tolerate California wine?" he asked, in what I took to be an underhanded jab at the European tastes I'd acquired living with a Brit.

"Sure," I said, taking the glass he offered. Out the window, the tongue of silver cloud on the water had thickened and advanced deeper into the bay, engulfing all of the bridge except for the tips of its towers. "The fog seems to be moving in."

Michael came to stand right next to me and looked out the window, glass in hand. It was another opportunity for me to see just how jowly he'd become with the passage of years. And, of course, so had I. The flesh was beginning to droop and drape around the corners of my mouth.

"Yup," he answered. "We'll be engulfed by nightfall. Then the fog will go back out in the late morning tomorrow." He glanced sideways at me.

"You know, I ought to call Ben. Tell him I got here safely."

"Go ahead."

I left the kitchen, took my cell to the living room at the other end of the house. Ben picked up immediately.

"How was the flight?"

"Fine, my stomach was fine."

"And how's everything going? Michael okay?"

"He seems okay." The situation felt awkward. Michael might be able to hear me from the kitchen.

"And Esther?"

"I don't know. It's not clear." I didn't want to say "Esther" or "she," thinking that Esther, too, might hear me. It was a small house.

"Not much privacy, I guess."

"Not much. I just wanted you to know I got here safely."

"Okay. Love you," he said.

"Me too," I said.

"Talk tomorrow, then."

"Yes."

I hung up, went back into the kitchen.

"How's Ben doing?" Michael asked. Whatever he said, whatever I said, we were headed over a densely stratified geological zone.

"Fine," I said.

"So how *does* Esther strike you?" He'd overheard me talking on the phone and gathered that Ben had asked the same question.

"She seems to be doing pretty well." I couldn't fathom how a twelve-year-old would contend with her mother's absence.

He sighed. "You know, Anna can be very temperamental, and she and Esther used to fight a lot. But ever since she started going on retreat, she's always real sweet to Esther when she comes back. Out of guilt, or maybe it's the Buddhist teachings that have made her calmer. So mostly Esther *is* okay. But every now and then she starts acting out. You'll see it eventually. Maybe she feels abandoned or realizes something else is going on."

"So, what is going on?" I asked, as I began to wash the head of lettuce he handed me.

"I'm not sure. I think doing art always kept her mentally in balance in some way, but then the chemical sensitivity issue forced her to stop painting. Her lungs were always her weak point."

"I know. I remember her having pneumonia in her twenties. Go on," I said, sipping the wine. It had a pleasant weight on the tongue.

"I think she started imploding when she could no longer paint."

"Imploding?"

"Imploding—from the creative energy having nowhere to go."

I listened, thinking that self-expression is more vital to some people than to others. I hadn't written a poem in years and, yes, not writing had made me a little dead around the edges, but I was alive in other places. My business was thriving; I was making money hand over fist. I'd simply put my focus elsewhere. Wasn't Anna doing something similar by putting her energy into religion?

Michael opened the fridge and took out a big pot, which he set on the stove.

"Home-made chicken soup," he said. "Good for a cold summer night."

"You cook now?"

"A little. Anna taught me."

I had to adjust to the idea of Michael cooking instead of surviving on Chinese fast food. Family life changes a man.

"So where does Buddhaland fit in?" I asked.

"You're probably familiar with the Buddhist philosophy that it's our desires that make us unhappy, and we can only find happiness by releasing them through meditative practice and so forth. And she says that's what she needs to do."

"To release her desire to do art?"

"Yeah, exactly. Though she's still doing art—watercolors of Buddhist deities that they sell in the gift shop—she can't do big canvases with oil anymore. She can't even tolerate acrylic paint. So what she says she wants now is to feel peaceful with the 'nots' of life. Not working with her favorite materials, not being an artistic success in conventional terms, not making money, etcetera." He broke "etcetera" slowly into four syllables. "She wants to release what she calls the ego involvement of the artist."

Here I was being Michael's confidante again. Okay. I knew how to do that.

"Is she threatening to stay up there?"

"Not exactly. But she's been up there for three weeks now and won't say when she's coming back. She's never been gone for more than a week before. So Esther and I are getting nervous."

"Has she had any professional help?"

"You mean therapy? Yeah, but it hasn't helped. She says Buddhism is the only thing that works for her."

"But she could be a Buddhist here—"

"She says she doesn't feel okay unless she's on retreat," he said. He was setting the table now, positioning the forks and soupspoons with exaggerated precision.

"Do you, uh, think there could be someone else?" I felt brave asking such a sensitive question.

"Well, if there is, his head is shaven and he's wearing red-and-yellow monk's robes."

We burst out laughing together. It was the first time in years we'd done that.

He stopped laughing and looked at me.

"Speaking of which, I need to prepare you for something. She cut her hair real short," he said.

"Anna cut her hair?" Except for a couple years right after college, when she'd worn her hair cropped, Anna had always had long, auburn tresses that moved in constant flow around her face and shoulders. "How short is real short?"

"Really, really short. Which is what makes me suspect she's thinking of becoming a Buddhist nun. In which case she'll have to shave her head."

"I can't believe she'd become a nun."

"As far as I'm concerned," he continued, very controlled, "I don't give a fuck what she does, but she has a child, and she belongs here."

"Were the two of you getting along before she left for this last retreat?"

It was another sensitive question, but he didn't mind. He shrugged.

"What does it mean for a couple to 'get along' when they're working all the time and parenting? Our life revolves around"—he dropped his voice— "our child. The truth is, Anna's illness was only one of the reasons we began to drift apart. We started fighting when Esther was a toddler— she was a textbook case of the terrible two, except that the contrariness lasted until she was about five, and parenting her left Anna exhausted. Unfortunately, it was around that time that I started getting known in the Bay Area. I was not only teaching during the day, but also getting gigs in the evening with my regular band. Sometimes I had to travel out of town for the weekend. I was gone too much of the time and Anna resented it. But really, I was just trying to get ahead a little. Wanting to save for Esther's college education and all that. A musician's life is hard, Julia."

"I know." I stared down into the salad bowl as I tore up leaves of lettuce and dropped them in. Michael had turned out to be a dutiful husband and father, but it probably wasn't that much fun being married to him. I didn't know whether he was a workaholic or simply bound up by the economic difficulties of making ends meet. In either case, not much of him was available for relationship. This reflection made the old wounded part of me feel a little better.

"So how have you been managing when Anna's gone—I mean, with Esther?"

"Well, I'm not taking gigs on weekends right now. When I've had to, Esther has gone to stay in the city with Robin and Serena. Serena's seventeen now, and a fabulous babysitter."

Esther appeared, cutting the confidences short. "I'm hungry," she said.

"Coming right up."

She came over to me and shyly gave me a hug. It seemed the right moment to introduce a new topic.

"Esther, I wanted to tell you, Uncle Ben and I are talking about adopting a child. So I might be able to provide you with another cousin."

Her eyes widened. "Like how old?"

"Maybe a baby, maybe older."

"I'd like that. I'd like that a lot."

Michael concurred. "What a wonderful idea, Julia. What a wonderful thing to do."

"We had a single meeting with a social service agency, that's all. The question is whether we're too old—I mean, there's a lot to consider." I smoothed Esther's hair. "So I'm not making any promises."

"You wouldn't regret it," Michael said.

"The fact is, I've always had a hard time making major decisions." I stopped dead, realizing who I was talking to, and blushed as our eyes met.

"I remember that about you," he said. "I remember it very well."

Esther disappeared as soon as she'd eaten, and Michael explained his plan to me. The next morning we would drive up to Ukiah, where Buddhaland was. The three of us would visit with Anna, then I might have some time alone with her. She probably wouldn't agree on the spot to come back with us.

"So then what?"

"We'll drive over to the coast to visit some friends of the family. Do you remember Val Findlay from Yale?" he asked.

"Yes," I said, startled.

"Anna and I reconnected with him when we moved out here. His mother has become a kind of honorary grandmother for Esther. Anyway, Val has taught me everything I know about photography. He does these classes in the wilderness, and I sometimes go along as his assistant. If you don't mind, I'll leave you and Esther to help him out on Saturday."

"I like having time alone with Esther," I said, wondering what it would be like to see Val again. My memories of him were pleasant—and distant. It would be okay.

"I thought you'd enjoy that," he said. "Anyway, while I'm at the workshop, you can hang out in Mendocino with Esther. Val's mom is up there, too. You'll like her. Then we can always go back to Ukiah to see Anna again. We can play the situation by ear."

"But Michael, why wasn't Robin willing to talk to Anna?"

"You know Anna's always turned to Robin for advice, and—well, maybe Robin feels she's had enough influence."

"Meaning?"

"What Robin said was, 'I don't want responsibility for Anna's decisions one way or the other.'"

"Hmm."

"Did you know that Robin has found a Native American guru and she goes to a drumming group and that sort of thing? So she's on a spiritual quest, too, but of a very different kind. Maybe that has something to do with it. There are aspects of Robin's practice that Anna finds primitive. Like, once a year Robin goes to a sundance where they drive metal rods through their pectoral muscles and dance without food or water for three days straight."

"You're kidding me."

"The self-torture is supposedly a way of demonstrating to spirit— Great Spirit—the seriousness of one's commitment."

"Wow."

"I have to admit I've always liked the term 'Great Spirit,'" Michael said.

"Better than 'God,'" I agreed.

"One could argue," he went on, "that human beings are driven to invite suffering into their lives, in one way or another. I mean, look at how people destroy themselves with drugs and alcohol, not to mention toxic relationships. At least, the native tradition does it in a context of the sacred."

"Yes, but—"

"Anyway, far be it from me to defend Robin. The point is, you're the woman for the job. And you grew up with her."

"That was a long time ago. I don't think I have any special access now," I said.

"You brought us together, so on a karmic level you must have some special power—"

"On a *karmic* level?" I asked in disbelief.

He smiled. "I guess California has changed me, too. It's really the way people think here."

"Do you think there is such a thing?"

"As karma?" He reflected. "I don't know. I don't rule out the possibility."

"So it's my karmic duty to intervene here?"

"Yes, for Esther's sake."

After we finished our wine, Michael called Esther back into the kitchen to help him clean up. The sun was setting in the clear sky over the fog bank, slicing the summer atmosphere over the Marin hills into strips of fluorescent pink and gold. Maybe Michael's marriage wasn't perfect, but, wow, what a view. Jet-lagged and confused, I excused myself. On the way upstairs to take a shower, I glanced at the piano in the living room, recalling that time when each of us had been a catalyst for the other. I couldn't help but romanticize it in retrospect. Now, in contrast, there would be no point asking Michael to play something for me. He didn't need me any longer; he had found another muse—had married her. And if she was making him suffer now, he'd only be more prolific as a consequence.

It was with a feeling of complete dissociation that, washed and changed, I got into the bed that Anna and Michael shared. I'd gotten good at not thinking about certain things and *that* was one thing I certainly wouldn't think about now. Instead, I was wondering how much Ben minded my sleeping under the same roof as Michael, with a twelve-year-old as chaperone, when Esther appeared in the bedroom doorway, adorably decked out in a bright green fleece bathrobe over iridescent purple pajamas with a cat print. She approached with a Harry Potter book under her arm.

"Aunt Julia, can I read out loud to you?" she asked. "I'm reading this one for the third time. It's great."

"Sure." I was exhausted from the trip but wanted to be a good auntie. Esther climbed in under the down comforter and, fluffing up a pillow, placed it closer to mine. I rolled on my left side to look at her. I was struck by the way her face blended Anna's and Michael's most attractive traits— she had Michael's brown eyes and black hair, Anna's bone structure, and a mouth that combined the particular rosiness of her mother's with the broad sensuality of her father's. If Ben and I adopted, our child wouldn't look like either one of us. I was okay with that. I was okay with everything. Because I had to be.

Esther began reading. I hadn't read any of the *Harry Potter* series and was completely lost from the first sentence but pretended to understand with the occasional "uh huh" continuance signal. After she'd read me a copious portion of *The Order of the Phoenix*, we turned off the lights. She kept on shifting around in the dark.

"You okay?" I asked, touching her arm.

She moved closer to me. I felt her hand close on my pajama sleeve.

"Are you going to get my mother to come back?" she whispered.

"I'll try, honey. I'll do my best."

"Actually, I hate her. I don't care if she comes back."

"I know you're angry."

"I'm twelve. I don't need her anymore, anyway."

"You sure about that?"

"Yeah. Her being gone—it's just like being at sleep-away camp. I don't mind."

"I didn't know you'd been to sleep-away camp." I tried to keep up from a distance, but this I'd missed.

"Once. For a week."

"Do you want to cuddle?"

"Yeah."

I held Esther close, taking in her little-girl fragrance. Except she wasn't a little girl anymore, she would be a teenager the following winter. I vowed to myself that in the future I wouldn't let the distance between New York and California keep me from spending more time with her. If Ben and I adopted, I'd make sure Esther got to know her cousin.

With her heavy head on my shoulder, it was difficult to fall asleep. Soon she was breathing heavily. As I listened to Michael moving around in Esther's room on the other end of the landing, I decided that this whole adventure was fortunate. It was an opportunity to confirm—to *reiterate*—the decision Michael and I had made years before. If I'd had any doubts about whether we'd done the right thing, I could put them to rest now, by going up to Ukiah with him and trying to persuade Anna to come back. It was an opportunity—so rare in life—to make complete peace with the past. And after this, we would all be more of a family for each other.

Silence fell in the house. Michael was in Esther's bed, reading perhaps, or listening to music.

Gently I moved Esther off my shoulder and got up to rummage in my suitcase for a sleeping pill.

18

"YOU WANT TO DRESS in layers," Michael said the next morning. "It's cold by the bay because of the fog, but it could be boiling up in Ukiah."

It was early. As Anna would be unavailable during the noon-hour meditation service, Michael wanted to arrive midmorning. Anna expected us, as he had left a message for her informing her of our arrival.

Setting out on West 580, we crossed the north end of the bay over the Richmond Bridge. To the left, a couple of giant tankers sat on the silver water, looking still and abandoned. To the right, the bay narrowed toward its source, the Sacramento River. Straight ahead, the tallest of the Marin hills, Mount Tamalpais, was, like a mountain in a Chinese scroll, a charcoal blue against pearl-white clouds. As we approached the other side of the span, the gray gradually turned a dark, velvety green.

In my mind Marin was connected to that night I spent with Val. It was a pleasant memory, with a free, spacious feeling around it.

In the back of the car, Esther played a game on some digital device. Michael and I were quiet as the highway curved north. We passed a shopping center with ochre stucco walls and red tile roofing, then another. The Mexican-style construction and palm trees seemed at odds with the cold weather. But soon the fog cleared, and Michael turned on the air conditioner as I stripped down to a T-shirt. In a rolling, rural landscape, cows on stretches of pasture alternated with vineyards.

"It looks vaguely Italian," I said, remembering a trip through Tuscany with Ben.

"Speaking of which, I have a CD of lesser-known Vivaldi in the glove compartment..."

As I released the door to the compartment, I remembered the night he'd made me a Möbius strip after we saw *Teacher's Pet*. Everything reminded me of something else. I found the CD and inserted it. The land flattened out as we approached Ukiah; vineyards alternated with orchards. At the highway turn-off, a huge sign read PEARS.

We went down a side road for a couple of miles, past dull houses with white siding and rectangular lawns. Suddenly, bizarrely out of the suburban American context, there was a huge arch decorated with gigantic red Chinese characters, under which smaller English letters said BUDDHALAND.

Michael drove in through the gate and past some institutional-looking buildings to the visitor parking lot.

"What's with the peacocks?" I asked, looking at a group on the lawn.

"I don't know. Maybe a sacred bird."

"Or an antidote to the drab architecture?" I said.

"This used to be a mental institution," he said.

"Really? You're kidding me!"

"Weird, isn't it? You'd think that all those crazy people living here would have left a bad vibe that would make it hard for the monks to meditate."

He parked and turned off the ignition.

"So now what?" I asked.

"We visit with Anna for a bit as a threesome, then Esther and I will take a walk to see the peacocks, and you can talk to her alone. Then we'll go have lunch." He pulled into the visitor parking lot. "There's a vegetarian restaurant here for visitors."

"They make great tofu rolls," Esther said from the backseat.

We got out of the car. The sky was a perfect blue and the sun intense. The heat felt thick and heavy on my skin, and I began to perspire. A woman with a shaved head, dressed in burgundy-and-saffron robes, walked by. A high, squealing sound, like the meow of a cat in pain, broke the silence.

"What was that?" I asked.

"Peacock," Esther said.

There was another squeal and another. The cry had a mysterious, eerie quality.

"Her dorm is this way," Michael said, gesturing with his head.

Esther took my hand and Michael led the way, his head forward in sad determination. We stepped up to a one-story building painted a dirty, diluted yellow. Going in through the glass door, we reached a reception desk where a woman with a shaved head and dark robes greeted us. Michael politely requested to see Anna. The woman nodded and stepped out from behind the counter. We watched her walk down the corridor and knock on a door.

Anna came out in a novitiate's sleeveless black robe with a maroon sash. Her hair was cut like a boy's, as it had been in her early twenties. She wore a Buddhist bracelet of wooden beads inscribed with Chinese characters and, hanging on a necklace, a green jade pendant representing Kuan Yin, the goddess of compassion. Perhaps she'd been meditating cross-legged on a cushion in her room or reading a sacred text.

She approached smiling and gave Esther a long hug. Esther seemed at first receptive, then a surly expression passed over her, like the cold shadow of a storm cloud. Anna turned and kissed me on the cheek, then finally Michael.

"Let's go for a walk," she said.

Outside, I was so stymied by the strangeness of how she looked that I found it difficult to think, let alone make conversation. But she was occupied with her daughter.

"How was camp last week?"

"Boring," Esther said. "I don't like being a CIT."

"Well, honey, we're always open to suggestions if you want to do something else. But you don't seem to make any…"

Michael lagged behind, and I slowed down to keep pace with him.

"Let's sit," he said.

We sat on a bench and watched Anna and Esther walk around together. He had a grim expression.

They were out of earshot when he spoke. "If I'd married you," he said, "this never would have happened, would it?"

I was so shocked I couldn't respond.

"How is that Möbius strip going with you and Ben, anyway?" he continued, not looking at me. "Are you still miraculously renewing your relationship year after year?"

"Jesus Christ, Michael."

"I want to know. I want to know whether my prediction was correct."

A California jay, indigo blue in body with a black head and a Mohawk crest, landed on the concrete path in front of us, looked at Michael, and took off.

"Well, if you want to know, the marriage survives thanks to my letting go."

"Meaning?"

"I allow distance. I don't struggle for an intimacy that can't happen." I'd never articulated this to anyone, and it felt depressing to do so. "Because the intimacy that I want doesn't exist."

"Doesn't exist?"

"No. I want something that I'll never get. I'm wired for longing in perpetuity. Maybe because I had an alcoholic mother and never got what I needed from her. There was this early experience of lack, and I've never gotten beyond it." Now that my mother was dead, I could speak these truths without feeling I was blaming her.

"That sounds grim, but possibly accurate."

"The other side of the coin is that I really have achieved some self-acceptance, some equilibrium—" I stopped as I had a flashback to our conversation in the bar at Penn Station.

"Back to your philosophy of happiness?" He was having the same memory.

"I guess."

"So you're happy—or balanced—enough to think about doing an adoption?"

"Yes. We've taken the first steps."

"It's a great idea," he said. "Love for a child is the only kind of real love there is, anyway. And an adoption—what could be more worthwhile than that?"

"I'm not thinking of it as a philanthropic act. It's something I want to do for me."

"Of course." His eyes were still on his wife and child. "I can't get used to seeing her in those goddamn robes."

"All that black fabric must be really hot in this weather," I said.

Anna and Esther were approaching now, and we fell silent.

Esther broke away from her mother and ran up to Michael. "Let's go to the pond, Daddy."

"Sure." He turned to look at me with a neutral gaze. "There's a kind of watering hole for the peacocks. We'll be back in a while."

He stood up and they moved away, leaving Anna and me alone. She sat down next to me, where Michael had just been.

"It's good to see you, Julia," she said. "What are you doing in California?"

"I'm here to see you, obviously," I said.

"Oh." She laughed, making a bright, clean sound. "You're here to 'rescue' me, is that it? As though I didn't know what I was doing. But I do, you know. I really do."

Perhaps she was suffering from some kind of narcissistic personality disorder.

"Well, start talking."

She just laughed again.

"Julia, this isn't one of those 'crazy' California cults you hear about. It's a retreat and a teaching institution with a lineage that's thousands of years old. Master Lun-yi belongs to a tradition that goes right back to the Chan Buddhism of ancient China—most of which was destroyed by Communism. But fortunately for us, a branch went to Taiwan, where it was preserved."

"And do they teach that it's okay to abandon your children?"

"I was expecting that. Well, consider this: I've been so ill in Berkeley that I haven't been much good as a mother recently. Dad is number one for her anyway. It was him she asked—not me—to go see the peacocks. Anyway, I haven't abandoned her. I plan on still being involved. I don't think this is very different from a divorce situation, where one parent has custody and the other parent has less access."

"What's different is that it's your choice."

"I don't see the difference. Take a situation where a man leaves his wife for another woman and consequently ends up seeing his kids one weekend a month. Isn't that a choice as well? You do realize, don't you, that your shock about what I'm doing is based on old-fashioned ideas about the mother's primacy in child rearing?"

"So you feel okay about leaving her?"

"Not completely, because part of me has those same ideas. Every woman in our society does. Anyway, I'm not leaving her; I'm just taking a little time for myself. And I'll be the first to admit that I don't know what I'm doing. Or how long I'm going to stay on."

"Are you thinking of—I don't know how to put it—'joining' this order? I mean, becoming a nun?"

"Anything's possible. My destiny is up for grabs." She smiled.

I stood up impatiently. "The way you say that—it's ridiculous. As though you didn't have any part in the decision."

"You don't know how ill I've been. The asthma in Berkeley was making everyday activities almost impossible, and my energy was lower than it's ever been. So at this point in my life I gravitate toward anything that keeps me going. It's a matter of physical survival."

"I'm sorry you've been so ill." I felt chastened.

"Part of it is the chemical sensitivity thing. Basically, I've been poisoning myself for decades with art supplies. But I know there's an emotional component as well. I have to face that and do what I need to do to get better."

I waited for more information, but there was only silence, punctuated by the sharp meows of the peacocks.

"So what *is* it about?"

"A mix of things," she said. "I'm tired of my constant dissatisfaction with myself and the way things are—"

"With your marriage?"

"Michael has been a good husband, but some part of me hasn't settled down. I haven't been present in my marriage the way I hoped to be."

"And how is coming here going to solve that?"

"I want everything to settle in my mind so I can see things more clearly."

"All right then." I contained my exasperation.

"How about I take you for a tour? I want to show you the Great Hall."

"Okay."

We walked down a path, turned a corner around another building, and came to a one-story structure with a higher roof. A midcentury portico over the front entrance extended to the sides, where it sheltered two Chinese wall paintings about twenty feet high. To the left, a human figure with a massive, rectangular head and swirling robes played an elongated guitar-like instrument. To the right, another figure, with a red face and flame-like shapes coming out of his ears, danced furiously.

She led the way into the hall. Inside, the air was cool and spiced with incense. At the far end, a massive gold Buddha was the central object of worship. Hundreds or maybe thousands of smaller Buddhas, about a foot high, lined the walls on either side, sitting behind protective sheets of glass and illuminated by light coming in through the clerestory windows. About twenty people, some in monk's robes, others in street clothes, kneeled on cushions praying or meditating.

Anna turned toward me and whispered, "This is where I'm at peace."

"It's very…impressive." The space was sacred in a way both simple and exotic.

Anna moved forward and knelt. I heard her mumble something in a language I took to be Chinese. How far would she go—had she gone—into this whole thing? Was it right to bring her back out if she had found here some connection to a greater meaning?

She stood up and turned back toward me. We walked back out into a sun twice as hot and brilliant.

"I'm thirsty," I said.

"Let's find Esther and go back and get some water," she said.

She led me around to the back of the Hall and from there to a copse of trees near a shallow pond. Michael sat on a bench, watching Esther take pictures of the peacocks with her cell phone. The sight of his slumped shoulders made me sad in my bones. It had always worked that way for me—feeling sorry for him moved me as much as admiring or enjoying him. In this strange place, where time slowed down, there was a universe of reflection between each second and the next. And it was wordless and vast—the way Michael was a problem coming back again and again, needing to be worked out. Whether this was karma or Nietzsche's theory of eternal return, I didn't know, but this might be my last chance to make peace with our history. If I didn't work it out now, I never would. There was a commandment inside it that I had to obey.

"It's really quite odd," he said, gesturing toward the birds with his chin, "the way the males and females avoid each other. It's a wonder they ever get close enough to mate."

It was true. The males stood in all their glory on the right side of the pond, and the females, drab like brown pheasants, on the other.

"Maybe they stay separate because they're in a Buddhist institution so they're being chaste," Anna said, smiling. At least she hadn't lost her sense of humor.

"Do birds have penises?" Esther asked.

"Not really," Michael said. "They rub their cloacae together."

"What's that?" Esther asked.

"The cloaca is the bird hole that does everything," Michael said. "Don't they teach you anything at school?"

"How do you know so much about bird reproduction?" I asked.

"From going on photography shoots in the wild with Val."

We all fell silent, studying the peacocks.

"I'm really thirsty," I said again.

"Es, why don't you take Aunt Julia back to the water fountain at the reception hall?" Anna suggested.

"Would you mind?" I asked Esther.

Esther took my hand. As we walked away, I watched, out of the corner of my eye, as Anna and Michael moved closer together and sat down on a bench for conversation. They disappeared from view when Esther and I went around the front of the Great Hall. Passing by the gigantic, dancing Chinese gods, I felt a bit faint, dehydrated perhaps from the heat and the flight the day before. My heart rate was accelerating, too. I had the sense of a parallel reality converging upon me—a parallel reality that I was now, in a surreal flash, stepping into. A dream came back to me, of hovering above Michael in his house, watching his family life unfold. Esther was only three and running down the hall of the San Francisco apartment they'd lived in at the time—an apartment I'd never seen, yet clearly imagined. Then, in another dream, I was watching them move into their Berkeley home. Was it possible that I'd been dreaming about him regularly for years? And now Anna was leaving him, maybe, and he would be available again. Maybe. When we reached the fountain and I bent over and drank thirstily, my knees wobbled beneath me.

"I need to sit down, and I should call Uncle Ben," I said.

There was no bench; I checked that the grass was clear of peacock poop and sat down. I took out my cell and dialed Ben.

"Hi there," he said. "Esther is still chaperoning you, I hope?"

"She's right here. We're at the monastery. Anna and Michael are off somewhere talking." I told him about the peacocks and the Great Hall with the thousands of Buddhas behind glass.

"I guess you can't talk about Anna right now," he said.

"No," I said, looking at Esther, who was texting someone. "Except to say one word: weird."

"Weird?"

"She has turned into her opposite—the opposite of what she used to be."

"Call me when you can, okay?"

"Yes."

"Love you," he said.

"Me too," I said. I ended the call and put my phone away. "Who are you texting?" I asked Esther.

"One of my friends," she said.

Michael and Anna appeared across the lawn. Michael walked with sagging posture, whereas Anna stood straight and solid. I didn't know what she was going to do, but clearly she was separating out from Michael. She wouldn't go back to him. Hadn't Michael realized that? Why had he asked me to come to California?

A wave of nausea came over me. I was hit by cramps.

"I'm going in to use the bathroom," I said to Esther.

"Okay."

I went into the reception building and found the restroom where my bowels emptied themselves as I doubled over with painful intestinal cramps. When I came out, Michael and Anna and Esther were standing waiting for me.

"Are you okay?" Anna asked. "You're white."

"It's the heat," I said.

"You need some more fluids and maybe lunch," Michael said.

Anna looked at her watch. "And it's time for me to go to the midday service."

"We'll walk you," Michael said.

The two of them paired off ahead of us, while Esther finished texting.

"Maybe you should turn your phone off," I said.

"Sure." She put it in her pocket. "Let's talk about movies," she said.

"Movies?" I couldn't take my eyes off Michael and Anna.

"Like, what's your favorite musical? What's your favorite comedy? Or sci-fi—let's start with, what's your favorite sci-fi?"

"Sci-fi? That's easy. *Star Wars, Return of the Jedi*."

"What about *Star Trek: The Voyage Home*?"

"That's a good one, too."

"Let's imagine a conversation between Luke Skywalker and Spock. Luke says: I got to find my father, and Spock says: 'This desire of yours is just not logical...'"

We caught up with Michael and Anna at the entrance the Great Hall. The tall front doors were secured wide open, and men and women in robes were walking in, bowing to the Buddha, and taking their places kneeling on the cushions inside.

"I'm going in now," Anna said. "And after the service, there's afternoon meditation. Will I see you again?" she asked me.

"I think so."

"We'll stop on the way back down," Michael said.

She hugged Esther and me and kissed Michael on the cheek. We watched her go in through the tall doors and down the center aisle.

Michael looked at me. "Let's go have lunch," he said, "and then we'll hit the road."

I had no idea of what he was thinking or feeling. Of course, I hadn't for years.

19

THE BIT OF FRIED rice and tofu that I'd eaten in the sweltering monastery restaurant sat uncertainly in my stomach as the road to Mendocino swerved around and over small hills covered with wild bramble. Right when I thought I couldn't tolerate another turn, the land grew flat enough for a stretch of vineyard, and I was imagining an afternoon of wine tasting, complete with a picnic in the sun. Then all trace of humankind besides the road itself disappeared again, and we were taking turns so extreme that the road seemed to be going backward as much as forward. We were getting too far from civilization. As a typical New Yorker, I was more comfortable in Lisbon or Prague than in the "country" of my own nation.

"There's some Dramamine in the glove compartment if you need it," Michael said.

"It's too late for that," I said. I had my own supply, but without Ben to remind me to take it, I'd of course forgotten.

"You'll love Mendocino. It's beautiful. Worth the drive."

"I hope so."

"What about some Yo-Yo Ma? Everything's better with Bach. Balances the brain."

He put on some music, and I tried to settle in. Pines and eucalyptus alternated with redwood, and branches of low bramble formed a tunnel over the twisting road. A field opened up, offering a few cows and a couple of hawks spiraling smoothly overhead. We reached the junction with 128 and made a right, passing through a stretch of flatness to tiny Boonville—the very name of which lent respite—and then the road started winding forward again. The temperature dropped as we moved under a low bank of gray clouds, and I reached for Anna's sweater. We passed a dilapidated barn of rusted tin, then moved back into forest. Moss grew thick on the trees here; in some places it hung, curiously, like pale green beards, from the lower branches.

I glanced into the back seat. Esther had fallen asleep.

"So what do you think?" I asked Michael.

"About—?"

"Your situation."

He looked in the rearview mirror at his daughter.

"We can talk about it later."

"Tell me about Val and his mother, then."

"Val bought twenty acres of land on the Comptche road—"

"The what?"

He laughed. "Com-chee. It's a road so windy that only locals drive it—and live on it. So the land is cheap but beautiful. He built a house some years ago and lived there with his girlfriend until they split up. He also built another, smaller house for Stephanie—his mother. Esther loves it up here. She can run around like a wild Indian. Oops, I suppose that's politically incorrect now. And Val has a daughter from his girlfriend, who's just a little older than Esther. During the school year she's up in Arcata with her mom, then she comes down in the summer. The girls are great pals."

"Is the mom the same girlfriend he had...years ago?"

"Suzanne? Yes."

"But they split up?"

"Yeah."

We fell silent. I thought about my night with Val. Then I thought about my night with Michael. Glancing sideways at Michael, I saw again the way the skin had slackened under his chin, and reflected again that I wasn't looking so good myself. Did he still find me attractive? Did it matter? What was this irritating impulse inside me to move toward him? Why was it still there, after so many years?

"I need to close my eyes," I said.

"Go ahead and nap. We'll be there soon."

The privacy behind my closed lids felt good and my stomach grew calmer. But each time I drifted off, my head dropped, yanking my neck and waking me again.

"We're here," I heard him say.

He pulled into a dirt driveway that cut through the redwoods to a clearing where a two-story wooden house looked inviting with its large, modern windows and long clean lines.

"This is Val's house."

Esther opened her eyes and we unloaded our bags and went in. No one was home, so Michael opened the unlocked front door to a main living area that, thanks to multiple skylights, was bright in spite of the fog overhead.

I immediately noticed an upright piano. "Who plays?"

"Val's daughter," Michael said.

On the walls hung numerous photographs in simple black frames, many of them taken on the California coast, others in more exotic locations, like South America and Asia. I was drawn to some pictures of human figures taken from the back, studies of silhouettes against natural settings. In one, a woman with straight brown hair, wearing a dress, stood leaning against a wooden fence with her back to the camera. I studied the dark shape of the body, the hair cut at the shoulder, the posture tilted so that one hip was higher than the other—provocatively, perhaps—and realized it was me, at the goat farm that morning long ago.

Michael came up from behind me and looked at it.

"Hmm," he said.

"I'm going out to look for them," Esther interrupted.

She ran out the door.

"She'll run over to Stephanie's to get Val," Michael said.

"Where's that?"

"Further down the driveway. Not far. Steph had hip surgery a couple of weeks ago. We'll probably eat there tonight."

This landing in the midst of an odd assortment of people, some of whom I knew intimately and others not at all, left me feeling disoriented. I took a breath.

"Cuppa tea?" he said, smiling.

I smiled at the reference to those evenings at Yale, when Ben shut himself up in his bedroom to prepare for his exams, and Michael and I would have a cup of tea together halfway though the evening's studying.

There was an open kitchen with an island breakfast counter. I sat on one of the stools and watched him put the kettle on and rummage for teabags.

"So how was your conversation with Anna?" he asked.

"I don't have much to report. She seems pretty confused."

He nodded. "You asked me last night how Anna and I have been getting along. It's such a difficult question. Compared to what? What's marriage supposed to be like?" As he sat down next to me at the counter, his knees brushed mine.

"What did you think I could accomplish by seeing her? You didn't think I'd get her to drop everything and go home, did you?"

"I wanted the moral support, I suppose."

"Well, I'm here."

"I'm glad you're here, Jul." The nickname signaled a change in register.

"I don't think you really know why you called me," I said.

"You're right. I don't. But in some way you're part of the puzzle."

"Am I?"

"Of course."

The front door opened and Esther walked in followed by Val and his daughter.

Val looked exactly the same, as wiry and fit as seventeen years before, with the same beard, barely tinged by gray, and Mediterranean tan. He was, if anything, more interesting and handsome for the time that had passed—sculpted and beaten by the years into something beautiful, like a piece of driftwood polished by sand and water. He shook my hand and drew me toward him to kiss me on the cheek.

"This is my daughter, Jackie," he said proudly.

"So you're living in the woods now?" I asked. "I love your house."

"It's great, isn't it?" he said. "And it costs me nothing to live here, so I have money to travel."

"All over the world, I see." I gestured to the photographs with my head.

"I have no complaints," he said.

"What are you girls up to?" Michael asked.

"We're going to play Scrabble with Stephie."

"I think I'll take Julia into town. What do you think?" Michael turned toward me. "And we can go out to the headlands, too, for a walk."

"Sure."

"Get some wine, won't you?" Val said. "Then come out to Mom's when you get back. We'll have dinner there."

"You'll need an extra jacket," Michael warned me. "It's cold on the bluffs."

I grabbed something and we went out. Getting into the car, I saw Val and the girls head down the path deeper into the woods.

"The girls like his mother?"

"They adore her. She's like a grandmother to Esther, which is great since my own mother was useless, and Anna's relationship with Linda— well, as you know, it was pretty awful."

Michael pulled off the property and we headed into town, taking the Comptche road to the coast, then swerving on Route 1 along the bluffs until Mendocino appeared, quaint, Victorian, proud of its time warp. Dotted with cylindrical water towers on stilts and widow's turrets roofed with brown shingles, it's a town where many a forlorn wife once looked at the ocean, praying for her sea-faring husband. Michael parked on the main street in front of a small supermarket. At the north end of the street was a stunning view of black cliffs beaten by frothing, white waves.

"You can look in the shops if you want, while I get some wine for dinner."

He disappeared, and I stepped into the jewelry store next door. I felt excited. For years I'd dreamed of this—of being alone with Michael again. I decided to call Ben again to steady myself, but on taking my cell phone out of my bag I found there was no service. We were far from everything here. I turned my cell off and applied myself to looking at the earrings on display. There was a pair of large hammered gold hoops that caught my attention, and I bought them. It was the kind of impulsive purchase I never would have made at home.

"I think I'll put them on now," I said to the saleswoman, a hippie in her fifties with long graying hair and an ethnic-looking tunic. I took off the topaz studs I was wearing and placed them in the box she offered me. I was fastening the hoops, looking at myself in the mirror, when, holding a paper bag with a couple of wine bottles sticking out, Michael appeared in the reflection.

"Good choice," he said.

"You think so?" I asked, turning toward him.

He lifted his free hand and brushed my hair away from my face, tucking some of it behind my ear. There was a sweet familiarity to the gesture.

"They balance the thinness of your face," he said.

We got back in the car and drove through the town, past a tiny, burgundy-colored church housing the health food store and a sprawling, shingled art center, onto a neck of uninhabited land leading to the ocean. Cutting through a grassy plateau, we reached a parking lot overlooking the Pacific.

"Let's walk."

We set out over headlands stripped of trees, covered only by grasses and the occasional bush. Up and down the coast the ocean crashed loudly against dark stony cliffs. I could hear sea lions faintly barking in the distance. Michael walked ahead of me, silent, on the narrow dirt trail. After being in the car all day, I relished the movement and revivifying cold air. I was so far from everything familiar that it was hard to believe I'd left New York only the previous morning. Again I felt I had fallen into an alternate dimension where time was spreading the minutes further and further apart.

We walked and walked.

"I'm getting tired," I said.

"Let's sit."

Cross-legged, we looked out at the ocean. I wondered how he saw it. Reading my mind, he said, "Today it looks like it's in E-flat."

"Any modulations?"

"Oh, yes, all over the place." He gave me that grin I used to adore. "I love the ocean," he went on. "It makes everything all right the way nothing else can. It's the reason I could never leave California—the coast here is so amazing."

He looked at me.

"This is difficult, being with you like this again," I said, hoping to diffuse the awkwardness of it.

"You mean—because we made a mistake?"

"A mistake?" I was taken aback.

"Sixteen years ago."

"I didn't know we'd made a mistake."

"Yeah, maybe not. Maybe if I'd married you instead, you'd be the one checked into a monastery now—what do you think?" His voice was flat, detached.

"You wanted me to leave Ben first, and I wasn't brave enough. That's what it boiled down to." Talking about it made me hot and cold, even so many years later.

"You don't blame me for that, do you?" he asked.

"No, of course not. You were justified," I said. "What you said about my wanting to 'try you out' before breaking with Ben—you were right."

"So things couldn't have been different than they were, could they have?" He looked at me earnestly, as though I was the one with the answer.

"No," I said. "But I really—I really suffered."

"Did you?" he said, and he reached for my hand. "So did I."

"You seemed...not to. The way you took up with Anna so quickly."

He looked down. "I was so confused, and there was so much going on in my head that it was just a noisy jumble. I couldn't really think or feel under the circumstances. The only thing I could hold on to was what I wanted for myself—stability, kids, simplicity—and it didn't seem like you could offer me any of those things. I didn't want to be dragged into another complicated love triangle. I'd already had enough of those." He looked back up at me. "So I had to go—run, really—in the opposite direction."

"So there it is. We each did what we had to do."

"So then why does it feel like a mistake?" He stroked the back of my hand with his thumb. His voice had never been deeper or graver. I had always loved the sound of it. And I still did.

"I don't know, but it can't be, because you have Esther."

"Well, I guess this is an opportunity to figure it all out, isn't it?"

He let go of my hand as we stood up, then reached for it again. Waves twenty feet high crashed noisily below, and I had the vision of an earthquake propelling us over the edge and to our deaths. At the same time, holding his hand made me feel a peacefulness that was broad and bright, like a mountain valley filled with a still noon light. Here was something I'd wanted for years—an opportunity for resolution.

The path was narrow and we walked back to the parking lot shoulder to shoulder, holding hands.

When we got to the car, he said, "We'll have a nice dinner with the others and then we'll feel better."

Glancing sideways at him, I noticed that with every passing hour he was looking years younger.

Back at the house, I felt overwhelmed by jet lag and sea air and the unease created by our conversation. I needed to lie down. Michael led me upstairs to Val's room.

"Val has been sleeping at his mom's since her surgery. This'll be your room."

He left, closing the door behind him, and I pulled off my jeans and got into bed. On the walls hung more of Val's nature photography and a small acrylic painting of horses whirling in space that might have been Anna's. A skylight overhead admitted a greenish-gray light. I rolled onto my side and pulled the covers over my head. There was too much to digest here—the visit to see Anna, the stalemate in their marriage, Esther's situation. And there was my implied part in all of it. The deadness in Michael's voice during our talk on the headlands expressed my own feeling about what had happened years before. The past felt heavy and incomprehensible.

What made it worse was that Michael's presence made me think about Ben differently, as it had years before. Instead of seeing the sweetness and the good times, I felt again a yearning for intimacy that hadn't been met. Certainly something had changed recently. Was it the anticlimax after the success of *Women, Be Rich*, or Ben's involvement with his own career? Over the past few years, I had stopped desiring him; maybe the reason wasn't approaching menopause, as I'd thought, but that the bizarre commuter's life we'd led for sixteen years had taken its toll. How sad that it felt like an enormous relief to be away from him and the pretenses that kept our relationship going. How could I bring an adopted child into this weird marriage I'd made for myself? Clearly I was hoping to infuse new life into a moribund relationship.

The intensity of the sorrow jogged something in my brain. I got up and looked around for a scrap of paper. There was none. Going to my bag, I took out my journal and wrote:

I can't say how it happened,
the slow sad fraying of thread
and pleat and cotton nap
as I stood outside, against the wind,
and you huddled inside.

I was almost fifty, and I'd made a mess of things. Was it too late to break out of the trap I'd created for myself?

The thought of Ben, of going back to New York, made me want to zone out for a while. Val's house in the woods was absolutely quiet. I dived into a deep nap.

I was awakened by a feeling of movement—Michael sitting down on the bed next to me, his hand on my arm shaking me gently.

"Jul, if you don't get up now, you won't be able to sleep tonight," I heard him say. "And it's time for dinner."

My neck felt stiff on the pillow. I'd hurt it earlier in the day when, dozing in the car, my head had dropped and rolled around. Opening my eyes, I looked at the way Michael's hairline moved forward into a widow's peak, at the size of his head, at the brown of his eyes. And for the first time since my arrival, he looked exactly the same as he had twenty-six years before, when I'd first known him at Yale.

20

"LET'S TAKE THE PATH through the woods, instead of the driveway," Michael said as we stepped out of Val's house.

Obediently, I followed him. Brown fronds crackled underfoot as we took a narrow path toward Stephanie's. The deeper we went into the magnificent forest, the farther I felt from my life back home. In the damp, cold summer evening, I was happy to have both the sweater and jacket Michael had advised. Although the light was dimming now, I had the sense of starting a new day after my nap.

"I thought redwoods were supposed to be taller," I said, looking up through the lacy canopy that floated about thirty yards above us.

"This is all second-growth," Michael explained. "The original forest was logged and destroyed at the turn of the century, but later came back."

"So this isn't the forest primeval."

"No, it's more like the forest of eternal return."

The path dipped down to a low area crossed by a trickle of a creek. Then we made a short climb, our feet sliding back at times on the fallen branches. We heard barking and a golden retriever bounded toward us happily.

"It's Maxie—Stefanie's dog. We're almost there."

With Maxie in the lead, we reached a clearing. Through the windows of an A-frame cottage, complete with a smoking chimney, I saw Val. A little tent was set up on a redwood deck next to the house.

"Who sleeps outside?" I asked.

"The girls are probably planning on it."

Michael opened the door for me, and I stepped in. A strikingly beautiful old woman with a heavy gray bun at the back of her head approached leaning on a walker.

"So you're Julia," she said.

Val had spoken to her about me.

"And you're Stephanie."

"Stephie." She had a wide smile.

"Hi, Stephie." Something about the way she held her head forward caused me to step toward her and, careful of the walker, kiss her radiant, fine-lined face.

"Help me sit down." She spoke with an indefinable, highly musical accent.

I supported her as she sat on the couch. The living area of the cottage was a miniature version of the main house, with the kitchen, dining area, and living room all in one space. Esther and Jackie were playing Monopoly on the floor by the fireplace. Val, who was standing in the kitchen cooking, offered me a glass of wine.

"Something smells fantastic. What are you making?"

"Hippie lasagna. Like the kind Robin used to make."

Robin used to tuck spinach and eggplant between layers of pasta and sauce, always in a pan large enough to feed whoever dropped in.

Michael helped Stephanie sit at the table and we took our places. The table was set with hand-blown glass plates, each with a different swirling pattern and color scheme. The wine glasses, too, proclaimed some glass worker's gift and vision. Soon wine and food were being served.

"Did you take Julia to the Art Center?" Stephanie asked Michael.

"It was closed," Michael said.

"I was very involved, once," she said to me.

"Are you an artist?" I asked.

"I was an actress first."

"My mother was an actress, too," I said to Val.

"Something we have in common, then," Val said. "My mother's had a fascinating life."

"Yes. Born in Turin, married a Scotsman, followed him to Edinburgh..."

"And then to London," continued Val, who clearly enjoyed reliving her story.

"Your English is perfect," I said, now hearing the Scottish and Italian inflections in her speech.

"I studied hard because I wanted to go on the stage. And I did. I was on the stage in London."

"So how did you end up here?"

"My husband was a drifter as well as an artist. He fell in love with Mendocino so we moved here. I was involved with the town theater. Then when he began blowing glass, I gave up the stage to work with him."

"So you made these?" I asked, amazed, picking up the wine glass to examine it.

She laughed. "These are warm-ups—like scales for a musician. Val, show her some real things."

Val went to a cabinet and brought out a vase, which he held before me. I didn't ask to touch it because I was afraid to. A pattern of tall green grasses with tiny blue flowers floated inside the glass. A bouquet placed in it would appear to be springing up from a field of bluebells.

"Did you mind giving up the stage?" I asked. As beautiful as the vases were, the feminist in me bristled at this story of a woman who had abandoned the art of her choice for one chosen by her husband.

"Not at all. It turned out I was better at glass than acting. And glass-blowing is the perfect craft for this climate because you're always near fire." She laughed. "The Italian in me liked being toasty."

She seemed happy. I wondered if I could be so happy, alone in the woods, widowed, no longer practicing my art. But it seemed she still had an occupation.

"Of course I'm not strong enough to do that anymore, so I do other things," she said, a little mysteriously.

"Like?"

"I make lotions and potions." She chuckled again. "I'm a witch now."

After we ate, the girls went back to their Monopoly game, and the adult conversation took a more practical direction. Val and Michael started discussing the class they would teach on Saturday, confirming who had signed up for it and which points of photography they'd cover. They would camp out with the group and return on Sunday.

"Aunt Julia, we're stuck, come help us out," Esther said.

I went over. Both girls were penniless and had mortgaged all their properties.

"You girls are finished. I say you start all over again."

"How about we each get a thousand dollars from the bank to keep going?" Esther suggested.

"That's cheating," I said.

"Not if we both do it," Jackie said. "Then it's equal."

"Yeah, and not if *you* give us the thousand dollars," Esther said. "Then it's like a surprise bonus or something."

The financial advisor in me resisted, but I sat down on the floor with them and counted out the money.

"You look tired," Michael said to me a little later. We were eating a cake the girls had made under Stephanie's direction.

"It's past midnight in New York."

"The girls are sleeping in the tent tonight," Val said. "And I'm staying here to help Mom. So the house is yours." He gave me a look, both roguish and wry.

"Thanks for dinner," I said.

"Julia, it's always a pleasure to see you," Val said.

"Take a flashlight," Stephanie said, gesturing to a basket near the door with several.

Michael and I stepped out into the night. "We'll take the driveway back," he said.

Light from a three-quarter moon filtered down through the redwood canopy onto the dirt road. He turned on the flashlight.

"Hope we don't meet any bears or wildcats," he said.

"Really?" I was startled.

He laughed. "Just teasing. I mean, there are bears and wildcats here, but we won't meet them."

We started to walk. Knowing that we'd be alone in Val's house, I couldn't help but want him again. But the way back to intimacy felt closed as we walked in silence. Michael's mind was probably elsewhere—on his wife, who had sequestered herself with a bunch of shaved-headed monks, and on Esther, who would suffer most if the marriage failed. But why was I thinking *if* the marriage failed? Hadn't it failed already in some way?

Hadn't it been a mistake? But—I kept coming back to it—how could one speak of mistake when they had a gorgeous child? Thinking about what it would be like to have a daughter like Esther, all I could do was ask myself why, when natural conception had failed, I hadn't initiated an adoption earlier. I'd been slow, almost paralyzed, around every major decision in my life.

And I'd wasted opportunities. Being "childfree," I could have followed my muse and written poetry, but I got busy doing other things. In spite of all my financial and professional accomplishments, I felt disappointed in myself.

I had to consider Ben's role in my artistic block. By hooking up with an expert in contemporary poetry, I'd set my inner critic up with a job for life: whatever I wrote wouldn't be as good as some poet Ben had read, taught, and dissected. But if Ben had been partly responsible—hadn't supported my agenda to generate either life or poetry—in the end the fault was my own. I'd lived my life with a contracted, defensive attitude.

As Val's house came into sight, Michael interrupted my gloomy reverie.

"So what do you think we should do next?" he asked. "About Anna, I mean."

He held the door open for me.

"I don't know." I went in, plopped myself down on the couch. "I really don't know what I can do here."

"I guess I was hoping not so much that you'd *do* anything, but that you'd *see* something for me—have some insight into the situation. As a woman and her cousin and all that."

He sat down on the couch next to me.

"It's your marriage, Michael." I couldn't hide my irritation.

"All right, then."

"Sorry. I don't feel well. My neck really hurts."

"Wait a minute. I have something for that." He got up and went upstairs. A minute later, he came back down holding a glass jar.

"Some homemade salve, courtesy of Stephanie. You want a neck rub?"

I blushed. "That's an offer I won't refuse."

"Come sit in a chair." He pulled a chair out from the dining table.

I went over and sat in it.

"Don't be shy, open your shirt collar up a bit. By the way, this has cannabis in it."

"Cannabis?"

"Cannabis—you know, marijuana."

"Stephanie makes salves with marijuana in them?"

"It's a vasodilator. Which means it promotes blood flow."

He rubbed some on his hands, which he placed on my neck.

"Do you know what you're doing?" I asked.

"I've practiced a lot on Anna," he said.

It wasn't exactly what I needed to hear.

"Okay."

My emotional reaction to his touching my neck was so intense that it took me a moment to enjoy the massage.

"Can you relax a bit?" he asked. "You know, neck tension is a sign of a disjunction between the head and the heart."

"That sounds like California-speak to me."

"It is."

I closed my eyes and let the feeling of his warm hands on my neck come in. Just as I was starting to relax and enjoy myself, he gave me a pat on the shoulder.

"There—you're done. I have to go wash my hands." He went to the kitchen sink.

I buttoned my shirt up, went back to the couch and sat down. Why were we "hanging out"? Shouldn't I just get up and go to bed? Well, why not? I was wide-awake now.

He came back to the couch and showed me his hands, which were bright red. "See how the cannabis improves the circulation." His eyes met mine. "You want something to drink? Brandy or something?"

"*Brandy?*" I laughed. "Since when do you drink brandy?"

"I don't, but Val does." He went back to the kitchen, opened a cabinet door. "He's got brandy and, uh, let's see, some weird Italian bitters that Stephanie made, and whiskey."

"I'll go with the brandy," I said.

Outside the crickets were impossibly loud. I imagined the males, huge, in the forest floor, rubbing their wings together to please the females. The old tension was rising in me again, and it wasn't simply sexual. It was the pressure of all the things we'd never said to each other. Could there possibly be so many, after all the conversations we'd once had? Yes, because we were starting all over again, from a different vantage point this time.

He brought the brandies over and set them on the coffee table. "Okay," he said. "We're alone now. Let's talk."

21

IT FELT LIKE A summit meeting.

"What are we going to talk about?" I asked.

"Anna. And everything else. Life. Like we used to." He sat down next to me, a large and comfortable man sinking into a large and comfortable couch.

"I don't know what's going on with Anna," I said, "but I don't think she's coming back."

"It doesn't look like it, does it?"

"How will Esther be with that?"

"I don't know. I'll have to take her up to Ukiah a lot to visit." He seemed a little numb.

"If Anna becomes—takes orders—whatever—I don't know the Buddhist vocabulary for it—would she be allowed out? I mean, could she go home to visit Esther?"

"I don't know. I've never been married to a Buddhist nun before." He smiled wanly. "Let's talk about you instead. I want to know more. Your book must have made you a lot of money. And now you're going to adopt a child. It sounds like things have really come together for you, even without that intimacy you wanted."

"I've been hugely successful and yet I feel I've made a mess of things."

"Meaning?"

"The only thing I wanted most was to write poetry, not books about money. And the other thing I really wanted was to have a child. If Ben and I adopt now, we'll be seventy when our kid graduates from college. Unless we get an older child. But older children usually come with problems—like attachment disorder or developmental issues—that I'm not sure I'm ready for."

"Isn't it a case of better late than never?"

"It's a case of not knowing what I'm doing."

"Well, regret—as we both know—is just a fantasy about something that couldn't have been. Like our regret about us."

He was looping back to our conversation on the bluff.

"If things couldn't have been otherwise, why do we regret?" I asked.

"Unprocessed grief," he said, with that clinical detachment he fell into when a topic became painful.

I couldn't be as detached. Suddenly it was all coming up for me—not only the regret and the grief, but also the thoughts about those feelings that I'd kept to myself for sixteen years.

"You made me feel completely alive. And I needed you to feel creative," I said. "I mean, when I knew you, I wanted to write and play music, and then when you stepped out of my life, I no longer wanted to. The urge just crumbled, and I couldn't force it." I paused, and then I said something that felt huge: "Michael, you were my muse."

I was admitting to him that he had touched some place in my soul that no one else had or could, that he had awakened me through some kind of mysterious alchemy. Perhaps that was the meaning of the Sleeping Beauty tale: love wakes you up. In therapy, Sandra had suggested that I was after some missing part of myself and that, if I kept searching with her, I'd find it. But I had stopped looking and let the dream go underground.

"We sparked each other," Michael said. "We set each other on fire." The flatness of his voice suggested the spark was dead. "We gave each other the intensity that artists need to create."

"But you were able to continue—to find that spark in Anna—whereas I haven't found it anyplace else."

"For the first few years, yes, I tried to find it in Anna, and there were moments I thought I had found it. Then it sort of—dissipated."

"Then how did you keep going?"

"Honey, I found it in you." The word "honey" glimmered, a warm ray of light in the dark place we were in.

"In me?"

"In remembering you, thinking about you, keeping you alive inside me. It's you I've composed for, again and again."

I remember it all exactly—every sentence, gesture, act of that night. Because I preserved it, like strawberries in sugar, or olives in brine.

I started to cry. "Oh, Michael. We were so stupid."

He cried, too, the way men do: silent, slow tears. "You were my muse, too, but a difficult one, Jul. After all, you decided I wasn't good enough for you. That's what it boiled down to. If you hadn't judged me—things might have turned out differently."

Guilty as charged, I fell silent with remorse.

"The irony," he went on, "is that you judged me harshly because you knew me too well. You decided—at the very beginning, when we were at Yale—that I was unreliable because I'd had so many relationships. And later, when I let you see my self-destructiveness and depression, you didn't think it could work. Basically, you just reflected the negative opinion I had of myself. But Anna, who didn't know me as well you did, was able to imagine me differently."

"If I hadn't judged you, I would have had the courage to go with my feelings and leave Ben." I wept noisily and my shoulders heaved.

He scooted over and put an arm around me. "Enough crying, Jul. It's wonderful that we can sit here and talk about it, don't you think? It makes the grieving less lonely."

I rested my head on his shoulder and put an arm around his waist. There had been nights, alone in New York during the workweek, when Ben was in Princeton, that I'd allow myself to think of him and would fall asleep after pleasuring myself to memories of my single night with Michael. It was a ride of minutes, after which—in the first years—I sometimes cried, then fell asleep. It was the ritual of the broken-hearted, who even after the cord has been cut, look back hoping to taste again, somewhere in the body and the mind, the incredible sweetness that's been lost. And the ritual had been an attempt to contain and ultimately exorcise the grief, but what it did instead was to preserve my relationship with him on a subterranean level. With the passing years, yes, the longing had diminished, but it had never disappeared.

"Why are we doing this? I thought I was finally getting over you," I said.

"Was this a mistake, then, having you come out to visit?"

"Maybe. Maybe we'll have to start the grieving cycle all over again."

"It's karmic, Jul. All this is happening for a reason."

"You once said there was no one up there orchestrating our opportunities for us."

"I did say that, didn't I?"

"I remember everything you've ever said, Michael. Every word."

He laughed. "Well, I take it back. What I mean by karmic is that you and me—it's like a problem that'll keep coming back until we solve it."

I had a vision of us meeting every ten years until we died—each time renewing the wounding, so that the whole cycle of grieving would start again. I saw myself at seventy and him at eighty, sitting before the fire rehearsing our regrets. It was too pathetic. But then I felt his hand gently stroking my neck. He had a different solution in mind.

"So what you're suggesting," I said, "is that we need to solve it now?"

"What do you think?"

Here was desire again, after a long absence. My stomach fluttered. Yes, I desired him, but I had a keen sense of my own fragility: what would it be like to spend a night or a few nights together and then part again? I didn't think I was strong enough for that. I couldn't go through another round of having and losing. And if he meant something else, something more drastic and permanent, there were even more obstacles this time—not only Ben, but the adoption we were planning, and Esther and Anna, too.

But I saw myself leaving Ben; I could even give up the idea of adopting a child.

"Are you talking about just now—or are you talking about more than now?"

"I'm talking about you moving out to California to be with me. I can't move back to New York because of Esther."

"And—what about Esther? How do you think she'll take it?"

"She'll resent you at the beginning, I suppose. But she already loves you."

"And Anna?" We were on a super highway now, and my heart beat hard.

"We have to tell Anna—and Ben—as soon as possible."

In that moment, everything seemed easy. The impact on Esther, the divorces we'd need, what I'd do with my business, starting over again in California—I had faith that it could all be resolved. I was sure this was

the right thing to do, because I had—in a secret corner of my brain—
imagined, for years, that we would find our way back to each other.

He kissed me gently on the lips, then looked at me inquiringly.

"Let's go upstairs," I said.

"Yes," he said, kissing me again.

"I'm a little nervous. I haven't had sex in a while."

He laughed. "Well, I'm an old man—don't think I can do it three
times in one night anymore!"

"It doesn't matter," I said, "because we'll have a lot of nights now."

I'd yearned so long and so hard for him that I was barely conscious of
what was happening. How do you remember, record all the details of
union with another, when, in that union, you were so obliterated as to
have no vantage point? No part of the "I" as an observer able to jot down
everything that happened?

Cherries preserved in honey. Flowers between pressed pages.

I remember standing face to face upstairs, in Val's room, next to the
bed. The sudden exultation. No more tears, just wanting to laugh with
cosmic joy. He put his fingers to the zipper of my jeans, and I said "too
fast" and repositioned his hand on my waist, wanting to slow him down,
so that I could savor it, but he wouldn't be controlled. It was like being in
a sudden storm sweeping up and across a prairie when there's nowhere to
go for cover besides a tree—which is the most dangerous place to go when
there's lightning. So you just stand and let the rain and wind take you, you
risk being struck by a bolt of fire. Which is what I did, as he kissed me,
sucking on my tongue too hard, and I felt the pull at the back of my throat,
and he grabbed me harder between my legs and then pushed me onto the
bed and then back till I was lying down with my legs off the bed, my feet
on the floor. He picked my legs up and slid my jeans off and my panties.

"What do you want?" he asked me.

"I want you to do to me all the things you didn't do sixteen years ago."

"Me, too." He reached up to take my hand and gently sank his teeth
into me. "How many times I've thought about all the things I didn't get
around to doing to you. I didn't look at you enough. I want to look at you."

He spread my knees, opened me up. "You're beautiful," he said.
"You're gorgeous."

His tongue moved across me, like a finger of sun tracing a groove of warmth and light in sand, and I, like sand, let myself soften, be pushed and probed and played with. I was parted in two, and he was the divider, and I could only give way, melting and dissolving. It was the same thing Ben had done to me hundreds of times, but it felt new, as though it had never been done to me before. Michael's tongue was exact, insistent, and his teeth grazed me with a daring precision that filled me with a primordial, rapturous terror.

"You get naked, too," I said.

I took off my shirt as he took off his pants and got in the bed next to me, his brown irises caressing my face like a warm breeze. My desire mixed with a compassionate tenderness for the way he'd aged as I touched his body thickened by the passage of time, his skin marked by age spots. Only his erection, when my eyes and fingers met it, looked and felt the same. I wrapped my hand around him and the warmth in my hand felt like perfume. He moaned with pleasure as my palm slid down to cup him beneath. He was avid, impatient, and placing a hand on my shoulder, pushed me down so I could take him in my mouth. I thought, *He's almost sixty. I wonder how many more years we have here.* I was hit by the fear of not getting enough before he was too old to get it up anymore and I was too dry to let him in. I was stricken by the pathos of the years we'd wasted. But then the thoughts vanished as, with his hand in my hair, he pulled my head up and down, controlling my movement. The only thing I wanted was to give him pleasure and to do it for the rest of my life. He pushed my head down again and I opened for him. This was my way of possessing him, and everything we did would bind us, making our decision to be together irrevocable. There would be no going back after this, because we'd wanted it too much, too long. I pushed back up against his hand and moved up to look at him. I had to tell him how profound it was for me.

"I made love to you in my head hundreds of times," I said, "and would weep afterwards."

"You don't have to weep anymore." A pause. "I love you," he said— for the first time. I'd waited twenty-five years for those words. He climbed on top of me and bent my legs, lifting my knees up to my shoulders.

"I'm not so flexible anymore," I said.

"Yes, you are," he said.

Holding my legs up and apart with his arms, he entered me. I was soft and wet and open, and the warmth was not only in me but all through and around me. I felt more naked than I'd ever felt before, I was flying through a swirling red space with tiger teeth in the nape of my neck and yellow fires blazing on the horizon. I was his, as I had been since we'd first done it so many years before. I crossed my ankles across the small of his back, hooking my feet together. His rhythm suited me perfectly, and I was a fluid helix moving tighter and tighter around him.

He paused, kissed me on my neck. "I want to fuck you till you're unconscious. Till you give yourself over to me completely."

"Do it," I said, and then the youthful sex energy returned, flaring and firing—poignant so long past the years of fertility, piteous in middle age—and we mated like a buck and a doe in the woods, or a pair of wolves in moonlit snow, or wild horses on a prairie. I was the she-animal in heat, wanting to be stamped and marked and he was the male, stamping and marking; we rode the spiraling pleasure energy faster and faster. There was no arguing with everything in me that wanted to give in, give up, and give over to him.

Truly, after this, there was no way I'd ever go back to Ben.

22

SHIFTING IN BED IN the early morning, moving closer. Putting my arm around his waist, moving a hand down, taking his erection in my hand, holding it, then letting go, drifting back to sleep.

Waking again, the square white beam of day coming through the skylight overhead, the sounds of birds outside. Lying on my other side now, him behind me, cradling me.

Feeling perfectly peaceful, the immensity of the heart when it finally agrees with itself, and body and mind soften around it, murmuring a gigantic yes to what is.

Then the consequences of what has just happened rouse me. The pain we'll cause. Tell Ben, tell Anna, tell Esther. About Ben, it will be a ripping of sorts, but less than it would have been sixteen years ago, and I've had enough of not having enough. About Anna, I go blank. She's a cipher, I don't know what to think or feel about her. Mostly Esther worries me. How will she react? My niece will become my stepdaughter. She'll grieve for her mother, and, as Michael said, probably be rejecting of me initially, but eventually we'll be okay.

And I'm okay with the thought of leaving New York. I've put myself in a box, and it's time to get out and leave everything behind. I like California.

Starting my business all over on the West Coast won't be easy.

Well, none of it will be easy, but I have no choice but to flow with the energy of events.

As Michael's arm pulls me in closer, the feeling of solution—the equal sign—comes to the fore, and I drift back into sleep.

We were both awakened by noise downstairs.

"Shit," Michael said, "I wonder if that's Esther."

We leaped up and put on our clothes from the previous day. We stood face to face, running our fingers through our hair.

"Am I going to tell her now?" he said. "Maybe after breakfast."

We went downstairs and found Val, making coffee in the kitchen.

"Hey, guys, good morning," he said. "What do you want for breakfast? Oatmeal? Eggs?"

"Toast," I said.

"And eggs," Michael added, "if you're cooking. What are the girls up to?"

"They're making breakfast for Stephanie. I decided to come back here for my double-kick fair-trade Costa Rican blend." Val crossed his arms and looked at us, grinning like a gremlin or a sprite. "So?" he asked.

"So?" Michael repeated.

"What are you guys going to do?"

Was it that obvious that Michael and I had spent the night together?

"Julia's going to move out to California to live with me," Michael said, drawing me toward him.

It sounded like a rehearsal of something he was getting ready to perform many times, for many people.

"Julia," Val said, "I always dreamed of you in that bed upstairs—but not with someone else."

"I knew I could trust you to say the right thing," I said.

"Or not to say anything at all," he said, and I knew he'd forever be discreet about the night I'd spent in his van. "It sounds like you two should spend the day together," he continued. "I'll take care of the girls."

Michael turned toward me. "Should we take a walk on the beach after breakfast? And then we can drive back to Ukiah and tell Anna."

On the edge of Mendocino there's a little white church, with a tall steeple covered with gray shingles, and behind it a staircase leading down, through a patch of bramble, to the cove where Big River, exiting from the coastline forest, broadens at its outlet and flows into the ocean. As we descended the concrete stairs covered with sand people tracked up, I took in the tall green waves crashing on the rocky coast. Closer in, the beach was strewn with enormous weather-beaten tree trunks and strands of kelp, some of them twenty feet long. A chilly wind, coming in over the water, hit us.

"I wonder what kind of day we're going to have today," he said, and I knew he wasn't talking about the weather.

"Should I call Ben before we leave?"

"Why don't you call him from Ukiah," Michael said. "That way we can break the news at the same time."

A dozen albatross appeared out of nowhere, flying low out toward the sea. Perhaps it was the size of the birds' heads, almost as large as their bodies, which kept them from soaring higher.

We sat on a log polished gray by sun and water. I traced the black lines in the wood with a finger as the conversation turned to practical things, like whether I should return to New York on Tuesday as planned or take a few more days, and how much time I'd need to sell my business and sublet my apartment for the remainder of the lease. That this was *finally* happening seemed miraculous. On the other hand, there would be pain in doing what needed to be done in order to take everything to the conclusion we desired. Internally, I had already separated from Ben, but on the surface of things we were still a couple, and his agreeing to an adoption was a huge victory that wouldn't be easy to relinquish. For a split second, I wondered whether Michael might be willing to adopt an older child with me. Probably not. I had to face it—his age. The cruelty of the number fifty-eight. Well, I'd have my hands full being Esther's stepmom. Whatever the complications, holding Michael's hand gave me a sense of total power over my happiness: I was so sure this was meant to be that I wouldn't feel guilty for long about Ben or Anna or even Esther.

We got up and followed the edge of the river across the wide sandy cove to the ocean's edge. The wind was stronger and colder by the sea, the sky overcast with morning fog. I put my arms around Michael's waist and he dropped his cheek against my head, lifting it occasionally to kiss my hair. I was peaceful in a way that felt completely new. I reveled in it—the wind, the warmth of his face, the clear brightness in my heart. This was joy.

As we drove back to Ukiah a couple of hours later, weaving along the infernally looping road, our mood became more somber.

"How are you going to tell Ben?" he asked.

"I'm just going to say: I've decided to move to California to be with Michael." I needed to rehearse it. I opened my handbag to check that my cell was sufficiently charged. We were still in an out-of-service zone. "What are you going to say to Anna?"

"I'll say: Julia has decided to move to California to be with me."

"Do you want me there?"

"Sure. I mean, you *are* here."

"Did you—uh—did you ever tell her about the night we spent together in New York?"

"No."

"And she never guessed?"

"I don't think so. Why should she have?"

"I don't know."

We drove along the north side of the Navarro River, which cuts through an area of dipped land. I looked at my watch.

"Can we stop and get something to eat?"

"We'll stop in Boonville."

Exiting the forest, we came to the town in question—just a few shops on the north side of the street. We stepped into a little bakery and found what we needed, some focaccia with cheese and olives and a couple of lemonades. We got back in the car to eat.

"Sky's clearing," he said, nodding at the low clouds clearing overhead.

"Yup."

"Do you think you'll be okay living in my house?" he asked.

"What do you mean?" I picked the olives off the focaccia to eat them first.

"I mean, in a house where I lived with Anna."

"I hadn't thought about it."

"I'm halfway through the mortgage, just starting to pay off the principal in a big way. I'd hate to sell and move."

"Maybe we could just buy a new bed and repaint the bedroom?"

It made me ecstatic to talk about it. There might as well have been rainbows in the sky and fairies dancing on the hood of the car. But I'm a practical person, and my brain likes to crunch figures. "Maybe I could buy her out of her portion of the house. Then it would feel more like mine." The idea of buying Anna out sounded smart but felt surreal.

"I wonder what she would do with the money," he said. "Maybe donate it to the monastery."

"You think she's that crazy?"

"I don't know." He shrugged and changed the subject. "You know, Jul, I realize all this means giving up that adoption you were thinking of doing with Ben, and I wanted to say, well, if I wasn't so old..."

"That's all right," I said. "I mean, it's painful, but it's all right."

"One never felt like quite enough," he said. "But at fifty-eight, I just can't imagine it."

"It wouldn't be fair to Esther," I said.

The road for rest of the drive was straighter, easier, sweetened by our fantasies of a life together. He put on Simon and Garfunkel and we sang "The Sounds of Silence" and "Bridge Over Troubled Water" in unison. The songs seem transcendental in a way I'd never appreciated before. We were so high, we could have been angels with wings.

But when we exited the woods and turned onto 101 North, reality hit me. I glanced at my cell. We were back in a service area. I'd be calling Ben soon.

Silent now, we followed the same road we'd taken the previous day, through the town of Ukiah and up to the monastery, through the big gate with the Chinese characters and in to the visitor's parking lot. As soon as I opened the car door, the inland heat hit me, and I heard the peacocks crying.

We went into the dorm and asked for Anna. She was out, probably in the midday meditation. In our bliss, we'd forgotten her schedule. So we walked over to the Great Hall and sat on a bench with the plan of going in to the temple and looking for her when the service ended. It was a long wait in the hot sun, with the peacocks making their uncanny feline calls in the background. I took Michael's hand and leaned my head on his shoulder. He hummed to himself. Some melody he was working on. A half-hour passed. My nervousness faded as I became bored with waiting.

And then Anna came out and saw us. It hadn't occurred to me that we might end up telling her not with words but with actions—with a public display of affection, or PDA, as we used to call it way back when. But that's how we did it.

Startled, Michael and I let go of each other's hands and stood up, but the message had already been conveyed. She approached, looking shocked.

"You're here again. I gather there's been a development," she said dryly.

"Yes, Julia is going to move out to California to live with me and Esther," Michael said, exactly as rehearsed.

"That was fast," she said.

"Well, you've been coming and going for a while now," Michael said.

"I've been going on retreats. Is that what you call 'coming and going'? Couldn't you give me the time to work things out?"

"You haven't seemed interested in working things out. You've been too busy running away."

"Fuck you," she said and began walking away. Michael followed her. They stopped and she yelled at him, her closed fists punching downward.

I watched, thinking, *Let them have their scene—this would be a good time to call Ben. May all the bombs drop at once!* I took out my cell and called my husband.

"Where are you?" he asked.

"In Ukiah again." I told him about meeting Val's daughter and mother. "Ben," I finally said after the preliminaries, "I've decided to move out to California to live with Michael." Just as rehearsed.

"What? Goddammit!" he said. "Goddammit."

"I'm sorry," I said. "I'm so sorry."

"Are you sure about what you're doing? I don't even know what to say. Jesus, I had a feeling this was going to happen if you went to California. I can't believe we were thinking of adopting."

"I'm sorry," I repeated.

"We've been together twenty-six years. How can you give up so easily everything we built up together?" he said.

"I'm not doing it easily. I feel terrible about it. I hate hurting you."

"And what about Anna and Esther? How can you do something so destructive?"

"We're in the twenty-first century, Ben. People do this all the time. It's not like I invented divorce."

"No, but I thought you were different. I thought *we* were different. I thought you valued things like shared history, commitment, common values—"

"I do value those things. But Ben, it's just gotten too"—I so didn't want to say the word, I almost choked on it— "empty."

After we hung up, I sat for a minute, wondering if he'd call me back. He didn't. I'd burned all my bridges.

I felt a little sick on the return drive to Mendocino, and it wasn't just the winding roads. Not only had I broken up with Ben, but I'd done it over the phone, from across the country: the coward's way out, a path both grotesque and contemptible. And there was something else, too. Ben had accused me of being destructive, but what I had to face was that our relationship had been on the wane for years without either of us realizing it. Why had I been willing to make do with so little? I had refused to see the facts staring me in the face: Our sex life, once so gratifying, had eroded over the previous decade to the point of virtual nonexistence, but I'd attributed that to the hormonal changes of midlife and the aging of the relationship itself. The previous summer there had been another shift. After returning from a successful trip to Istanbul, we had gone for a month without meeting. Ben was in Princeton and I was in New York, and every weekend we were too busy or too tired to get on the train to see each other. I had thought, *Busy time for Ben—beginning of the school year,* and complimented myself on being a successful, autonomous woman with a twenty-first century marriage, while another layer of thinking underneath whispered, *Truth is we've reached a kind of take-it-or-leave-it attitude about spending time together.* I kept lying to myself because it was the path of least resistance.

I was suddenly afraid of the unknown. A dream I'd had in the early morning floated into consciousness. Michael and I were swimming in the middle of a lake surrounded by forest. We lost our bearings and couldn't figure out which was the shore we needed to return to. Of course, we could have swum back to any part of the lake, but there was a desire for certainty of direction that threatened to pull us under, and the longer we treaded water trying to decide, the more exhausted we became and the more in danger of drowning. The dream went on, but I couldn't remember the rest of it.

I had a splitting headache from the winding of the road.

"Could you slow down a bit?" I asked. "I don't feel great."

Going slower, Michael had to keep pulling over into the turnouts to let traffic pass. I noticed his forehead was lightly perspired.

"Are you okay?" I asked.

He looked in the rearview mirror and pulled over again. After three cars zoomed past, he just sat there, not pulling back onto the road.

"I'm freaking out," he said. He leaned forward and rested his forehead on the backs of his hands, which were still gripping the wheel. "You're not going to make up with Ben when you go back to New York, are you?"

"No! Why should I?"

"Because you hate change."

"Maybe, but God, Michael, please believe me."

"I could go to New York with you," he said, his voice slightly muffled from his hunched posture.

"What about Esther?"

"She can come, too."

"Don't you think that might be a little much for her? Not only Aunt Julia taking Mom's place, but hey, how about a trip to New York to watch her undo her marriage? Shouldn't you two just stay here while I take care of business?" I couldn't imagine the two of them underfoot in my little apartment while I consulted a divorce lawyer.

"I think a trip to New York might be a nice distraction for her."

"You're not worried about custody, are you? Anna seemed pretty pissed today, but I gathered from a previous conversation that—" I stopped. How do you talk about a mother's willingness to leave her child?

"She'd welcome the freedom?" he prompted, finishing my sentence. "Anyway, she's the one who's been disappearing—in a court of law, I don't think she'd stand a chance, if she decided to fight, which she won't."

"But you're nervous—"

"I'm nervous about everything. I'm worried about Esther and I'm nervous about being separated from you. I wish we could get married straightaway."

It was the sweetest thing he'd ever said to me. "It'll be fine."

"I'll buy you an engagement ring," he said. "On Monday." He picked his head up from the wheel and looked at my left hand. "Would you take those fucking rings off?"

"Oh, Michael. Open the window, okay?"

He opened the window and I slipped the wedding band Ben had given me off my finger and threw it out into the woods. Then I slipped the more valuable sapphire engagement ring off my finger and tucked it into my bag.

"I'll sell this one."

"Okay. Let's get out and walk down by the river," he said.

We got out, and my headache dissipated as I took in the forest air. Michael went to the trunk of the car and reached for a blanket— "for us to sit on," he said—and we crossed the road and walked, with dead leaves and pine needles sliding under us, down the embankment. The sound of crickets rolled out from the bramble and the woods, mixed in with the humorous ribbeting of frogs. The late-afternoon sun struggled through the layers of advancing fog, and the temperature dropped.

When we reached the edge of the water, he turned and led me upstream to a spot under some low-arching trees, the branches of which were hung with pale green sheets of moss. I followed obediently until he stopped and spread the blanket out. He sat down and I sat next to him.

He took my hand. "I can't stop thinking how ironic it all is. I didn't want to go forward with you sixteen years ago because of all the suffering it would cause, and now, because we waited, we'll cause suffering to more people than we would have back then."

"Well, these sixteen years have given me the opportunity to get to the end with Ben." I needed to put a positive spin on it in order not to go under.

"Yes, and me the chance to have Esther."

"So, it's been for the best."

"Everything happens the way it's supposed to?"

"I don't know," I said.

"How does your head feel now?" He was caressing my neck.

"I'm fine now."

He laid back and unzipped his pants, revealing a bulge inside his briefs.

"Take your pants off and get on top of me," he said.

"I'm not a fan of doing it outdoors," I said, looking around nervously. It was unlikely that someone speeding by on the road above would see us, but the possibility made me uncomfortable.

"Come on," he said. "We won't be able to do it when we get back to the house, and I can't wait till everybody's gone to bed tonight. I'll wrap the blanket over you. I want to feel you on top of me. Desperately."

The way he needed me was so raw. It was the way I wanted to be desired—urgently, impulsively. I slid my pants and underpants off and got on top of him, and he pulled the free half of the blanket over the top of us.

"Help me out," he said.

I put him inside me and we began to move gently together.

"Promise me," he said, holding my face between his hands and kissing me tenderly.

"Promise you what?"

"That you won't change your mind."

"I promise I won't change my mind."

"And that you'll love me forever."

"I promise. Please don't worry. I promise I'll love you forever."

I wanted him inside me so I could be inside him: if I could be completely filled by him, not only my sex, but my hips and chest and my arms and legs as well, we would coincide. I wanted him inside my head because I was already inside his. We moved faster together and he came very suddenly and then I came a moment later, pressing up against his leg. *Too quick*, I thought, as he wrapped the blanket around us tighter and burst into tears, sobbing in a heavy male way, and I cried, too. We cried for the marriages we were breaking and for the years together we'd lost. With my cheek up against his stubbly face and his forehead buried in my hair, I cried for the person I might have been—a poet, perhaps, or at least a woman wide awake, living from the heart—had I chosen him years before.

We lay in each other's arms, sobbing and mourning on the embankment, until we were drained. In the silence that followed, as I looked into his eyes and he stroked my hair, there was only the occasional whoosh of a car passing above and the loud drone of crickets coming up all around us as a second softer layer of chirping shimmied up from the woods across the stream. The needles and fronds beneath us, the dense forest above, and the river nearby wove themselves together around us into a fabric capacious and crannied enough to contain our grief.

The second part of my morning dream came back to me: as I treaded water in the lake, feeling that if I didn't decide which way to go I'd drown,

I looked downward through the crystal-clear pool and saw shining at the bottom a tawny slab of granite, striated with sparkling veins of rust-orange and turquoise that danced as rippling currents refracted it. The mica sparkled like gold in a Klimt painting.

I traced his large face with my fingers and told him the dream.

"I guess it was about finding beauty in the middle of terror," I said.

"Change is always terrifying," he said. "But as long as we keep fucking we'll be okay."

I reached for my panties, stood up to put them on as Michael pulled on his briefs. The two of us, our middle-aged bodies naked from the waist down, standing in the woods putting on our underwear—an undistinguished scene. The ridiculousness of it made me smile. As we zipped up our jeans, Michael caught my eye and smiled, too.

He rolled the blanket up under one arm and took my hand with the other and we climbed back up the embankment to the car. Every time he took my hand I felt more peaceful. The different parts of me were coming together like pieces of a puzzle. Yes, I was assembled now. I was put back together at last.

It was only as I put my seatbelt back on that I remembered we still had to tell Esther.

23

THE SENSE OF BEING in a moral storm came over me as we pulled into Val's driveway. I cringed at the thought of roiling Esther's world. Glancing at Michael's face, I saw the discomfort spreading over his face, which was turning as gray as the fog overhead.

We sat in the car for a moment before getting out.

"We should just tell her straight," he said. "Like we did Anna and Ben."

"She's going to hate me," I said.

"Who knows."

"If you'd told me twenty-four hours ago that all this was going to happen, I never would have believed it."

"I know. I'm kind of in shock, too. It's such a mixture of wonderful and horrible."

As Val's house was empty, we deduced the girls were probably at Stephanie's. After washing up, Michael and I set off on foot to the little cottage.

As we approached, we heard screams and laughs coming from the tent on the deck.

"Hey," Michael said, opening the flap of the tent. Inside, Esther and Jackie were sitting in their sleeping bags, playing Monopoly by the light of a battery-operated lantern.

"We're both broke again," Esther yelled. "It's crazy."

"Yeah, but I'm more broke than she is," Jackie yelled.

"No, *I'm* more broke."

They rolled on their backs, screaming with delight.

"Later," Michael said to me, letting go of the flap.

We went inside the little cottage to find Val heating up the leftover lasagna and Stephanie sitting on the couch with a magazine, her walker nearby. She was wrapped in a shawl bright with yellows and oranges. Returning to her house on this second night, it felt like a home away from home, and I wondered how often Michael and I would visit Val and his mother, and whether they would become a second family to me.

"How did things go today?" Stephanie asked.

"I hope you don't mind. I told her," Val said.

"It's okay, it'll soon be public knowledge," Michael said. "But you didn't tell Esther, did you?"

"Of course not," Val said. "I thought you'd want to have a conversation alone with her about it."

"So how did things go?" Stephanie repeated.

"Difficult," I said.

"We got the job done," Michael said.

"If you don't go with your heart," Stephanie said, "you might as well be dead."

Michael and I looked at each other.

"We've had a lot of experience with that," I said. "With being dead, I mean."

Val poured us a couple of glasses of wine.

"Let's drink to your happiness," he said. We clinked glasses.

The girls burst in, and Esther ran up to me and, bringing her face close to mine, batted her eyelashes. She was wearing smudged black eyeliner and mascara that had splattered in a semicircle on her cheeks.

"You're wearing makeup," I said.

"Don't you think it's vamp?"

"And goth?" Jackie said, coming up and putting her similarly blackened face up next to Esther's.

"It's definitely vamp *and* goth," I said.

As we took our seats around the table, Val started talking to Michael about the next day.

"You haven't forgotten we're teaching a class tomorrow, have you?"

"No," Michael said.

"Are you still going to camp out with us?" Val asked.

"You're camping out?" I asked, dismayed. They'd mentioned it the previous day, before Michael and I had slept together, but I hadn't processed it. Now it was my turn to have separation anxiety.

"That's what we usually do. We drive up to Jackson State Forest with a group of students and camp and take pictures," Val said.

I looked at Michael.

"I think I'll take my car so I can drive back tomorrow night to sleep here," he said to Val. "And then I can get up early Sunday and be back up with the group by nine."

"That's fine with me," Val said. "And Julia can have Steph's car over the weekend."

"I can't drive, anyway," Stephanie said. "You're going to be my babysitter for a couple of days, you realize."

"I don't mind," I said. "Thanks," I said to Michael.

"Obviously," he said and took my hand to reassure me.

And then we realized that, by forgetting Esther in our self-centeredness, we'd just told her.

"So you're going to be—like what?—Dad's girlfriend?" she said.

The crickets suddenly got louder.

Michael put his fork down delicately. "Esther, I was going to tell you before dinner—"

"You guys are really sick. That's like—like incest or something."

"Esther," Michael said, "Aunt Julia is Mommy's cousin, not mine."

"It's still really weird."

"Do you want to go outside and talk a bit?" Michael asked.

"I don't need to talk," she said, her face stiff with anger. "Half of my friends have divorced parents." She looked at me. "But I'm not going to call you Mom or Julia. Just Aunt Julia, like normal. You're just Aunt Julia, visiting. Visiting for a long time. Maybe."

"That's fine," I said.

"It serves Mom right," Esther said, her little brain tacking against the wind. "She's never around, anyway. She's been a real asshole."

Nobody corrected her language. There was an excruciatingly long silence.

"Let's make lava cakes for dessert," Val suggested. "I've got these frozen things that explode when you put them in the oven."

"Oh, they're *so* yummy," Jackie said. "To *die* for." And she swooned to the side until she purposely fell off her chair.

It was the kind of evening when it seemed fitting to go over the top with everything, so it was no surprise when one of the lava cakes erupted all over the inside of the oven, and we ate a fabulous dessert with the smell of burnt chocolate in the air.

I'd assumed Esther would spend the night outside in the tent again, but she had something else in mind. As Michael and I got up to leave, she said, "Hey, wait a minute, I'm going with you guys."

"You're not staying with Jackie?" Michael said as he grabbed a flashlight.

"No, I'm sleeping in your bed tonight," she said, taking my hand.

I'd anticipated rejection, not clinging. Or maybe this was a passive-aggressive maneuver to keep Michael and me apart.

"Aren't you a little old for that?" Michael said as we stepped outside.

"Your dad and I will be sharing a bed now," I added.

"I don't mind sleeping with you guys tonight. It's lucky Val has a king—there's plenty of room."

Mastering my disappointment, I looked at Michael.

"Just this one night, Es. We're not going to make a habit of it," he said.

I nodded in agreement. It seemed a reasonable compromise. After all, we'd just turned her world inside out.

As I walked with her small hand in mine—with the feeling of holding something delicate and precious, like an injured bird—my mind made a brief excursion to the adoption with Ben that I was abandoning. Thankfully a child hadn't yet been referred to us. That would have been harder—perhaps impossible—to relinquish. In this whole messy story with Michael, at least there had been this one element of fortunate timing. And the adoption plan seemed abstract compared to the reality of the young person who was now with me. I was finally inhabiting the place inside me capable of "being here now"—a place so much more accessible when there's love and joy than when there's dissatisfaction and yearning. (Funny how the mystics and philosophers never mention that.) It had taken me so long to get there.

When we got back to Val's house, Michael sent Esther upstairs for a bath and we sat on the couch holding hands.

"You don't mind, do you, about tonight?" he asked.

"Of course not. I'm just glad we did it by the river this afternoon. It must have been that prophetic sense of yours, knowing there'd be an obstacle later in the day."

He gave a sad laugh. "You know, Jul, I've given up the predicting thing. Been wrong too many times."

"You never know how things are going to turn out, do you?" I said.

I held his hand, traced the age spots on it as I remembered Ben. It was past midnight back on the East Coast. Was he sleeping or lying awake cursing me?

"What are you thinking about?" Michael asked.

"Ben."

"You feeling bad?"

"Well, on a certain level, of course; but on another, not at all."

He nodded. "The time comes when you have to live things as they are. The worst thing would be to continue living a lie."

I reflected on it. "It wasn't a lie—with Ben. I really loved him. It just wasn't—a good fit. So I had to live apart, in order to be me." I would have to find a way to honor what I'd had with my husband, and the time to start doing that was now.

A little later, after Michael and I had also gotten ready for bed, the three of us got into Val's bed. Esther settled in happily between us, like the sword between Tristan and Isolde.

"Can we go out to breakfast?" Esther asked me. "To the Wizard of Oz place?"

"What's that?"

"It's a coffee shop in Fort Bragg that's full of Oz photos and memorabilia," Michael explained.

"And everything on the menu is, like, Scarecrow waffles and Tin Man pancakes. It's really fun."

I agreed to take Esther and Jackie and Stephanie, too, if she felt up to it, out for breakfast.

She fell asleep quickly, and Michael and I laid on our sides looking at her. Then at each other.

"Are you going to be able to sleep okay?" he asked me.

"Sure. This is cozy," I said.

It felt more than cozy. It felt right in some way that was literally extraordinary. I remembered how Sandra used to say that new relationships are ideal places for projection. She talked about it as though all relationships were ultimately equal. What enables us to fall in love, she said, is the blankness of the slate before us. Not knowing the object of desire, we can see him or her as the perfect catalyst for whatever aspect of our personality needs to be born.

But I knew Michael. I knew he could be depressive, difficult, abrasive. And I loved him anyway because there was some element of *fit* between us, some harmony of temperaments that made me feel less alone.

I fell asleep secure in my immense happiness.

I had a disturbing dream before waking the next morning. I had gone on a photo shoot with Michael, and we were climbing a gentle hill toward a mature tree at the top that was loaded with pale pink blossoms. But when we reached it, we found that all the blossoms had fallen off and we were standing with our feet deep in a blanket of petals. There was nothing to photograph. And I looked at the tree aghast, as though it had been bombed.

I woke up. Esther was still sleeping but Michael was gone. I got out of bed and went downstairs.

He was sitting on the floor cross-legged, with his camera bag in front of him, checking lenses.

I looked at him and had a premonitory flash. I saw him in trouble in some way. Maybe out hiking, an accident, a broken leg, alone, too far to call for help.

"You'll—you'll be with the others the whole time, won't you?" I asked.

"Yeah, with Val and the students." He looked up at me. "You okay?"

"I had a nightmare. It's my turn to have the separation anxiety."

"We'll probably have an early campfire dinner and I'll be back by nine or ten."

"You won't change your mind and decide to camp out?"

"I'll be back tonight." He stood up and took me in his arms. "And if I'm not completely exhausted, I'll make love to you."

"And if you are completely exhausted?" I nestled my nose in the warmth of his neck.

"There'll be the night after and the night after and the night after that. And days, too. Early mornings and late afternoons." His fingers in my hair still felt new and fresh, as though he were touching me for the first time.

There was a gentle knock at the door and it opened. It was Val. Michael unwrapped himself only partly from me, leaving one arm around my waist.

"Hey. Good morning." Val said. His van was parked right outside the house.

Michael reminded Val that he would take his car and ride separately, as he wouldn't be staying over at the campsite.

"I hear you," Val said and, looking at me, smiled.

"You don't mind, do you?" I asked him.

"Not at all. I can babysit the group." Val was wearing one of those khaki vests with ten pockets, all of them stuffed with photographic equipment.

"All right, then," I said.

Michael gathered me up for a last squeeze and went out the door.

24

I MADE MYSELF SOME coffee and sat on the couch, wrapping a throw around me. I was preoccupied with the practical issues ahead of me. Divorcing Ben. Liquidating my business and my apartment. How much money would be required for the transition.

Divorce. All the consonants in the word are ugly. D for death. V for vacant. C for ceasefire.

Ceasefire? There had never been a war between Ben and me, just a steady, slow pulling back from intimacy.

I scrounged around for my journal. I continued the apology poem for Ben that I'd started—was it possible?—only the day before.

> *We should be honest before it's too late,*
> *find the one tree in the savannah*
> *and in its shade speak*
> *of the desert and how it encroached.*
> *How everything there disappeared,*
> *including the oasis where we once lived.*

I'd get through it all by writing. Somehow.
I dozed off.
I was awakened by Esther sitting down next to me.

"Would you rather die by fire or by ice?" she said.

"What?"

"It's a game," she said. "You have to choose one. Fire or ice?"

I was awake, finally. "Ice, I guess. You just go to sleep, I think." It was a hard choice, because I didn't want to be numb anymore. I wanted to be on fire.

"We're going to the Wizard of Oz for breakfast, right?"

"Sure."

"I think I'll have Scarecrow Waffles," she said.

We got dressed and walked down the road to Stephanie's, to find her and Jackie awake and waiting.

"I am truly hungry," Stephanie said. She sat on one of the dining chairs, dressed in some baggy pants and a sweatshirt. Jackie stood behind her, brushing her long gray hair.

"So we're going out?" I asked.

"Oh yes," Stephanie said. She was obviously in pain but had a radiant smile, nonetheless. "Jackie, Esther, can you go find Maxie? Julia, would you mind braiding an old woman's hair?"

The girls went out in search of the dog, and I took my place behind Stephanie. Her hair was thick and cool in my hands.

"How are you doing today?" I asked.

"Looking forward to being better. What about you? Did you sleep all right?" she asked.

"I did."

She chuckled. "With a little girl between you."

"It was okay," I said. "I love Esther, and I want to make this easier for her."

"I'm looking forward to getting to know you," she said. "And I'm glad you've decided to come out and be with Michael."

"Thanks for saying that," I said.

"I don't know what your story was with your husband," she said, "but I sense you've never blossomed completely and you're hoping for that with Michael."

I might have felt awkward talking about my plans with such a new acquaintance, but standing behind her afforded the privacy I needed to speak.

"My husband has many wonderful qualities, but there wasn't space in our marriage for all of me, and probably he would say the same, that there wasn't space for all of him." I paused to wonder what aspects of his character Ben had needed to lop off in order to fit the rest of him into the structure of our marriage. In my selfishness, I'd never asked myself the question before. "Probably there isn't, in any relationship, space for all of any one person, and I guess the question is whether a given relationship allows room for whatever is most urgently in need of being born—for both parties."

A given relationship. Both parties. Here I was being completely swept off my feet by someone I'd never stopped longing for—and I had to make it sound like a rational and reasonable choice. Wasn't it time simply to speak the passion in my heart?

"The thing is," I continued, "I'm so completely in love with Michael that if I weren't to choose him, the life force would just run out of me."

More than the life force—the sense of my life as a meaningful whole, of my self as being of a piece, coordinated, integrated—an organism where everything was connected to everything else. In a flash, I considered what it would mean not to choose him: how I would feel like I was falling off one of those cliffs buttressing into the ocean at the end of Main Street, Mendocino, California.

Stephanie's nodding head pulled the strands I was braiding out of my hands. I latched onto them again and finished braiding the tips. As I slid a hair tie around the bottom, she reached a hand back over her shoulder and touched mine.

"Then let yourself vibrate with passion, my dear. Because it may not come around again."

"I know."

"And a single moment of being completely yourself can be worth much sacrifice."

"I'm beginning to understand that, too."

As I helped Stephanie into the passenger seat and put her walker in the trunk of the car and then, with the girls and Maxie in the backseat, drove up the coast the few miles to Fort Bragg, I was glad for the distraction of the outing. Being separated from Michael, if only for twelve hours, was hard, and I vowed to myself that in the future we would spend as little time apart as possible. I would go back to New York to do what I needed to do, then come back to California, and we would never again be separated. Better yet, I'd agree to the idea of him and Esther coming to New York with me. Why had I objected to it? We could visit the zoo and South Street Seaport; we could take the Circle Line cruise around Manhattan. Esther would love it. I wouldn't need more than a day in Princeton to settle things with Ben.

In the passenger seat Stephanie was quiet, her pain perhaps aggravated by the movement of the car. I sensed she wanted to be quiet about it. Glancing at her sideways, I could see her cheerfulness was being challenged by the noise in her body.

Esther and Jackie were playing "would you rather" in the back seat.

"Would you rather eat worms or crickets?"

"Would you rather wear your pajamas to school or your underwear to the supermarket?"

"Would you rather lose an arm or a leg?"

The choices became more macabre as the game went on.

"The game is a good preparation for the impossible choices of life," Stephanie said.

The road north to Fort Bragg cut through more redwood and pine, occasionally opening up on the left to the rocky coast. The ocean spread out like brushed steel under fog. The way it didn't feel like summer but like some in-between season not on the human calendar deepened my sense of moving in an alternate dimension, in which the usual laws of time and space might be bent. Here, a river meeting an area of raised rock might go right over it, or you might even go backwards in time and rewrite things the way you would have liked them to be. Certainly there was much I'd like to rewrite. I couldn't deny my grief over the time together Michael and I had lost. What had I been waiting for? Stupid, stupid girl.

We passed a few quiet shopping centers that created open sky where dense forest had been, then reached Fort Bragg, a flat, unpretentious town with galleries and shops housed in old buildings that had never been spruced up for tourists. Their open doors were inviting. I'd come back sometime with Michael, and we'd browse together.

Luckily there was a parking spot in front of the coffee shop. The girls climbed out, and I tied Maxie up to a parking meter. She wagged her tail and barked, giving us her big-dog, black-gummed smile. The happiness of dogs—something worth studying. As I got Stephanie's walker out of the trunk, I sighed internally. Dealing with the elderly takes patience, but, approaching fifty myself, I was old enough to have a sincere compassion for her suffering. Besides, her delight at being up and about was my reward.

"We'll have a beautiful afternoon," she said, gazing at a blue crack in the cloud bank above. Then, looking at me: "I want a booth. A nice, soft surface."

The walls inside the café were crowded with movie posters and stills from *The Wizard of Oz*. The girls climbed into the booth first, still playing "would you prefer," while I helped Stephanie settle in and the waitress stored her walker out of the way. Gazing at the menu offering Scarecrow waffles, Tin Man omelet, Munchkin pancakes, I felt my internal clock ticking loudly. I wanted the day to go by as fast as possible so I could be with Michael again. A feeling of enormous good fortune came over me every time I thought of him, as though I'd just won the lottery. I was having one of the most beautiful weekends of my life—this sumptuous love affair was happening to *me*. I was blessed and blissed, exhilarated like a child running down a hill, arms aloft, ready to fly. The sexual energy coursing through my body again felt terrific.

I ordered Yellow Brick Road French Toast. I'd have it with lots of syrup.

I can't say exactly when my mood changed. A dull feeling crept into my head when the sugar rush wore off, and I dragged my feet a bit through the rest of the day—taking Stephanie back to her house then playing Monopoly with the girls. Later, I went into town by myself, bought some chicken and vegetables, came back, and made dinner for the four of us. Some churning was inevitable: the reunion with Michael was infinitely precious, but in between waves of joy, I contemplated again the coming upheaval of everything I was used to—my business, my routines in New York. I didn't waver for a minute, but there was a bracing for the difficulties to come.

The sun climbed the sky, then slowly descended, as though this day were like any other.

After dinner I helped Stephanie get ready for bed while the girls brought their little tent inside and set it up in the living room. They needed to be within Stephanie's shouting range for the night Val was gone.

I stopped outside the tent.

"Knock knock," I said.

"Don't come in! Private!" they screamed.

"You girls settling in?" I asked.

Esther stuck her head out between the tent flaps.

"When's Daddy going to be back?"

I looked at my watch. "Maybe in an hour or two. I don't know. I'll bring him over for breakfast in the morning—how about that?"

"Sounds great."

I got down on my hands and knees and kissed her forehead. "Good night, Esther. Good night, Jackie."

It was darkening quickly as I walked back to Val's house alone. A blanket of fog rested over the redwoods like a canopy on high poles. I thought about my phone conversation with Ben—how he'd said it made him sad to throw away what we'd built together. He saw a relationship as a kind of cathedral under endless construction. But I saw it—now—as a living organism with its own peculiar cycles of growth and aging. Woody Allen's words in *Annie Hall* came back to me: A relationship is like a shark; it needs to keep moving or it dies. And then he pauses and says to Annie, "What we've got on our hands is a dead shark."

I showered, got into my pajamas, and settled into Val's bed to wait for Michael's return. Taking up my diary and a pen, I savored the memory of the two nights we'd spent together—the first one so passionate, the second so sweet, with Esther lying between us. The journal entry came in verse, again.

> *I have looped backward and forward*
> *like the dancing road and the loaded river*
> *that persist forward*
> *through hills of rock and woven bramble*
> *away and toward you*
> *away and toward*
> *again and again.*
> *If only I'd had the dynamite,*
> *we could have been together sooner.*

I put my pen down. The writing voice was there again. I welcomed its return.

The road and the river, they know
how to get where they're going,
even as they wander they unfold,
obeying laws of purpose and gravity.
If only I had obeyed the laws
of desire, which dictate another
kind of gravitational pull
and operate another kind of
wisdom.

I glanced at the clock. It was getting late, and I was drowsy from the day's activities. The fog outside the window glowed eerily in the moonlight. Putting down my journal, I closed my eyes, the heel of my hand resting in stillness on my pubic bone, my body quietly hopeful for a reunion later that night. For some years now, I'd been hovering in a disembodied relationship with Ben. But, as it turned out, I wasn't quite ready to give up the life of the senses. The sense of time running out made everything more precious. I was almost forty-nine, Michael was fifty-eight—how much more time did we have to make the beast with two backs? (Though the women's magazines would have you believe that, with the help of estrogen cream and Viagra, you could keep it going until you were dead.)

It was midnight when I woke up, chilled. The bed was still empty. Had Michael been detained by a dinner at the campsite that had started late? No, that didn't make sense.

Maybe he'd run out of gas or had a flat tire and was waiting for someone to flag down for help. He wouldn't be able to call AAA, because cell phone service was spotty in these parts. At night, a back road in Northern California would be sparsely traveled, and passing drivers might not see or stop for a man in the dark. If his car had broken down, he would simply have to wait until morning.

I got up and wandered around the house. Downstairs in the living room, I looked at Val's photographs again and at the picture of me taken that morning in Marin, then browsed his bookcase to distract myself from my fears. There were some thick tomes on his shelves, like James Michener's *Hawaii* and Umberto Eco's *The Name of the Rose*. It seemed Val shared the taste I'd recently developed for historical fiction—something I wouldn't have guessed about him. It made sense: you have to be either single or childless (which he was when Jackie was up north with her mom) to tackle books like that. It pleased me that Val and I had a common interest; it suggested that our encounter years ago hadn't been arbitrary. He had, with his lightness and humor, disarmed me and helped me step out, opening the way to what would happen later with Michael.

I looked at the clock again. It was almost one. Horrible scenarios flashed through my brain. I rummaged around Val's living room and found a map, thinking I might go out and look for Michael, but I didn't know which route they'd taken to the woods or exactly where they were camping. I could drive around anyway or call the park service. No, that would be overreacting. When I first lived with Ben in New Haven, there were nights like this one, when he was out late at a university function or a party I'd declined to go to, and I'd stayed up waiting for him, imagining the worst—that he'd been beaten or knifed and left for dead. I used to calm myself by attributing my worry to the Holocaust mentality—the Jewish expectation that someone (in tall leather boots) is going to knock at the door and take away your beloved. Well, just as Ben always had been fine, so would Michael be. The roads were empty and quiet at night. Whatever had happened, it was unlikely he would be either assisted or harmed.

In the long hours I struggled with my anxiety, I got to take the measure of my love and commitment. Whether the explanation for his delay was a flat tire or an accident, I would be without defense. I had to surrender to whatever happened, to accept as right whatever came my way. *Amor fati*, the love of one's fate, is what it's called, and that was the only way to go here. It made me both more vulnerable than I'd ever been before and more resilient, because I knew I could handle whatever came up. Finally, overcome by exhaustion, I went back to bed, where I dozed fitfully, clinging to the only story I could tolerate: Michael's car had broken down and he was sleeping in it, waiting until morning for help.

25

LIGHT WAS BREAKING WHEN the phone rang. It was a nurse, calling from the Mendocino Coast Hospital in Fort Bragg.

"Is this Julia Field? Michael Chambers was in a minor road accident last night. He was picked up this morning. They're keeping him here for observation."

"Is he okay?"

"There's some problem with his arm, but otherwise he seems fine."

"What happened?"

The woman told me the little she knew. Michael's car had gone off the road at one of the curves leading out of the forest and slid into a bramble-filled vale. Had it skidded on the moistness that the evening fog sometimes mists onto the road? It wasn't clear.

"I'll be there as soon as possible." There was a tremor in my voice.

"He's fine," the nurse said. "Cold from being out all night and kind of shaken up, but hardly a bruise. You can take your time and have breakfast."

"No," I said. "I'll be right there. Should I bring his daughter?"

"You can if you like. You'll find him in the emergency area. They haven't put him in a room yet."

I hung up. Michael, in an accident! And I felt responsible, because he'd been on his way back to see me. Maybe he had even been racing along the road.

Vibrating from the adrenaline running through my body, I rummaged in my valise for a clean pair of jeans, then layered on a T-shirt, sweater, and jacket. Brushed my teeth in a hurry, ran my fingers through my hair. Forget makeup. Out the door.

The early morning forest, dim under clouds, was alive with birds. Walking over to Stephanie's cottage, I debated what to tell Esther. Selfishly, I didn't want to take her to the hospital with me. It seemed like an extra complication, and wasn't that what children were—complications? Maybe that's why I'd kept postponing parenthood. Lifting a flap of the tent the girls had set up in the living room, I saw they were both sound asleep. I got on my knees, gently shook Esther. She took a breath and, ignoring me, rolled onto her side. Getting up and stepping quietly into Stephanie's room, I saw that she, too, would be difficult to rouse. Something in me wanted to contain and minimize what had just happened. I wasn't in the mood to be cross-questioned by Stephanie and the girls when I didn't have much in the way of facts. So I stood there for a moment in the gray light and decided to tell a lie. Taking up a pen in the kitchen, I wrote a quick note: *Went into town. Back soon.* And I left.

The ride from Val's up to the hospital in Fort Bragg took only a few minutes. When I got there, I parked and made my way into the emergency area, which consisted of a small lobby with a central desk and a few curtained cubicles off to the side. A country hospital like this probably didn't get much action.

I was stopped at the entrance by a nurse.

"I'm looking for Michael Chambers," I said.

She looked down at her admissions log.

"Jul! I'm over here!" The voice came from behind one the curtains.

The nurse nodded me in.

In a room that was barely private—a space between two walls with a curtain half-drawn across the front—Michael, looking oddly asymmetrical, was propped up in a folding hospital bed, one arm connected to an IV. He was wearing the same pants and shoes he'd left in and they stuck, somewhat comically, off the end of the mattress, while his shirt—or rather, his usual two shirt combo—was open at the top, revealing part of an electrode they'd attached to him. A pilled electric blanket looked comforting. It was a shock seeing him this way—not as lover or friend, but as patient and invalid. I remembered my last visit to my father, in intensive care, before he died. How he'd been connected to too many machines, how he'd hated the noises of the hospital always going in the background. Now here was Michael being old and getting older, and that meant I was, too. A shiver of resistance went up my spine, then evaporated as I leaned forward and kissed him. His lips were warm and dry.

"I was worried all night about you. You really okay?"

"Something's wrong with my left arm." He paused. "They think I've had a stroke. I've already had a blood test and a CAT scan."

I must have blanched. "Something wrong with your arm—"

"Not much feeling. I can barely move it." He budged his arm out an inch, then back in. "Lifting it is even harder."

We looked at each other, thinking about the piano. I didn't know much about strokes, except that recovery depends on rapid diagnosis and care. Michael had been out in the wilds of Mendocino County for ten hours, and whatever damage he'd suffered was likely to be permanent.

Michael cleared his throat. "The doctor's going to be back in a moment with the results—" He stared off into space with the corners of his mouth pulled down.

"Michael—" I began.

"I'm scared stiff. But the crazy thing," he said, "is how hungry I am. I'd give anything for some scrambled eggs and a cup of hot coffee."

"You want me to go get—"

"You probably need clearance first. Everything is procedure here." He paused. "Did you tell Esther what happened?"

"Not yet. They were all fast asleep."

"That's okay."

"Maybe I should have woken them up before I left—"

"Val will be here soon. And Anna. They called her as 'my next of kin.'"

We fell silent.

"So what happened?" I asked.

"I was driving very slowly. There was a thick mist on the road and I couldn't see very well, so I really was being careful. I remember I had this headache, and I had one of these moments when you notice two opposite things at once—the fog was so beautiful with the moonlight coming through, and my head felt like it was splitting—and I must have lost consciousness, because next thing I knew I was rolling into a ditch."

"Rolling?"

"Rolling. Slowly, because I'd been going slowly. The fog was lucky, I guess. Maybe I lost consciousness for a few minutes or fell asleep, I don't know. As soon as I woke up, I realized something had happened to my arm, I thought maybe there'd been an impact and I'd broken it, but there wasn't any pain, so that didn't make sense. I got out of the car, walked up to the road, and I stood there for a long time, hoping someone would come by, but of course no one did. I realized I'd never be able to flag anyone down till morning, so I got back into the car and fell asleep. Good thing I had that extra blanket."

"So the stroke, if that's what it was, caused the accident—"

"Yeah. Anyway, when I woke up at dawn, there was this black cow standing on the other side of a fence, staring at me. It was kind of surreal. I walked up to the road and flagged someone down."

I felt horrible. If he hadn't been returning to see me, he would have been at the campsite with Val, who could have gotten him help sooner.

"And did you—panic during the night? I would have."

"For a moment I was frightened, but then, I don't know, not really. I was worried about you, knowing you would worry about me, and I was annoyed my cell phone was out of range. Mostly I was confused. And tired. We did a lot of walking yesterday with the group, and I was carrying a lot of photo equipment, so I was physically exhausted. It was easy to sleep in the car."

An older woman in a white coat with a clipboard appeared and introduced herself as Dr. Whiting. She inspired confidence.

"Hi," Michael said. "This is my"—he paused a fraction of a second—"fiancée, Julia."

"I've got the results of the CAT scan here. You've had what's called an ischemic stroke, caused by a blood clot in the brain. Fortunately, it was limited in extent, which is why your only symptoms are in that arm. Unfortunately, because you were out all night, you missed the three-hour window of opportunity for immediate treatment, which might have dissolved the clot." She went on to speak, much too fast, about the different types of stroke, the relationship between the cardiovascular and neurological systems, the organization of the brain, what can be done in that first window of opportunity he'd missed and what can be done afterwards. Not speaking medicalese, I was unable to take in some of the information; I could only parse what she said for the outcome. *Fortunately, unfortunately, fortunately*—the language of doctors, as they tread between the hard facts and the job, almost forgotten in present times, of giving hope and comfort.

Whiting looked down at the chart. "You live in Berkeley? We'll refer you to a stroke specialist there, who will arrange physical therapy for you and discuss medications and lifestyle changes to prevent a recurrence." *Michael in physical therapy. A possible recurrence. What does this mean for him? What does it mean for me, for us?* "We're going to run a couple more tests in a bit. We'd like to keep you here for observation for a couple of days, in case there's a recurrence."

The doctor stood up to leave. Michael stopped her.

"I need to know more. I'm a musician," he said.

A shadow passed over her face. Was it compassion, or a closing down to compassion? How many horrid stories had she seen, how many sad prognoses had she delivered?

"We're discovering that the brain is more plastic than we thought—if the areas designated for motion are destroyed, other areas can be trained to take their place."

"So recovery is possible?"

"Some people recover almost completely, some don't." She sighed. "Either way, you will adjust. People do. You're fortunate the stroke was so limited in scope."

"All right," he said. I saw him struggle with terror. But he wouldn't give into it. *We* wouldn't give into it. "Uh, one more thing," he said, catching her again on the threshold. She stopped, turned. "Could you authorize breakfast?"

She smiled. "Sure."

After she left, I scooted my chair closer to him. I was on his right side, and I reached for his good hand. He squeezed my hand in return.

"So you'll get physical therapy and—" I stopped. It was hard to imagine that he might never recover the pianistic dexterity he once had.

"At least," he said, "the melody hand is okay. Who needs the left hand, anyway? Chords, bass lines, who needs 'em?"

"I'll be your left hand," I said.

"I bet you could be. You used to be pretty good."

"For an amateur."

"Jul, I know this isn't what you signed up for."

"On the contrary. I had the whole night to think that I never, ever want to be separated again from you, not even for a single night. And you were right, you and Esther should come to New York with me when I go to wind things up there."

"I'd like to come with you. If they'll let me. I wonder if it's safe to fly after a stroke." He sighed. "Do you think there's some kind of computer up there that works things out, so that as soon as you get one thing you want in life, something else gets taken away?"

"I don't know," I said, feeling the tears well up. I stopped them. He was the one who had the right to cry, not I. "But it seems that things work that way, doesn't it?"

I went to the hospital cafeteria to get a bagel and cream cheese for me and some scrambled eggs and sausage for Michael. "I want a feast for my last breakfast," he'd said, "before they put me on some militaristic antistroke diet." I picked up a couple of newspapers at the hospital gift shop on my way back.

It felt bizarrely like camping out, as we ate breakfast in the emergency room cubicle, serving ourselves from the red plastic tray I perched on his lap. I held Michael's coffee cup for him and passed it to him on command. We ate in silence, gazing through the open curtain at the comings and goings of personnel in the emergency room corridor. An orderly wheeled a patient out of the cubicle next to us, a nurse went in with a stack of clean linens. Another nurse walked by, carrying a Starbucks paper bag and a cup of coffee. There was something so casual about the way everyone behaved here. A snippet of conversation between two nurses floated in. One of them was driving to Sacramento the following Sunday for a baby's baptism.

"Jul," Michael said. "Whatever happens, I'm going to do my best not to be bitter. I'm through with being bitter."

"If you need to be bitter sometimes, you're allowed."

"'Sometimes'?" He smiled.

"Just sometimes."

We finished eating. The longer we sat there, hoping for a doctor or nurse to check back in with us, the more our waiting diluted the sense of disaster. We fell into a kind of daze, with our eyes fixed on the hallway as the minutes passed, then a whole hour and another. The drabness of it all—the body malfunctioning, the doctors unable to provide a satisfactory fix. Our physical fragility—the dark underbelly of life that keeps returning. Michael closed his eyes and hummed to himself. I tried to read the newspaper.

Finally, there was a punctuation mark in time, when Anna and Esther appeared. Anna had traded her novitiate's robes for jeans and a heavy green turtleneck sweater.

Anna didn't greet me; she just nodded to Michael politely. "You okay?"

Michael nodded. "Julia, can you give her the story?"

I relayed what the doctor had said, and Anna listened, barely looking at me.

"Sorry about your arm," she said to Michael.

"Yeah," he said. "I'll be okay."

Esther looked frightened. "I want to go back to Berkeley with Daddy," she said.

Anna's lower jaw slid forward. It was an awful moment to witness—Esther's choosing her father over her mother.

"I think," Anna said, "we should go back on our own, and Daddy and Julia can follow. We'll go visit Aunt Robin for a few days. Julia can take care of Daddy. Isn't that what's going to happen here?" Anna gave Michael and me a look that was more blank than questioning. Then she turned to Michael. "Would you mind if Julia and I went out for a walk?"

"Go ahead. Esther and I will hang together for a while and play twenty questions or hangman."

Anna and I stepped outside. The July coastal weather, absurdly unpleasant, stuck its cold fingers down the back of my shirt. Anna walked with her shoulders forward, leading me I didn't know where.

"There's a bench up here," she said.

We sat down. A couple of galleries across the street were still locked up. It wasn't even nine o'clock yet. Looking at Anna, I could only think, *A home-wrecker. That's what I am.*

"You want to talk to me," I said.

"You know, when you gave me the news at the monastery, it was like, for God's sake, I've been meditating in this sacred place, reading texts about compassion and forgiveness, how could I express all my—my rage and shock—and—" She stuttered.

"I'm so sorry, Anna."

"That's not enough, and it'll never be enough. Do you understand what I was doing there on retreat?"

"Not really."

"I was praying and meditating to calm myself, to sort certain things out and gather myself, my—my peace of mind, my energy, my sense of priorities—in order to return to Esther and to my marriage—and then you come—barging in—I'm really appalled."

Chastened like a child, mortified about the pain I'd caused her, I couldn't object. I couldn't say, *It was Michael who asked me to come—and what were you doing leaving your child?* or *Your marriage was really a mistake following upon another mistake, and I never stopped longing for him, so this has got to be right.* Because there was no right or wrong here. Just a mess.

"I'm sorry," I repeated.

"You're a real shit."

I had to defend myself. "Anna, you're the one who left."

"You didn't hear anything I just said?"

"Okay, you had health problems, okay, you needed to go on retreat—"

"It's hard living with Michael, in ways you perhaps haven't thought of."

"His being moody, is that what you mean?" I wanted to take the question back as soon as I asked it. It felt vulgar to compare notes about him, and I hated that she had extra information from their years together.

"No. His being a genius. It's crushing living with a genius," she said. "It was one of the reasons I stopped doing art."

She was painting a scenario completely opposite to what I imagined living with Michael—my source of inspiration—might be like.

"But you were always so prolific as an artist. I always envied that in you. Prolific and really good."

"Really good? Maybe. But Michael is brilliant, and I couldn't help feeling competitive with him. And as he became more and more successful and his music started gaining recognition, his work took precedence over mine—in practical terms, I mean, like who got to travel for their work, who had to stay home with Esther—and I had a hard time playing second fiddle."

That this might have been part of their dynamic had never occurred to me. No one can make you feel inferior without your consent, Eleanor Roosevelt said. But Anna was talking about more than feeling inferior—she was talking about the delicate juggling act that goes on inside a couple, whereby one party (more often than not male) creates the agenda and the other party goes along with it. If I had been with Michael and had a child with him, I might have fallen prey to the same male/female pattern. I might never have gotten to be the protagonist of my own life. Maybe I had chosen the commuting arrangement with Ben—and the slightly more distant relationship that went with it—because I knew, instinctively, that in this man's world, it was the only way I could be sure to have the freedom I needed to make something of myself.

"You felt trapped," I said.

"I felt like his genius was feeding off of me in some way. Like he was sucking the creative energy out of me so he could use it himself. So that the more productive and famous he became as a musician, the less motivated and engaged I became as an artist."

"God, Anna. You make him sound like a—a—"

"A leech or a parasite?"

"Or a vampire!"

"But this is the thing, Julia. When I was on retreat, I saw that I was the cause of my own unhappiness. I saw that I was letting the demands of my ego run my life and ruin my marriage. I was like a child wanting to 'win' all the time. And after I saw all this, I was ready, truly ready, to step back into my marriage and turn it around. And now you've ruined it."

"No, you weren't ready to return. You're saying that as an afterthought. You're saying that because it's too late now and you blew it and you want to make me feel bad."

"I don't want to make you feel anything, Julia. I just want you to disappear."

"Well, I'm not going to disappear."

"You'll see, Julia. You'll see that living with a genius ain't no picnic."

"Whatever it was for you, it'll be different for me."

"We're not going to resolve this," she said, standing up.

"There's nothing *to* resolve. The ways things are is the way things are."

I stood up, too, and we headed back to the hospital in silence.

26

I PUT OFF MY return to New York because the doctor said Michael shouldn't fly for three months and I had vowed to myself that we would never again spend a night apart. Besides, after the stroke, he needed me. The first weeks were extremely difficult. We do so many things with two hands, and Michael had to learn how to do them all with one—putting toothpaste on a brush, getting into a pair of pants, reading the newspaper. The struggle with objects—the dropping and fumbling—made him irritable, yet he was, thankfully, not above asking me for help with tasks, like the cutting of meat, that he couldn't figure out how to do on his own.

In this period he was, justifiably, self-involved, and sometimes I felt that I could have been anybody in the slot of helper and soother, of cook, driver, and caretaker. Other times, he would take my hand or give me a deep look and say, "Jul"—just my name, nothing more than that—in a way that reminded me I was exactly where I was supposed to be, that I was appreciated and needed in the way I wanted to be—with no holding back.

Certainly it was not how I'd imagined I would begin my life with Michael. I drove him to one medical appointment after another. I went to the drugstore to fill his prescriptions and helped him implement the recommended dietary and lifestyle changes. I took him to physical therapy, where he was given hours of strengthening exercises that left him exhausted and frustrated.

In the first weeks, he careened into morbid self-pity and stayed there, flailing like a fly stuck to fly paper. He slept a lot.

He described the arm as heavy, a kind of dead weight pulling at his shoulder. He said he felt lopsided, like he was carrying a heavy bag of groceries that was yanking at his collarbone. The doctor called it "spasticity" and prescribed medication to ease the pain.

I spent hours surfing the Web, finding stories of recovery from stroke. When Michael gained speed typing with one hand and joined me in the search, he found nothing but dismal stories of chronic pain and lives and careers ruined.

"Maybe I'll be able to use my arm to get dressed or hold a book, but to play again? That seems unlikely. And I don't know how I'm going to continue if I can't play music." As promised, he didn't go into bitterness. He went straight into despair. "I can't even feel happy about your being here. I feel like I'm damaged goods and this isn't fair to you."

"If I wasn't here with you, I'd just be wondering how you are and wanting to help you and take care of you."

"Are you sure?"

"I'm sure."

"But what am I going to do with myself? So what if I have to give up performing, but how am I going to compose? Or teach? How am I going to survive?"

"You'll figure something out. Or we can use my nest egg if we have to." I had a small inheritance from my father and savings from years of frugal living and the sale of my book.

"I don't want to use your savings."

"It doesn't matter. Anyway, I think you'll go back to work. You'll find a way."

He lay down on the couch to rest. I looked around. The house was a mess, which sometimes bothered me, sometimes didn't. I went to sit outside on the back steps and take in the afternoon sun. At the back of the yard, which gently sloped up the hill, stood a garden shed Anna had turned into an art studio. She would empty it eventually, and I would repaint the interior and use it as a home office, because I would want a room of my own that could be quiet and orderly. I gazed at the flower beds, a little scruffy, which needed sprucing up. Anna's flower beds, probably. I didn't imagine Michael had ever helped her in the yard. Well, I would buy her out, redo every corner of the house and garden in my image. I would have liked Michael to sell the place, but Esther was too attached to her home—we'd never move.

I got up, went over to a magnolia bush in flower and plucked three crimson blooms, then headed back into the house to rummage in the cabinets for a glass bowl. My job was to lift Michael's spirits and be hopeful about his recovery. It was hard to keep my bitterness to myself when there was so much of it. Why did this have to happen and why had it happened right after our reunion? What maleficent force in the universe was intent on making things as difficult as possible for us? Fate had snuck out from behind a corner and mugged us at gunpoint, robbing us of the happiness we might have enjoyed in the special period of first living together. But engaging in hand-to-hand combat with bad luck was pointless. The sooner I submitted to the realities, the better off I'd be. I found a bowl, filled it halfway with water, set the flowers to float inside and placed them on the side table next to where Michael was now dozing, so that he would see it when he woke up.

There was no escape, and in any case, I didn't want to escape. Looking at Michael sleeping, the only thing I felt was the enormity of my love for him and the necessity to let events unfold as they would. Resolution would come not in his recovering or not recovering from his stroke but in how I—in how we—met events, with what grace or lack of grace, with what generosity and kindness to each other and ourselves. Strangely, it was almost a relief not to have control. The more I let go, the more I came into being with him exactly as he was in body and soul, and the better I got along with myself, whether I was feeling frightened or resentful of the hand dealt us.

> *The reef is inside, there*
> *where things crash*
> *against the unyielding.*
>
> *Each tide is a storm equal*
> *to the puzzle of whirling*
> *moment by moment.*
>
> *It's all froth,*
> *air and water mixed*
> *and in movement.*

I give in, not up.
When I am carried
it hurts less.

The surging is true
and all the breaking
to be trusted.

If writing poetry felt like a darning of the places where my courage frayed, it was taking care of the practical stuff that kept me grounded in the realities of my new life. I took Michael's car to a specialized mechanic to have it adapted for a one-armed driver. A knob had to be attached to the steering wheel and the direction indicators moved to the right side. Then I bought myself a blue preowned Honda. These were optimistic acts, which assumed that Michael would return to employment or at least to independent activity and that I would remain in California. Buying myself a vehicle before I'd wound things up in New York felt frightening and liberating at the same time.

I also bought a new laptop and set it in the kitchen, which became my headquarters for managing my business back east. I'd taken on a partner when I became certified as a financial planner, and Rachel, who was now managing my clients, checked in with me daily, sending questions my way as needed. I soon chucked my plan of opening a full-scale branch of my firm in the Bay Area: between Michael and Esther I'd have my hands full. I would start out modestly, subletting an office and seeing clients who found me through reading *Women, Get Rich*. In the meantime, I started to do research and take notes for the book's sequel, with the working title, *Women, Make Your Daughters Rich*. I didn't realize until later that I was writing it as an act of atonement toward Esther.

Robin called to ask how Michael was doing and whether I needed anything. I'd been living out of a suitcase and requested a loan of T-shirts and sweaters.

In the middle of all this, there was the matter of Anna exiting the household. About a week after we all returned to the Bay Area, she called to say she had rented an apartment in Berkeley and would be coming over with Robin to get some of her stuff. She said Esther wanted to come back to stay with us. Michael said okay.

I wanted to hide when I heard the sound of her car in the driveway. There I was, living in her house and plotting how to erase her from it—what colors I would use to repaint the walls, how I'd rearrange the furniture and order another bed for Michael and me. I saw Robin getting out of the car, and I imagined pulling her aside to ask how long I might expect to feel guilt. Since she was a psychotherapist, I imagined she might be able to give me a precise answer, like, you can expect an alleviation after exactly so many weeks or months. And then, looking out the window and seeing Anna approach with Esther, I realized I would always feel guilty. The best I could do would be to train myself not to think about it too much.

Anna knocked on the door before opening it with a key. I came into the foyer, and Michael, who'd been reading the newspaper in the kitchen, joined me. With Esther close behind her, Anna walked in no longer wearing her Buddhist jewelry, but a simple gold locket instead. I felt almost paralyzed by remorse and sympathy. In a series of missteps, tragic for her and beneficial for me, she had relinquished her husband and compromised her relationship with her child. But I could reduce my sense of responsibility with the reflection that she'd been a lost soul long before I'd entered the scene. I muttered a greeting and looked down to avoid meeting her eyes as she passed by me and walked upstairs to the bedroom.

Robin carried in some empty boxes. Although Michael had warned me of her going "native," I was unprepared for her appearance. She was as dark as I'd ever seen her, having spent days outside at the last sundance, and wore several silver necklaces around her neck, heavy with turquoise and carved pendants of a hawk, a wolf, and a creature with horns. Around her waist was a western type of belt, made of thick leather with more turquoise and a silver buckle. She put the boxes down and hugged Michael.

"I'm so sorry," Robin said, and inquired after his progress. "Hello, Julia." She hugged me and stroked my hair, as though to say she wasn't passing judgment for what was happening. "I brought some clothes for you to borrow."

Esther put her arms around her dad; he put his right arm around her.

"I was thinking," he said to his daughter, "why don't the three of us go out to brunch, maybe to that place in the Berkeley Marina, while Mom and Robin pack? What do you think?"

"Can I bring my kite?"

"Yeah, we can go to the green afterwards and fly it."

Esther went upstairs to get it.

Anna came back downstairs, carrying a packed valise. She looked at us with a face of steel. "She's still saying she wants to live with you," she said to Michael. "I imagine you'll let me have her on weekends."

"Of course," he said. "Whatever she wants and whatever works for you, too—for all of us."

"I think we can save a lot of money if we do this with a mediator."

For the first time I wondered about the economics of her situation. I'd been so involved with taking care of Michael that I hadn't pondered the obvious—that she might have been economically dependent on him. My conscience would require us—or me, if Michael couldn't go back to work—to supplement her income.

"I've got some more empty boxes in the car to bring in. A guy will be showing up with a van soon," Anna added, and she followed Robin back out to her car.

Michael and I stood there, waiting for Esther to come back with her kite. I wanted to get out of there as soon as possible.

We had brunch at a restaurant on a pier at the edge of the water, where the cold July morning offered a dull view of San Francisco, blurred by the summer fog. Afterwards, we drove over to a field nearby, where the sky was dotted by soaring kites in the shapes of bright butterflies, olive drab airplanes, and complicated box and cellular structures dressed up as stars and dragons.

We watched Esther run across the grass until her blue-and-green hummingbird lifted off.

"Gee," Michael said, "it could almost be a day like any other." He put his arm around me, drew me closer with a small smile. "Hello there."

We were walking back to the car when Esther stopped and said to her father, "How long?"

"How long for what?"

"How long till your arm is better?"

"I don't know," he said. "Maybe it won't get better."

"But isn't it like broken or something?"

"No," he said. "It's not broken. It's just not—communicating with my brain."

She had obviously assumed that it would, like a fracture, be mended soon, and now she looked puzzled. "I don't get it."

"To tell you the truth, I don't really get it either," he said, not in the mood to go into the details.

"I think it's going to get better," she said. "Everything gets better, eventually, doesn't it?"

He held her as she leaned her head into his comfortable waist, and I saw he didn't want to disappoint her. "Yes, usually it does."

We stayed out all afternoon to give Anna the time she needed. After flying the kite, we went to a bookstore and a video store, then Esther and I did a little grocery shopping while Michael snoozed in the car.

When we got back to the house, Anna was gone. Michael lay down on the couch, and I went up to the bedroom and found that Anna had taken not only her dresser but also the night table, the quilt cover from the bed, and the art work—hers—that had been hanging on the wall. Well, I had furniture in my New York apartment that I would move out here. Esther followed me upstairs, looked at the empty spaces, and scrutinized my face.

I sat on the bed, facing her. "I guess I'll have some redecorating to do. What would you think if I repainted the inside of the house? I'm thinking of softer colors."

"Can I help choose them?"

"Of course."

"I want my room to be light blue."

She sat down next to me, and it was my turn to scrutinize her. She'd done a lot of growing up in the ten days since I'd last seen her.

"I'm sorry, Esther, for all the disturbance that—has happened." I stopped myself from saying "that I've caused." I wouldn't take it all on my shoulders.

She shrugged. "Everybody gets divorced sooner or later."

"No, not everybody." Her words left me grief-stricken.

"Almost everybody." She paused. "Do you want to play Monopoly with me?"

She was obsessed with the game. Once, long ago, I'd been, too. I was around Esther's age when I played for three hours at a time with Anna, one week I stayed on Long Island with my aunt and uncle. Maybe one day Esther would remember this as the summer of Monopoly instead of the summer her parents got divorced.

"Yes, I'd love to play Monopoly with you."

I can't overstate how much having Esther there helped us. It was still summer, and when she returned to camp, I found myself taking on a mother's duties, packing her bag lunches, driving her up to Tilden Park after breakfast, and bringing her back in the afternoon. Esther's schedule lent a welcome structure to our day, which now had something to revolve around beside Michael's medical appointments. I had a pleasant moment every morning after signing her in at the campground in the wooded hills above Berkeley, when I would stand for a moment in the forest fragrant with eucalyptus and pine, watching her run off and join her friends. The kids congregated in a shaded clearing dotted with picnic tables, then fanned out to activities in the fields and woods nearby. Their joy was contagious.

One afternoon I persuaded Michael to go up to Tilden with me to get Esther. After picking her up, he suggested we hike a short trail out to a pond Esther liked to visit. The path ran at the bottom of a fold in the hills protected from the ocean fog, and the air had a crackling dryness laden with summer pollen. Esther scampered ahead as Michael and I followed behind.

"It feels good to be out walking," he said. "I need to get more exercise, not just at the physical therapist's."

We held hands walking, something Ben and I had never done much of, not even at the beginning of our relationship. I loved the feeling of Michael's hand in mine, though now it always evoked in me a silent prayer for the other one.

We reached Jewel Lake and sat on a bench. Esther crouched by the pond to get a closer look at the turtles sleeping on the lily pads. Heavy-bodied dragonflies with iridescent wings grazed the surface of the water, which had a skin of dust and bubbles over it, like scalded milk about to froth. In the middle of Michael's ordeal and my empathetic suffering, of our anxieties about his health and Esther's adjustment, here was this moment of quiet beauty, of delicate, breathable happiness knocking at the door. It was the same sense of peacefulness that I'd experienced holding his hand on the bluffs of Mendocino. A streetlight in the heart saying, *Take shelter here.*

Michael must have felt it, too. His outlook shifted after that afternoon.

Having dropped Esther off one morning, I came home and, upon opening the door, heard him at the piano. He was playing intervals of a fifth, as though doing ear-training, an exercise he certainly didn't need.

Entering the living room, I saw he was gently supporting his left arm with his left knee and right hand as he practiced his old swing-and-drop technique between pinkie and thumb. The movements were painfully slow, evincing an enormous focusing of mental concentration and physical energy.

Not wanting to disturb him, I headed toward my computer in the kitchen, but he heard me and, swinging around on the bench, looked at me with that old smile of his, full of childish enchantment.

"You're playing," I said.

I approached him, and he took my hand, made me sit down on the bench next to him.

"I've decided I'm not going to let this stop me. As long as I'm learning how to tie my shoelaces again, I can learn how to play again, too."

"Good."

"Look what else I've been doing."

He moved over to the electric keyboard, hit a button, which started the playback of a bass line he'd recorded, and launched into accompanying himself with the right hand, improvising as he went along. It was a slow, melodically rich piece, with mournful undertones.

When he was finished, he turned back to face me. "I'm going to figure out how to compose, and I'm going to figure out how to teach. With all the technology out there, there must be a way. I can take a medical leave in the fall to figure it out. And I've been thinking about teaching kids with disabilities. There's a lot for me to learn, and a lot I can do—for others, as well as myself. It's the only way I'm going to be able to stop feeling sorry for myself."

I took his good hand, placed it on my knee, and stroked it.

"Can I help?"

"It's crossed my mind, and yes, actually, you might be able to help."

"Anything you want."

"Of course, I want to figure out how to do as much as I can on my own, but I'm going to need help from time to time with transcription, and I might need an assistant teaching."

"Wherever I have the skill, Michael."

This was all very different from what I'd expected. I had imagined two arms around me, now I had one. I had looked forward to watching his two hands making music, now I would have to be one of those hands. And this was the silver lining—that he felt so at ease asking for my assistance.

"If there's such a thing as a blessing," he said, "that's what you are, Jul." He put his arm around me, and I buried my head in his shoulder.

That night, I stepped out of the shower and found I'd forgotten to bring my bathrobe in with me. Wrapping myself in a towel, I went into the bedroom, where Michael was already in bed, listening to music. We hadn't made love since his stroke and suddenly I felt shy and self-conscious about my body—my double-scarred abdomen, my breasts a little lower and ass a little flatter than I would have liked. But as I finished drying myself and, putting the towel down, reached for the big white shirt I slept in, he took his headset off and looked at me with blushed animation, and I hesitated with the shirt in my hand, conscious now of something else—that I still had a waist, that my breasts were still soft and my legs shapely.

"Jul," he said, "you do manage to raise my spirits." And he threw the blanket to the side and invited me in.

I placed my nightshirt over the lamp to soften the light. "Do you think Esther's asleep?" I asked.

"I think so. But why don't you lock the door, just in case."

I locked the door and went over to him.

He gave me a wistful look. "I'm kind of hobbled here, with only one arm. Do you mind taking charge till I'm better?"

His optimism made my heart surge with joy. "Of course not. As long as this works," I said, touching him, "I'll be fine."

Michael filed for medical leave in the fall and began working out new courses he could teach using recordings for his left hand or, on certain occasions, asking me in as a visitor. We planned on making a trip to New York in late September. I had a lot on my agenda: emptying my apartment, winding up my business, getting the divorce rolling. As far as terminating my marriage was concerned, the task list was straightforward. When I'd moved into New York and started paying rent on my Fourteenth Street apartment, I'd stopped contributing to the mortgage on our house in Princeton. I wouldn't ask Ben for money there. As for my clothing and possessions, I had already transferred things I valued to Manhattan. Slowly and methodically, I had separated myself out over the years, as though to minimize the eventual mopping up.

Ben sent me short e-mails that varied so widely in tone and content that I never knew what to expect when I opened them. One was angry and hurt, another was forgiving, a third asked whether I needed him to do anything for me while I was gone—the assumption being I'd soon be back for good. Then there was the phone call in which he asked if he could come to California to talk things over. I replied, no, absolutely not, it was pointless—I'd be going east soon enough anyway.

One morning Michael and I were in the kitchen having breakfast when my cell rang. It was Ben. He had arrived in town the previous night. Appallingly, he had, without telling me, made arrangements to fly out and stay at the Shattuck Hotel in downtown Berkeley.

"I'm here. I want to see you," he said.

"How could you fly out without clearing it with me first? Supposing I'd been busy?"

"I need to see you. And you owe it to me to see me, Julia."

I suggested we meet at the Rose Garden, which was down the hill from Michael's. I wanted to meet in a public place so that neither one of us could get too emotional. Hanging up, I looked at Michael.

"Well, he's still your husband," he said philosophically.

"It's horrible, but I really don't want to see him."

"Because you don't want to think about how much pain he's in."

"And because I must be a horrible person to be inflicting the pain on him."

"You'll get used to it. Or you'll get used to not getting used to it. I'm getting used to not getting used to it with Anna."

When I reached the Rose Garden, I found Ben already there, pacing the sidewalk in front of the entrance. Unlike Michael, he had barely aged over the decades: he still had the straight stance of a fencer, his skin was still taught over his cheekbones. The flesh had slackened a little under the jaw, but that was all. It rang a bell inside me to see him—an off-key gong, both familiar and faraway. I parked and walked to greet him. He kissed me on the cheek.

"It's nice here, you'll like it," I said, as though this were an ordinary encounter, with me playing the tour guide.

We entered the garden through a wooden bower to stand at the top of an amphitheater formed by a half-dozen arched rows of roses arranged along cement terraces descending to a small bridge over a creek. The Rose Garden was built as a WPA project, and when Michael had shown it to me for the first time, I'd read the explanatory plaques with the sense of being in a horticultural museum. Now it occurred to me that this was an inappropriately romantic spot for my meeting with Ben.

"Not much of a view this morning," he said. The bay was under its blanket of morning fog.

"It'll open up later," I said, like a long-time resident. We sat on a cement bench. "I'm not sure why you flew out," I continued, "when I'll be in New York in September."

"I'm here because I think you're making a mistake."

"No, Ben."

"Listen to me, Julia. It's like you get hypnotized around Michael and forget everything we've had together. We've had wonderful times together—traveling and pursuing our careers—and now I'm happy to do an adoption with you if that's what you want. I'll move into the city. We'll have a regular family life."

"No, Ben."

"No one, Julia, no one can take care of you the way I can. No one can be there for you the way I've been." He took my hand.

That gave me pause. It was true that Ben had been loyal, caring, and generous. And holding his hand in mine, I remembered what a good lover he'd been. Now that Michael was one-armed, would I ever miss all the good sex I'd had years before with Ben? Probably.

"Maybe safety's not what I need anymore. I'm happy to take care of Michael. I'm okay with the uncertainty. I'm sorry I'm hurting you, but that's the way it is."

"It just doesn't make sense."

"Maybe it doesn't. Maybe I won't even be happy, or maybe I'll feel burdened or disappointed, but this is what I have to do."

"Supposing Michael has another stroke? You could end up taking care of a vegetable."

That was going too far. "Stop it, just stop it, okay?" I let go of his hand and stood up.

Resting his elbows in his knees, he placed his head in his hands and covered his eyes. "I should never have let you move into New York seventeen years ago. Or I should have moved in with you. I don't know."

"I don't want to discuss this anymore. There's nothing more to say." I wrestled with the temptation to walk away and leave him alone in the painful stew I'd put him in. No, I couldn't. He'd flown so far—not that, for a world-traveler like him, a trip from New York to California was more than a hop—and I felt I owed him a certain chunk of time. How much? An hour? Two? Enough time to apply bandages, to give him reason to imagine that we'd still be connected in some meaningful way. "Do you want to take a walk? There's a nice park on the other side of the street."

He stood up, his cheeks wet. "You're a real fuck, Julia, you know that?"

"You're probably right," I said.

"Okay, let's go for a walk."

"Hug first," I said.

Putting my arms around him, I took in the leanness and strength of his body. He was, in his early fifties, as fit as he'd been in his twenties. In terms of emotional stability, health, and longevity, not to mention income, he was a real prize and there was some truth to what he'd said: the trade I was making wasn't sensible. I felt like a heel for hurting such a good man, but I could take consolation in the thought that another woman would snatch him up soon enough. As much as Ben was suffering, he wouldn't remain single for long.

27

IN THE YEARS THAT followed, I would learn to navigate the ups and downs of life in a family where a child was shuttling between a father recovering from a stroke and a mother going through an interminable midlife crisis. I would have to hold the center for Esther and help her negotiate the field between her divorced parents, a field I was partly responsible for creating. It was as though all the messiness of relationship and family, which I'd successfully avoided in my commuting, "childfree" marriage, had come back to me sevenfold. I wouldn't have had it any other way, but the mix of satisfaction and difficulty took time to get used to. The emotional place I found myself in—where what I had creaked from the cracks, but I didn't want anything else—was new and strange after the years with Ben, when longing had come to feel like a natural state of being.

My first months of living with Michael were the most difficult. I think back on that time as a kind of necessary inoculation that made the ensuing complications more manageable in comparison. As we dealt with the misfortune of his stroke, negotiated with Anna, and helped Esther adjust to the new arrangement, I often wondered what it would take for me to feel that the Bay Area was home and that Michael and Esther were my new family. Ultimately, it was the trip back east to sublet my apartment, sell my business, and say my good-byes that gave me the closure I needed to move ahead.

Almost three months after his stroke, Michael received his doctor's permission to travel. It was late September, and Esther, who was in school, stayed with Anna while we flew by ourselves to New York for a week. I found myself in my apartment and bed with the man I'd fantasized about during the years I'd slept next to Ben.

We had some pleasant days of hanging out in Lower Manhattan, and then there were hours of me packing up my apartment and taking care of business at my firm while Michael browsed music stores and visited old friends. About halfway through our stay, I got my courage up and, leaving Michael in the city for the day, took the train out to New Jersey to meet with Ben. It was eerie to see him on the train platform, waving an arm at me, as though I were coming out, as usual, to spend the weekend with him.

Driving me back to our house, he said that he was determined to be my "friend," that we'd lived through too much together to disappear from each other's sight.

"With the whole country between us, I don't know what being friends might mean," I said. I kept my eyes fixed on the landscape outside the window. We were on Cherry Hill Road, moving toward our home in rural New Jersey. Even with the late September desiccation of foliage, the landscape still had a summer density to it.

"We'll e-mail, maybe even use the phone sometimes. We'll stay in touch."

"Okay," I said. I knew that, once the divorce was finalized, we'd be in touch less and less until nothing was left. But I wanted to make this as easy as possible for him. "We'll stay in touch."

"And who knows? Maybe you'll change your mind."

"You're not thinking of contesting the divorce, are you?"

"Of course not. It was just a—reflex."

"I mean, I'm selling my client list to my partner. I'm subletting my apartment for the rest of the lease. This is permanent."

"I know. I said the words just slipped out, like a reflex."

"And if I feel you're waiting for me to change my mind, I won't be able to stay in touch."

"All right, then."

We fell into a surly silence. What I wanted to say was, I won't change my mind, not only because of Michael, but because you're like an old shirt that shrank in the wash and doesn't feel right anymore, or an old sweater with holes in the elbows that I can't wear in public. But I kept the cruel metaphors to myself in order not to hurt him more than I already had.

When we got to the house, he offered me something to drink, as though I were a guest, which I guess was what I'd become, and I stood awkwardly in the kitchen as he poured me a glass of apple juice. Then we began going through stuff. I'd thought I would want to ship out to California only the things, stored in the attic, that I'd inherited from my parents. But Ben kept asking me, did I want any of the dishes or pots, the art on the walls, the furniture. At first, I kept declining, saying I didn't need any of it, but he got my interest when he mentioned the rug I'd chosen in Istanbul. Yes, as a matter of fact, I did want that, and I wouldn't mind if we threw in the abstract painting over the mantelpiece. I could add everything to the shipment of furniture coming from my apartment in New York. Simple enough to arrange.

The reflection I didn't share was that all these objects would make Michael's house feel more like home.

Ben had assembled tags, boxes, and newspapers to help me pack. As we did the work, one object at a time, the tension we'd felt in the car began to dissipate. It was a warm afternoon, and I couldn't help but enjoy the breeze coming in through the open windows.

"You really don't have to do this with me," I said.

"It's faster this way. And therapeutic. It makes the separation real. It gets more real with every object I place in this box," he said, securing a newspaper-wrapped plate into place with more newspaper. "As much as any of our being together was real."

"Meaning?"

"Meaning when we started commuting, I got used to being in this house by myself."

I stopped wrapping and sat down to listen, sensing he had more to say.

"I know it often bugged you," he went on, "that I wasn't more expressive. I know that sometimes you wanted more of my gut reactions to things, but you—you also had a way of keeping yourself separate and apart. You moved into New York right at the moment I was achieving the security I needed to engage myself deeper—" He stopped himself.

"Though you would probably say it was a matter of emotional style, of my patterns of communication—or non-communication."

I shrugged, ready to take my share of the blame. "I guess I was passive. I was always willing to take my cues from you. When I saw you pull away, I was all too willing not to push. I guess I wasn't so great at intimacy, either. Maybe if we'd gone into couples therapy, we might have connected more."

"But with Michael, it's okay?"

I didn't want to talk much about Michael. It felt like a violation of privacy. So I answered it sideways. "With Michael, I'm more intimate—with myself. I guess that's why I've been able to write again." Whenever Michael settled in at the piano, I worked at the computer on *Make Your Daughters Rich*, or I took out my notebook and, with a sense of steady purpose, made poems. Poetry was no longer a sporadic project, but focused and intentional, like beading or setting mosaics. And it was easy now because I had my tools and I knew where to mine for materials.

"I guess that's what you needed all along—to live with another artist." He gave an odd emphasis—bitter? contemptuous?—to the last word, pronouncing it "artiste."

"Maybe," was all I said. I wasn't going to vaunt my relationship with Michael to Ben.

"I'll be miserable for a while, but I'll move on," he said.

"I'll miss you," I said.

"Of course you will. It's only natural." And we went back to packing.

I rode back to New York with combined sorrow and relief, thinking I might not return to Princeton for years, or maybe ever, and meditating on the cruel abracadabra of divorce, whereby parts of your history disappear and are replaced by the submerged parts of the self that you get back. Years of imagining, subliminally, how painful breaking up with Ben might be, if it ever happened, had made the actual event less traumatic than expected. And I had to wonder whether the commuting lifestyle I'd chosen for us hadn't been my way of pulling out so gradually as to mute the impact of the break. Whatever the case, I felt only an aching numbness around my action.

I called Michael to tell him when I would get in, so once the train pulled in to its underground platform at Penn Station, I climbed up the stairs, pushing against the usual, aggressive crowd, to find him waiting at the top. He wasn't shaven, but his two shirts, one on top of the other, were clean and tucked in. We beamed at each other, happy to be reunited after a day's separation. It was the reverse of the first parting we'd had twenty-six years before, the night of the sushi dinner and the famous kiss, and I had the lovely sense of time and events being put right, like a self-healing zipper, or the bark of a tree growing over a patch of naked wood where a limb has been removed.

"How did it go?" he asked, hugging me first with his strong arm, then with the weak one. He had made progress with his left arm after months of physical therapy, and he used it as much as the shoulder pain permitted.

"Long day," I said. I told him how Ben seemed to be in a better place, how we'd packed together, and what I'd chosen to ship out.

Michael and I made our way past the food stands toward the escalator up to Seventh Avenue. The station was still a bit of a catacomb downstairs, but cleaner now, with the homeless gone and the air more breathable.

Outside on the street, Michael said, "Hey, how about we see if that sushi restaurant is still there?"

"It was on Thirty-Ninth, wasn't it?"

"Between Sixth and Fifth, I think."

"And it was a September night, wasn't it?" I asked.

"Sure was."

We walked up Seventh a few blocks, then went east on Thirty-Ninth. We were stymied when we reached the midpoint of the block between Sixth and Fifth to find that several more Japanese restaurants had opened up on both sides of the street.

"Uh-oh," he said. "Do you remember which one it was?"

"No idea. Except, south side of the street, I think."

We gazed in the window of one, then another.

We looked at each other and started laughing.

"So much for memory lane," he said. "Well, this one might be it. What do you think?"

I peered inside. It looked familiar, the way all Japanese restaurants do, with its sushi counter and little square curtains stamped with navy woodblock prints. I shrugged. "Beats me if it's the same one."

We laughed again and went in.

"It's absurd," I said, "remembering that evening so well, but not remembering where we ate." An end-of-the-day gloom came over me.

"At least you didn't smoke too much pot in your youth. I can't remember half of my life." He drew some reading glasses out of his chest pocket.

"As long as you remember the parts with me in it."

"That I do, Jul."

I took up a menu. "One thing I do remember: That night, I could barely eat. I was so wound up about your leaving New Haven, so upset you wouldn't be around anymore—and I wanted to kiss you so much."

"Me too." He spread the menu on the table, put his glass of water on it to hold it open. His arm got tired at the end of the day.

"But that didn't stop you from eating like a horse."

"No, it didn't, did it? Male-female thing, I guess."

The waitress came over, and we ordered, each of us pretending we were ordering the same thing we'd had twenty-six years before.

After dinner, we stepped out and instinctively headed toward the New York Public Library, in the opposite direction of my apartment. It was a walk of only a couple of blocks up Fifth to Forty-First Street. Approaching the front of the library, we saw the big white lions waiting for us, their paws extended in feline self-contentment.

"The scene of the crime," Michael said.

We sat down on the step beneath the south statue, holding hands. The night was warm and soft, the way it almost never is in Northern California. There was the same flow of yellow taxis down Fifth Avenue, the honking and speeding coalescing into a current of sound and movement.

"Do you think that if I'd gone home with you that night," I asked, "that everything would have been different? That I might have broken up with Ben?"

"Probably not."

"Why couldn't you just have swept me off my feet?"

"Slung you over my shoulder and carried you off to my cave?" He smiled. "Wish I could have, Jul."

Maybe it was the emotion of packing up with Ben, or the enormous sense of time lapsed that came over me when we couldn't find the sushi restaurant, or maybe it was the bittersweetness of holding Michael's hand on the steps where we'd had our first kiss—I was suddenly overcome by sorrow. "The twenty-six years we didn't get to have together—it feels tragic to me," I said.

"I have those moment of regret, too, but, Jul, it wasn't tragic. A child not having enough to eat, a teenager killed by a drunk driver—that's tragic. What happened to us—what we did—was just a lot of stupid bungling, that's all. We thought we were so smart, but we bungled it. We were both too terrified, for different reasons. I'd had too many triangular relationships and you, you just needed that security Ben gave you."

"Maybe Sandra was right. Having an alcoholic mother made me want to be safe more than anything else. God, I've let so much of my life be ruled by fear. Sometimes I just can't forgive myself for that."

"Honey, don't torture yourself—" He let go of my hand to caress my cheek.

"Remember how we said that everything happened the way it was supposed to?" The attitude of acceptance that I'd so carefully cultivated was quickly crumbling. "Well, I don't buy it. Even when I tell myself that things had to go the way they did because you had Esther, I still don't buy it. If we'd been together, we would have had a child like Esther— or adopted one—and then Esther would have been spared the mess of divorce. I'm always going to feel guilty about what we've done to her."

"So will I, but Jul, Esther's probably going to be okay, and you—you got to stop trying to figure it out. You got to accept what we've done, where we've been. And who knows where you really got your fearfulness from. Maybe it had nothing to do with your mother's drinking but with some kind of weird fear gene. Look at Anna. Her mother drank more than yours, and that didn't make her want security. She did the opposite, speeding through relationships for a decade before she married me."

"But the first one," I said, referring to Anna's high-school boyfriend, "it took her a long time to shake him." I was reluctant to abandon my hypothesis.

"Yeah, it wasn't until the Italian guy that she really dumped Doug."

"I met the Italian guy and never understood what she saw in him."

"All I know," he said, "was that between Doug and the Italian, it was a double train wreck."

I calmed down as we pondered it. Talking about Anna served to remind me that I couldn't blame everything on my own cowardice because our story was intertwined with hers. If she hadn't hooked up with

Michael at my Christmas party, maybe things would have gone differently. And certainly, if she had held on to him later, I wouldn't be with him now. The funny thing was realizing that, as close as Anna and I had once been, I didn't know what made her tick, and it seemed Michael didn't know either.

"Anyway, as far you were concerned," Michael continued, "the fact is, Ben was a good starter husband for you."

I laughed. "'Starter husband'? Excuse me?"

"Yeah, like a starter house. At twenty-five he was more mature than I would be at forty. I was too caught up in every passing mood. You might have been miserable with me."

"Maybe," I said, doubtful.

"No maybes about it," he said. "The fact is, having a child and now this stroke—it's forced me to drop the bitter thing. You either embrace what you got—or bust. I've finally grown up, so I'm okay for you now, and you"—he squeezed my hand— "you are perfect for me."

We looked at each other. The way his brown eyes could hold my gaze for a long time, without swerving—that was the only security I needed now.

"You're right," I said. "Except you're more than 'okay' for me. You're perfect, too."

"Even with the arm?"

"Even with the arm."

"Thanks." He leaned toward me for a kiss. "Let's try not to get stuck in looking back, okay? The important thing is that we're together now. And we've got too much to do—we've got to help Esther grow up and you've got to write and I've got to compose. There's all kinds of good stuff ahead."

"Okay," I said reluctantly, because I had one last memory to share. "But—remember how, when we crossed the street, you swung me toward you for a kiss? And all the taxis honked at us?"

He grinned. "That was a wild moment, wasn't it?" He touched my face, cradled it with his hand. "And now here we are."

I gazed at him, thinking, the muse doesn't come to you dancing in a field, with daisies in her hair. She appears in the battlefields of life, in the messy, painful places where old dreams get fragmented and something new has to be born. And she asks you to give birth in the most difficult places—in the desert, on the mountaintops, under water. Thus she had come to me, in the shape of this wounded, complicated man, who could take me higher and lower than anyone else. Michael, my aging, unshaven muse.

"What is it?" he asked softly.

"Michael, you ruffle everything in me until it wants to come out. In poetry, I mean."

"Me, too," he said. "In sonatas and symphonies."

Suddenly we were aware of a surreal urban silence. The traffic lights at the corner of Forty-First had turned red, and the river of cabs was stopped before us, waiting. Was there perhaps, among them, one that had witnessed our crazy kiss in the middle of the avenue twenty-six years before? We'd never know. The lights turned back to green, and we instinctively craned our necks to look south and watch them change on Fortieth and Thirty-Ninth, one after the other all the way down Fifth Avenue as far as the eye could see, while the flotilla of taxis started moving again, honking and whooshing its passengers toward who knows what destination.

Acknowledgments

MY DEEPEST GRATITUDE GOES to my agent, April Eberhardt. Before guiding me toward She Writes Press, she provided invaluable feedback to various versions of the novel and helped me craft a more fitting ending to it than the one I had initially envisioned. Without her guidance and support, this novel would have been a lesser thing destined for the drawer. She truly was its midwife.

I was also very fortunate to find two wonderful readers and friends in my fiction-writing group, Kristene Cristobal and Veronica Reilly-Granich, who offered constructive criticism chapter by chapter. Additionally, I'd like to thank everyone who read portions or earlier versions, including Lily Chien-Davis, Jenny Glasgow, Tim Hampton, Katherine Ibbett, and Elizabeth Rosner. Thank you also Gina Kovarsky for helping me think of myself as a writer early on.

I am lucky to be in a poetry group and have benefitted from the community provided by the members of Fresh Ink, including Madeline Aranda, Rita Flores Bogaert, Gail Entrekin, Chantal Guillemin, Ellen Levin, Barbara Minton, Kimberly Satterfield, and David White.

Special thanks also go to Jeff Mink and Jeanie Iams for their gifts of presence and care.

Thank you to Brooke Warner and the staff at She Writes Press for making publication a transparent and positive experience. Grateful acknowledgment is also made to *The MacGuffin* for publishing a version of the first chapter entitled "The Unshaven Muse."

Finally, writing is a lonely activity, and I am most grateful for the love and encouragement of my husband, Tim Hampton, and daughters, Emily and Sophia, who bring endless joy into my life.

About the Author

JESSICA LEVINE'S fiction, essays, poetry, and poetry translations have appeared in many publications, including *Amarillo Bay, California Quarterly, Forge, Green Hills Literary Lantern, Poetry Northwest, North American Review, RiverSedge, The Southern Review, Spoon River Poetry Review, The MacGuffin,* and *Willow Review.* She earned her PhD in English at the University of California, Berkeley, and is the author of *Delicate Pursuit: Literary Discretion in Henry James and Edith Wharton* (Routledge, 2002). She has also translated several books from French and Italian into English. You can visit her at www.jessicalevine.com, where you will find links to some of her shorter works.

SELECTED TITLES FROM SHE WRITES PRESS

She Writes Press is an independent publishing company founded to serve women writers everywhere. Visit us at www.shewritespress.com.

Duck Pond Epiphany by Tracey Barnes Priestley. $16.95, 978-1-938314-24-7. When a mother of four delivers her last child to college, she has to decide what to do next—and her life takes a surprising turn.

Beautiful Garbage by Jill DiDonato. $16.95, 978-1-938314-01-8. Talented but troubled young artist Jodi Plum leaves suburbia for the excitement of the city—and is soon swept up in the sexual politics and downtown art scene of 1980s New York.

Cleans Up Nicely by Linda Dahl. $16.95, 978-1-938314-38-4. The story of one gifted young woman's path from self-destruction to self-knowledge, set in mid-1970s Manhattan.

Clear Lake by Nan Fink Gefen. $16.95, 978-1-938314-40-7. When psychotherapist Rebecca Lev's father dies under suspicious circumstances, she becomes obsessed with discovering what happened to him.

Shanghai Love by Layne Wong. $16.95, 978-1-938314-18-6. The enthralling story of an unlikely romance between a Chinese herbalist and a Jewish refugee in Shanghai during World War II.

Fire & Water by Betsy Graziani Fasbinder. $16.95, 978-1-938314-14-8. Kate Murphy has always played by the rules—but when she meets charismatic artist Jake Bloom, she's forced to navigate the treacherous territory of passionate love, friendship, and family devotion.

CPSIA information can be obtained at www.ICGtesting.com
Printed in the USA
BVOW01s1010010514

352276BV00006B/197/P